Maggie Craig wa[...] Glasgow, the young[...] father and a mother who worked in the typing pool of John Brown Land Boilers. Maggie was working as a medical secretary when she met her Welsh husband, Will, when he was doing part of his apprenticeship in a Clydeside shipyard, and she and Will subsequently sailed the world on oil tankers before settling in Glasgow and starting a family.

Maggie now lives in an old blacksmith's house in rural Aberdeenshire with Will and their two children. She is the author of DAMN' REBEL BITCHES, which tells the story of the women of the Jacobite rebellion. Her three earlier novels, THE RIVER FLOWS ON, WHEN THE LIGHTS COME ON AGAIN and THE STATIONMASTER'S DAUGHTER, are also available from Headline.

Also by Maggie Craig

The River Flows On
When the Lights Come on Again
The Stationmaster's Daughter

The Bird
Flies High

Maggie Craig

headline

First published in hardback in 2001
by HEADLINE BOOK PUBLISHING

First published in paperback in 2002
by HEADLINE BOOK PUBLISHING

10 9 8 7 6 5 4 3

ISBN 0 7472 6392 2

Typeset by Avon Dataset Ltd, Bidford-on-Avon, Warks

Printed and bound in Great Britain by
Clays Ltd, St Ives plc

HEADLINE BOOK PUBLISHING
A division of Hodder Headline
338 Euston Road
London NW1 3BH

www.headline.co.uk
www.hodderheadline.com

To Saint Mungo's Bairns:
both native and adopted,
and to all those who love the Dear Green Place.

Here is the bell that never rang,
Here is the fish that never swam,
Here is the tree that never grew,
Here is the bird that never flew.

And to assorted members of the animal kingdom without whom this book would have been written in half the time.

'Let Glasgow Flourish'

Acknowledgements

I should like to extend my sincere thanks to everyone mentioned below.

To Lillian Kelly of Lillian's Flower Shop in the High Street, who generously shared with me her deep knowledge of the local area.

To my good friend Chris Longmuir, Assistant Principal Officer, Adoption and Fostering, Angus District Council, who gave me crucial information relating to Scotland's long tradition of boarding-out (and shipping abroad) children taken into care.

To Brenda Smith and Anne Wood of Tennent Caledonian's Wellpark Brewery for very kindly and patiently showing me around their Heritage Centre and pinpointing the location of the old stables, and to Fiona Nicoll for being my oldest friend. She knows what I mean.

To Donald Smith, whose vivid memoir of his own and his family's long involvement with the Wellpark Brewery – *From the Bottom of a Barrel* – provided very useful background information and inspiration.

To Ricky Simpson and Anne Galbraith of Glasgow City Council for a point of information relating to Glasgow's cemeteries.

To Evelyn Tiefenbrun for assistance in finding the *mot juste* and to Evelyn Hutchison for being Evelyn Hutchison.

To my clever and beautiful daughter for sitting on my

desk and coming up with exactly the right idea, and in the nick of time too.

And, as ever, may blessings rain down gently upon the heads of all those gallant and knowledgeable men and women who toil at the Mitchell Library in Glasgow. Research for this book led to many happy hours spent rummaging through the newspaper archives stored in that treasure-house of knowledge.

Prologue

Saturday nights were the worst. Without the inhibition of having to get up for their work the next morning, the men who thought the solution to life's problems could be found at the bottom of a bottle could start early and finish late. It began with bonhomie and snatches of song and a desire to call the whole world their friend: particularly those other men who lived and worked with them in the warren of streets and lanes clustered around Glasgow's cathedral and High Street.

At the top of that sloping part of the city's oldest thoroughfare known for centuries as the Bell o' the Brae lay the Drygate, home to Josephine Collins and her family. Tucked in behind Duke Street Prison and the local brewery, the south side of the short street had been sacrificed to the expansion of the gaol. Its north side lay under the shadow of the Necropolis, the sprawling Victorian cemetery on the hill above St Mungo's great church.

Josie knew, because her teacher at the Ladywell School had told her so, that the Drygate had once been a very posh place indeed. In the old days, so Miss French had said, canons of the cathedral and well-off citizens of Glasgow had lived there in pleasant townhouses. Now those townhouses had been subdivided too many times, into tiny, overcrowded tenement homes in a permanent state of poor repair. The back courts were full of dirty puddles and broken glass, and rubbish and rusty old prams on which the children played. Some folk tried to keep their closes and stairs swept and washed. Others had given up the unequal struggle.

Humble or grand, tenement dwellers throughout Glasgow always called their homes houses, never flats. Each back court had its midden, a place to dump ashes from the fire and household refuse. The scaffies lifted it once a week, but whilst it lay there rotting and waiting for the dustmen, it inevitably attracted rats. Sleek and glistening and looking better fed than many of the local children, they slithered up from the Molendinar burn to scavenge in the closes.

The Molendinar had once been a tumbling and sparkling stream, full of fish and clean water. That was why Saint Mungo had chosen to found his religious settlement on its banks all those hundreds of years ago. Where it wasn't culverted, the burn was now little more than an open sewer. It stank to high heaven in the summer, which didn't stop children playing in it.

Josie and her younger sister Rachel were forever dragging their wee half-brother Charlie away from its mucky banks. He always howled in protest, too young to understand that they and their mother Dorothy were only concerned about the dangers the filthy stream might pose to his health.

Once, coming home from school in the winter when it was dark, Josie and Rachel had experienced the icy terror of a rat sliding over their feet on its way through the close. Although the leerie had already been on his nightly rounds, the flickering gas wall light which gave some illumination to the entrance passageway had served only to make the experience more frightening. Seeing the creature slink away into the shadows was a picture which refused to leave Josie's head.

Now the two sisters always made sure they each picked up a stone somewhere on the short journey home from school. Then they could fling the pebbles through the close to startle anything which might be lurking in the gloom before speeding to the door of their ground-floor home as though the hounds of hell were snapping at their heels.

They shared that home, small though it was, with their mother and Charlie, their stepfather Arthur Collins and his two almost grown-up sons. Somehow Josie could never quite manage to think of Billy and young Arthur as her brothers. She also hated her stepfather for insisting she and Rachel take his surname. Just because their real father had died in the Great War didn't mean they had stopped being his daughters. As far as Josie was concerned, their name was still Shaw but she had learned the painful way to keep that point of view to herself.

Like many of the local men, the three Collins males worked in the nearby brewery. Like some of them, they were a wee bit too fond of its product.

Yes, Saturday nights were the worst.

PART I

Chapter 1

1924

Even in the long, light summer evenings Josie and Rachel's mother always made sure her girls and young Charlie were safely indoors by eight o'clock on a Saturday. However, with windows facing on to the street, it was impossible not to be aware of what was happening out there: what was happening out there right now.

First the clatter of running feet, tackety boots striking the cobblestones of the roadway. Curses and oaths being hurled backwards and forwards. A drunken challenge issued, the words slurred. 'Aw right, then. If ye think ye're hard enough!'

There was a grunt and the unmistakable sound of fabric being ripped. Someone had grabbed someone else by the jacket. Josie had seen the manoeuvre more than once. She had her dark head turned away from the window but she could visualise the free hand being drawn back to power the punch which would inevitably follow.

More than likely the combatants had been best pals half an hour ago. What started as relaxation after a hard week's toil could so quickly turn ugly. The over-crowded houses, poor living conditions and dead-end jobs created a potent situation in which slights and resentments, real or imagined, often festered and exploded into violence. Long before closing time, men would spill out on to the streets looking for trouble. All too often they found it.

Huddled together in the box bed, the furthest they could get away from the window, Dorothy Collins sat with one arm around a trembling Charlie, her other hand resting on Rachel's hair. Legs drawn up, the girl lay with her head in her mother's lap, eyes squeezed tightly shut. It was impossible to shut out the noises.

Another unmistakable sound. Punches being thrown. Hard knuckles against soft flesh. The windows rattled as someone was thrust against the glass.

'What'll we dae if they break the windae, Mammy?' Rachel whispered. Josie caught her mother's eye. What *would* they do if the brawling men broke the window? And where were Arthur Collins and his two big galumphing sons when you needed them? Josie's generous mouth twisted in reluctant amusement. Probably off causing trouble outside some other respectable person's house.

She patted her sister's arm and put as much reassurance into her voice as she could muster. 'They'll move on soon, Rachel. Don't you worry, pet.'

Her mother sent her a grateful look, woman to woman. Josie experienced a quick little surge of pride and pleasure. Ma was coming to rely on her more and more, and she was glad of it. Dorothy Collins didn't have it easy. She'd never had it easy.

A household of seven people, three of whom never did a hand's turn, generated a huge amount of cooking and cleaning and washing. The never-ending housework was accompanied by the continual struggle to make ends meet, exacerbated when too much of the money which came into the house went straight back out again, squandered on the pleasures the Collins men considered so indispensable to their well-being.

Then there were the babies: those who had lived and those who had died. Josie knew she'd had another wee sister, stillborn between her own birth and that of eight-year-old Rachel. Although Charlie had come into the world hale and hearty less than a year after her mother had married Arthur Collins, six months later Dorothy had miscarried another child.

Last year, like a bright little candle flame in the darkness, there had been Jamie. Josie had hoped he would be the one to mend her mother's broken heart but the wee lad had lived for only six weeks, dying just before Christmas. She knew Dorothy remembered and grieved for all of her lost children.

The fight did move on. Unfortunately, it only went as far as the family's close. Horrified, they listened to what could only be the sound of one man banging another man's head repeatedly off the solid wooden door to their small home, mere yards from where they cowered together on the box bed. It had to stop eventually. Unless murder was going to be done.

Once all that could be heard beyond the door was a low moaning, Josie and her mother went out to see what they could do for the young man lying in a bloodstained heap on the cold stone floor of the close. They were joined by Mr and Mrs Fitzgerald from across the lobby, closely followed by Mrs Paterson and her son Thomas from the second floor.

'He wanted tae come doon and break it up,' she said breathlessly, clutching nervously at the sleeve of her son's striped shirt, 'but ah wouldnae let him.'

Tam Paterson let out an exclamation half of dismay and half of disgust as Dorothy Collins used the damp cloth she had brought out with her to wipe the semi-conscious man's features free of blood.

'D'ye recognise him, Thomas my boy?' asked Mr Fitzgerald, taking a step back to allow his young neighbour an unrestricted view.

'Aye,' said Tam grimly. 'Alan Thomson. I was at the school with him.' He glanced at Josie before hunkering down beside the injured man. 'D'ye no' know him yourself, hen?'

She edged round the little group to get a better look at the battered face. 'You were a couple of years ahead o'me, remember.' Then: 'Oh, aye. Lives round the corner in John Knox Street?'

Nodding his head in a quick gesture of agreement, Tam stretched out a hand to assess the damage. He was Saturday night casual, sleeves rolled up to the elbows, collarless shirt open at the neck. Realising she was blocking his light, Josie moved to one side, allowing a bright shaft of evening sunlight to fall on the two young men. It struck sparks from the fine copper-coloured hairs on Tam's forearms.

'In the name o'God, Alan man,' he said, 'you're no' a very pretty sight.'

Astonishingly, a smile broke through the streaks of blood. When Alan Thomson spoke, Josie realised what had saved him from more serious injury.

'Tam!' he yelled and then winced at the sound of his own voice. 'Ma head's swimming,' he complained, trying – and failing – to raise a shaking hand to it. 'I think mebbe ah've had a wee bit too much to drink.' His attempts to focus on his former schoolmate's features were obviously causing him some difficulty. 'Is that whit's wrang wi' me, Tam, old pal?'

'You're three sheets to the wind, me lad,' said Mr Fitzgerald.

'Three sheets?' queried Ella Paterson, sitting hunched forward on the second bottom step of the stairs, arms wrapped around her drawn-up knees. 'Three hundred, mair like.'

Mr Fitzgerald straightened up. 'Indeed, Mrs Paterson, indeed . . . But it would seem the demon drink has afforded our young friend some protection on this occasion. The deadening of the senses arising from the ingestion of intoxicating liquors has perhaps prevented the contraction of more serious injury.'

'Sure, and you would know all about that, Mick Fitzgerald,' said his wife. Her barbed look would have flattened a lesser man. 'We all know the devil looks after his own.'

Tam and Josie exchanged a private smile. A drayman at the brewery, Mick Fitzgerald helped deliver the company's products to hostelries and hotels throughout the city. Like most of the carters, he was known to take a wee refreshment now and then, though the only discernible effect was to make him even more loquacious and eloquent than usual. He liked to declaim poetry when he'd had a few.

Particularly fond of Wordsworth and Shelley, he was so admiring of their verses he was prepared to graciously overlook the fact that both gentlemen had belonged, as he liked to put it, to the race which had oppressed his dear old mother country for centuries. As his wife Bridget had spent a large part of her girlhood and young womanhood in the East End of London, this comment was always met with a vociferous defence of the great good nature of your average Cockney, and by logical extension, every other decent Englishman and woman.

'The salt of the earth, Michael Francis Fitzgerald. And don't you forget it!'

When she was really annoyed with him, Bridget's husband always got his full given name.

Between them, the women doing what they could to help, Tam and Mick got Alan Thomson to his feet. He groaned, his head flopping forward as though an unseen hand had cut the string holding him up.

'Will you manage him like that?' asked Dorothy Collins doubtfully, eyeing the lifeless arms draped heavily over the two rescuers' shoulders.

'We'll be fine,' Tam assured her, splaying his hand out

over Alan's chest to steady him. 'It's no distance.'

'Ready, lad?' asked Mick, bracing himself to take his share of what was now a dead weight.

'Eh . . .' said Tam, carefully not looking in Josie's direction, 'will I maybe chap the door when we get back, Mrs Collins? Let you know we got him home safe?'

Dorothy Collins's eyes were kind, but there was a teasing glint in them. It lent sparkle to her face, displacing the look of permanent tiredness she wore these days. 'You do that, son. I doubt Josie'll be able to get to sleep tonight unless she knows the laddie got home safely.'

Standing behind Tam, Josie saw the tops of his ears turn a delicate pink. Their respective mothers hadn't finished with him yet. Folding her arms, Dorothy propped one shoulder against the solid wooden post at the bottom of the bannister and addressed herself to Ella Paterson. 'Would ye no' agree with me on that one, Ella?'

'I have absolutely nae dubiety about that, Dorothy.' There was devilment in Tam's mother's face too. 'How could any o'us rest easy the night if we didnae know that my Thomas had reassured your Josie on such a very important point?'

Hampered though he was by the arm around his neck, Tam managed to throw a long suffering look over his shoulder. Just eighteen, three years older than Josie, he had been the mainstay of his widowed mother and his younger brothers and sisters for so long he had acquired a gravity and self-possession well beyond his years – except when it came to his liking for Josephine Collins. That transformed him into the stumbling and gawky youth his chronological age entitled him to be. 'We're off,' he said gruffly. 'See youse all shortly.'

When, as promised, he knocked on the door twenty minutes later, Josie was busy helping her mother get Rachel and Charlie ready for bed.

'Away on out,' insisted Dorothy Collins. 'Hello there,

Tam.' She had followed her elder daughter to the door, a half-undressed Rachel clutching at the washed-out apron she wore over her long dark skirt. 'Give the wee yin to me.'

Josie handed over her naked and squirming brother. She'd been about to bath him in the jaw-box, the deep sink under the kitchen window whose cold tap provided the family's only running water. Charlie would have a nice warm bath thanks to the water she'd put on to heat well before the fight had broken out. The huge black kettle which sat more or less permanently on the range took a long time to come to the boil.

'Come out to the close mouth?' Tam suggested as Josie pulled the door shut behind her. 'It seems to be all quiet on the western front now. We'll be safe enough till closing time.'

They stood on either side of the narrow entrance to the tenement, unconsciously mimicking each other's posture: leaning against the wall of the building with their hands behind their backs. The stone was warm from the sun, lingering still in the long Scottish evening.

The position in which they stood naturally directed their gazes towards the great mediaeval cathedral, visible where the Drygate opened out into Cathedral Square. Josie's eyes found one of the lamp standards up there. It was decorated with the figure of Saint Mungo and the symbols associated with him: a salmon with a ring in its mouth, a tree, a bird and a bell.

Even before she had learned about it at school, her mother had told her the story behind all of those. Dorothy had explained also that while the holy man had two names, sometimes being referred to as Saint Kentigern, the inhabitants of the city he had founded preferred to call him Mungo and themselves 'Saint Mungo's bairns'. There was a nonsense rhyme which went with what had become Glasgow's coat of arms.

Here is the bell that never rang,
Here is the fish that never swam,
Here is the tree that never grew,
Here is the bird that never flew.

'You and Mr Fitzgerald got Alan Thomson home all right?' she asked.

'Aye.' A brief smile kissed Tam's sunlit features. 'You should have heard the names his ma called him! He's in for a right doing the morn.'

'When he comes round?'

'Aye,' he said again, and left it at that.

One of the things Josie had always liked about Tam Paterson was that he didn't expect you to talk all the time. He was a man of few words himself, a gentle lad doing a job he loved. An apprentice carter at the brewery, he worked directly under Mick Fitzgerald. Like the Irishman, Tam loved the horses and had a real way with them.

A lone drunk lurched past on his way home. The way he was zigzagging over the pavement it was a miracle he hadn't stumbled into the gutter and cracked his head open long before he had made it this far. 'Another Saturday night in the Drygate,' Josie observed drily.

Tam's clear eyes followed the man's erratic progress, his handsome face troubled. 'I would never have thought Alan Thomson was the type to hit the bottle.'

Josie shrugged. 'Men drink,' she said.

Tam shook his head decisively. 'No' all men, Josie. No' me. I'm never going to take strong liquor.'

'I'm very glad to hear you say that, Tam.'

He took his eyes off the departing drunk and turned them on to her instead. 'Are ye, Josie? Are ye really?'

'Of course I am. I've seen the heartache drink can cause.'

Tam nodded. 'Heartache. Aye, that's the word, right

enough. You're a dab hand at finding the right word, Josie.' He repeated it with a kind of bleak satisfaction, separating the two syllables and expelling them on a sigh. 'Heart-ache.' Then he dropped his head and his eyes to the pavement.

It occurred to Josie to wonder if his father had been too fond of the demon drink. She could remember some muttered comment Mrs Fitzgerald had made to her own mother ages ago about Ella Paterson being well rid of that man of hers.

That might explain a lot: Tam's resolve to have absolutely nothing to do with alcohol, his protectiveness towards his mother, the strong sense of responsibility he felt towards her and his wee brothers and sisters. Josie was gazing compassionately at his bowed head when it suddenly snapped up.

'You can count on me never touching a drop, hen. I can promise you that.'

'I'm glad to hear it,' she said again. 'It's not easy turning down liquor in your job, is it?' She knew it was common practice for carters to be offered a drink at each establishment to which they made deliveries.

'No,' he agreed, 'but if you put your mind to something you can dae it, Josie. I really believe that. If you want something enough.' The passion in his voice was unmistakable, his eyes eloquent with longing.

Now it was she who dropped her gaze and turned her head away. You couldn't grow up in an area like this and be ignorant of the facts of life. Once, coming in through the back court late one moonlit night, she and her mother had surprised a couple. The man had the woman pressed up against the wall of the building and his hands had been everywhere.

'Doing what comes naturally,' Dorothy said calmly once they had passed them. 'Only I wish they would dae it somewhere else than in our back court.'

Lying in bed that night, Josie had thought about the couple. The woman's head had been tilted back against the hard stone wall, her body bowed out awkwardly to meet those questing hands. Yet she hadn't looked in the least uncomfortable. Quite the reverse. Josie had flopped on to her back and allowed herself to wonder what it would feel like to be held and touched like that. What it would feel like with Tam Paterson.

He was so nice. Och, he was so handsome too with his eyes as blue as the sky and his hair the colour of a shiny chestnut. He had a way of looking at Josie which made her feel as if she was the most important person in the world. Her cheeks were growing hot. She lifted her eyes towards the Necropolis, its monuments and obelisks standing up like accusing fingers against the darkening sky.

'Josie . . .'

Startled, she turned her head. Despite the heavy boots he wore, she hadn't heard him approach. Their faces were inches apart, so close she could see herself reflected in his eyes. He said her name again, five soft letters of longing and desire. Like the Molendinar in days of old, her blood began to tumble and race through her veins.

Then, from somewhere not too far away, she heard a raucous laugh she recognised. Arthur Collins and his sons were coming up Hangman's Brae.

'That's my stepfather and the boys,' she said breathlessly. 'I'd better be getting in.'

Tam stepped back, hastily putting some distance between the two of them. Woman enough to be excited by what had happened, there was sufficient of the child in Josie to feel relief at not having to respond to his tentative advances quite yet. Tam might be only three years older than her but he was a man, with the status which came of being out in the world earning a living.

In most ways Josie considered herself quite grown up

but she was still a schoolgirl. For a few more weeks at least, she thought, suppressing a quick stab of regret. She'd have left at Easter if her stepfather had had his way but her mother had insisted on her being allowed to stay on till the summer.

The response of the Collins males when they spotted the two young people standing together at the close mouth was entirely predictable.

'Aw, would you look at that!' yelled Billy. 'Romance blossoms in the Drygate.'

'Love's young dream,' agreed his brother Arthur, giving Josie the sly and sleekit smile which never failed to make her feel uncomfortable. 'Ah hope you two havenae been doing anything you shouldnae. Have you had ma sister up against the wall, Tam, old pal?'

Tam's face flamed into painful colour.

'Naw,' said Billy, 'he just wishes he had, but little Miss Prim here wouldnae let him!'

He let out a coarse guffaw, his father and brother joining in. Tam sent all three of them a look of disdain and spoke quietly to Josie. 'I'll say goodnight then, hen.'

'Aye,' she said, following him into the close. 'Thanks for coming to the rescue this evening.'

Embarrassed as they both were, he stopped at the foot of the stairs and turned to face her, one hand resting on the newel post, a small decorative globe crowning the bannister. 'Nae bother.' His fingers tightened on the dark wood underneath them. 'I'd do anything for you, Josie. Anything at all. Ye know that, don't you?'

She opened her mouth to assure him that she did, but was interrupted by young Arthur, coming up behind her. 'Still trying tae persuade her tae let ye have a feel, Tam?'

Stony-faced, Josie pushed the door open and she and Tam watched the three of them file in, noisy and heavy-footed and demanding their supper.

'I'll need to go and help Ma feed them.'

17

The tension emanating from Tam was tangible. Josie placed her left hand on his right arm, felt the contraction of the muscles as he reacted to her touch. 'It's not worth it,' she murmured.

He looked outraged. 'Not worth it? Josie, you know I'm no' a violent man, but for two pins, I'd lay that lot out cold.'

'I know you would,' she said sadly, gazing up at him as he stood on the second step. 'But there's been enough of that here tonight. D'ye no' think so?'

Lips clamped tightly together, he sucked air in through his nose, then exhaled it angrily. 'If you say so,' he said at last.

'I do,' she responded, and gave him a lopsided smile. 'Good night, Tam. And thanks again.'

She disappeared into the house before he could say anything else. Touched by his wish to defend her good name, she knew he would come off worst in any encounter with her stepbrothers. They would fight dirty, and think nothing of going at him two against one.

Walking into the kitchen and seeing them lolling at the table waiting for Dorothy Collins to serve them, she thought bitterly that Billy and Arthur Collins wouldn't recognise gentlemanly behaviour if it came up and hit them in the face. Biting back the observation that her mother needed nothing so much as her bed, Josie busied herself with putting out cups and saucers and plates.

'Thanks, pet. Will you read Charlie and Rachel their story now and tuck them in?'

'Will ye no' read us a wee bedtime story and tuck us in, Josie?' called Billy. 'Arthur and me would really like that. Especially the tucking in bit!' He laughed uproariously.

Josie caught her mother's eye. Unable to bear the bleak look in it, she forced herself to toss a careless bit of banter back to Billy before going through to the front room. Oh, how she wished her gentle mother had never met Arthur Collins!

She understood why Dorothy had married him. After Andrew Shaw had fallen at the Somme, it hadn't been easy bringing up two daughters on the few shillings a week a grateful country gave its war widows. When Arthur Collins had come a-wooing the widow Shaw five years ago there had been a certain rough and bluff charm about him. That hadn't lasted long – only until he and his two sons from his previous marriage got their feet under the table.

An hour later Josie was lying beside a sleeping Rachel and Charlie on the pull-out bed in the front room, trying vainly to shut out the low murmur of voices coming from the curtained box bed in the corner. The older boys slept in the kitchen, the rest of the family in the only other room.

Even with her pillow over her head, she could hear Arthur Collins's deep voice, wheedling and persuasive. Then her mother's reluctant acquiescence. Too tired to resist.

Josie pressed the pillow harder to her ears.

Chapter 2

'So what happened then, Josie?'

Standing on one of the sloping paths of the Necropolis, Rachel's face bore an expression of eager anticipation. She loved her big sister's stories, especially when told in these suitably spooky surroundings. Burial ground of Glasgow's great merchant families of the Victorian era, the grassy hill above the cathedral was dotted with replica Greek and Roman temples. Some were as large as small chapels, with locked metal doors or ornate wrought-iron gates guarding shadowy interiors.

'Is that where the bodies are, Josie?' Rachel always asked in horrified delight.

Josie would nod wisely and stretch out a dramatic hand to those other memorials surmounted by a massive Greek urn or ornamental stone casket. 'And inside those,' she pronounced solemnly, 'lie the bones and dust of those who chose to depart this earth by means of a funeral pyre.'

Sometimes she managed to terrify herself as much as Rachel. Charlie couldn't really be expected to display the same sort of interest in her tales but he had been happy enough to toddle along with his big sisters this Saturday afternoon. He stood now at Rachel's side, grubby hand held fast between her much cleaner fingers. *Born to be a lady*. That's what Dorothy always said about Rachel.

Although all three children were barefoot, they had started the day clean and neat. The two girls were still as smart as their mother had been able to make them that morning, their long and glossy hair brushed and caught up in a navy ribbon at the back of their heads. They wore crisply starched cotton pinafores in the same colour, but the heavy brown skirts and pale blue blouses they wore underneath were much mended and darned.

Josie seldom had new clothes and as the younger of the two, Rachel's wardrobe consisted entirely of hand-me-downs. Despite that handicap, she always managed to look neat and well-groomed. There was something very refined and rather proper about Rachel. Her mother summed it up with a good old Scots word: perjink.

Charlie had got his hands dirty five minutes after they'd left the house, grubbing about in the gutter for a bright pebble he'd seen there. It reposed now in one of the bulging pockets of his short trousers, jostling for position with his other treasures.

There was a shiny copper penny Josie had given him, a handful of marbles, an extremely sticky toffee he was saving for an emergency, a half-eaten biscuit he had kept for the same reason but which was rapidly going mouldy – and a dead worm. They were all objects irresistible to a small boy, but he was beginning to have an inkling that his sisters might not be too keen on some of them. Particularly the worm.

Josie prepared to answer Rachel's question. She lifted her arms, hands open and palms facing outwards in the kind of gesture the minister in the great cathedral below used when he delivered the benediction at the end of the service each Sunday. She'd chosen to tell the story in front of a mausoleum which did look quite Egyptian, decorated as it was with carvings of palm leaves and stylised eyes.

'Then,' she intoned, 'Howard Carter walked forward and looked into the tomb. Lord Carnarvon asked him if he could see anything, and he said, "Yes. Wonderful things".'

She paused, caught anew by the simple eloquence of that description. *Wonderful things.* Funny how two little words could capture so well the substance and atmosphere of the discovery of King Tutankhamun's burial chamber. Since the initial breakthrough at the end of 1922, almost two years ago now, she had been fascinated by the story.

So had the rest of the world. The newspapers often reported on it and Josie was an avid reader of them. She'd been introduced to their pleasures by Mick Fitzgerald, who routinely passed on to her whichever one he had bought that day, delighted when he discovered his young neighbour shared his interest in how the different publications reported the same stories.

The *Irish Times*, the *Glasgow Herald* and the *Manchester Guardian* were Mick's favourites. Occasionally he took *The Times* or the *Daily Telegraph* because, as he put it, 'It never hurts to know what the enemy is thinking.' Josie enjoyed reading all of those and every other newspaper she could get her hands on. She lived in a city well-served for them.

Apart from the *Glasgow Herald*, there was the *Daily Record & Mail* and the *Bulletin*, which specialised in picture stories. There were evening papers too: the *Evening Citizen*, the *Evening Times* and the *Glasgow Evening Dispatch*. She found them all interesting, although the *Evening Dispatch* could sometimes be a wee bit staid.

Over the past year she and Mick Fitzgerald had noticed a change of style in many of the newspapers they read and discussed. The articles were being written in a different way, more modern and up-to-date. Instead of the traditional headline followed by several subheadings which more or less summarised – and gave away – the whole story, one snappy headline was now followed by a tightly written piece of journalism which enticed you to read and appreciate all of its words.

Not only that, long columns of text were now being broken up and enlivened by lots more photographs. The *Evening Dispatch* didn't seem to have caught up with either of these trends yet. Nevertheless, it had published a wonderfully spine-tingling account of what had become known as the Curse of the Pharaohs, the mysterious deaths which had befallen so many members of Lord Carnarvon's Egyptian expedition, including Howard Carter himself.

The report had used splendid expressions like *ill-fated*, and had suggested that the archaeologists might have called down *the wrath of the ancient gods of Egypt upon themselves*. Inspired, Josie had sat down and written up the story herself, trying as far as possible to put it into her own words, although she'd been unable to resist keeping those two particular phrases.

Rachel had heard her big sister's version several times before, but she seemed to enjoy it as much this time as she had on the previous occasions. Bored with standing still, Charlie toddled off along the path. Once the story was told Rachel reverted to practicalities.

'Should we maybe go back down the hill now, Josie?' she suggested. 'I think Charlie's getting a bit bored.'

Josie followed her sister's pointing finger, and then both girls exclaimed in unison. 'Och, Charlie!'

The wee boy was on his knees, happily pushing his hands into the loose earth surrounding the base of a tall obelisk. He had managed to give his worm Christian burial before Rachel reached him, grabbed his muddy hands and drew them along the grass to clean them.

'You go on down with him, Rachel. I'll be right behind you.'

Josie waited until they disappeared out of sight as the path switched back on itself and dropped a few feet. Then she moved away from the mausoleum and struck out across the springy grass past a slender Celtic cross which commemorated a young man who had drowned in a boating accident on the Firth of Clyde. She'd always found that particular inscription real sad.

When she reached the highest point of the hill she stopped and turned. Spread out at her feet, the great city of her birth stretched as far as the eye could see: a sprawling mixture of houses, churches and public buildings, locomotive and chemical works, foundries and shipyards. Over to her left, glimpsed through warehouses and granaries, the Clyde snaked its way towards the sea.

Beyond the river rose the gentle plateau of the Renfrewshire hills. Enclosing the other side of the Clyde Valley, the Old Kilpatricks and the Campsies were more rugged. Josie had a dim recollection of once having been there, before the Great War when her real father had still been alive. Recently she had asked her mother about it.

Dorothy Collins had smiled sadly and said aye, once they had taken the bus out to Lennoxtown, climbed the Crow Road up to the Campsies and had a picnic. It had been before Rachel was born, so there had only been the three of them.

'Your father made a daisy chain for both of us,' she had told Josie. 'Crowned us his Queen and his Princess.' There had been such a wistful look in Dorothy's eyes, and Josie had tried her hardest to remember Andrew Shaw laying the circlet of daisies on her dark cloud of hair.

Her eyes left the hills, tracked over to the city centre. It was no distance from the Drygate but the family seldom went there. The High Street was like a great river, a psychological barrier far wider than the Clyde.

Harbouring a secret ambition of taking her Higher Leaving Certificate and becoming a teacher like her beloved Miss French, there had been a time when Josie had thought education might be her passport to a wider world. She'd had some wonderful daydreams about that but in her heart of hearts she had known there was as much chance of it coming to pass as there was of her travelling to the moon.

She'd have to be content with the education she had received. As it was, with her fifteenth birthday falling in August, she'd had a year more than she might have done. She could have left last June but her mother had somehow managed to bamboozle Arthur Collins into not realising that.

Josie had promised Miss French she would keep on reading after she left school. Her teacher had introduced her to the local library, spoken up for her when the librarian had looked askance at Josie's address. Angry and embarrassed, she had listened to a whispered conversation about the woman's reluctance to allow any of her precious books to spend time in the Drygate.

'The books will be quite safe,' Miss French had insisted. 'A very nice family. Exceptionally clean and well turned-out. You can see for yourself.'

As the librarian peered at her, Josie had experienced a sudden rush of sympathy for the cows and calves she sometimes saw being driven along Duke Street to the cattle market on the corner of Melbourne Street. That was how some folk gawped at them.

There wouldn't be much time for reading once she was working. Arthur Collins had blithely suggested his stepdaughter apply for a job he knew was going at the abattoir attached to the cattle market. Observing Josie's horror-struck reaction, Dorothy had patted her hand reassuringly and told her later she was sure she would be able to get a good clean job in a shop, perhaps even one of the more exclusive ones in the High Street.

'You're a clever lassie. A bonnie one too. As long as you remember to speak properly, put on the pan loaf a wee bit, you'll do fine. Some nice respectable place will snap you up, you mark my words. Maybe that lovely dress shop on the corner of Bell Street, or the florist's at the top of the Saltmarket.'

Josie privately thought it highly unlikely either of those establishments would take her on. She didn't have smart enough clothes, for one thing. Or shoes. She was barefoot today because the only alternative was being hot and uncomfortable in the one pair of heavy boots she had to her name and which she otherwise wore all year round.

She'd better get a move on. Rachel and Charlie would be wondering where she was. Manoeuvring neatly around a steep hairpin bend in the pathway, the squawk of a seagull passing overhead attracted her attention. She paused, shading her eyes against the sun so as to follow its progress. It flew towards the city centre and wheeled round towards the river.

Lucky seagull. It could go where it liked: over the city, down the river, across to the hills. Josie cast a swift glance around her. There were no living people to be seen among the monuments and the dead folk wouldn't laugh at her.

She extended her arms as far as they would go, straining with her fingertips as though she were trying to touch invisible walls. Standing on tiptoe, she tried to make herself as light as possible, a feather which the summer breeze caressing her smooth cheeks might easily lift.

Then, laughing at her own foolishness, she let her arms fall to her sides and ran down the hill after Rachel and Charlie.

They were waiting for her on the Bridge of Sighs, Charlie hanging over the parapet perilously high above the gulf which was now Wishart Street and had once been the valley of the Molendinar. Clinging on to the threadbare seat of her brother's short trousers, Rachel looked up with relief as her big sister approached. The anxious expression on her pretty face turned to delight as the three of them walked out into Cathedral Square.

'Oh look, Josie!' she cried. 'There's a wedding. Let's

wait and see the bride coming out. Maybe there'll be a scramble!'

'Don't be daft, Rachel,' said Josie, eyeing the line of sleek black motor cars waiting to receive the wedding party. 'This looks like a posh do and rich folk don't throw their money away.'

However, she agreed good-humouredly that they could wait. The longer they were out of the house, the more likely it was their mother could have a decent rest, at least until Arthur Collins and his sons came home from the football. If their team had won, everything would be hunky-dory. If not, Dorothy and the girls would have to creep around them as if they were walking on eggshells for fear of earning themselves a coarse and profane tongue-lashing.

Less than excited at the thought of watching a wedding, Charlie had perked up at the mention of a scramble, even though he would have to compete with the dozen other urchins waiting by the wedding cars and obviously nurturing the same hope. There were several photographers there too with large cameras on tripods, getting ready to record the special moment when the bride and groom emerged from the great west door of the cathedral.

When they did, Rachel was overwhelmed with admiration. 'Oh . . .' she breathed, 'doesn't she look lovely!'

She did. Josie immediately composed a description in her head. *Looking perfectly radiant, the bride wore a modern interpretation of a classic design. Her ivory silk frock was up-to-the-minute in length, stopping just on the knee. Her hand-embroidered veil was exquisitely draped.*

She watched with unaffected pleasure as the other guests came out. This was like the fashion photos in the newspapers come to life and the men were as elegant as the women. Several of them wore Highland dress – kilts, velvet jackets and frothy lace jabots.

One tall and fair young man really looked the part, his

good looks enhanced by the plaid he wore over his shoulder and fastened to his black kilt jacket by a big silver brooch with a large amber-coloured stone in the middle of it. She caught his eye and he surprised her by smiling at her.

The children watched as a succession of photographs were taken: the bride and groom on their own; with the best man and bridesmaids; with the two sets of parents; with various combinations of the other guests. After they were done, Josie noticed one of the photographers was now writing busily in a notebook. He looked up and saw her studying him.

'Friends of the Cunninghams,' he offered, indicating the wedding party with a nod of his head.

'Oh?' she responded. From the way he'd said the name, she realised it was supposed to mean something to her.

'My bosses,' the young man supplied. 'Owners of the *Glasgow Evening Dispatch* – among various other newspapers and magazines. Look,' he said, 'there's old Mr Cunningham now.'

A press baron, no less. She'd read about them, usually in the newspapers belonging to their competitors. The tall gentleman in morning dress and top hat had a mane of white hair and reminded her of Mr Lloyd George. The young man who had smiled at her was helping him into a car. The first vehicles in the line pulled away, a handful of coins flung from one of their windows towards the waiting children.

'He looks a bit fierce.'

'He can be. We call him Old Father Time because he's always yelling the *Dispatch*'s motto at one of his poor hapless wage slaves. *Time and tide wait for no man* – "especially in the newspaper business, laddie",' Josie's informant mimicked. 'He's always on the telephone too but some of us reckon he could speak to most people in Glasgow if he just went up on to the roof and shouted.'

Josie laughed. 'So you're taking photos of the wedding for the *Evening Dispatch*?'

'Aye, and the bride's the old man's god-daughter, so I'd better make a good job of the captions that'll go with the pix.'

Pix, she thought. Short for *pictures*?

'Tell me what you think of this one,' he said. 'I'm really quite proud of it.' He cleared his throat and began. '*The bride wore ivory. Her short gown danced on the knee and in every other detail obeyed Dame Fashion's strictest commands for this season*.' He looked up expectantly from his notebook.

'Not bad,' said Josie, tickled both by the extravagant yet concise description and the fact that it was a man who had composed it.

'Would you add anything?'

That amused her too. In her starched pinafore and patched clothes she couldn't imagine she looked much like an authority on fashion but he had asked for her opinion so she gave it to him. 'I think you should mention that the dress is silk. And would you perhaps say something about her veil?'

'Like what, exactly?'

She offered him her own sentence. *Her hand-embroidered veil was exquisitely draped*. He nodded enthusiastically, inquired if it was all right with her if he pinched it, and wrote it down in his notebook in a series of squiggles – shorthand, Josie presumed. Then he asked what she was called and told her his own name in return, extracting a small white card from the inside pocket of the jacket of his smart suit in confirmation.

Josie took it and read the words printed on it out loud: *Ben Gold*, and on the line below, *Glasgow Evening Dispatch*.

'Short name,' she observed.

'Deliberately so. I think it sounds better than *Benjamin Goldmann*.' He gave her a rueful grin. 'Less Jewish.'

Josie's brow furrowed. 'Why would you want to sound less Jewish?'

There were quite a few Jewish families in and around the High Street, several of them owning local shops and businesses. Since the Necropolis had its own Jewish enclosure, she supposed there must always have been some of them in the neighbourhood.

Ben Gold smiled at her. 'Sweet,' he said. 'Very sweet.' When he raised his curly head and looked over her shoulder she had the oddest feeling he wasn't seeing the cathedral or the departing wedding guests but something which lay way off in the distance somewhere.

'There are all sorts of prejudices in this world, Miss Collins.' His gaze came back to her face. 'Would you know me again?'

'Sorry, was I staring at you?' Josie blushed, realising how that might have been interpreted. Mr Gold was a very handsome young man. She said the first thing which came into her head. 'I always imagined people who worked for newspapers were older.'

'Even old people were young once,' he said reasonably. 'Have you never heard of cub reporters?'

'No,' she admitted. 'I haven't.'

'Newspapers take some people on really young. Folk who've got a talent for writing. So they can train them up in their way of doing things.'

Josie felt a rush of excitement. 'I've got a talent for writing,' she blurted out. She was shocked at her own lack of modesty but those were the exact words Miss French had used. *You've got a real talent for writing, Josephine.*

'Maybe you should apply to the *Dispatch* for a job, then,' he said casually, slipping the notebook into his jacket pocket and beginning to dismantle his camera.

'Can girls be reporters?' she asked, surprised.

'Oh, aye,' he said. 'There's two or three on the *Dispatch*.'

Josie's heart skipped a beat. It resumed its normal rhythm all too abruptly as she realised that she couldn't possibly have anything in common with the girls he had just mentioned. Female reporters would be young ladies, well-educated and well-spoken. They were highly unlikely to have been brought up in places like the Drygate either. Yet still, painfully aware of all that, Josie posed another question. 'Writing about fashion and stuff like that, you mean?'

'Hard news too,' he said with a smile.

She thought she understood what *hard news* meant, so she decided not to ask him to explain it. Studying him intently as he packed away his equipment, she found that her brain was racing, a hundred more questions hovering on her tongue. An ambition had been born.

Chapter 3

All through this Monday, always the longest day of the week, it had been obvious to Irene French that her brightest pupil had something on her mind. Josephine Collins was screwing up her courage to ask something. That was why she was lingering behind now, hands nervously clutching at the folds of her pinafore as she watched the last of her classmates file out of the room.

Tidying up her own desk set on the low platform in front of the blackboard, Irene lifted her head and directed a smile towards the back row where Josie sat. 'Was there something you wanted, my dear?' She cocked her head towards the wood and glass-panelled door to the classroom. 'Oh, excuse me one moment, Josephine.'

Turning sideways to make her way through the closely packed wooden desks, Josie came forward, only to stand in an agony of impatience as her teacher began to speak to the other young woman who had come into the room. Her name was Miss Anderson, and she was nothing at all like Miss French.

Whilst Josie's teacher was enthusiastic and encouraging towards all of her pupils, Miss Anderson seemed to actively dislike children. She also made no secret of her opinion of the lowly social status of many of her young charges. Becoming aware of Josie standing a few feet away, she broke off from what she was saying. 'Run along, girl.'

The dismissive phrase was accompanied by an equally

dismissive flicking of the fingers, but Josie stood her ground. 'Please Miss Anderson, I need to speak to Miss French about something import—'

Despite her determination, her voice tailed off when Miss Anderson, who'd already turned her back to continue her conversation, swung round and glared at her. 'Did you not hear me, Josephine Collins? I told you to run along.'

Josie was scared of Miss Anderson. She'd been in her class two years ago and had hated every minute of it: the grudging way the woman imparted information, the cutting and sarcastic comments she made, the unjust way she meted out discipline and punishment. One day, puzzling out a complicated long division sum, Josie had been using the blackboard behind the teacher's head as a thinking post. Miss Anderson had accused her of staring at her, and of dumb insolence.

Refusing to accept any explanation, the teacher had administered three powerful strokes of the tawse. The humiliation of the undeserved punishment had been awful, as the sting of the brown leather strap on unprotected palm and wrist had been exquisitely painful. Josie's absolute resolve not to cry had only made it worse.

Yet what she needed to speak to Miss French about was too important for her to meekly turn tail and run. She stayed where she was and took a deep breath. Anger flared in Miss Anderson's cold eyes, but Irene French intervened, stretching out an arm to indicate that Josie should move closer to her platform.

'Just a moment, Daphne. I think I'd better hear what this young lady has to say. I'm scared she'll burst otherwise.'

'P-please, Miss French,' Josie stuttered, 'w-would you know how to write a letter of application?'

Irene French answered her pupil's question with grave

courtesy. 'Yes, I would. Are you wanting help with something like that, Josephine?'

Doing her damnedest to ignore Miss Anderson's silent and inhibiting presence, Josie poured it all out, transmitting the information she'd got from the astonishingly friendly young man she'd met at the cathedral on Saturday afternoon. She had to stop every so often to explain the words she was using, terms she herself had known for only forty-eight hours. She'd thought about what he'd said so often over the weekend they were already becoming familiar to her.

'I couldnae start as a cub reporter, of course, I'd have to be a message girl or something. Maybe for the copytakers. They sit in these wee cubicles and take copy over the telephone.'

'Copy?' asked Miss French.

'That's what they call the stories the reporters write.'

'Over the telephone?'

'Mr Gold – that's the young gentleman I met – says it's like taking dictation at school.'

'Well, you're certainly good at that, Josephine,' Miss French said stoutly. 'And your handwriting is very neat and easy to read.'

Josie tried to sound nonchalant. 'Apparently they take it straight down on to typewriters. If they think you might have an aptitude for it, the paper will pay for you to have typing lessons at night school.' She swallowed hard. The thought of using a typewriter was only marginally less terrifying than the thought of speaking to another human being by means of a telephone. She'd never used the instrument.

Seated behind her desk with her chin propped on her fists, Miss French's eyes were bright with interest as she listened to the words tumbling out of her pupil's mouth.

'It sounds like an excellent job for you, Josephine,' she said. 'Right up your street.' Her brisk and positive tone made Josie's spirits soar. An image of herself in the Necropolis last Saturday afternoon winged its way into her head. Airborne at last, she thought joyfully, the bird that never flew suddenly taking to the skies.

'How do you go about applying?' Miss French asked.

Josie repeated what Ben Gold had told her. 'You write a letter to the editor enclosing two or three examples of your writing. If they like them they'll ask you to attend for interview at their offices in Buchanan Street.'

That was another terrifying prospect. What would she wear, for a start? She put that problem to the back of her mind for the moment. She'd cross that bridge when she came to it. If she came to it. She swallowed hard, and went on. 'Apparently you need two people to speak for you as well. Mr Gold said he'd put in a good word for me and I was wondering maybe . . .'

'If I might supply you with a written reference?' Miss French interrupted. 'Of course, Josephine. I'd be glad to.' She tapped her desk with one finger. 'I have some of your compositions in here. I'm sure the *Evening Dispatch* would be impressed by any of them.' She smiled into Josie's eyes. 'Wouldn't it be absolutely *wonderful* if you became a reporter?'

Josie smiled back shyly. Since her conversation with Ben Gold that idea had grown and grown. She'd been astonished when he'd offered to be one of her referees. 'I've got a hunch about you, Miss Collins,' he had explained, adding with a grin, 'and you did give me that *exquisitely draped veil*. I owe you a favour in return.'

Encouraged though she had been by that, Josie was still hardly daring to hope this was a dream with the remotest chance of becoming real. But if her teacher had confidence in her . . .

'For heaven's sake, Miss French!'

Both Josie and Irene French jumped at the interruption. They had quite forgotten the other woman's presence. Taking no part in the conversation, Miss Anderson had been perched on one of the desks in the front row of the classroom, listening with an outraged expression.

Now she said spitefully, 'How far do you think her application will go when they see her address? Working on a newspaper is a profession and a vocation – like teaching.' She turned to survey Josie. 'Wee lassies from the Drygate don't do that sort of thing. They're not up to it!'

Feeling about one inch tall, Josie dropped her eyes to the floor. The hateful voice went on, damning her even further. Damning Rachel and Ma and Mrs Paterson and the Fitzgeralds and every other decent person she knew.

'Why should anyone give a girl like this a start when they know full well she'll be married and breeding within a couple of years? The first halfways personable brute who crosses her path and that'll be it. The same as her mother and her mother before her, and all the rest of them in that rabbit warren up there—'

Josie's dark head snapped up but Irene French got there before her. 'That's enough, Daphne.'

The simple comment was uttered softly, but there was something in Miss French's voice which stopped her colleague in mid-flow. Daphne Anderson looked like a fish which had newly been landed on a river bank, floundering and gasping for air and wondering just how it had got there.

'Josephine, could you come to my house right now? Would your mother be worried?'

'You're surely not taking the girl home with you, Irene,' said Daphne Anderson, shocked into the indiscreet use of her colleague's first name.

'As a matter of fact, I am. Josephine,' Miss French asked again, 'will your mother be worried if you're late?'

'I could send a message home by my wee sister,' Josie said breathlessly. 'She'll be waiting outside for me.'

'Go and do that now, my dear, I'll meet you at the gate in five minutes.'

Miss French, it turned out, lived at the foot of the High Street, in a lovely red sandstone building above a row of equally nice shops.

'Come away in,' she said, leading the way along a close lined with beautiful china tiles and up the stairs to the front door, 'and we'll get that letter written and work out which of your compositions to send with it.' She had put a selection of them into her briefcase before they left the school. 'I have an engagement tonight in town and I'll be passing the newspaper office, so I could deliver your application by hand if you like. How would that be?' She extracted a key from her jacket pocket, opened the door and ushered Josie in. 'Go on through, my dear. To the front room.'

The spacious and light-filled apartment made an immediate impact on Josie. 'Oh, what a bonnie room! And you've got a bay window! That's what my mother would love.'

She ran forward to stand in the window embrasure, looking out with pleasure on the busy scene below. Trams, cars and horse-drawn vehicles were making their way around the tall and narrow Tolbooth Steeple. The historic tower stood in the middle of Glasgow Cross, the meeting point for five busy thoroughfares: the High Street, the Trongate, the Saltmarket, the Gallowgate and London Road. At midnight on Hogmanay, people gathered there to welcome the New Year, listening to the Tolbooth bells ringing it in.

Turning, Josie regarded the room in which she stood. The solidity of the beautiful cast-iron fireplace in the middle of one of the walls was lightened and comple-mented by two vertical lines of blue and white Delft tiles. The fresh flowers in the plain white china vase which stood on the empty hearth were also blue and white and the fireplace itself was flanked by two presses whose doors had been removed and which now served as bookcases.

In front of the fire sat a settee and two big armchairs, all of them draped with colourful cloths and piled high with cushions. Josie's eyes darted round the room, spotting the bed recess – as brightly decorated as the sofa and chairs – and a small writing bureau and upright chair close to it. Apart from one or two knick-knacks and a few lovely pictures on the walls, there was very little else in the room.

Perplexed, she addressed a question to Miss French, standing in the doorway watching her. 'Where do you cook?'

'Oh, I have a kitchen as well. Ben the hoose,' Irene said, dropping into the vernacular she would never have used at school and indicating where she meant with a wave of the hand.

Josie's grey eyes grew wide. 'You have a room and kitchen all to yourself?'

'I'm afraid so, Josephine,' Irene said wryly. 'I'm sorry if you disapprove.'

Josie blushed. 'Och, no. I'm sorry, I didnae mean . . .' She stopped and pulled herself together. Normally she did her best to speak nicely in front of Miss French. 'I don't disapprove at all. I've aye dreamed of having a room of my own.'

That simple ambition made Irene French's expression even more rueful. 'Be careful what you wish for, Josephine. Sometimes dreams come true.' Smiling at the obvious incomprehension which greeted those observations, she came forward and gave her pupil a gentle pat on the cheek. 'You don't know what I'm talking about, do you?'

Moving over to the bureau, she pulled out the chair which stood in front of it. 'Let's hope you never find out,' she said softly. She turned, her voice stronger. 'Come and sit down here and we'll get started.'

Josie was still studying her curiously, her interest piqued by the odd turn the conversation had taken. Irene became brisk, patting the back of the chair and repeating her invitation to sit down on it. 'Work, Josephine,' she said firmly, 'that's the thing. Satisfying work is a great blessing.'

Try as she might, sternly telling herself not to count her chickens before they were hatched, Josie couldn't help spinning daydreams as she walked home from Miss French's house. The *Evening Dispatch* would be so impressed by her compositions they'd offer her a job as a cub reporter straightaway and at an enormously high wage too. She would progress and progress, writing ever more exciting and important stories. In a couple of years she'd be earning enough to pay the rent on a home of her own. In her imagination the house bore a marked resemblance to the one she'd just left, although she couldn't imagine living on her own as Miss French seemed to do. That must surely be a lonely kind of life.

Josie's daydream included her mother and Rachel and Charlie. She wasn't sure where Arthur Collins and his sons fitted in and she didn't much care. She wasn't letting them into her castle in the air.

It would be a nice big house in a decent and well-kept building, with high ceilings and a bay window in the front room. Josie would go out to work to earn the money and her mother would keep the house. Dorothy would be able to buy nice food she would enjoy cooking for all of them and have plenty of time to put her feet up as well. She could sit in the bay window and watch the world go by or entertain friends to tea. Ella Paterson and Mrs Fitzgerald would call past now and again.

Rachel could stay on at school. Maybe she could become a teacher, Charlie too if he turned out to be clever. Josie hugged the happy hopes to herself. If she could give her wee brother and sister a hand up and a better start in life they could become anything they wanted to be.

When the reply to her letter came on Wednesday morning asking her to attend for interview on the following Friday at 5.45 p.m. her dreams shot up into the stratosphere. Convinced that the speed of the reply must indeed mean that Ben Gold *had* put in a good word for her, Josie was dancing on air despite the terror occasioned by the notification that Mr Cunningham himself would be interviewing her. As the letter explained, it was his policy to personally interview every job applicant seeking a position at the *Dispatch*. Standing reading the business-like sentences over her shoulder, her mother was as excited as she was.

'In Buchanan Street? The best street there is? Right, hen,' said Dorothy, a new determination about her. 'You're going to put on the pan loaf and wear your Sunday best.' She chuckled. As always, amusement transformed her from a tired-looking woman into an enthusiastic girl, not a great deal older than her daughter. 'Or my Sunday best, more like.'

'Apparently old Mr Cunningham has a real thing about shoes,' Josie said anxiously, remembering something Ben Gold had said after glancing in a rather embarrassed way at her bare feet. 'Says you can tell a lot about a person from the shoes they wear and the way they keep them.'

As one, the two of them looked down at each other's footwear. Then they looked at each other. Josie left it to her mother to state the obvious. 'Your boots are getting a wee bit disreputable, no' to mention the fact that they're gonnae look a bit heavy with my suit. You could have

40

borrowed my shoes but they're falling off my feet. No,' Dorothy murmured after a moment's reflection, having apparently had a silent discussion with herself, 'we havenae got time to wait for the Barras at the weekend, so it'll have to be Paddy's Market for us, hen. I'll meet you after the school and we'll go down then.'

Rachel volunteered to stay at home with Charlie the minute she heard of the plan. She would have been mortified if anyone she knew had seen her anywhere near Paddy's Market. While the much bigger weekend Barras attracted customers from far and wide, its weekday counterpart was somewhere only really poor people went.

Clothes which would have been reckoned rags elsewhere were sold here to folk who could afford nothing better. That was how the market held in the lane next to the fish market had acquired its name. When the first great waves of Irish immigrants had come off the boats at the Broomielaw Quay half a century and more before, they had often been completely destitute, with nothing to sell save the shirts off their backs. With no other means of raising money, that was precisely what many of them did.

Josie and her mother weren't thinking of those old sad stories on this sunny Wednesday afternoon. Enjoying the outing and each other's company, they made their way slowly along the lane between the Briggait and Clyde Street, laughing at the banter being tossed about between stallholders and customers alike. Josie clutched Dorothy's arm.

'Look, Ma. That looks as if it might fit me.'

The shoe positioned along with several others on a piece of cloth lying on the cobbles was in remarkably good condition. It was also more up-to-date than Josie had dared to hope, with a low but elegant heel and a T-bar strap. It was even brown, and would therefore go with her mother's costume. She watched anxiously as Dorothy stooped to pick it up for a closer examination. Would it fit? Would it be too costly for their meagre resources?

Spotting their interest, the stallholder, a good-looking man with a mop of wavy red hair and a lilting Irish accent, launched into his sales pitch. 'A silver sixpenny will secure you that bargain, missus. Is that not a darling wee shoe ye're holding there in your fine white hand?'

'Mebbe,' Dorothy said grudgingly. Necessity being the mother of invention, she was extremely adept at striking a bargain, never giving any ground until she had what she wanted at the price she was prepared to pay for it. Josie did her best to help by keeping her face poker straight, although it was gey hard. Only sixpence for a lovely pair of shoes in such good condition? They didn't really need to beat down a price as low as that.

'Where's the other one?' her mother asked. 'She'll need to try them on.'

'Sure,' the man said, looking her straight in the eye and speaking without a hint of embarrassment, 'there's only the one shoe in this pair. The price reflects that small problem. What a lady like yourself might consider nothing more than a minor inconvenience.' He smiled roguishly.

Watching the interchange, Josie noted with interest that it was the sort of smile a handsome man gave a pretty woman. She glanced at her mother. Dorothy *was* pretty, especially at the moment, her face animated and her eyes sparkling with life. She needed more of this: time away from the never-ending round of household chores; the opportunity to get out and about in the world; conversation and contact with other folk.

To her further delight, Josie saw that her mother was blushing a little, responding to the stallholder's evident and unabashed admiration of her. Dorothy rallied well, slapping the single shoe down into the man's hand. '*You* might call it a minor inconvenience,' she said with a magnificently haughty air, 'but I can see very well that ma lassie's got two feet, you great gomeril. Good-day to ye.'

They made it out into Clyde Street before the giggles overcame them.

'Minor inconvenience?' spluttered Dorothy, barely managing to get the words out. Seeking support, she placed one slim hand on her daughter's shoulder.

'Sure, and does the price not reflect that?' responded Josie, putting on a very creditable Irish accent. '*There's only the one shoe in this pair*,' she howled. Then, like her mother, she found herself unable to speak for a minute or two. 'Maybe I could hop along to Buchanan Street, Ma,' she suggested eventually.

Dorothy nodded. 'That's-just-what-I-was-thinking,' she managed. Recovering, she gave Josie's shoulder an encouraging squeeze. 'Don't you worry,' she said, 'we'll find something. Come on and we'll take another wee walk through.'

However, apart from an ostentatious wink from the would-be shoe salesman, which Dorothy just as ostentatiously pretended to ignore, they acquired nothing on their second trip through the market.

'Och well,' she said philosophically as they made their way back along the Briggait to the Saltmarket, 'we'll polish your boots till they shine. You'll wear my costume and best blouse and I'll do your hair real nice. You'll look so lovely they won't even notice your feet.' Her eyes were soft with love as she turned to look at her daughter. 'They'll be that dazzled by your pretty face and your bonnie hair.'

'Aye, Ma,' said Josie gently. 'Plus my brilliant compositions and Miss French's reference, of course.'

'Those too,' said Dorothy. 'Nae doubt about it.' She lifted her chin. 'And once you've got the job you'll be able to put some money by each week. Get yourself a really nice pair o' shoes.'

'Aye, Ma,' repeated Josie, taking her mother's arm. Linked by bonds both visible and invisible, the two of them headed for home.

Chapter 4

The first half of Josie's journey from the Drygate to Buchanan Street late on the following Friday afternoon took her through surroundings which were familiar enough. She walked along George Street, in the man-made canyon formed by the tenement houses which lined it. Every so often she had to cross one of the roads, also full of tenements, which rose steeply to her right, climbing up over the ridge of Rottenrow towards Cathedral Street and Parliamentary Road.

The area on the opposite side of George Street was full of warehouses and workshops. Rickety wooden staircases on the outside walls of stone buildings led to garment factories in lofts where seamstresses and tailors toiled under huge skylights to satisfy the demands of exclusive shops in Buchanan Street and Sauchiehall Street and beyond. Albion Street was home to one of the city's cigarette factories. Behind it lay Candleriggs and the wholesale fruit market. Full of hustle and bustle from early morning till midday, by this time in the afternoon the area around it was quiet and still.

It was the familiar mix of homes and workplaces, punctuated at the further end of George Street by the rather more imposing Royal Technical College and the long side elevation of the City Chambers. Obeying the directions Miss French had given her, Josie crossed into George Square and struck out diagonally across it.

She paused briefly by the newly erected cenotaph. Field Marshal Earl Haig himself had presided over the

dedication ceremony, a large crowd assembling to pay
tribute to all those citizens of Glasgow who had fallen in
the Great War. Josie allowed herself a moment's silence to
remember just one of them. Wish me luck Daddy, she
thought, touching the paw of one of the two great stone
lions which guarded the memorial to reinforce that plea.

Negotiating flower beds and statues, she crossed Queen
Street and entered St Vincent Place. The buildings here
were very grand, all ornate stonework and highly-polished
granite and marble pillars and gleaming brass plates
bearing the names of solicitors and banks and shipping
agents.

She passed the headquarters of the Anchor Shipping
Line, a tall and elegant building faced with white tiles
from which the pollution caused by Glasgow's heavy
industries could be more easily cleaned off. Next door,
the *Evening Citizen* newspaper was housed in compact
splendour, its red sandstone frontage adorned with a twin-
faced clock turret.

The building in Buchanan Street with the beautiful
brass lettering set into its large portico declaring itself to
be the *Glasgow Evening Dispatch* was similar in style to the
Citizen building and equally as impressive. It too had a
clock, with a single but rather beautiful face surrounded
by Gothic lettering.

Standing on the opposite side of the street, Josie tilted
her head so as to be able to read what it said. It was the
motto Ben Gold had mentioned. *Time and tide wait for no
man.* Perhaps not, but her appointment wasn't for another
fifteen minutes. Too early was as bad as too late. She
would wait for a wee while before she went in.

She retreated to the back of the pavement and took
in the scene. As the office day drew to an end smart
businessmen, dapper in bowler hats, dark jackets and
pin-striped trousers were leaving their places of work for
homes in the affluent suburbs. Girls a few years older

than herself hurried past carrying important-looking envelopes and packets.

On the opposite side of the road, a young woman stepped out from behind the wheel of a car, shrugged into an elegant coat and strolled off down Buchanan Street. As fashion decreed, something Josie had learned from reading the fashion pages of the *Bulletin* last week, the young motorist was clutching the buttonless garment about herself with one artfully positioned hand.

Josie glanced down at herself. It was all very well being familiar with the theory but the practice fell sadly short of the mark. When she had left the house she had felt rather smart and quite grown-up in her mother's Sunday best, ready to take on the world. Now she realised just how old-fashioned her outfit was, the skirt far too long and the heavy tweed completely unsuitable for a warm summer's day. All the women around her were wearing lovely knee-length frocks in lightweight colours and fabrics.

Many of them also wore neat little cloche hats over bobbed hair. Josie's headgear was a home-knitted tammy, and although Dorothy Collins had indeed done her hair nicely, its length must make her look exactly what she was: a schoolgirl dressed up in her mother's clothes.

Then there was the sheer awfulness of her footwear, big heavy boots in June. They must make it crystal clear what sort of a home she came out of, that she belonged in a cramped and gloomy tenement. Miss Anderson's words rang in her head. *Just a wee lassie from the Drygate*. It was as if she had the sentence stamped on her forehead, as easy to read as the motto around the *Evening Dispatch*'s clock.

Her carefully nurtured confidence, buoyed up with the enthusiastic good wishes extended by Miss French when she had left school this afternoon and the same from her mother and Rachel before she had set off half an hour ago, began to wobble. How could she possibly fit in here, among these well-dressed and capable people? She might be only a mile or so from her home but she was in a different world.

She let her eyes travel up the *Dispatch* building, trying consciously to calm herself down by thinking of the best words to describe it. Tall. Stately. Airy. There were lots of windows. She supposed you would need those in a building where people spent the day writing and typing.

Josie took a deep breath. If she turned tail now and ran, Miss Anderson would have won. She had to go through with this. For the sake of her mother and Rachel and Charlie. For Tam. For Mick Fitzgerald, who had been so pleased when he had heard she'd got an interview for a newspaper job. For her own sake. She gave herself an order. *Get across there, you.*

Once she reached the portico she hesitated again, standing at the bottom of the sweeping short curved staircase which led up to the front door.

'Can I help you at all?'

She turned, and found herself being addressed by an Egyptian sheikh with laughing green eyes.

'Have you lost your camel?' she asked mildly, startled out of shyness by the surprise of meeting a man dressed in flowing robes and headdress in the middle of Glasgow. Blinking, she saw that her cavalier was with a group of people similarly attired: an Egyptian princess and a couple dressed in white linen suits and pith helmets.

The green-eyed sheikh laughed. 'Fancy dress party this evening,' he explained. 'On the theme of—'

'King Tutankhamun and the excavations,' Josie supplied.

'A pretty loose interpretation of them,' he agreed, rewarding her answer with an appreciative curve of the lips. He seemed vaguely familiar and she wondered if she'd met him before. Somehow she doubted it. She didn't

48

tend to mix with the kind of people who went to fancy dress parties.

'Roddy!' came an impatient female voice. It was the Egyptian princess. 'Come on, darling,' she called. 'I absolutely must have a whisky and soda before I die of thirst.'

'In a minute,' he said absently over one of his broad shoulders, his attention focused on Josie. 'I noticed you hovering across the street there and I thought maybe you were lost. If you're looking for the *Evening Dispatch*, you've found it.' He indicated it with a tilt of his head. The gesture made the folds of material framing his firm-jawed face sway and dance. 'Reception's just inside the door. They'll help you out.'

Grateful for his kindness, she found herself confiding in him. 'I've got an interview. I'm trying to get my courage up to go in there.'

'Och,' he said, the merry eyes softening, 'you shouldn't be scared. Who's interviewing you, Mr Cunningham?'

Josie nodded. 'I hear he's a bit fierce.'

'Really? What else do they say about him?'

'Apparently he shouts a lot. Doesn't need a telephone to make himself heard on the other side of Glasgow.'

'I've heard that myself,' murmured the sheikh. The smile playing about his mouth widened.

'He's also supposed to have a big thing about shoes,' Josie said, her brow furrowing in concern, 'and mine aren't up to very much.'

The sheikh leaned back and squinted down at her feet. 'They look very clean and well-polished,' he assured her, adding casually, 'I wonder if they have a nickname for Mr Cunningham in there.'

'Seemingly they call him Old Father Time.'

The young man gave a short bark of laughter, encouraging Josie to pass on more of what Ben Gold had told her.

'Because he's always quoting the words round the clock and because they think that's what he looks like. I thought he looked a bit like Lloyd George myself.'

The young man laughed again. 'He wouldn't like that comparison very much. He's an old Tory.'

'You know him?'

'I have that honour and privilege,' he said grandly, but with a twinkle in his eye. Being ironic, she supposed.

'And is he fierce?' Josie asked anxiously.

'His bark's a lot worse than his bite. He also likes people who stand up to him. Don't be a wee mouse, that's my advice to you. And if Old Father Time' – he chuckled as he said the name – 'asks you for suggestions on how the *Evening Dispatch* might be improved, think along the lines of attracting new readers. Newspapers are always interested in doing that.'

'Roddy!' came an imperious voice, not the Egyptian princess this time but the female member of the couple dressed as archaeologists. Her gaze slid over Josie without interest.

The sheikh made a grimace. 'My big sister,' he offered. 'Pain in the neck.' He raised a hand in farewell and swung the cloth of his headdress over the bottom half of his broad face, as though he were about to plunge into the sands of the Sahara rather than the crowds of Buchanan Street. His voice came out muffled. 'Good luck with your interview.'

He strode off in a swirl of robes, Josie gazing bemusedly after him. This was a different world indeed, where young ladies drank whisky and grown men played the fool and allowed women to boss them around. Then she thought about Mick and Bridget Fitzgerald. Maybe the differences weren't that great. Resolutely, she pushed open the big half-glazed door of the *Glasgow Evening Dispatch*.

At close quarters, she thought Mr Cunningham looked

even more like Lloyd George and however much she tried to hide her heavy boots by tucking her feet in beneath her she was convinced that his piercing gaze kept falling to them. Another man introduced Mr Cunningham as the editor-in-chief and himself as his deputy, though in her nervousness Josie failed to catch his name.

Her interviewers sat together behind a massive desk set in front of a large window. She'd been seated on a single bentwood chair placed in the middle of what felt like several acres of empty floor. It all made her feel very small – apart from her clompy feet.

'So, young woman,' the editor-in-chief began, leaning forward over the desk and booming at her. 'Tell us why you want to work for this newspaper.'

She was struck dumb, so sure they would think her appearance shabby and trying so hard to mind her ps and qs when she did speak she couldn't think of anything to say. She had to say something. Both men were looking at her expectantly.

'B-because I'm g-good at writing,' she stuttered.

The deputy editor wrote something down on a piece of paper. Mr Cunningham barked out another question. 'Anything else?'

'I l-like reading n-newspaper articles.'

Under the folds of her mother's heavy skirt Josie was digging her nails into her palms. She knew she should say more than that, expand on the topic, but her brain seemed to have seized up. Mr Cunningham turned to his deputy and murmured something. He could obviously speak in a low voice when he wanted to. Josie heard the whispered response. *Not much self-confidence.*

She might have known this wasn't going to work. She felt like bursting into tears. Miss Anderson's voice was echoing round her head again, in the empty spaces which should have been filled with intelligent answers to the questions which were being put to her. *They're not up to it.*

51

She could see the sneering face, feel the disdain and condemnation.

Did they think it was easy having self-confidence when you were born and brought up in the Drygate? When everybody looked at you as though you were dirt because of your address and tarred everyone who lived there with the same brush, the good and the bad alike? Oh, but that made her so angry! There were lots of good people in the Drygate. So many of them had never been given the opportunity to show what they were made of or what, given half a chance, they might be capable of.

She had her chance now, right here in this office. Her heart thudding against the walls of her chest, Josie coughed to clear her throat. 'I like reading articles and comparing how different newspapers deal with the same topics.'

As one, the two men swivelled their heads and stared at her, for all the world as if she had disturbed some private and fascinating conversation they'd been having. She remembered what the sheikh had said. *Mr Cunningham likes people who stand up to him.*

'I can write,' she said. She gestured towards the sheets of paper lying on the dark wood of the desk in front of him. 'My teacher says so, and she's given me a reference to go along with my compositions. Have ye no' read any of them?'

Damn, damn, damn. She'd said *ye no'* when she should have said *you not*. And that last question, delivered with her head and her dander up, could be seen as bordering on cheekiness. As Mr Cunningham loomed over the desk – he seemed to be very good at looming – she braced herself for the dressing down. They'd probably be able to hear it in Paisley. But the words he fired at her weren't at all what she expected.

'What do you think of the *Dispatch*'s coverage of the Irish Question?'

Now there was a big subject, but she'd listened carefully to what Mick Fitzgerald had to say on that score, and developed a few ideas of her own into the bargain. She told Mr Cunningham what she thought, giving him a succinct summing up, and sensed the sharpening of interest emanating from both men. Maybe this badly dressed wee lassie sitting in front of them might have something to contribute to the paper after all.

'You seem to have thought about it very carefully,' observed the deputy editor. 'Is there a particular reason why you're interested in the subject?'

More relaxed now, Josie answered him fluently. 'I was there when the IRA ambushed the prison van in Duke Street.' Her face grew sombre. 'When the policeman was killed.'

'In the course of trying to prevent the Republicans from forcibly releasing one of their number,' Mr Cunningham confirmed. He frowned. 'That was three years ago. You must have been very young.'

'Old enough to be scared,' she told him, 'but interested too. It was odd,' she said reflectively. 'When the shots were fired, other people were running away. I was as terrified as they were but part of me wanted to stay and see what was going on.'

The deputy editor smiled. 'And did that part win?' he asked.

Josie nodded. She'd been slightly ashamed of herself at the time but the men behind the desk were now looking approvingly at her.

'The newsgathering impulse,' Mr Cunningham said. 'Everyone else runs away from burning buildings. Journalists run towards them. Tell us what you think about the *Evening Dispatch* features.'

She presumed they were the lighter items, not the *hard news* Ben Gold had mentioned. 'I think they're good . . .' she began cautiously.

'But?' demanded Mr Cunningham. She looked at him, and decided she might as well be hung for a sheep as a lamb.

'They can be a wee bit dull sometimes.'

There was an audible intake of breath from the deputy editor, but the big chief posed another question. 'In what way?'

'Well, it's an evening paper . . .'

'Does that make it inferior to a daily paper?' Mr Cunningham banged the desk with his fist, and Josie jumped. 'Dammit, the *Dispatch* has a very wide and intelligent readership. And it's my favourite out of all the newspapers and journals in my stable. This is where I started in this business, you know. When I wasn't a great deal older than you are now, young lady.'

Stand up to him, she thought. If he allowed her to answer he would see that she agreed with him. Evening papers weren't inferior to daily papers, just different. She told him as much and he sank back into his chair and asked her to explain what she meant.

'People sit down with an evening paper after their tea. They want to read the news but they want to relax a wee bit too. The *Glasgow Herald*'s got this column where they poke fun at what's going on in the news. It's very witty. Something like that would be ideal in an evening paper.'

The deputy editor gave her a sharp look and wrote something on his piece of paper.

'Some of the other papers have started including a page every day on women's topics. The *Dispatch* could do that too.' She remembered the advice the sheikh had given her earlier. 'Attract more female readers.'

Mr Cunningham grunted. 'Not backwards in coming forwards, are you?'

'You asked for my opinion, sir.'

'So I did,' he agreed. 'Can you work hard?'

Josie swallowed. Her heart was beating a tattoo against

her ribcage again. Could that question possibly mean what she thought it meant? In her mounting excitement she forgot all about putting on the pan loaf. 'Aye,' she said.

'Start at the bottom and take years to work your way up to something better?'

'Aye,' she said again.

'Can you put up with long hours and shifts and having to run up and down the stairs a hundred times a day? Fetch and carry for people who'll give you very little thanks for it?'

'Aye,' she said for the third time.

To her astonishment, Mr Cunningham stood up and came round the desk to shake her hand. 'I like a lass who's got spirit. The job of copy and messenger girl is yours, my dear. My secretary will let you know the details of pay and conditions.'

Back in the outer office without any clear recollection of how she had got there – perhaps she had floated out – Mr Cunningham's secretary looked at her over her spectacles. 'We'll require you to be smart, Miss Collins. A clean, fresh blouse every day. Will that be a problem?'

'N-no,' Josie stuttered, furiously reminding herself to speak nicely. 'Not a problem at all.'

Back in the Drygate half an hour later, Dorothy Collins threw her arms about her daughter's neck. 'Och hen! I'm that pleased for ye. We'll have a wee cup of tea to celebrate. Come and sit down and tell me all about it. I want to hear everything they said to you and everything you said to them.'

For the next ten minutes Josie satisfied her mother's curiosity, then tentatively mentioned what Mr Cunningham's secretary had said about smart clothes.

'Don't you worry about that. I've got it all worked out. You can keep my Sunday best skirt and blouse—'

'No, Ma.'

'Aye, Ma,' insisted Dorothy with a smile. 'When do I ever wear them? At least wi' you giving them a regular airing they'll shake off the smell of mothballs.' She bent back her thumb to indicate one outfit taken care of and began ticking off other items on her fingers. 'I've spoken to Mrs Fitzgerald. She used to be a seamstress when she was young. If we get the material, she can make a new skirt and two new blouses. That'll give you enough to ring the changes.'

'But Ma,' Josie protested, 'how can we afford all that?'

An odd look flitted across Dorothy's face. She stood up and walked over to the shelves on the opposite wall. Snaking her slim hand in behind the drum in which she kept flour, she brought out a flat round tin which Josie recognised as having once held boot polish. As she returned with it to the range, there was the unmistakable sound of rattling coins.

Josie watched her flipping it open, wondering how on earth her mother had managed to squirrel anything away. She saw the glint of silver, realised what she was looking at and uttered an immediate protest. 'No Ma, not wee Jamie's lucky money!'

The small hoard of cash which Dorothy had tipped out on to the table was largely made up of sixpences and shillings, although there were two florins and one half crown in amongst it. All of the pieces of silver had been gifts from the women of the neighbourhood to Josie's wee brother whose too-short life had ended before Christmas last year. Studying the money now, she thought sadly that the tradition of placing each coin gently into the baby's own tiny palm before it was handed on to his mother had failed to confer the hoped-for luck and good fortune.

Her mother gave her a level look. 'There's eighteen and six here. I'll leave the sixpence in for luck.'

'But it was for Jamie!'

Dorothy's voice trembled. 'Well, he doesn't need it any more, does he?'

Josie had to repeat the whole story of her interview to an excited Rachel when she returned from yet again retrieving Charlie from the Molendinar. When her step-father came in he evinced no interest other than to ask what her pay would be. It was Dorothy who told him, blithely knocking half a crown off the real sum. Josie felt a great rush of love for her. Her mother was making sure she would have some money for herself.

'She'll still have to do her share around the house,' Arthur Collins said gruffly. 'She needn't think she's getting out o' that.'

Do her share like he and his sons did? She'd be contributing wages to the house now too, which was their argument for never lifting a finger to help.

Josie didn't express any of those mutinous thoughts out loud. It wasn't fair on her mother. Besides, she was too happy. She had a job on the newspaper, a humble one admittedly, but it was a start. As she lay beside Rachel and Charlie that night, she hugged the knowledge to her like a precious jewel.

Chapter 5

Josie's head was spinning. She suspected it might actually burst if her poor beleaguered brain was called upon to absorb one more name or one more fact. As for remembering all the different rooms and departments she would have to become familiar with ... Well, that was surely going to take weeks.

From the outside the *Dispatch* building was deceptively small. Inside it was like a rabbit warren, extending upwards over six floors and sprawling backwards to a narrow lane which ran parallel with Buchanan Street. That was where the print room was and the loading bays from where each afternoon bundles of papers were dispatched to newsagents and kiosks all over Glasgow and beyond.

The space which housed the noisy, hot and smelly printing presses was huge, walls having been knocked down to accommodate the machines, but the rest of the building was packed with what seemed to Josie like hundreds of offices, most of them on the cramped side. Even those which were larger, like the newsroom and the library, were overflowing with people and desks and typewriters and telephones. Each of the six floors also appeared to have its own fascinating selection of nooks and crannies.

She was being shown round the building by one of the senior copytakers, a rather solemn middle-aged gentleman who had introduced himself as Mr Robert Bruce. Josie would have thought any man who bore that name would have considered it a cause for celebration but the namesake of Scotland's hero king had pronounced it with an air of weary resignation. Presumably he'd spent half his life listening to jokes and smart comments about it.

Her first day in the newspaper business began with an instruction to leave her things in the small staff locker room on the first floor. Mr Bruce announced that she was to have a comprehensive tour of the premises. Comprehensive was the word. As the morning wore on it became clear that he wasn't the kind of man who believed in hurrying things.

They had, for example, spent an awful long time in the print room, Mr Bruce emphasising what a great concession it was for Josie, as a female, to be allowed in there at all. Up to a point she found the head printer's description of the actual printing process quite fascinating. By the end of his impromptu forty-minute lecture, both her technical knowledge and her powers of concentration were somewhat stretched.

'That was the father of the chapel,' her guide said after they left. 'We've aye got to keep him and his members sweet. If the printers decide to get shirty, we're all snookered.'

Josie found the newsroom much more interesting. There was a large desk for the news editor, so covered with papers and notes and cups and saucers she wondered how he ever managed to find anything, and an equally large round table for the reporters under his command. It was easy to see that this was the nerve centre of the whole newspaper. In the twenty minutes she and Mr Bruce spent there, the telephone on the news desk rang constantly.

Several of the calls were followed by the news editor bellowing out a command to his men and, Josie noted with interest, one woman. About the same age as Mr

Bruce, the lady in question was introduced to her as Miss Clarke.

'With an *e*,' she said sternly, wagging an admonishing finger at Josie. 'That's the most important thing you have to learn about working for newspapers, young woman. Always spell people's names correctly. Accuse them of any crime or social or sexual deviancy under the sun and they won't protest. It gets their names into the paper, doesn't it?' she inquired cynically. 'But woe betide you if you spell those names wrong.' The warning finger came up again and Miss Clarke's voice, deep already, sank even lower. 'Woe betide you, my girl.'

Like most of her male colleagues, Miss Clarke with an *e* smoked constantly. The air was heavy with the aroma of tobacco, the atmosphere so thick Josie wondered if that was why the news editor yelled so loudly. Perhaps he thought his staff couldn't see him through the fug.

'Gibson! Get down to the Broomielaw right away. We're getting reports of a fire on board a cargo ship.'

'McKay! I trust it hasn't slipped your mind that the Lord Lieutenant of Dunbartonshire, his lady and their charming daughters are being honoured at a reception in the City Chambers in eight and a half minutes' time!'

'On my way, boss,' said a younger man, grabbing a shorthand notebook and smiling winningly at Josie as he ran out of the room.

'McKay!'

The young reporter put his head back round the door.

'Don't forget to take a snapper with you! And we'll need a description of the frocks, may God and all His angels help us!'

Deducing that a snapper must be a photographer, Josie wondered if Ben Gold might get the job. He seemed to know something about ladies' fashions.

'Clarke!'

As Mr Bruce ushered Josie out – she was beginning to

think of herself as a stray sheep and him as the collie dog – she registered that Miss Clarke wasn't accorded any extra courtesy because of her gender.

The picture editor and his assistant were busy too, but both were courteous and took the time to explain their work to Josie. 'We're trying to increase our photographic coverage. Catch up with our main rivals,' said the assistant. 'Not quite to the levels of the *Bulletin*, but a lot more than we do at the moment.'

Then it was on to the library where reference books and back copies of the newspaper were stored. 'You'll be sent to fetch some of these from time to time,' the librarian said. 'A reporter checking the facts on a story we've covered before. Or perhaps checking how we covered it.'

'Aye,' put in Mr Bruce. 'And if anyone wants you to run an errand they'll either phone downstairs or shout out for you. If you hear anybody in the building call for a copyboy, you respond to it instantly and do what needs doing.'

Josie considered pointing out that she was actually a girl, then decided against it. From what she had seen so far this morning the female sex was in a distinct minority here. Besides, she didn't want to prolong her tour by asking too many questions.

It was now twenty minutes to one. Having left home at half past seven so as to run absolutely no risk of turning up late on her first day at work, she was beginning to feel a wee touch hungry. She was also developing a keen interest in the location of the nearest ladies' lavatory. If Mr Bruce didn't decide he needed his midday meal within the next twenty minutes she would be facing the excruciatingly embarrassing prospect of asking him where it was.

She thought she might have seen one in the wood-panelled corridor next to the staff locker room where she had left her things, but she wasn't sure. The building was full of wood-panelled corridors. They were walking along one on the top floor now. Mr Bruce indicated a dusty passageway which led off to their right.

'Don't go along there on your own,' he said. 'Always ask someone to accompany you.'

Intrigued, Josie followed his pointing finger. 'Is that how you get on to the roof?' There had to be a great view from up there, right across the city's rooftops. Probably as good as from the Necropolis.

'Aye, but there's this big room down there before you reach the door to the roof. It's used for storage now but formerly it belonged to one of the old editors. Seemingly he liked to say he was always on top of things. That's why he chose to have his office on the top floor.'

'So why shouldn't I go there by myself?'

'There are those who say the old boy still drops in from time to time.' Her companion paused. Deliberate or not, the delay was just long enough to give the second half of his answer the emphasis it required. 'Which is pretty gey impressive when you consider that he jumped off the roof back in eighteen seventy-two.'

Josie glanced at the man, wondering if he was pulling her leg. It seemed unlikely. Whilst having been perfectly civil to herself and everyone else they'd met, Mr Robert Bruce hadn't smiled or laughed once throughout this whole long morning.

Her interest in the whereabouts of the lavvy was growing by the minute but a ghost story was a ghost story. 'Why did he jump off the roof?' she asked. 'Does anybody know?'

Mr Bruce shrugged. 'Who knows why editors do anything?' He pointed Josie towards a set of double doors which led out into the stairwell and lift shaft. 'We'll take the quick way down.'

Freedom at last. That happy prospect allowed her to rise above the terror occasioned by the rickety lift. Not only did it shake alarmingly as it headed towards the ground floor, there was only one word to describe the speed of its descent. It plummeted.

'Maybe he went mad.'

'Pardon?' Lost in happy thoughts about the imminence of her release, it took Josie a second or two to realise Mr Bruce must still be thinking about the ghostly editor.

'It happens, you know,' he said gloomily. 'Especially in this place.' He pulled open the noisy metal gates and stood back to let her go out in front of him. 'I'll take you to see the copytakers now.'

Josie meekly followed her gaoler. His attitude of doomed resignation was catching.

The copytakers sat in little cubicles in a group of three interconnecting rooms whose internal doors had been removed for ease of access. They were all wearing headphones and transferring what they heard through them on to typewriters which filled the tiny desks built into their individual booths. Mainly men, there were a few women dotted amongst them.

'Take copytakers,' said Mr Bruce, as they walked over to stand next to the cubicle nearest to the external door. 'They're all mad. The whole lot of them.' Like the mills of God, his thought processes appeared to grind exceedingly slow.

'Got it. Aye. Fine. Cheerio, then.'

Pulling a sheet of paper out of his machine, the young man they were standing next to looked up and pulled a daft face as he removed his headphones. 'It's the voices in our heads,' he told Josie cheerfully, having obviously heard his colleague's comment. 'Filling our heads all day long with the deathless prose produced by the scribes who work for this mighty organ. That's enough to drive anyone off their rocker.'

He lowered the head in question forward and banged it gently on his typewriter. 'Nouns, verbs, adverbs. Not to mention all those prepositions. Our poor wee brains are subjected to the relentless march of words through them and the constant clatter of typewriter keys outside them.'

The girl sitting in the cubicle next to him removed her own headphones. 'Don't frighten the lassie. She looks intelligent. Which means she'll be in here with us soon.'

Looking remarkably sane, her colleague raised his head and winked at Josie. 'Where you'll have to deal with eejits who dictate things like *full stop, new sentence*. Don't they think we know that a new sentence follows a full stop?' His voice was full of wounded outrage. Then he straightened his shoulders and yelled for a copyboy.

Josie wondered if Mr Cunningham made it a condition of employment that everyone who worked for the *Glasgow Evening Dispatch* should shout their heads off at regular intervals. Seeing her jump, the copytaker laughed and apologised, sticking out his hand. 'Tell us who you are, flower.'

'Josephine Collins,' she responded shyly. 'I've just started today as a messenger and copygirl.'

'Alan Dewar, at your service. Copytaker and unemployed novelist. Serving time with hard labour in this bear pit when all I really want to do is write the Great Scottish Novel.'

That earned him a look of affectionate exasperation from his female friend, who reached over and ruffled his dark brown hair. 'Aye, one day the world will recognise his genius.' She smiled at Josie. 'Deirdre Smith, Miss Collins. Welcome aboard. You'll be spending quite a lot of your time with us, taking copy up to the sub-editors on the fourth floor.'

'That'll keep you fit.' The messenger boy reaching across Josie for the article seemed to have materialised out of thin air.

'Are we not allowed to use the lift?'

'A lassie after my own heart,' said the boy, clutching the sheets of paper to his chest and making exaggerated sheep's eyes at Josie. 'If you're actually volunteering to travel in that contraption ye obviously enjoy dicing wi' death. Of course,' he continued, 'the odds against it being on the ground floor when you need it are about a million tae one. If a story comes in just before it's time to put the paper to bed, you're gonnae have to dash up those stairs like Eric Liddell.'

'Like you should be doing now, you wee toerag,' said Alan Dewar. 'Our new recruit may indeed be a very attractive young lady, but kindly refrain from mooning over her in that revolting manner. Love lives must be conducted outwith office hours. You know the rules.'

'You're embarrassing the girl,' chided Deirdre Smith. She stood up, pushed back her chair and walked over to Josie. 'You're looking a bit pale and interesting pet. Are you needing your lunch?'

'Yes,' said Josie gratefully, hoping her sheepdog would relinquish control before she had to rush to the ladies' with the speed of an Olympic sprinter. He did, although he muttered something about lunch breaks being a luxury in the newspaper business, especially on an evening paper. Some people knew they couldn't relax until the late final hit the streets and there was no possible chance of getting any more news out that day.

'I'll meet you back here at two o'clock sharp,' he told Josie. 'You haven't met the people in features yet.'

'And I bet you can hardly wait to spend more time with our Robert,' murmured Alan Dewar as the door swung shut. 'It's a psychosis, you know.' The man sitting on his other side lifted his head.

'Of the liver, do you think?'

'Not Robert the Bruce,' scoffed Alan. 'He just loves being miserable. Why look on the bright side when it's so much more fun to look on the black?' He leaned back in his chair and put his hands behind his head, interlacing his fingers. 'I blame the Kirk, of which I understand he's a pillar. I bet he revels in all that Presbyterian guilt. Thou shalt not enjoy thyself.'

'Isn't it cirrhosis anyway?' queried Deirdre. 'Of the liver, I mean.'

Alan shrugged his shoulders. 'Psychosis, cirrhosis, what's the difference? Everyone in here is suffering from one or the other.'

'They're all either aff their heids or hopeless drunks,' explained Deirdre, seeing Josie's puzzled look. 'Come on, I'll point you in the direction of the locker room. There's a toilet up there too,' she murmured as she led the way out into the hallway. 'If you've spent all morning with Mr Bruce I imagine you'll be needing to make a visit there by now.'

'Oh, aye,' said Josie gratefully. 'Thank you.'

Ten minutes later, considerably more comfortable in body, she was standing in the staff locker room wondering if *putting the paper to bed* meant what she thought it did. They seemed to have their own form of English here, not to mention speaking it in an extravagant and flamboyant way.

Still, almost everybody she'd met had been friendly. That copyboy was maybe a bit fresh but she would set his gas at a peep if he tried anything on. You didn't grow up in the Drygate without learning how to dampen the ardour of an over-enthusiastic youth.

She surveyed the large square table which dominated the centre of the room and wondered if someone as lowly as herself would be permitted to sit at it. Maybe folk had their favourite places. While she was considering the problem, she heard voices in the corridor outside.

The girl standing in the open doorway of the locker room was tall and slim, with glossy dark auburn hair cut in the short fringed bob which was currently the height of fashion. Hand on doorknob, she threw a laughing comment over her shoulder. When she turned to say hello to Josie, her hair swung beautifully with the movement. 'Your first day? How's it going?'

'It's been absolutely fascinating,' Josie said slowly, and speaking nothing but the truth. The girl laughed and came confidently into the room. Her striking looks were enhanced by her fashionable clothes. She wore a very short box-pleated navy skirt in lightweight wool and over it a long and lacy jumper in palest cream, belted to give her ensemble the necessary low-waisted look. Josie was sure her matching stockings were real silk and she would have died happy if she'd possessed a pair of shoes like the ones the girl was wearing. They were navy too, with low heels and a narrow strap over the instep secured by a pretty little button.

'It's always a bit daunting when you start a new job,' observed the newcomer, placing a small packet wrapped in greaseproof paper on the table in front of her and proceeding to unwrap it. Like Josie, she had sandwiches, only hers were dainty triangles of bread and cold meat with the crusts cut off. Josie's were two thick slices with a small amount of cheese between them, grated to make the taste go further.

The young woman didn't seem to notice what she was eating, too intent on quizzing the new girl on her reactions to her first day. After a few questions, she laughingly apologised for it. 'Sorry, I'm not letting you eat your lunch. Reporter's instincts, I'm afraid. We never stop asking questions.'

Josie's grey eyes widened. 'You're a reporter?'

'A very humble one. Sorry, I should have introduced myself before I started interrogating you.' She offered her hand. 'Sally Fleming, Features Desk.'

Josie shook hands and gave her own name. 'It must be great to actually be a reporter,' she said feelingly.

'It has its moments. Although currently I feel like I'm banging my head off a brick wall.' Responding to Josie's look of interested inquiry, she expanded. 'I'm trying to persuade the editor to institute a page exclusively for women readers.'

'Oh, I think that's a great idea! I suggested that to him at my interview.'

Sally grinned. 'I could warm to you, Miss Collins.' She took a healthy bite of one of her little sandwiches and chewed it reflectively. 'I only wish I could think he was actually listening to you at the time. The only other female journalist in the building is totally against catering for the *Dispatch*'s women readers.' She shuddered theatrically. 'Have you met our Miss Clarke yet?'

'Is that the lady in the newsroom?'

'Yes. Fearsomely intelligent and not an ounce of sense of humour in her. Nor would she ever dream of working in features. Considers that sort of thing to be beneath her. Like too many people, unfortunately.'

'I thought she might be a bit of a dragon,' Josie confessed.

'Comes from a long line of dragons,' came a voice Josie recognised. 'All of the fire-breathing sort.'

She looked up and saw Ben Gold, fingers curled around the staffroom door. 'You got the job then, Miss Collins? Congratulations!' He came forward, laid a camera bag on the table and shook her warmly by the hand.

'You must have given me a good reference,' she said shyly. 'Thank you. Thank you very much.'

'Think nothing of it,' he said with a smile. 'It was my pleasure. I'm sure you're here on merit anyway.' About to join the two girls at the big table, something outside the open window attracted his attention. He walked over to it and waved to Sally and Josie to join him. 'Look, it's the son and heir.' There was an unexpectedly harsh edge to his voice.

The tall young man with his foot on the first step of the entrance stairs one floor below was casually dressed.

He wore a soft-collared shirt, light-coloured linen trousers and a jacket in the same material and a similar shade. It wasn't the sort of outfit you expected to see in the city centre. Unless they were workmen, most of the men you saw around these parts wore formal and rather sombre business suits.

Most unusually, especially for Buchanan Street, he wasn't wearing a hat either. Looking down on the top of his head, Josie saw the July breeze lift the ends of his dark blond hair. As they watched, a petulant voice floated up to them.

'You're not *really* going back to work, Roddy?'

Josie transferred her attention to the car which sat at the kerb. The girl behind the driver's wheel was pouting prettily.

'Afraid so, my love.' Laughing, the young man turned and blew her a kiss, then took the stairs two at a time, disappearing into the building.

Josie's stomach gave a great lurch. It was that laugh which had done it. When she had last seen the light-hearted young gentleman he had been dressed as an Arab sheikh. Oh dear.

Chapter 6

'The son and heir?' Josie repeated, stalling for time. It had just come to her why she had thought he looked familiar when they had met on the steps on the day of her interview. He was the young man who had smiled at her at the cathedral, whom she had seen helping Mr Cunningham into the car. Pity she hadn't remembered that and put two and two together before she had opened her big mouth and put her equally large foot right in it.

Sally nodded. 'Yes, Roderick. Mr and Mrs Cunningham's wee afterthought and the apple of the old man's eye.'

'What about his mother?' Josie asked, only half paying attention. She was wondering what her chances were of avoiding young Mr Cunningham for the next six months, or at least until he had forgotten both their meeting and her rudeness about his father.

'Oh, she died when he was quite young, apparently.' Sally's eyes, their lashes lightly coated with mascara, were still fixed on the road below. 'Looks like the young master's been out for lunch with one of his girlfriends.' Her pretty mouth turned down in a mocking gesture. It too was discreetly painted, in a shade of lipstick which perfectly complemented her hair colour. 'He does seem to have rather a lot of them.'

'I wonder when the novelty of working for a living will wear off,' said Ben sourly. 'I don't suppose he has the faintest idea of how lucky he is to walk out of Glasgow University and straight into a job here.'

70

'Maybe he's a good writer,' Josie said doubtfully, moving back over to the table and resuming her seat. Sally followed her but Ben stayed where he was at the window. His response to Josie's comment was uncompromising.

'He's one of the enemy. The over-privileged son of a press baron. Destined from birth to join the ranks of the filthy capitalists.' He spat the words out as though they would make him sick if he kept them in his mouth any longer. 'Happy to exploit the misery of the poor to maintain themselves and their purely decorative wives and daughters in positions of comfort and power.'

Josie was unsurprised by his grim tone. Politics was a serious business these days. It might be seven years since the guns on the Western Front had fallen silent, but industry and commerce were still trying to recover from the effects of four years of world war. How you thought that crucial recovery might be achieved depended on which side of the political fence you stood.

Ben Gold was obviously a socialist. Lots of people were. Mick Fitzgerald for one, probably herself for another. She knew it wasn't right for some people to have so much when others had so little, especially when so many of the former hadn't worked for what they had. Josie also firmly believed that when it came down to it, the difference between her and the young lady who had just dropped the boss's son off was nothing more than an accident of birth.

'It's the arrogance of the ruling classes that I can't stand,' Ben declaimed. 'Asking working people who're struggling hard enough already to tighten their belts and make sacrifices. People like Roderick Cunningham and his kind don't understand the meaning of the word.'

Hands clasped on the table in front of her, there was a note of reproach in Sally's voice. 'People of every class lost loved ones in the war, Ben.'

'I suppose,' he admitted grudgingly. He thrust his hands into his pockets and propped himself against the window frame. 'Well, now we've got a Labour government at last, we'll maybe see some changes.'

The expression on Sally's face grew sceptical. 'And can we look forward to Mr Ramsay MacDonald and his cabinet addressing one of the major injustices of our age?'

Ben shifted uncomfortably. 'Sally, he may have other priorities—'

'Hah! That means no, I take it. Explain something to me, Ben. How is it that you've got the vote now while Miss Collins and I will have to wait until we're thirty?' Her voice grew heavy with sarcasm. 'The thanks of a grateful nation for the work done by women during the Great War. But only to those who're ratepayers.' Sarcasm gave way to indignation. 'Or the wives of ratepayers, of course. Appendages and chattels of some man.'

Josie regarded Miss Fleming with renewed interest. There was obviously a lot more to her than good looks and fashionable clothes. Ben Gold was studying her too, an expression of great affection on his handsome face.

'Not that I'm being ungentlemanly here but whilst I recognise that Miss Collins might have another lifetime to live before she's able to exercise her democratic rights, don't you yourself have rather less than eight years to go, Miss Fleming?'

'You know exactly what age I am, Benjamin Goldmann.' She turned to Josie. 'We went to school together.'

That explanation made Josie wonder if they had been childhood sweethearts. They certainly seemed very close. Despite Miss Fleming's current belligerence, there were sparks flying between her and Ben Gold which spoke of a deep and loving bond. That impression was confirmed when she pulled a face at him and dropped the argumentative stance almost as quickly as she had adopted it, turning once again to Josie. 'Fancy a quick walk round the shops, Miss Collins?'

'I'd love that,' she said shyly. She wouldn't be able to afford to buy anything but she would enjoy looking. Miss Fleming was very stylish. It would be fun looking at things with her, hearing her opinions on the latest fashions.

'Can I come too?' asked Ben eagerly, standing back to let the two girls precede him back into the room.

'But Miss Collins and I want to look at the clothes shops,' protested Sally.

Ben gave her an arch look. 'What makes you think I don't, sweetie?'

It wasn't until the end of her second week at the *Dispatch* that Josie came face to face with the son and heir. Running upstairs with some copy, not yet exactly sure what happened to it after she placed it in the wire basket on top of the cupboard inside the door of the sub-editors' room, she found herself putting the sheets of paper into his hand as he stepped into the open doorway.

'Thanks,' he murmured, scanning the first few lines of the article. 'We've been waiting for this.' He glanced up in a polite smile of acknowledgement which broadened into a real one when he recognised her. 'Hello there! You made it through the interview, then?'

'Yes.' The only way to go about this was to brazen it out. She took a deep breath. 'So did you, I see.'

He chuckled. 'Well, at least you don't pussyfoot around the issue like the rest of them do.'

Pleased that she had made him laugh, she tried again. 'Was your interview *very* tough?'

'As a matter of fact it was.' He tucked the typescript under one arm and sank back against the cupboard, half-standing, half-leaning. 'Although I don't suppose anybody in here would believe that,' he observed.

'I believe it,' Josie said impulsively.

'Why?' he demanded

'Because it obviously matters to you that you're here on merit and not simply because you're your father's son.'

He acknowledged that with a grave nod of his head. 'Thanks. I appreciate that.'

'So what is your job then?' He was the boss's son and she the humblest of copygirls but he seemed disposed to be friendly.

'Sub-editor.'

'Oh aye, of course.' Josie nodded wisely. Two weeks into the job and having applied herself to the issue, she was convinced there could be very little journalistic jargon left for her to learn. 'What with your father being the editor.' Presumably the deputy editor who'd helped interview her had simply been filling in.

Roderick Cunningham laid the typescript to one side, pushed the heels of his hands against the cupboard on which he was sitting and grinned at her. It was hard to believe that a man whose eyes could crease at the corners like that was a filthy capitalist. 'Sorry,' he apologised, 'I'm not really laughing at you. It's an understandable mistake.'

He explained to her what sub-editors did. Far from being the editor's deputy, they came pretty low in the pecking order.

'Particularly as far as reporters are concerned,' he added wryly. 'They seem to think we crawled out of the primeval slime. People get very precious about what they've written and it's the subs who edit that before it goes into the newspaper. We write the headlines and make sure the copy itself is grammatical. Check the spelling and punctuation. Sentence structure and suchlike.'

'Is that what you studied at Glasgow University? English?'

'Yes. And Scots.'

Josie wrinkled her nose in puzzlement. 'Scots?'

'What we all speak when we take the marbles out of our mouths,' he explained.

'But you're so well-spoken.' She thought he had a beautiful voice, rounded and mellow. You could tell he was Scottish, but only just.

He grimaced at the term she had used. 'Only because certain people made it their business to knock any hint of a Glasgow accent out of me.' He fixed Josie with a stern look. 'Do you really think there's something wrong with the way you talk? I think it's lovely.'

'Well,' she pointed out, 'people are always telling me there's something wrong with it.'

He lifted one of the hands with which he was bracing himself against the cupboard in a gesture of exasperation. 'That's so wrong! Scots is the language of Burns.' The hand travelled to his hair, his fingers ploughing impatiently through it. 'Lots of other great writers too. Take Robert Fergusson, for instance, one of the great neglected geniuses of Scottish literature.'

'I'm afraid I've never heard of Robert Fergusson,' she confessed, 'but I do love Burns. I get that from my father, I think.' Her mother had told her of Andrew Shaw's love of poetry, pointing to the framed print in her kitchen which had belonged to him and which depicted a scene from *The Cottar's Saturday Night*, one of Burns's most popular poems.

'I'm a real enthusiast for the Bard of Alloway too,' Roderick Cunningham said warmly. 'I get that from *my* father.' Mischief crept into the green eyes. 'Or as you know him, Old Father Time.'

Josie blushed, and posed an anxious question. 'You haven't told him, have you?'

'Of course not. I can keep a confidence, Miss . . .'

'Collins,' she supplied. 'Josephine Collins.' She blurted out an apology. 'I'm awful sorry if I was rude about him.'

75

'Not at all,' said Roderick easily. 'You were only repeating what other people had said and it was very naughty of me not to tell you who I was.' He folded his arms across his broad chest. 'Sometimes I find it embarrassing to have to admit that I'm the boss's son. People start treating you differently, you know?'

She didn't, but she thought she understood what he meant. 'Did your father teach you about writing for the newspapers?'

He nodded. 'I've always haunted the office during my school and university holidays. My mother died when I was eight. My sister wasn't long married then and I was rather in her way. Whenever my school wasn't keeping me out of her hair, she used to dump me in here. Not wanted on voyage, as it were.' He gave an odd little shrug of the shoulders, dismissing the subject. 'Do you want to write yourself, Miss Collins?'

'Oh, aye – I mean yes.'

'You mean *aye*,' he said firmly. 'Tell me what you've learned so far.'

She answered him without missing a beat. 'That a news report always puts the most important information right at the beginning.'

'The result first.'

Josie nodded. 'Say there's been a big robbery somewhere. The first paragraph tells you what, where, when, why, how – and who if they know it. Which they usually don't. Then each subsequent paragraph adds more information.'

'In descending order of importance,' he contributed, 'so that if it has to be cut we're not losing too much.'

'Because it's always cut from the bottom up.'

'Aye,' he said, giving her a smile to acknowledge his use of the word. 'Because we don't always have time to read what we're cutting. It can get a bit frantic in here sometimes.'

'I've noticed.'

Roderick Cunningham laughed. 'Do you know why articles are written like that? The fearsome Miss Clarke told me.'

'And if she says it, it must be true?'

'It would take a braver man than me to doubt her,' he agreed. 'According to her it goes back to the American Civil War. They were sending information back by Morse code, tapping it out on the key. They had to get the important information over quickly because there was always the danger they would be cut off. By the other side presumably, or marauding Red Indians.'

'Or some sort of natural disaster,' Josie offered. 'Like those rock falls you see in the cowboy pictures.'

'Exactly.' He smiled at her again. 'Shall we be friends, Miss Collins?' he asked. 'Since we're both starting out together in this daft business?'

'Yes,' she said. 'Let's be friends.' Even if he was the boss's son and, according to Ben Gold, a filthy capitalist, he was a human being. What's more, he seemed to be a nice one – what Tam's mother called a really *genuine* sort of a person.

'First-name terms?'

Josie hesitated. 'We've been told to call you *Mr Roderick*.'

'Oh no!' he exclaimed. 'Really? That sounds positively Dickensian. I'm not having that. Roderick's fine,' he said. 'Or Roddy.'

It was only when she was on her way home that she realised she was now friendly with the undoubted future editor of the newspaper for which she worked. Aye, she thought, that'll be right. She startled a woman walking in front of her along George Street by laughing out loud.

Chapter 7

'Oh, Lord!' Sally Fleming's face was a picture of dismay. 'It's snowing!'

Josie, who'd just taken charge of an article to go upstairs to the sub-editors, followed her horror-struck gaze to the tall windows overlooking Buchanan Street. Like scraps torn from a sheet of white tissue paper, large snowflakes were floating gently past on their way down to earth.

'It is Christmas Eve,' she pointed out. 'It's appropriate. I like the snow. It makes everything look clean and fresh.'

'Until all the wheels and horses' hooves and feet churn it up into grey slush,' moaned Sally. 'Not to mention the fact that if this keeps up all afternoon I'll have to put on my horrible rubber galoshes to go home tonight.'

Josie left the Features Department hiding a smile. The weather had to get really bad before the fashionable Miss Fleming plumped for practicality over fashion. While she envied Sally her collection of smart footwear Josie had to admit, reluctantly as she heard herself clomping up the stairs in them, that her own heavy boots were much more suitable for this kind of weather.

Although she'd been out working for six months now she hadn't yet saved up sufficient money to be able to buy herself shoes. There were always so many other calls on her small wage, and the proportion of it she was able to keep for pocket money was tiny. Och well, maybe she'd manage to get a pair before the spring arrived.

The scene which greeted her up in the subs' room was one to which she'd grown accustomed since she'd come to work at the *Dispatch*. Roddy Cunningham was holding forth, long arms outstretched as he regaled his colleagues with a funny story. One of them spotted Josie standing in the doorway.

'There's a lady present, Roderick my boy. Keep it clean.'

'As if a gentleman like myself would descend to smut in order to get a cheap laugh!' Roddy clapped a dramatic hand to his chest. 'I'm wounded, I really am.' He swung round and flashed Josie a quick smile. 'Hang on a wee minute before you go back downstairs, Jo, would you?'

He always called her *Jo*. It was an abbreviation of her name she found she liked and its informality was typical of the man. Her first impressions of him had been accurate. Despite his wealth and social position, there *was* something awfully down to earth and genuine about him.

He certainly didn't expect people to bow and scrape because he was the boss's son, although he could play the haughty young gentleman when he wanted to. Josie had seen him do it and deduced it was usually when he thought someone was being insufferably pompous. His normal demeanour was one of relaxed friendliness, an attitude which had won over many of the people who'd been doubtful about him at the beginning. He also had an immensely attractive verve and enthusiasm for life. He liked to fling himself at it: often quite literally.

Back in October he had returned from a house party in the Highlands with a broken nose. The girls at the front desk had shrieked when they had seen him, alerting everyone in the vicinity to his battered appearance. With typical insouciance, Alan Dewar had sauntered out of the copytakers' room and greeted Roddy with a 'Mr Boris Karloff, I presume?'

Undaunted by the bandages swathing his face,

Roderick had launched into a detailed account of how he had incurred his injury. He'd been staying near the twin villages of Kingussie and Newtonmore, deadly rivals in the small matter of shinty. Kingussie had been short of a man for a practice match and . . . well, he should have known better.

When Sally Fleming inquired archly as to what exactly shinty might be he grinned at her wickedly, or as wickedly as the dressings criss-crossing his face allowed. 'A cross between hockey and clan warfare.'

'So some ferocious Highlander smacked you on the nose with a big stick?' asked Alan.

'It's called a *caman*, dear boy,' Roddy said loftily. 'And the perpetrator was a merchant banker from Edinburgh.'

Josephine waited until he had concluded his current story, a perfectly clean but somewhat convoluted account of an incident at some other weekend house party he had attended. Once the tale was told, he walked over to where she stood next to the door. Bandages now removed, everyone agreed that he had been remarkably lucky. His nose was perhaps just a little broader than it had been before.

'Those shorthand and typing classes?' he said. 'I'm hoping we might have some news on them by the end of the day.'

'Oh, that would be great,' she said enthusiastically. 'I'm really grateful to you for speaking to your father about them.'

'Nonsense. I want to do them too, you know, and lots of people have put in a recommendation that you should go on a course as soon as possible.' He laughed softly when she blushed. 'Don't look so embarrassed. Everyone's keen to see you get on. Even the fearsome Miss Clarke,' he teased.

'She's not fearsome at all once she finds out you're interested in writing.'

'No,' he agreed. 'She's not.'

Discovering Josie in the lift intently reading a piece of copy on one of those rare occasions when that means of transport had been on the ground floor at the right time, the older woman had explained a few of the basic principles of newspaper journalism. Since then she had passed on more tips. She wasn't the only one. The foot soldiers of the *Glasgow Evening Dispatch* liked to think of themselves as cynical and hardbitten, but many of them had responded to Josie's evident curiosity and eagerness to learn.

'Don't mention the classes to anyone yet,' said Roderick. 'You know how my father likes to make these announcements himself. With luck we'll hear before the holidays anyway.'

'Are you going away somewhere?'

'Dinner at my sister's house tomorrow.' He rolled his eyes heavenwards. 'Still, it'll be fun being with my nephew. He's just turned thirteen.'

'You're a young uncle, then.' She took a step towards the door.

'Aye. I don't think my sister thinks there's much to choose between Matthew and myself. She finds us both equally juvenile.' He raised his eyebrows, passing the comment off as a joke. 'Then Dad and I are off to friends in the Borders for a few days from Boxing Day onwards. I'm looking forward to that. Does your family celebrate Christmas, Jo?'

'Not really,' she said, sliding off the subject of her home life as she usually did. 'It's not really a Scottish festival, is it?' She paused in the doorway, one small hand resting on the frame. 'So I've not to say anything about the classes?'

Roddy adopted a mysterious look. 'No names, no pack drill.' As usual, he was unable to resist hamming it up. Raising a hand to his face, he tapped his nose significantly with his index finger to emphasise the need for secrecy. Josie laughed when he winced.

'Where's your womanly sympathy?' he grumbled.

'Self-inflicted injury,' she said blithely. 'Caused by sheer stupidity on your part. You admitted as much yourself.'

Shy at first, she now treated him as he expected to be treated. It was the way things were done at the *Dispatch*, especially among the younger members of staff: a cheerful trading of friendly insults within and between the various groups which made up the workforce. The Newsroom and the Features Department pretended to sneer at each other, the copytakers complained constantly of the idiocy of journalists and reporters of all persuasions while the printers knew they were the only people who were really crucial to the production of the paper.

Two hours later Josie stepped out into a wintry but picturesque Buchanan Street. Darkness had fallen along with the snow and the brightly lit shop windows were festive.

Like most Scots, even those not in the newspaper business, she would be at her work tomorrow as usual. Rachel and Charlie would be hanging up their stockings tonight but that was as far as it went. It was Hogmanay and New Year which was the big festival for ordinary folk. That didn't prevent Josie from appreciating the efforts the shops had gone to, vying with each other to create the most luxurious displays of Christmas cheer and plenty.

Enjoying the scene, she stood for a moment with one mittened hand resting on the balustrade of the entrance steps, partially protected from the deluge by the ornate overhanging stone canopy. Whoever had left the building shortly before her must have run their own hands down the curved stone bannisters. She could see the tracks on both sides. The copyboys gathering up snowballs, no doubt.

The heavy door behind her opened and Alan Dewar

and Deirdre Smith came out. They stood and chatted for a minute or two – until they were all struck by snowballs launched with pinpoint accuracy by the three copyboys standing grinning at them from the other side of the street.

'Honestly,' Alan said, brushing the snow off his coat and the red woollen scarf Deirdre had given him for his last birthday, 'some people never grow up. I'll sort out the wee blighters.'

Watching him dart through the traffic to the other side of the road, Josie thought that Sally was right. The snow would soon be churned up into horrible slush. Alan caught up with one of the boys, stooped to lift a handful of fresh snow, pulled the boy's collar back and tipped it down his back. The lad howled with delight: in much the same way as Alan did when one of the other boys retaliated in kind.

Deirdre patted Josie's sleeve. 'What was that he just said about some folk never growing up? Good night, pet. Merry Christmas.'

Josie returned the salutation cheerfully, made her way down the steps and headed up towards St Vincent Place. By the time she got there her dark coat, knitted tammy and hair were sparkling with snowflakes. She negotiated the busy thoroughfare and was trudging past the Clydesdale Bank when she heard her name being called.

Peering through the snow and traffic, she spotted Ben Gold. She would have crossed back over to him but he indicated with a wave of his hand that she should stay where she was. When he reached her he pulled her into the light being cast by one of the low ornamental globes set into the wall at the front of the bank building.

'It's confirmed,' he said, almost out of breath. 'You start shorthand and typewriting classes in January!'

Josie's grey eyes opened wide with delight. 'How do you know?'

'The son and heir's just told me. Wanted to give you the good news himself but his old man's nobbled him to discuss something.' Ben took a deep breath to recover from his run through the snow. 'He said he thought it would make a nice Christmas present for you and asked if I'd mind trying to catch up with you. I'm to wish you Merry Christmas from him as well.'

Being one of those people who continued to maintain a hostility towards Roddy, Ben had the grace to look a little embarrassed. The boss's son generally met any such aggressive unfriendliness with calm good manners, as he obviously had this evening.

'It's a lovely Christmas present,' Josie said, gazing up at Ben. He was covered in snow too. It twinkled like stars on his dark curls. Since she would have to wait a few days to thank Roddy, she settled for thanking the bearer of the glad tidings instead. 'Oh, Ben!' she said, and threw her arms about his neck in sheer gratitude. His own arms came lightly about her waist in automatic response.

Behind her, she was aware of a slow-moving horse and cart, the customary clip-clop of hooves transformed into a squelching sound by the snow which covered the road surface. A familiar voice gave the animal the command to stop.

The soft lamplight falling on Tam Paterson's face didn't make his expression any less stormy. Josie hastily let her arms slip off Ben's shoulders and introduced the two young men. Ben was all charm. Tam barely acknowledged his friendly greeting, his lips compressed in a thin line of disapproval as he addressed Josie. 'I'll give you a ride home.'

'Have you finished all your deliveries?'

'Of course,' he said, his voice clipped. 'I wouldnae be going home otherwise, would I?'

'This'll be a busy night for you, I expect.'

Lobbed into a potentially awkward silence, Josie knew

that Ben's comment had been designed to be helpful. It evoked a mere grunt in reply.

'Up you go then, madam,' said Ben, giving her a hand to climb up beside Tam. 'Your carriage awaits.'

She beamed back down at him. 'Merry Christmas, Ben,' she said.

'Wrong religion, sweetie. But thanks all the same.'

As they pulled away from the kerb, she could feel Tam's reaction to the casual endearment. It was in his rigidity as he flicked the reins to get the horse moving again without so much as a backward glance at Ben. That was plain silly. He must know he had nothing to worry about. Their relationship had progressed a lot over the past six months.

Only yesterday evening they had exchanged kisses and cuddles in the most shadowy corner of the close. Somehow Josie never worried about four-legged visitors when she was with Tam. Their late-night trysts had become a regular occurrence – despite a private decision that since she wanted to concentrate on her job it might be as well to hold him at arm's length a wee bit.

Once she allowed him to put his strong arms about her all of her good resolutions were forgotten. When his gentle but firm lips kissed her forehead, her neck or her mouth she could think of nothing else but returning his caresses. Surely her reactions proved to him that he was the only one she cared about in that way?

They travelled along to George Square and halfway around it in silence. The breeze turned sharp, and Josie shivered.

'There's a rug there. Put it over your knees.'

He reached behind him with one hand and gave it to her, his eyes never leaving the road ahead. She obeyed him with a murmured thanks. Unable to keep it to herself any longer, she told him her good news. He reacted with another grunt.

'Tam,' she said gently. 'You don't need to worry about Ben. He's not like that.'

'Grow up, Josie. All men are like that.'

She studied his stiff profile through the swirling snow. How could she explain? Either he wouldn't understand or he'd be shocked and disapproving. *Grow up*, he'd said. She'd done a lot of that since she'd been at the *Dispatch*, acquiring a sophistication which sometimes surprised her. She often felt as if she was living in two different worlds. No, she knew she was.

She laid a hand on Tam's arm. He didn't shake her off but he didn't soften at her touch either. 'Everybody behaves that way at the paper,' she said. 'They're like actors on the stage. You should meet the boss's son some time. I was so pleased to hear about the shorthand and typing classes, that's all. I wasn't giving Ben a *real* kiss.'

Tam was still staring straight ahead, taking a sighting on the road in front of him through the ears of Jimmy, the great Clydesdale horse which was pulling the dray. 'Weren't you?' he asked, and Josie heard the thawing she'd been waiting for. Tam Paterson wasn't a moody person. He'd been jealous, that was all. There was something quite nice about that. It was touching . . . and rather flattering. Josie was far too fond of him to take advantage of it.

'Definitely not,' she said briskly. 'You know something, Tam? I'd be much warmer if I sat closer to you.' She edged nearer, flicked the corner of the blanket over him too. Under cover of it, she laid her hand on his leg.

'Oh, Josie . . .' he moaned, and she chuckled softly when she saw his own big hands relax on the reins.

'Keep your mind on your work, Mr Paterson. We're no' wanting to end up in the gutter.'

'I'm needing a kiss, ye wee bisom.'

'I'll give you plenty later on tonight.'

'A hundred,' he said.

'A dozen,' she teased. 'We wouldnae want you to get spoiled.'

'I'll make ye forget tae count them,' he promised. He took his eyes briefly off the road and snatched one to be going on with.

'Ma?' Josie pulled her key out of the lock and closed the front door behind her. The house seemed strangely quiet, especially for this time of day when her mother was usually bustling around preparing the evening meal. Curious, she went through into the kitchen.

Dorothy Collins was in the rocking chair by the range staring blindly into the flames, her hands lying loosely in her lap. Josie searched her memory. She couldn't remember when she had last seen her mother sitting doing nothing.

'Ma? Are you all right?'

Dorothy looked up. She blinked once or twice, as though her daughter's softly spoken inquiry had recalled her from somewhere a long way away.

'Are you all right, Ma?' Josie asked again, moving forward as she spoke the words. She crouched down beside the rocking chair. 'Where are Rachel and Charlie?'

'Across at the Fitzgeralds' house. The menfolk have gone out for a drink.' She attempted a smile. 'Since it's Christmas Eve.'

Any excuse. Dorothy made an obvious effort to rouse herself. 'How did you get on at your work today, lass?'

She had answered one of Josie's questions and not the other. Noticing the omission but not quite sure what to do about it, she told her mother about the shorthand and typing lessons. Animation lit up Dorothy's weary face.

'And the paper will pay for them? That must mean they're thinking of starting you as a copytaker, hen. That's great news. I'm real pleased to hear it.' She raised one of her hands from her lap and smoothed her daughter's luxuriant dark hair back from her brow. 'Your father would have been very proud of you.' Dorothy's eyes drifted to the print of *The Cottar's Saturday Night* on the wall above her head.

Her daughter peered anxiously up at her. 'Are ye no' feeling very well today, Mammy?'

Dorothy laughed. 'I'm feeling fine,' she said. 'Blooming, you might say.' She gripped the arms of the rocking chair and slid forward in it, preparatory to standing up. 'Come on then, this'll no' pay the rent. Will you help me get the tea?'

'Aye, and I've got a couple of wee things for Charlie and Rachel's stockings. Here, I'll show you before they come back.'

Rising to her feet also, she began to rummage in her bag. She'd saved up her pocket money for the last few weeks so as to be able to buy the small gifts.

Her mother regarded her with soft and loving eyes. 'You're a good lass, Josie. Whatever would I do without ye?'

'Merry Christmas, Ma,' she responded impulsively, passing on the greetings given and received so often today in Buchanan Street, in her other world.

'Merry Christmas, my lassie. Come and give me a hug.'

Dorothy felt so small and thin, as though a puff of wind might blow her over. Scared of hurting her, Josie held her as tightly as she dared. Let her have a Happy New Year too, she thought, squeezing her eyes shut so that the wish would take. Please God, let my mother find some joy in the year to come.

Chapter 8

The page did eat the date. The date did eat the page. The
second sentence had raised a laugh when the short hand
teacher had first dictated it to her students. Now it didn't
provoke the merest flicker of a smile. With Easter and
the RSA examinations only a fortnight away, every
head in the room was bowed in fierce and silent concentration.

In half an hour's time in the classroom along the
corridor those same heads would be bolt upright, eyes
fixed on the large chart at the front of the room which
showed a much-magnified layout of the typewriter key-
board. Looking down at the real thing was a mortal sin,
punishable by being shouted at in front of your fellow
students. They were learning to be rapid and accurate
touch typists and the only way to do that was by touch. A
glance before you started to ensure your fingers were
poised above the correct guide keys was all that was
allowed.

Josie had taken to the twice-weekly evening classes at
the commercial college in St Enoch Square like a duck to
water. Despite her initial fears about getting to grips with
a typewriter, Josie now loved the fact that her own ten
fingers could tap words into a machine which then
transformed them into a neat and professional-looking
printed page. As long as you practised enough, of course,
and their teachers made sure of that.

Since the course had started at the beginning of
January she had lost count of how many hundreds of

times the quick brown fox had jumped over the lazy dog. Then there were all those good men who needed to be told that now was the time to come to the aid of the party. Despite the monotony of the practice sentences Josie understood the point of the endless repetition. It was all about gaining the confidence that the relevant keys were where your fingers thought they were.

They had progressed on to copying business letters and longer passages out of stiff-backed textbooks propped up beside the large and solid Underwood and Remington typewriters they used. So far, all the words Josie had typed had been someone else's. One day they would be her own: well-researched and well-crafted articles on a myriad of fascinating and topical subjects.

Crafted. It was one of the formidable Miss Clarke's words. She had told Josie that a good piece of journalism, or indeed of any kind of writing, had to be constructed. It needed a shape: a beginning, a middle and an end. Miss Clarke had also emphasised the importance of the hook, the snappy beginning which encourages the reader to read on, not turn the page to read another article with a more enticing first sentence.

'You've got more leeway in a features article,' she'd said, unbending sufficiently to admit she herself had once written such pieces. 'You can be more descriptive, offer some of your own impressions of what you're writing about. Although,' she continued, raising her usual warning finger, 'you must always guard against the use of the first person singular. Unless it's a personal experience piece, of course, although even there it pays to be careful. It sounds arrogant and self-obsessed if you keep saying *I*. And unlike a news report, you don't have to give all the information in the first paragraph. You can tantalise, perhaps ask a thought-provoking question which you then proceed to answer.'

'You mean,' Josie said, thinking about some articles

she'd read recently, 'like: *What Do Women Really Want? How Much Longer Must Glasgow's Citizens Put Up With This Scandal?* That kind o' thing?'

Miss Clarke nodded approvingly. 'If that question comes from someone you've interviewed for the piece, so much the better. Good quotes are crucial, particularly when you're investigating some sort of scandal or injustice.'

'You don't look down on feature writing then?' Josie asked interestedly. 'Some people seem to.'

'There are features and features,' said her tutor darkly. 'The best are equally as valuable as the best news reports. Indeed, the boundaries between the two can sometimes be hard to distinguish.' The warning finger came up again. 'What you must always bear in mind, young Josephine, is that it's all too easy for female journalists to find themselves being shunted into the frothy siding, never to emerge again. Especially attractive young ladies like yourself,' she admonished. 'Then it's all fashion and cookery tips and bonnie baby competitions and writing about the social lives of aristocratic ladies.' Miss Clarke shuddered.

Josie nodded. 'That's what Miss Fleming says. She calls it the doings of *The Honourable Miss Double-Barrelled*.'

Miss Clarke let out a surprisingly girlish peal of laughter and patted Josie on the shoulder. 'Very good. Don't betray my dark secret to anyone, will you, Josephine? And never forget about the beginning, the middle and the end. And the hook.'

It was a different kind of hook which was worrying Josie at the moment: the ones attached to the shorthand outlines she was copying down in her notebook. Like everyone else in the class, she had initially found it quite tricky becoming familiar with the symbols which Roderick Cunningham referred to as *these blasted wee hieroglyphs*. Determined to succeed, she had enlisted Rachel's help.

Each evening after they helped their mother clear away
the tea things and wash the dishes, the sisters sat down at
the table and for at least half an hour Rachel read out
passages for her sister to take down in shorthand.
Sometimes it was an article from the newspaper, sometimes a text from one of her schoolbooks. As Dorothy
pointed out, smiling at her girls, that killed two birds with
one stone, helping Rachel with her schoolwork too.

Thanks to those extra practice sessions with Rachel,
Josie now had one of the fastest speeds in the class. As a
result, the teacher was putting her in not only for 80 and
100 words per minute but also the stage above. She had
thrilled and challenged Josie last week by announcing in
front of the whole class that she saw no reason why Miss
Collins shouldn't achieve 120 wpm at the Easter exams.
The shorthand teacher wielded a merciless stopwatch,
smilingly ignoring the groans and pleas for mercy as she
proceeded in rapid succession from one passage to the
next.

Mind you, as Roderick had been the first to notice,
their teacher did suffer along with them. A charming lady
in her early forties who always addressed her young
students as *ladies and gentlemen*, she started each evening
session with her glossy brown hair pulled back into a
smooth chignon. An hour of relentless dictation and
timing, not to mention sitting hunched over the book
from which she read out, invariably took its toll on her
coiffure.

Several strands of hair always managed to work themselves loose long before the hour was out. She was prone
to absentmindedly shoving them back in wherever they
would go, the resultant effect on her otherwise *soignée*
appearance being a source of much harmless amusement
to her pupils.

One of the first to finish taking down the current piece
of dictation, Josie lifted her head and glanced across at

the neighbouring desk. Roddy was having hair trouble too, one of his corn-coloured waves falling forward over his brow. He blew it away impatiently, concentrating hard on the task in hand.

'Quite sore on the fingers this lark,' he observed as they chatted together in the ten-minute break before they went on to the typewriting section of the course. 'Especially the pinkies,' he added, stretching out his hands and surveying the digits in question. 'Don't you find, Jo?'

'Does it no' all just add to your battle scars?'

His hand went protectively to his nose.

'How is that now?' she asked.

'An awful lot better.' He raised his eyebrows twice in quick succession. 'Even if it has spoiled my good looks.'

'Och, no,' she said immediately. 'It gives your face more character.'

He laughed. 'Is that a compliment or an insult?'

As they came out of the college after the typing class, he offered her a lift home. He always did that, as she always refused. Josie would have loved a ride in his car but she knew he was only being gallant. She had another reservation too.

She could never be ashamed of Ma or Rachel or Charlie but the Drygate was something rather less than humble. She didn't want Roderick Cunningham pitying her because of where she lived. Struggling together to master shorthand and typing, him treating her in the easy way that he did, they were equals. She liked that.

'I'll say good night, then,' he said in his lovely voice, deep and soft in the darkness. 'See you in the morning, Jo.'

As ever when she came home in the dark, Josie had armed herself with a small stone to fling along the close in case there were any rats lurking. It had no sooner left her hand than she heard a sharp yelp of pain. Very human-sounding pain.

'What the fu—'

Emerging from the close mouth on to the pavement, her stepbrother Billy stifled the curse when he saw her. 'Och, it's wee Josie. Home from the night school.' He made it sound like something she ought to be ashamed of. Arthur was at his shoulder, a bottle of beer in his hand. He passed it to Billy, who took a swig before handing it back to him. Arthur raised the bottle in a mocking salute.

'Care to join us? We'll even wipe the top of it,' he added with an unpleasant leer. 'If you insist, wee sister.'

'No, thank you.'

'Oh, get her!' said Billy, his words slurred. He raised the pitch of his voice, mimicking her. '*No, thank you*. Och, we're very pan loaf now that we work in Buchanan Street!'

She looked at him coldly and made to enter the close, willing them to stand aside and let her through. Neither of them moved.

'Excuse me, please.'

That got her more mimicry. Billy looked her up and down. 'I must say our wee sister's looking very smart since she started work. Would ye no' say so, Arthur?'

'I would indeed. Now she's no' wearing pinafores and we can see a wee bit mair of what she's made of. Very tasty. Tell ye what, hen,' he said, 'we'll let you by in return for a wee kiss. How's that?'

He made a horrible smacking noise with his tongue and his lips, as though he were relishing a piece of food. Josie choked back the revulsion and gritted her teeth.

'Let me through or I'll knee the both of you where it hurts.'

Arthur laughed. 'No' so posh now, eh? What would your toffee-nosed friends up the town think if they could hear ye?'

She locked eyes with him. 'Let me through,' she repeated, wondering what her chances were of making good on her threat. If there had been only the one of them . . . but, as usual, they were hunting in a pack. 'I'll start screaming my head off if you don't,' she said, and had to fight against allowing the relief to show on her face when Arthur took two or three steps to the side.

By the time she got there he had closed the gap between himself and his brother up again, forcing her to brush against both his and Billy's bodies as she went into the close. Once she had squeezed through she turned and glared at both of them, defying them to try anything else. Arthur had one hand stretched out towards her. There was little doubt as to its intended destination.

'Just you bloody dare,' she whispered, slapping it down.

Arthur thrust his face towards her, his voice as quiet as her own. 'Gonnae get Tam Paterson to me? Jesus Christ, ah'm terrified.'

Billy's guffaw followed her into the house. How different from her other world where charming young gentlemen laughed at the things she said and politely asked if they could see her home. She made a mental resolution to ask Rachel to come out and wait for her in future when she came back from night school.

It was lunchtime and Sally was teaching Josie how to do the Charleston in the wide corridor outside the locker room whilst simultaneously propounding some of her theories on fashion. 'You see,' she said, 'people think it's all about frivolity and female vanity, but there's a serious side to it as well. No, bring that hand back up now.'

Josie negotiated the next series of steps. 'What's the serious side?'

'Short skirts,' said Sally. 'And flat chests.' She pulled a

comic face. 'The latter being something neither you nor I naturally have.'

Josie laughed. 'Too true. Is it the hands and knees bit now?'

'Yes. Quite hard doing it without the music, isn't it? Now, where was I?'

'Short skirts and flat chests.'

'Short hair too. What's all that saying to men?'

'Dunno,' said Josie. She carried on dancing and thought about it. 'I'm not sure about the short skirts, but I suppose the rest of it could be saying that we're not so different from them?'

'Exactly,' said Sally triumphantly. 'I knew you had a brain.'

'Thank *you*,' said Josie in mock-outrage. She was growing more confident, able to give the banter as well as take it.

Sally grinned and touched her fingertips to her heels. 'It's announcing that we're ready to be their companions and playmates.'

Josie thought about it some more. 'Because nobody wants to take anything seriously these days?' she asked breathlessly. Dancing and talking at the same time was quite tricky. 'Because-of-the-war?'

'It's the whole Jazz Age thing,' Sally agreed. 'Everyone's disillusioned, so the people who can afford it—'

'The-Bright-Young-Things?' Josie managed.

Sally inclined her head in acknowledgement. 'The very same. They'd rather bury their heads in the sand than pay attention to the misery round about them. Everyone's had enough misery.'

Josie nodded her head. It made sense. She waited till she'd caught her breath again. 'What's the next progression in fashion?' she asked. 'Back to long skirts?'

'Search me,' said Sally. 'If I knew that I could make a fortune on the Paris catwalks. Gosh, this *is* difficult without the music, isn't it?' She began supplying it. 'Pah-pah. Pah-pah. Pah-pah-pah-pah-pah-pah . . .'

'Young ladies! What *do* you think you're doing?'

The two girls froze in mid-step.

'Is this a seemly way to behave in the offices of the *Glasgow Evening Dispatch*?' bellowed the all-too-familiar voice.

'Let's face the music,' murmured Sally.

'That's very good,' responded Josie, fighting a highly inappropriate attack of the giggles. The two of them were for it. Turning awkwardly, Sally stumbled and grabbed on to Josie's arms for support. Eyes downcast as she steadied herself, her head flew up when she heard Sally speak.

'And what are you grinning at?'

'Not a thing,' Roddy Cunningham said smoothly. 'It wasn't a bad impersonation though, was it?'

'You didn't fool us,' Sally said grandly. 'We knew all along.'

'No, we didn't,' said Josie, a giggle escaping. 'We were terrified!'

He laughed and sketched them both a bow. Sally asked if he'd care to join them in the dance.

'Ladies,' he said, 'I'd love to. Unlike my respected parent, I absolutely adore the Charleston. However, I have about my person an item of mail which our Miss Collins might find strangely interesting.'

He held out a small blue cardboard cylinder. Guessing immediately what it contained, Josie flew to his side, breathless now with anticipation rather than exertion. 'The results are out? How have we done?'

'I've got thirty-five words per minute typing and a hundred words per minute shorthand,' he said smugly. 'How you've done is in here.' He raised his hand above his head and made her jump for it.

'Well?' Sally demanded as Josie extracted a rolled letter

and two certificates from the cylinder, stretched them out and began rapidly scanning them.

'The same as Roddy for typing.' She handed that certificate and the letter to Sally, wrestling with the second piece of parchment as it began to roll itself up again. 'And a hundred and twenty words per minute for shorthand. With Distinction!' she squealed. 'I've won a silver medal!'

'Oh, well done!' Sally threw her arms about her neck and hugged her.

Roddy shook her warmly by the hand and asked if there was an official presentation of the medal. Josie bent her head once more over the letter. 'They want me to go to the college on Friday. At twelve noon prompt.' She looked up. 'That's the day after tomorrow. Do you suppose it'll be all right for me to take my lunch break early?'

'Of course it will,' Roddy said immediately. 'I'll fix that for you if you like. In fact I'll go and see about it right now. I'm so pleased for you, Jo. Listen,' he said, already halfway towards the stairs and walking backwards as he made the suggestion, 'why don't I come with you on Friday and then take you out to lunch to celebrate? I'll get us both the afternoon off so we can take our time over it.'

She and Sally both yelled in unison. 'Look out!' He'd been a step away from tumbling down the staircase.

Bursting with pleasure though she was, Josie decided to keep her wonderful news to herself for the next two days. On Friday she would surprise her mother by arriving home early and proudly displaying her medal to her. She would further astonish Dorothy by relating how the boss's son had taken her out to lunch. Fancy that. She'd never been out to lunch with anybody. She only hoped she'd know the right knives and forks to use.

Waiting by the reception desk on Friday morning she was wondering why the stylish couple standing a few feet away seemed familiar when the receptionist spoke to her out of the side of her mouth. 'Old Father Time's daughter and son-in-law,' she volunteered.

That explained it. She had seen them before, on the day she had come for her interview and they had been heading off for their fancy dress party.

'Isn't their son handsome?' whispered the receptionist. 'Going to be a heartbreaker in a few years' time, I reckon.'

Roddy's nephew, Josie thought, sneaking a surreptitious glance. His parents were very good-looking too, although the whole family had a vague air of discontent about them. Perhaps they'd been quarrelling. The father sauntered across to speak to one of the other receptionists.

'Did you see my theatre review in last week's paper, my dear?'

'I'm afraid I didn't, Mr Campbell.' The girl sounded nervous and uncomfortable. When Josie saw the way Roddy's brother-in-law was looking at her she realised why. It was horribly reminiscent of the way Arthur and Billy looked her over. He was that type, then. No wonder his wife was glaring at him.

Roddy came breezing in. 'All set, Jo?'

He wheeled round when his sister said his name, seeming surprised to see his family there. 'Shona? Are you in to see Dad? Hello there, Charles. How's it going, Matt?' He strode over and ruffled his nephew's hair.

'No, Roderick,' said his sister, sighing heavily. 'We are not in to see Father. We have an appointment for luncheon with you. Don't tell me that you've forgotten.'

'It looks very much like it,' he said cheerfully, already moving back across the hall. 'Sorry, Shona. I've promised to take Miss Collins out to lunch today. She's just won a silver medal for shorthand, you know.' He beamed at Josie.

His sister's gaze swept over her as it had once before, cool and uninterested. Josie didn't think she was imagining the extra edge of disdain as she took in her youth, simple clothes and obvious lowly position. 'I hardly think it's fair of you to disappoint Matthew in favour of one of Father's junior employees.'

Roderick was opening his mouth to respond to that when the main door was pushed confidently open. The girl who swept in was most definitely a Bright Young Thing, fashionably dressed and oozing confidence. 'Roddy, darling!' she exclaimed. 'You're ready and waiting for once! Do tell me where we're going for lunch, sweetie!'

'Oh dear,' breathed the receptionist, 'now he's really in trouble.'

Josie decided to take herself out of the equation, stepping forward and placing her hand on Roddy's arm. He protested, but she insisted that she'd enjoy her afternoon off anyway. Then she left them all to it.

Despite her dizzy about the lunch, she was dancing on a pink cloud as she made her way home after the presentation. The principal himself had handed her the medal. He told her she'd brought honour on the college, her employer and most of all, herself. She must have worked very hard and she was entitled to feel enormously proud of her achievement.

Her shorthand teacher had looked benignly on, nodding so vigorously in agreement with everything the principal said that the destruction of her hairdo could only be a matter of time. She pummelled Josie's hand before she left the building. 'Well done, my dear! Very well done!'

She could hardly wait to show the medal to Ma and Rachel. Secure in its own little satin-lined box, it was tucked safely into a corner of her bag. Tam would have to see it too, of course. He'd be so happy for her.

Crossing the road at the corner of George Street and High Street, the Ladywell School no distance away on the other side of the crossroads, she paused for a moment, wondering about popping along to show the medal to Miss French. She might run into Miss Anderson, that was the trouble. More importantly, she really wanted her mother to be the first person to see it. She could call on her old teacher at her house sometime over the weekend. Aye, that would be better.

By the time she reached the end of the wall which ran round the prison and had turned into the Drygate, she was walking so fast she was almost running. Plunging into the close, she rapped smartly on the front door, too excited to delve into her bag for the key. She tried to control the smile spreading all over her face. She had every intention of spinning the telling of this out for as long as possible.

She knocked on the door again, shifting impatiently from one foot to the other. 'Come on, Ma,' she muttered. Judging by the last clock she'd seen it must be about ten to one. Her mother was never normally out at this time of day. Frowning, Josie fished out her key, unlocked the door and pushed it gently open. 'Ma?'

There was no answer. She checked both rooms but the house was completely empty. Walking back into the kitchen it struck Josie that it was also eerily quiet, reminding her of that occasion on Christmas Eve when she had come home to find her mother sitting staring into the fire. She tried to shake off the memory. She didn't much care for it.

Lifting the lid of one of the pans beside the range she found mince, cooked and ready to serve. Tatties were steeping in the other pot. That seemed odd. Her mother usually left their preparation till the late afternoon, maintaining they lost much of their goodness if you did them too far in advance.

Laying her bag on the table, Josie pulled out a chair and sank down on to it. The low wooden rocking chair beside the range which Dorothy had occupied that Christmas Eve was empty too. Propping her chin on her fists, Josie gazed at it for several minutes, as though she could will her mother to be sitting there, smiling gently up at her from its depths.

Lowering her hands and straightening her shoulders, Josie did her best to rid herself of the gloomy sensations. It was only because it was so unusual for her to be in the house on her own. When had that last happened? Her mother must have had to run some unexpected errand, that was all. She would be back soon.

Chapter 9

Ten minutes later, with an exclamation of disgust at her own stupidity, Josie leaped to her feet. Dorothy would be up with Tam's mother, or across at Mrs Fitzgerald's house. Leaving the door on the latch, she hastened to check. Tam's mother was out and Bridget Fitzgerald knew nothing of her neighbour's whereabouts.

'You're home early, pet,' she said, looking at Josie round the edge of the door. 'Was she expecting you?'

Josie shook her head. 'No. Oh, but Mrs Fitzgerald,' she burst out, 'I'm beginning to get really worried!'

Bridget opened the door wide and pulled Josie inside. 'Now, now, she'll be fine. Sure, what on earth could have happened to her? Come and sit down and I'll make you a wee cup o' tea. Your ma will probably be back before you've even finished the brew.'

Only she wasn't. Nor was there any sign of Dorothy once another half-hour had passed. Rejecting the offer of a second cup of tea and far too restless to sit still, Josie insisted on going out to the street to wait for her mother. Bridget went with her. At first she kept repeating that everything would be fine but soon she fell silent, her motherly face lined with concern as she observed Josie's rising distress.

Josie couldn't explain that to herself. Hands behind her back, her body pressing them hard against the stone of the tenement, she only knew that a terrible sense of foreboding was growing within her. She fixed her eyes on one of the lamp-posts in Cathedral Square which bore St

Mungo's symbols and prayed harder than she ever had in her life. Twenty minutes after she and Mrs Fitzgerald went out to the close mouth, her worst fears were justified.

Alerted by a stifled exclamation from Bridget, she turned her head from a rigid contemplation of the bell, the fish, the tree and the bird and saw a little procession wending its way along the pavement. Its progress was slow and tortuous and it was made up of three people, two women and one young man. One of the women was her mother.

Dorothy was being supported on either side. Josie recognised the woman as Ma Robertson from round the corner in Wishart Street. Without quite knowing why, she had always disliked her.

'Take your mother,' she said curtly as Josie ran up to meet the group. 'I've got to be getting back and I'm no' wanting to be seen wi' her.'

'What's happened?' Breathless with worry, she shoved the woman out of the way in her anxiety to reach her mother. Dorothy swayed and stumbled. She would have fallen forward on to the pavement if one arm hadn't still been around the shoulders of the young man, one of Ma Robertson's children, Josie realised now.

'Keep the heid,' he said roughly. 'Help me get her into yer close.'

She hurried to obey. Her mother's face was as colourless as a sheet of paper and her eyelids kept fluttering shut. The hundred questions screaming through Josie's brain crystallised into one. 'Has she been in an accident?'

'Aye,' Ma Robertson said sourly. 'Ye might say that. Only the accident took place a couple of months back. Too many months back. That's whit's caused the trouble the day.'

They had Dorothy inside the close now, Ma Robertson's son extricating himself out from under her arm, Josie doing her best to support her mother on the other side. With the faintest of sighs, Dorothy tilted her head back against the wall. Bridget Fitzgerald was still out on the pavement. She was staring at Ma Robertson and her eyes were gleaming like bonfires.

'May God forgive you,' she said, her voice trembling. 'May God and Our Blessed Lady forgive you.'

'Ah'm used to no' being appreciated for the work ah dae.'

'Work!' Bridget spat out the word. 'It's a sin you've committed here, ye foul bitch.'

The young man turned, aggression evident in every aspect of his stance. His mother pulled him away. 'Naw, son, let it alone.'

'The sin is mine.'

Dorothy's voice was faint but Bridget heard it, spinning round towards the close. 'Oh darlin' girl,' she said sorrowfully, 'I'll not be blaming you for what's happened here today.'

'You should . . .' The voice was fainter still.

'There's another who has to take responsibility,' said Bridget, her voice sombre. 'And I'm not meaning that ould hellhag.' Ma Robertson and her son were already disappearing round the corner of the street.

'Mrs Fitzgerald,' begged Josie, 'can you help me get her into the house?'

When they got through the front door they tried to steer her towards the box bed but she would have none of it, indicating the rocking chair and trying feebly to make her own way towards it. 'Too much mess for the bed . . .'

Scared of hurting her further, Josie and Bridget gave in, lowering her as gently as they could into the rocking chair.

'Cloths and towels and plenty of water, Josie me girl,' murmured Mrs Fitzgerald. 'That's what we'll be needing now.'

It was only when Josie came rushing back with what

Bridget had asked for that she saw the blood. Below the waist, her mother's clothes and underwear were stained the brightest of crimsons. One of her slim hands clutched desperately at Bridget's arm and her voice was strong and impassioned.

'I knew it was a sin, Bridget. I knew it was. But I just couldnae cope with another wee one. It's hard enough to manage as it is.' The brief spurt of energy dissipated. Her next words slid painfully out of lips which were beginning to acquire a bluish tinge. 'Couldnae face going through it all only to lose the baby, either. Like wee Jamie,' she said in a jagged whisper. 'And all the others . . .'

Watching in anguish, Josie saw her mother swallow, gathering up her fading resources before she spoke again. She peered up at Mrs Fitzgerald. 'Will God forgive me, Bridget? Will He?'

'Hush now,' said Bridget, dipping a cloth into the bucket of cold water which Josie had placed on the floor beside her. 'God is merciful. He knows full well that ye've never had your troubles to seek.' She wrung out the cloth and began gingerly dabbing. 'Don't look,' she murmured to Josie. 'Look at your mother's lovely face instead.'

That face was growing paler and paler but Dorothy did her best to smile at her daughter. 'Come here, my lassie,' she said, feebly lifting her other hand.

Josie took it between the two of hers. It felt thin and cold, so she gently pressed her own palms more tightly around it, trying to imbue her mother with some of her own warmth and strength. 'It'll be all right, Ma,' she whispered, scarcely knowing what she was saying. 'I know it will.'

Dorothy's eyes closed, but the smile stayed. 'You're a good lassie. A . . . good . . . lassie . . .'

Panic-stricken as the faint voice drifted off into nothing, Josie looked in mute appeal at Mrs Fitzgerald, kneeling at her mother's feet.

'Passed out,' she said, 'and just as well.' Pressing a damp cloth in place, she watched tight-lipped as blood continued to seep through it. She rose slowly to her feet. 'It's no use. It'll have to be the infirmary. Lassie, away you down to the stables and see if my Mick or your Tam's there. They can take her up there on one of the drays.'

'No!' Dorothy's eyes snapped open, the weakened voice all at once sharp and decisive. 'No' the infirmary, Bridget. We'll get into trouble.'

'We're in trouble now, Dorothy,' said Mrs Fitzgerald grimly.

Josie found both men and they came immediately to help. Mrs Fitzgerald had done her best to staunch the bleeding with cloths and had wrapped her mother in a blanket in readiness. As she hurriedly explained what had happened Tam scooped Dorothy up as though she were a baby and strode towards the door. Mick Fitzgerald laid a comforting hand on Josie's shoulder as they followed him out of the house.

Harnessed up to the dray, Jimmy the Clydesdale was waiting patiently at the kerb. He turned his huge head at their approach. Within the blinkers he wore to save him from being distracted or frightened by passing traffic, his big eyes were soft and curious.

'I'll come with you now,' Mick said, 'and drive the cart back so Tam can keep you company while you're waiting. Then I'll help Bridget clean up before the wee ones get in from the school.'

His wife nodded. 'Don't you worry about Rachel and Charlie. I'll see to them.'

'We'll not alarm them unnecessarily,' Mick said. 'We'll tell them you and your mother had to go out for a wee while.'

'Aye,' said Bridget reassuringly. 'That'll be the best way.'

Josie's eyes were brimming with tears. 'Thank you,' she said. 'Thank you both so very much.'

It was only a few hundred yards, up Castle Street and into the hospital. Josie knelt beside her mother holding her hand, although Dorothy Collins seemed barely to be aware of what was happening to her. Passing the end of Rottenrow, Josie glanced along it. That was where the maternity hospital was. Should they be taking her there instead of to the Royal? She didn't know. In any case, it was too late now. They were pulling into the forecourt of the infirmary.

Tam jumped down and ran into the massive building, Mick pausing only long enough to secure Jimmy before following suit. Dorothy's eyes flickered open. Flat on her back, all she could be seeing was clouds and sky but her mouth curved in a smile of great sweetness. It was still there when her gaze travelled downwards and landed on Josie.

'We're at the Royal, Ma,' she said urgently. 'You'll soon be getting help.'

Dorothy said nothing, simply continued to smile at her daughter.

'Mrs Fitzgerald's going to see to Rachel and Charlie,' she volunteered. 'I'll bring them in to visit you as soon as I'm allowed to, Ma.'

The voice was faint but the words were clear. 'You'll look after them for me, Josie?'

'Of course I will, Ma.' She looked up, alerted by a trundling sound. Two hospital attendants were pushing a trolley over the cobbles, Mick and Tam running along behind them. Her mother gripped her hand and she glanced back down in surprise. Dorothy's touch had been firm. Oh, surely that must be a good sign!

'Promise me, Josie. Promise me you'll look after them. And yourself, pet . . .' The voice trailed off again but her mother's eyes remained firmly fixed on her face.

'I promise, Ma,' she said, more concerned with how Dorothy was going to be transferred to the trolley. Once that had been accomplished, Tam put his hands on Josie's waist and swung her down from the back of the cart.

She wanted to go after the trolley, following it with her eyes as it disappeared through a set of double doors but Tam kept his hands where they were, preventing her from moving. 'Come on, now,' he said. 'We've got to let the doctors and nurses get on wi' their work. Your Ma's in good hands.'

When she began to protest he gave her a little shake, forcing her to look at him. There was care and compassion in his clear eyes. Love, too. An ocean of it.

'Come on,' he said again and she put her hand in his and let him lead her to the casualty waiting room. The seats in there were hard benches, arranged in rows like school desks. Tam sat her down on the end of the one right at the back of the room. 'Shove in a wee bit,' he whispered.

As she slid along the polished wood he sank down beside her and put his arm about her thin shoulders. She turned towards him, placing one hand on his chest. He put his own free one over it. 'Coorie doon, lassie,' he whispered into her hair. 'Coorie doon.'

She obeyed the instruction, placing her head on his shoulder. Her eyes were open but all she could see was Tam's pale blue shirt and dark waistcoat. They filled her vision completely, as the only sensation she was aware of was the beat of his heart underneath her fingers.

Tam had his eyes fixed on the big clock set high up on the tiled wall at the other end of the room. He'd been staring at it for precisely nine minutes when a movement below it attracted his attention. The young doctor who had just that moment stepped out into the waiting room paused in the doorway, scanning the people who were waiting.

Tam saw him glance at the middle-aged women sitting chatting together in the front row and at the young girl with the bandaged wrist who was obviously waiting for someone to take her home. Then he spotted Tam and Josie.

He ran a hand through already untidy hair, squared his shoulders and headed towards them. Tam took a tighter grip on Josie's sweaty fingers. He knew what the doctor was coming to tell them. It was written all over his face.

Hearing the approaching footsteps, Josie straightened up.

'You're the patient's daughter?'

She nodded in confirmation. Looking up at him in a mute appeal for good news, her grey eyes were enormous.

'I'm sorry,' the young man said. 'I'm really most terribly sorry.'

Chapter 10

Dorothy Collins lay on a hospital bed in a side-room which was flooded with sunshine. Even when the nurse who had escorted them there tutted under her breath and stepped over to the window to lower the pale yellow blinds, there was still plenty of light: more than enough to see how peaceful she looked.

A thick white blanket was tucked in over her chest so that only her head, shoulders and arms were exposed. They had washed her and put her in a long-sleeved white gown and someone had brushed her hair. Dark like Josie's, it made a startling contrast against the white linen of the pillow. She might have been asleep.

She looked well rested, the skin of her face smooth and free of the lines which the cares and worries of her life had put there. Drained away, Josie thought, as her life has drained away. She bent forward and touched her mother's hand, then glanced up at the nurse, who had come to stand at the foot of the bed.

'She's still warm.'

'It takes a while,' the woman said, her voice and her face full of compassion. It was that sympathy which shattered Josie's composure. With a sob, she fell to her knees beside the bed, unheeding of the pain caused by the sudden contact with the floor.

She leaned forward so that her forehead rested on the white blanket close to her mother's still-warm hand. Those careworn fingers had done so much for her: cooking and cleaning and cherishing. She longed to feel them smoothing her hair, as they had done so often in the past. Now she would never feel that loving touch again. Nor would Rachel or Charlie . . .

Josie never knew how long she knelt there. She knew only that time seemed to stand still for a while, each occupant of the room as silent and unmoving as she who lay on the bed. Eventually Josie felt another loving touch, a big hand being as delicate as it knew how, gentling her as he would one of his beloved horses.

'Will ye maybe come now, lassie?'

He was doing his utmost to be strong and sensible, a pillar of support in her hour of need. She choked back the tears and looked up at him. 'In a minute, Tam. Give me a minute or two more.'

She turned for one last farewell before they left the room. The figure lying on the narrow hospital bed was like a doll. A beautiful, lifeless doll.

The doctor was waiting for them in the corridor outside, leaning back against the wall with his arms folded over his white-coated chest. He looked dog-tired. 'I don't suppose you'll tell me who did this to her, will you?'

Tam coughed. Josie watched two nurses walking briskly away down the corridor and said nothing.

'No,' the young man said bitterly, 'I thought not. Why do women persist in putting themselves at the mercy of these butchers?'

Like a pale ghost, Josie walked at Tam's side through what seemed like miles of corridors. The tiled walls were so clean, the overpowering and pungent smell of disinfectant wafting off them and rising up from the hard floors. She made it out into the fresh air just in time.

Tam steered her towards a patch of grass near the cathedral and she bent over, retching. He splayed his big hand out over her back and when she straightened up she saw that his handsome face was solemn and sad and full of care and concern for her.

'I'm all right.'

'Josie,' he said, his hand still on her back. 'Ye're no' all right. I think I should get ye home.'

'Home?' she queried. 'What's home without my mother?'

'There's Rachel and Charlie. They need you now.'

She stared at him. He was right. He was absolutely right. She heard her mother's voice in her head. *Promise me, Josie. Promise me you'll look after them.* Dorothy had been so insistent, gripping her hand with that unexpected firmness. Oh, dear God. Had she known? The thought was agonising.

'Oh, Tam . . .'

He had raised his head, was looking away from her. Josie followed his gaze. Ma Robertson was waddling towards them, coming past the Laigh Barony Church. Her son was with her. 'Yer ma?' she asked when she reached them, puffing and out of breath as she struggled to keep up with her son.

'Dead,' Tam said brutally.

'Och, ye poor wee soul.' When the woman extended a hand towards her, Josie jumped back as though she'd been stung. 'Don't touch me!'

Ma Robertson's eyes narrowed. 'Ye'll be glad enough o' my touch if ye get into the same kind o' trouble your mother did.' Her eyes roamed over Tam. 'This laddie's desperate to tumble you on to your back.'

Hands clenched, Tam stepped forward. 'You watch your mouth, ye old bitch!'

Ma Robertson's son had stepped forward too. 'Want to make something of it, pal?'

'I might,' Tam said coolly. He indicated Josie with a nod of his head. 'And so might the lassie's stepfather and brothers.'

Real fear flashed through Ma Robertson's eyes. 'Ye'll no' tell them, will ye?'

'Don't you worry, Ma,' said her son aggressively. 'We can take on that lot, nae bother.'

'*God Almighty*,' breathed Tam. 'Have you no respect? This lassie's just lost her mother, for Christ's sake! Fuck off the both o' youse! Now!' he roared

They stared at him in astonishment. Tam Paterson was well known to be a mild-mannered lad.

'Sorry for the cursing and blaspheming, hen,' he murmured as the Robertsons retreated.

'It got rid of them,' she said dully.

'Aye,' he said. 'Am I taking you home now?'

She shook her head. 'I need to be by myself for a wee while, Tam. Please.'

He refused to leave her completely on her own but agreed to wait for her on the Bridge of Sighs while she walked up one of the sloping paths of the Necropolis. The city of the dead. It seemed appropriate.

She knew exactly which mausoleum she was looking for. It lay towards the back of the hill and it was flanked by two beautiful white-robed figures. One of them held a baby in her arms and her serene face had always reminded Josie of her mother.

Before they had been allowed in to see Dorothy an apologetic nurse had asked if she might take down some details. Tam had answered most of the questions, forced to refer to Josie only for her mother's maiden name and date of birth. Doing the arithmetic in her head now, she realised that Dorothy had been only thirty-four years old.

Thirty-four years old. It wasn't old at all. It was young. Josie turned from her contemplation of the statue's face and gazed in the other direction, over at the Royal Infirmary where her mother's lifeless body lay.

Bled to death. Bled dry. Drained of life by all she'd had to contend with.

Josie lifted her face to the sky. 'Not for me,' she

whispered. She took a deep breath and said it in a stronger voice. 'Not for me.'

PART II

Chapter 11

1926

'It's not fair!' burst out Rachel. 'I'm fed up doing all this work.' Her pretty face mutinous, she threw down the cloth she held.

'*You're* fed up?' Josie demanded. She was at the jawbox, up to her elbows in hot soapy water and dirty plates, Rachel drying the clean ones as her big sister placed them on the thick wooden draining board. Arthur Collins and his sons had come home from work, eaten their meal and gone out again. As usual, there had been no word of thanks, not even a grunt of appreciation.

It was daft of her to expect anything. After her mother's death a year ago it had simply been assumed that Josie would take over the household duties. It didn't matter to the Collins men that she was also holding down a full-time job. Their only interest in her work was for the sake of the money it brought in each week. The more she contributed to the household budget, the less they had to.

She'd grown a little wise about that. At the end of the week she opened her pay packet and laid the money out on the table as soon as she came in, ready for her stepfather to inspect when he got home an hour later. She hoped Arthur Collins thought she was being dutiful. In reality, she was tucking a few coins away every week, using the boot polish tin which had held wee Jamie's lucky money and emulating her mother by keeping it well hidden behind the flour crock. Nobody but herself was liable to lift that down from the shelf.

Her modest savings had been boosted by a promotion and a raise in pay. According to everyone at the *Dispatch* Josie had made the transition from copygirl to junior copytaker in record time, a tribute both to her newly acquired shorthand and typing skills and her eagerness to learn. Old Father Time himself had congratulated her.

Coming two short months after her mother's death, her success had provoked violently mixed emotions, which was why Sally Fleming had found her sobbing in the ladies' toilet an hour after she'd been given the good news. Josie told Sally only that her mother had died following a miscarriage.

With the Fitzgeralds' backing, it was what she had told Rachel and Charlie and everyone else too. Despite her condemnation of Ma Robertson and her trade, Bridget had also begged Tam and Josie not to tell Arthur Collins what had really happened. It would only cause trouble and fighting with the Robertson clan which might go on for years.

Fearful of Josie and the children getting caught in the crossfire, Mrs Fitzgerald had also pointed out how awful it would be for Rachel and Charlie to learn the truth about their mother's death by it being flung at them as a taunt by one of the younger Robertsons. In the end, that was the argument which had swayed both Josie and Tam.

Horrified that she had come straight back to work without requesting a few days' compassionate leave, Sally had asked if she didn't think she needed to take some now. Slumped in a corner of the ladies' with the other girl bending solicitously over her, Josie had looked up, her eyes brimming with tears. 'I wouldn't be paid for that, would I?'

'I'm afraid not. Maybe if we asked Roddy . . .' Sally's own eyes were soft and full of pity. She saw her own mother infrequently and without her father's knowledge.

Mr Fleming had thrown her out when she had refused to stop seeing Ben; his objection being that the young man was Jewish. As she said wryly, he didn't know the half of it.

Josie turned down the suggestion of approaching Roddy, and asked Sally not to tell anyone else at the *Dispatch* about her bereavement. It was hard enough coping with the sympathy of the neighbours, shocked and saddened by the passing of such a young woman as Dorothy. It was kind of people to offer their condolences, but every time her mother's name was mentioned Josie wanted to howl with anguish. If she was going to keep both her job and her promise to look after Rachel and Charlie, she simply couldn't allow the grief to overwhelm her.

Arthur Collins hadn't betrayed much emotion at the death of his wife and took little notice of the younger children either, reacting to their presence only if they irritated him in some way. Then it would be a shouted reprimand or a smack, both usually accompanied by foul language. Josie worried constantly about what Charlie might come out with at school if he started mimicking his father – or his elder brothers.

While they also paid very little attention to their brother and half-sister, they paid far too much to Josie. There were the smutty comments and the knack they had of being wherever she wanted to go, forcing her to run the gauntlet of their greedy eyes and searching hands.

She said nothing at home about her promotion. Like her mother before her, she found that the housekeeping money thrown grudgingly at her each week never stretched far enough. They all spent too much on drink and cigarettes and betting on lame greyhounds, that was the trouble. If they knew she'd had a pay rise, they'd keep even more of their own money back.

So she handed over the same amount of money each

week to her stepfather and allowed herself a brief spurt of unholy glee as she consigned her small brown pay packet to the flames of the range. She felt a glow of a different sort when she thought of the money in the boot polish tin. Over the past year she'd managed to accumulate a whole three pounds in there. Some of it was earmarked for a wee treat.

She was planning a trip *doon the watter* one Saturday or Sunday in May or June, a cruise on the Clyde in a pleasure steamer. It would be a thank you to her sister for all the extra housework she'd done over this past year and Charlie would love it. No doubt she and Rachel would have their work cut out keeping him back from the rail of the boat. She would ask Tam to come too, both for his own sake and also because he would help keep Charlie in order. He was much more of a big brother to the boy than Charlie's own flesh and blood were.

They'd be on the river, gliding out into the firth, getting lots of fresh air into their lungs and sunlight on to their skin. Josie was looking forward to seeing their wee faces light up with pleasure and anticipation. Charlie had cried for their mother for months . . .

So had she, but only late at night when she was certain everyone else was asleep. Almost from the very beginning, Rachel too had done her grieving in private, locking her emotions away even from her big sister. That worried Josie but she didn't know what to do about it. A few months off her seventeenth birthday, she often found herself wishing for an older head on her young shoulders.

She was sure one or two outings over the summer would help them all, the wherewithal provided by the money in her war chest. She'd heard that expression last week when she'd taken down an article through her headphones speculating on how full Britain's coffers would be should the unthinkable come to pass: another world war.

122

That particular eventuality didn't keep Josie awake at night. Europe was exhausted after the last round of hostilities, Germany and Austria defeated and broken. She couldn't imagine anybody had the appetite for more conflict. Come to think of it, nothing much kept her awake at night. Her days were too full. There was her job and then there was the housework.

She did as much as she possibly could by herself, gratefully accepting the help offered by Mrs Fitzgerald and Mrs Paterson but remembering always that they had their own households to look after. Rachel had to lend a hand too. Since Josie was out at her work all day, it fell to her little sister to start preparing the tea each evening, peeling potatoes and scraping carrots when she was actually itching to get on with her homework.

Although Josie had been surprised and dismayed to hear that Miss French had abruptly resigned her job and left the neighbourhood, Rachel was very fond of the teacher who had replaced her and whose class she was now in. A bright girl who loved her lessons, Josie had high hopes for her. If she could only build up the war chest, perhaps Rachel could be the one to go on to college.

That would really be something: herself a reporter and Rachel a teacher, not to mention what Charlie might achieve if the two of them were there to lend him a helping hand. Ambitions like those were worth a bit of hard work. Her own momentary spurt of irritation past, she turned to her sister, still regarding her with a rebellious air.

There were some ruffled feathers to smooth here. Nae bother. She could do that. Working at the *Evening Dispatch*, where strong personalities and fragile egos clashed on a regular basis – particularly as the daily deadline hove into view – had taught Josie nothing if not diplomacy. She had observed how some people managed to fan the flames while others had the knack of extinguishing them. She had come to the conclusion that honesty tempered with tact was the best policy and credit where it was due.

She took her hands out of the sink, wiped them on her apron and gave her wee sister her full attention. That was important too, letting people know you really were listening to them.

'Look Rachel,' she said, 'I'm very sorry you're having to do all this extra work but the fact is I just couldnae manage without you. You know that, pet.'

Since the small face looking up at her seemed marginally less belligerent, Josie dared to place a damp hand on one of Rachel's shoulders and give it an encouraging squeeze. 'You're a big help to me. And I appreciate it, I really do. I cannae do all the housework by myself. I've got my job to go to and I'm trying to do well there and get on.'

Should she tell Rachel of her plans for the future? No, perhaps not yet. Dreams were fragile. Expose them to the cold light of day and they might go up in a puff of smoke, leaving nothing but a few blackened fragments of destroyed hope dancing along the gutter.

'I've got school to go to. I'm trying to do well there.' Rachel's chin was jutting out, what Ma had always referred to as *the wee petted lip*. A wave of longing for Dorothy Collins swept through Josie. She would have known how to coax Rachel out of this mood.

'You are doing well at school,' she said firmly. 'I'm very proud of you.'

'Are you, Josie?' The tone in Rachel's young voice stopped Josie in her tracks, as did the look in her eyes. Like her own, they were grey, sombre and full of longing. For something both of them knew they could not have. No, not for something. For someone.

She pulled her sister to her, enfolded her in a bear hug. 'I miss Mammy too.' Secure in her sister's arms, Rachel let out a sob. Josie held her all the tighter, biting back her own tears and forcing down the painful lump in her throat.

When they eventually separated, she lifted an end of her apron and wiped Rachel's tears gently away. 'I'm very, very proud of you,' she said again. 'Not only because you're doing well at school but because you're working so hard in the house too. I know it's difficult, Rachel, but we've got to pull together. It's the only way we're going to get through this.'

Rachel gave an almighty sniff and picked up the tea towel. 'They never help.' Her contemptuous tone left little doubt as to who *they* were.

'Men don't,' said Josie briskly, plunging her arms once more into the sink. After they were finished here she would call Charlie in from the street and get him washed and ready for bed. If she read him his story and got him off to sleep quickly she might have time to read a couple of chapters of the book Roddy Cunningham had loaned her before the hordes tramped in from the pub demanding their supper.

'That's not fair.'

'I know it's not,' said Josie matter-of-factly, 'but it's the way it is.' She was on to the pans now. She lowered them carefully into the sink, pausing briefly from her labours to allow the water and washing soda to get at them before she started wielding the steel wool scourer. Bending forward over the jawbox, she twitched back the lace curtain and craned her neck to see if Charlie was still where he had been last time she had checked. He was, sitting on the edge of the pavement playing a game of marbles with two other small boys. All three of them looked as though they'd been dragged through a hedge backwards, the wee toerags.

'Anyway,' said Rachel, carefully drying the serving dish which had held tonight's mashed potatoes, 'not all men are like that. Tam Paterson helps his mother in the house.'

Josie's eyes were still fixed on Charlie and his pals.

Rachel's observation changed the affectionate reproach in them to something more tender. She lifted the scourer from the edge of the sink. 'Tam's different,' she said. 'Tam's very different.'

Alerted by Rachel's lack of response to those two softly spoken statements, she glanced over her shoulder. A few moments ago, her younger sister had been a lost child. The expression her features now bore was all too womanly. Josie straightened up and wheeled round.

'What are you looking at me like that for?' she demanded, her hands settling on to her hips.

'Nothing,' Rachel said airily. 'Nothing at all.' She was grinning from ear to ear.

'Cheeky wee bisom.' Josie flicked a soap bubble at her. Not that she really minded being teased. It was worth it to see Rachel smile like that.

Walking out into the street to fetch Charlie ten minutes later, it occurred to her that she had been dead right about one thing. Tam *was* different. She liked him an awful lot: his gentle ways and consideration for other people, the affection he had for his horses . . . the way his face lit up when he saw her.

Josie knew he longed to help her escape from the situation in which she now found herself. She knew also what his preferred solution was, but apart from the fact that they were both gey young to be contemplating marriage, he had his mother and his younger brothers and sisters to support, and she had Rachel and Charlie to provide for. Tam's modest wage was stretched enough as it was.

No, she thought as she bathed Charlie and got him ready for bed, that couldn't be the answer. She needed to keep her own job and she couldn't do that if she wed Tam. Married women might work pretty damned hard inside the house but it was almost unheard of for them to go out to work: certainly none of the women whom Josie knew did so. Only last month one of the copytakers at the *Dispatch* had got married. It had simply been expected that the girl would give up her job.

After she had supervised Rachel's ablutions and tucked her in beside Charlie, Josie sat for a while with Roddy's book in her lap and pondered what a waste it was to be trained up and work hard at a job only to have to give it up as soon as you had decided to walk down the aisle. Once you had children you had to be at home, of course, and there was all the housework, she supposed.

Josie let out a heartfelt sigh. She knew from experience how hard it was trying to combine that with a job. Maybe if more men were prepared to help around the house . . . although presumably that would be when hell decided to freeze over. She smiled ruefully and opened the book.

Much later, when the rest of the household was safely in bed, she stood in the close with Tam. At night she and Rachel and Charlie now had the front room to themselves. It was easier than ever to slip quietly out of the house.

She drew her fingers down over his rolled-up shirt-sleeves to Tam's bare forearms, feeling the little hairs spring up in response to her touch. When she slipped those same fingers inside the open neck of his shirt he sighed with pleasure and returned the compliment.

That felt so nice . . . but she couldn't let him go too far. Difficult though it was, there came a point when she knew she had to ask him to stop. 'I can't afford to get into trouble,' she whispered apologetically, all too aware of the denied need and desire coursing through both of their veins.

'No. Ye cannae.'

Tam placed his forehead against hers and his hands flat on the wall on either side of her head. 'To keep me away frae temptation,' he told her. He took a couple of shaky breaths. 'When a' I want to do at this precise moment is walk straight towards it. Make that run straight towards it,' he corrected, laughing softly in the gaslit gloom.

'Ride a Clydesdale straight towards it?'

He nodded, his mouth curving. 'I'd like fine to saddle Jimmy up and carry you off somewhere, Josie.'

'Over the hills and far away?'

'Aye. Over the hills and far away. I've got this dream,' he said hesitantly.

'Tell me.'

'Ye'll no' laugh?'

'Of course I'll not.'

'There's a nice wee house by a loch somewhere. A bit of land and a couple of horses. You and me. That's it,' he said, sounding embarrassed. 'Maybe it's no' much of a dream.'

'It's a lovely dream,' she said. 'I like it a lot.' She put a hand to the back of his head and gave him one last good night kiss.

This time his sigh was full of a different kind of longing. 'One day, lassie. One day.'

Roderick Cunningham put his head around the staffroom door. It was attractively tousled, as was customary on a Monday morning. He was always a bit more windblown than usual at the start of the week. This, Josie surmised, was not unconnected with his tendency to roll up at the *Dispatch*'s front door in a car being driven by some young lady with whose family he'd been spending the weekend, enjoying himself until the very last minute.

'How did you get on with *Fiesta*?' He curled his fingers around the edge of the door but didn't advance any further into the room. He was a little diffident about spending time in here, knowing very well that his presence inhibited some folk.

There were other people on whom his relationship to the boss had the opposite effect. They used Roddy as a conduit for their moans and complaints, assuming he would transmit them to his father. Ben Gold wasn't one of them but, currently sitting across the table from Josie and ostentatiously ignoring young Mr Cunningham, he was nevertheless a somewhat inhibiting presence.

Josie swallowed a mouthful of her sandwich – she knew now how to cut them every bit as daintily as Sally did – and sent Roddy over a smile.

He'd loaned her several books during the past few months. One had been an ancient tome containing a selection of Scots poetry. He'd pointed out one poem by Robert Fergusson entitled 'The Daft Days', gleefully informing her that this was the old Scots term for the Yuletide celebrations. Since Fergusson had written his cheerful stanzas in 1772, it was proof positive that whatever modern Scots thought, previous generations had celebrated Christmas as enthusiastically as they had Hogmanay.

Roddy had asked her to read the poem out loud. After some initial hesitation – apart from the poetry of Robert Burns, she wasn't used to seeing such broad Scots in print – she'd managed it easily. He had sighed admiringly and told her how much better she did it than he ever could.

'Managed to read quite a bit of it yesterday,' she said now in response to his question about *Fiesta*. 'I really like it. It's very modern.' She waved her triangle of bread and cheese in the air, searching for the right word. 'Very much in the here and now. Very . . .'

'Immediate?' he suggested.

'That's it,' she agreed. 'Very immediate.'

Ben Gold made an indeterminate sound somewhere at the back of his throat. He raised his curly head and regarded Roderick with cool dark eyes. 'Do you really think this Hemingway character is a writer a gentleman should recommend to a young lady?'

That was a ridiculous question. *Fiesta* might very well
have an adult theme, but Ben Gold knew where she came
from better than most. Did he think a lassie who'd been
raised in the Drygate didn't know all there was to know
about the facts of life?

Of course, his question didn't really have anything to
do with protecting herself from racy literature. It was
another way of getting at Roddy. Josie had always instinc-
tively understood why the boss's son so seldom chose to
retaliate when other people mocked or challenged, came
out with provocative statements or criticised the manage-
ment of the paper in front of him. His position imposed
penalties as well as privileges.

Given that one day he would be master of the *Evening
Dispatch* empire, it was expected of him to take without a
murmur all that was thrown at him while he was learning
the ropes. Some people, Ben being one of them, were just
downright rude and unpleasant to him. Surely no one
should be expected to put up with that, day-in, day-out?

Anger at social and economic inequality Josie could
well understand but it seemed hardly fair for one young
man to hold another responsible for all of society's
ills simply because of an accident of birth. Roderick
Cunningham had been born rich. She'd been born poor.
That was a fact of life. Noting his obvious reluctance to
respond to Ben's aggressive question, she leaped to his
defence.

'Do you really think I shouldn't be allowed to read a
book simply because I'm a female, Ben?' she asked lightly.
'The literary editor here said it was a great book, destined
to become a classic. Isn't that what he wrote in the paper
last week?' She tossed the question to Roddy.

His answer was an obvious attempt to defuse the
awkwardness of the situation. 'Yes. It's his review copy
you're reading just now. I pinched it from off his desk,' he
confessed charmingly.

Ben had been glowering at Josie. Now he turned his fixed stare once more on to Roddy. 'Rank has its privileges?' he queried archly.

That was another daft question. You didn't have to be the boss's son to take something from someone else's desk. Everybody did it, lifting books and magazines, pens, pencils and pins. The books and magazines were sometimes returned, the other items never were. That was another fact of life.

Roddy's grip on the door tightened. Watching his knuckles whiten, Josie was suddenly alert. Could it be that even his patience had its limits? If he was angry, it showed neither in his demeanour nor in his voice, which slowed to a lazy drawl.

'R-H-I-P? Absolutely. You do know the alternative name of Hemingway's novel, don't you?'

He raised his fair eyebrows and answered his own question. '*The Sun Also Rises*. Change one letter and that could be me. Obviously I'm only here because my old man owns the paper. Perish the thought that I might have got the job on merit. Or that I might actually have an aptitude for it and be prepared to work hard at it.'

Ben shifted uncomfortably in his chair. Despite his hectic social life, everyone knew Roddy put in his full complement of hours and more. He was no shirker. His face softened as he turned towards Josie. 'See you later, Jo.' A wave of the hand and he was gone.

Not wanting to lose her temper with Ben, Josie said nothing. He might not have been born into the poverty in which she had grown up but she knew he had first-hand experience of prejudice and injustice all the same. Coming from a part of the city where Protestants and Catholics had too much rancour for each other to have much left over for folk of any other faith, she only now knew how much intolerance people who should know better demonstrated towards Jews.

131

'All right,' Ben said defiantly. 'He's not quite so languid and effete as he likes to make out, but he's still one of the enemy.'

'He's a person. A human being, like you or me.'

'He's a capitalist,' Ben insisted, emphasising his point by banging the side of his hand on the big table, 'like his father. And the capitalists are the enemies of the working classes. The Prime Minister says that all workers, not only the miners, should be prepared to take a cut in wages to help the country get back on its feet.'

Disappointed though he was that Britain's first ever Labour administration hadn't even managed to see out the year in which it had been elected to power, the failure of Ramsay MacDonald's government hadn't dampened Ben's passion for politics. More comfortable now that they had left personalities behind, he leaned forward over the table.

'Tell me something, Josie. Will Stanley Baldwin be taking a cut in his wages? Will people like old Mr Cunningham? Will young Roderick maybe have to deny himself that second or third cocktail when he goes out on a Saturday night? Will his bossy big sister have to do without a new fur coat next winter? I can't imagine that husband of hers keeps her in the style to which she's accustomed.'

'Old Father Time supports them?'

'Of course he does,' said Ben contemptuously, throwing himself back in his chair. 'How could they survive on those few articles Charles Campbell writes? The occasional restaurant or book review isn't exactly what you would call work. It's not like going down a mine, is it?'

Josie held up her hands in a gesture of surrender. 'I agree with you about the miners, Ben, I really do. It's a disgrace. Who would do their job? For rotten wages too.'

'Which the bosses want to cut even further,' he said grimly.

The dispute between Britain's coal miners and mine owners had been dragging on for almost a year now. When the owners had broken an agreement guaranteeing a minimum wage and asked their employees to accept pay cuts, other unions had got involved. It wasn't only a matter of working-class solidarity but also the clear realisation that cutting rates of pay in one industry was the thin end of a wedge which would affect millions of working people and their families. The TUC had pledged that the miners would not be left to fight alone.

That stirring battle cry had been uttered in the middle of the previous summer, in July 1925. Since then there had been innumerable talks and conferences and committees. Josie couldn't see that any of them had produced very much other than threats and counter-threats. When the TUC called for a general strike, the government responded with plans to thwart one. It was April 1926 now and the talking was still going on.

At home that evening, standing at the close mouth enjoying the spring sunshine, she discussed the situation with Mick and Tam. 'It just aye seems to keep lumbering on,' observed the latter.

'It's gathering momentum,' Mick said. 'The showdown's coming and it's coming soon.' He put a match to the pipe he'd cleaned and refilled before coming out. 'I'm sorry to say it but I think both sides are spoiling for a fight.'

'What about you?' Josie asked. 'Will you strike? And the other carters?' She darted a quick glance at Tam. He was standing with his thumbs hooked through his belt loops, head cocked to one side. He was as keen to hear Mick's answer as she was.

The Irishman was sucking on his pipe to get it to draw. He removed it from his mouth, which twisted into a wry grimace. 'Well m'dear, whilst I'm in sympathy with the miners, I'm afraid the horses don't understand much about industrial disputes and class warfare, do they now?'

Tam straightened up, the worried expression which had been cloaking his features relaxing into one of enormous relief. 'Aye, they'll still need to be fed and watered and exercised, that's true enough, so we might as well keep on working. Folk will understand that, surely.'

'Don't be so certain of that, lad,' murmured Mick. His previous contribution to the conversation had sent Josie off in another direction.

'You think that's what this is then, Mr Fitzgerald – class warfare?'

'Don't you?' he asked shrewdly. 'We have one side which feels resentment and a burning sense of injustice. We have another – well aware of the strength of that feeling – which is running scared of what those feelings might unleash. The loss of their own privileges and superior position in society, perhaps. The revolution this country's never had. Of course they're going to dig their heels in and fight.'

She thought about it. He had a point. It was evident in the language now being used. People did talk about battle cries. Talks had become parleys. Both sides called for their supporters to rally to the cause. The unions wanted as many trades as possible to come out in support of the miners, the most vital industries first so as to cause maximum disruption. The government had issued an appeal for volunteers to do their jobs if they did.

'What about you, hen?' Mick asked. 'Will you come out?'

'Me?' Josie was taken aback. 'Surely the newspapers will have to keep going so everybody knows what's happening?'

'The press will be one of the first industries affected. The printers have always been a militant lot. If they come out . . .'

'. . . the rest of us are snookered,' Josie supplied, thinking back to what Mr Bruce had said on her first day at the *Dispatch*.

'Not only that.' Mick interrupted himself to take another few draws on his pipe. He pointed it warningly at her, stem first. 'Are you prepared to cross a picket line, young Josephine? Be a blackleg?'

'I couldn't do that,' she said, genuinely shocked. 'I think what they're trying to do to the miners is terrible.'

'So,' Michael Francis Fitzgerald persisted, playing devil's advocate and making a fine job of it, 'are you prepared to lose your job for the sake of the miners?'

Tam was looking worried again. Josie did her best to give him a reassuring smile, although she was deeply troubled at the prospect Mick had laid before her. What would she do if it came to the crunch? She couldn't bear to jeopardise the job she'd worked so hard to get and keep. Couldn't afford to, either. But if someone made a direct appeal to her conscience and sense of justice?

She tried, glumly, to look on the bright side. If the worst came to the worst, at least she had the money in her war chest. It wouldn't make the decision she might have to face any less difficult, but at least it was something.

Chapter 12

Sally was pacing the floor of the staffroom, the glint of battle in her eye. 'This is ridiculous. They're holding crisis talks at Downing Street and the Features Department is still publishing the doings of The Honourable Miss Double-Barrelled. We must tackle something more relevant to what's going on out there.' She waved an exasperated arm towards the window.

'Got something in mind?' Alan Dewar was sitting at the table between Deirdre Smith and Josie, quite literally twiddling his thumbs. The nonchalant air wasn't fooling anybody. It was the very end of April and over the past week the tension associated with the miners' dispute had been cranking up more tightly each day. Everyone was feeling it, particularly the large percentage of the workforce of the *Glasgow Evening Dispatch* which held political views at odds with those of the proprietor. Journalists, subs, copytakers and printers were unhappy about the editorials Mr Cunningham senior was writing damning the TUC and the unions.

Sally stopped pacing the floor and yanked out a chair for herself. 'Tell me what you all think of this.' She was proposing a double interview, two articles placed side-by-side which would illustrate the contrasts between the lives of two women: a miner's wife and a mine owner's wife.

'Not *angled* in any way though, Sally?' asked Deirdre Smith, frowning.

Sally shook her shining auburn bob with considerable vehemence. 'Absolutely not.'

'Two straightforward articles about two women's lives, letting the contrasts speak for themselves?' Deirdre's frown lifted. 'Well, considering practically the entire press is Tory and takes the government's side in all of this . . .'

'Not to mention bolstering the untenable position of the ruling classes,' chipped in Ben.

Deirdre gave him a long-suffering look and finished her sentence without breaking her stride '. . . your idea could be construed as giving some much needed balance, Sally.'

Beside her, Alan Dewar was looking sceptical. 'How are you planning to get this project passed by our leaders?'

Sally leaned back in her chair, looking just a little smug. 'Well, first I'll write up the interviews so brilliantly it would be a crime *not* to publish them.'

'Naturally,' murmured Alan. 'We'd all expect nothing less.' His eyes gleamed with amusement. 'Do let us know if you want any help with grammar or punctuation. We know you journalists often find such matters a wee touch tricky.'

'But seriously, Sally,' someone asked, 'Old Father Time's never going to wear it, is he?'

'He might if I enlist his son's help to persuade him,' she countered calmly.

Ben snorted in derision, but Alan's deep voice was thoughtful. 'Roddy's quite liberal in his views, right enough. I've had a few interesting conversations with him.'

'What about getting your interview subjects?'

Josie blushed as everyone in the room wheeled round to look at her. 'I m-mean,' she stammered, 'won't a miner's wife be scared of speaking out? And a posh lady wouldn't want to, would she?'

Sally gave her an encouraging smile. 'It's a very good point, Josie, but I've thought of a way round it. I'm going to do them both anonymously. No photographs either,' she said apologetically to Ben.

'You could do their houses,' he suggested. 'Not specifically, of course – that would identify them. A general view of a miner's row set next to a picture of a big villa or similar. We've probably got something like that in the picture library.'

'Great idea,' Sally said warmly, 'and very apposite considering the particular mine-owner's wife I have in mind does indeed live in a villa. She's a friend of Roddy's sister, apparently. I've already got an interview set up for Thursday afternoon. I'm going to take afternoon tea with her at her lovely home in Pollokshields.' Clearly enjoying herself, she said the last sentence in the sweetest of voices, the words tripping off her tongue.

Deirdre put her elbows on the table. 'She's agreed to take part in this double interview? She knows her life is going to be contrasted with that of a miner's wife?'

'Not exactly,' admitted Sally. 'She thinks I'm going to speak to her about her lovely home in Pollokshields and her interest in animal welfare.'

'Are you going to tell her what you're planning before you start the interview?'

Sally described a circle in the air with her index finger and affected an air of childlike innocence. 'No.'

There were some murmurs and uncomfortable shifting of feet before someone put the general discomfiture into words. 'Isn't that unethical?'

Now it was Alan Dewar who snorted. 'We're in the newspaper business. Ethics are a luxury we can't afford.'

His comment sparked off a debate which lasted for the rest of the lunch hour.

The ethical question bothered Josie too. Nevertheless, when Sally offered to take her along on both interviews, she jumped at the chance. This was exactly the sort of practical experience she needed if she was going to be a reporter herself one day.

The interview with the miner's wife was arranged for Wednesday. Josie met Sally at the railway station first thing that morning and they took a train out to the Lanarkshire coalfields owned by the husband of the lady in Pollokshields.

'The connection being entirely deliberate?'

'You're learning. We'll keep her name and where she lives confidential, of course. She and her family might get evicted otherwise. Her husband's ultimate boss owns the whole shebang – the mine, the houses the miners live in, the whole village. It's a form of serfdom, really.'

Both girls were surprised to find themselves in the middle of pleasant fields and rolling hills when they reached their destination. After a fifteen-minute walk, they reached a small village with two long rows of low houses on either side of a completely deserted street. Following a brainwave of Josie's, they went round the back of one of the terraces and discovered that was where life was being lived.

Narrow back gardens were full of neat rows of vegetables, bright clumps of flowers, women pegging out washing, cats and dogs lying in the sunshine, playing toddlers and slumbering babies. They were given a polite if cautious welcome and swiftly directed to the correct house.

The woman was nervous to begin with but Sally's skilful questions soon drew her out. Josie noticed how carefully phrased they were, designed to elicit much more than a simple yes or no.

'The thing is,' Sally explained as the two girls clambered on to the train back to Glasgow, 'an interview's not a conversation.' She put a hand to her chest and drew in some air, catching her breath. They'd only just made the train, having to run the last few hundred yards as they heard its whistle and saw the column of steam rising skywards as it rattled towards them through a fold in the hills. 'The interviewer must be careful not to talk too much. You're there to listen.'

'But you chatted a bit at the beginning.'

'That was to put her at her ease. She was quite uncomfortable at first.' Sally grimaced. 'Concerned that her house wasn't up to scratch, poor woman.' As the train gathered speed, she gazed out at the countryside rushing past them. Over in the distance, one of the tributaries of the Clyde sparkled in the sun. 'Wouldn't you think they could give them bigger gardens when there's all that space around them?'

'Her house was cramped too,' Josie said, 'but it was really clean and tidy.'

She had noticed that particularly. Her own home wasn't always as spick and span as she would have liked it. Keeping up with the housework was difficult when she was out at work all day. Sally had turned away from her contemplation of the beauties of nature and was giving her a curious look. 'You all right, Josie?'

'I'm fine.' She placed her hands on the upholstered seat, sliding her fingertips under her knees to sit like a schoolgirl, fascinated by the ever-changing view from the window of their compartment. The pits and coal bings were closer together now, the green fields and trees which dotted them less frequent. This part of the upper ward of Lanarkshire might not be the prettiest place in the world but she was enjoying her second train ride through it just fine, and all paid for by the paper too.

'You know how sometimes you didn't say anything after she had answered one of your questions?'

Sally crossed her legs, cupped her chin in her hand and put on a look of scholarly inquisition. 'Pray continue, Miss Collins.'

'You meant to do that, didn't you? Because often she added something that was really interesting.'

Sally beamed at her protégée. 'I call it the power of the

pause. People find silence uncomfortable and think it's good manners to fill it. If they've already answered your question they have to think really hard before they come up with anything else.'

Josie had the opportunity to observe the technique again on the following afternoon. Waiting for them in her parlour, the lady of the house greeted them both with a warm handshake.

'I do so admire the young women of today,' she said. 'Out in the world working and contributing. Man's equal in every way.'

She invited them to sit and waited until they were both settled before following suit. She seemed to be able to do so in some especially graceful way, lowering herself down in one fluid movement. Once she was there she swung both legs to one side, placing one foot behind the ankle of the other. It looked very stylish. Now that she had finally managed to buy herself a decent pair of shoes, Josie thought she might practise the manoeuvre at home.

Yesterday they had sat round the family's one and only table. Here they were ensconced in comfortable chairs and sofas, the tea things laid out on a side-table. Josie's worry as to how she could avoid spilling anything on to the beautiful silver-grey upholstery of the sofa in whose corner she sat vanished when the uniformed maid who'd admitted them to the house emerged from a corner of the room with three small folding tables. A flick of the wrist and one stood in front of each of them, the maid moving silently to the side-table.

'I do so like to be informal, don't you?' asked their hostess.

Josie murmured her thanks as she was asked whether she preferred her milk in first or last, tea was poured for her and the plate of cakes offered. This was going to make a good story to tell Rachel tonight, her big sister being danced attendance on by a maid in a black dress, white frilly pinny and starched cap.

The mine-owner's wife spoke easily and happily of her love of animals. With experience of Jimmy and the other Clydesdales at the brewery stables, Josie was able to exchange a few sentences with her about the foibles and little idiosyncrasies of horses whilst Sally took a break to sip some tea and nibble on a little cake.

Yesterday the miner's wife had served them home-made scones and jam. Pressed to eat more, Sally had accepted with alacrity. Josie had tactfully declined. Knowing what it meant to be really poor in a way the older girl never could, she had been well aware that the home-baking could only have been provided at the expense of the family's other food for that day. Yet she was pleased Sally had taken the second scone and praised the baking into the bargain. When you were poor, sometimes all you had was your pride.

The maid offered them another cake, refilled the teacups and asked her mistress if that would be all. Once she had been dismissed Sally got down to work, posing a series of questions about their hostess's home, family and charity work. She answered them all fully and comprehensively. Chatting knowledgeably about changing styles and the contemporary mode of furnishing houses, she laughed at the overcrowded and fussy Victorian style in which her husband's family home had been decorated.

Sally made a show of checking non-existent notes in the back of her shorthand notebook. 'That would be in Lanarkshire?'

'Yes. A great gloomy barn of a place. It's boarded up now.'

'You didn't like it out there? I understand the scenery is quite attractive in places.'

The woman gave a delicate little shudder. 'If you can

find it in amongst all those depressing mining villages full of unhealthy-looking children.'

'Your husband's tenants,' Sally said.

'Yes.'

Sally waited. The woman looked at her brightly. She obviously had nothing further to say on the subject.

'This dispute must make life uncomfortable for people like yourselves.'

'People like ourselves?' A perplexed wrinkle of the nose was followed by sudden realisation. 'Oh, you mean with interests in coal.' She laughed. 'I leave all that sort of thing to my husband. There's so much unpleasantness in the world, don't you think? I see it as my duty to provide the haven where he and our children can shut out that sort of thing.'

Sally waited again. Her interviewee frowned. 'Although,' she said earnestly, 'when I think of what some poor animals suffer . . . Well, it makes my blood boil.'

Josie hated cruelty to animals too, detested it with a fiery passion. However, it was on the tip of her tongue to ask this lady who was neither unkind nor stupid why she had so little concern to spare for the human animal, especially the ones whose labour kept her and her children in this beautiful house.

She thought back once more to the miner's wife, explaining with quiet and painful dignity how difficult it was to cope on her husband's wages as they were. A note of desperation had crept into her voice when she had speculated on how they would manage if he was forced to take a pay cut.

Sally wrote up the two articles in her own time on Thursday evening, bringing them in with her the following morning. She asked Alan, Deirdre, Ben and Josie to read them. Straightforwardly written as agreed, the author leaving her own political opinions out of the picture, they packed a powerful punch simply by nature of their juxtaposition. They went *en masse* to see Roddy, both to give Sally their moral support and also to show him how strongly they felt about the issue of balance in the coverage of the dispute.

Alerted by the heavy-footed arrival of a deputation in the subs' office, Roderick read the pieces slowly and carefully. When he had finished he raised his head and looked Sally in the eye. 'These are terrific pieces of journalism.'

She flushed with pleasure. 'So you'll persuade your father to publish them?'

'You want me to show these to him?'

'Of course.' As she frowned in puzzlement, the members of the deputation exchanged uneasy glances.

Roddy stood up, his chair scraping on the hard floor as he shoved it back. He was wearing his usual casual clothes, dark-green sleeve protectors over the cuffs of his creamy-coloured shirt. 'You really want to lose your job that badly, Sally?' His voice was as dry as sandpaper.

Josie saw Sally open her mouth and close it again. Roddy laid the tips of his long fingers on the article about the miner's wife. 'This I'm more than happy to plead for. I find it particularly moving when the lady talks of her hopes that her clever youngest son will somehow manage to escape the pit and go on to university. It puts a human face on this whole dreary dispute and I'm sure our readers will respond to that.'

He folded his arms across his chest and surveyed Sally with an air of cool authority. 'I'm afraid the other one will not be seeing the light of day.'

Sally's protest rose into a wail. 'The whole idea of the thing is to put the two pieces side-by-side!'

'I realise that. But you obtained the interview with the other lady unethically.'

'She wouldn't have spoken to us otherwise!'

'Exactly,' Roddy said grimly. 'That's the point. As a

journalist, one of your first duties is to admit who you are and what you're up to. It's a basic principle.' He unfolded his arms. 'For God's sake, Sally! You've been at this game longer than I have. You know what a low opinion people have of the press. If we're to have any hope of turning that around, we have to act responsibly. Play by the rules.'

'It's a good article,' Sally said stubbornly.

'It's a great article but you obtained it under false pretences. I would strongly advise against showing it to my father and I would suggest you rewrite it as a separate piece, angling it as originally intended.'

'As an innocuous piece of fluff!' Sally flung the words out as though she were hurling missiles into the sky. Her stormy eyes narrowed. 'It's because she's your sister's friend, isn't it? You're closing ranks. Like you people always do!'

Dismayed, Josie looked from one furious face to one which had gone carefully blank.

'She does happen to be a friend of my family, yes. But if you really think that's what my objection is here, I'm afraid you don't know me very well.'

Leaning forward, Sally snatched up both of her articles from the subs' table and turned on her heel. Ben took off in hot pursuit, leaving Josie and Deirdre and Alan to trade more uncomfortable looks. Roddy strode out from behind the table, extracted some copy from the wire basket inside the door and returned to his place. Sitting down heavily, he began to sub the article. 'Don't you three have any work to do?' he snapped.

'Exit our pal Roddy, enter the future owner and editor of the *Dispatch*?' queried Alan once they were safely out of earshot.

'I'm not sure if that's fair, Alan,' responded Deirdre. 'He does have a valid point.'

'You think so?' said Alan haughtily, giving her a cold look.

Josie chewed her lip. This was driving a wedge between everybody.

Chapter 13

Josie stared stupidly at the empty boot polish tin. Base in one hand and lid in the other, she examined the two pieces of shiny metal as though she could conjure up the money they had contained: all those yellow threepences and silver sixpences and shillings she had placed in there so carefully each week. With a sickening lurch of the stomach, it came to her that there had been no magic involved in their disappearance.

She'd had to stay back an hour last night, waiting for an overdue article being phoned in from a correspondent in Aberdeen. One of the Collins men would have been raking about for something she hadn't been here to fetch for him. Fitting the base and lid together again, she slipped the tin into the pocket of her pinny. Then she walked slowly over to the window and stood looking out.

For so long she'd gone out of her way not to provoke them. Fearful of earning herself or the wee ones a slap, she'd said nothing when they'd started bringing drink home or when Arthur Collins had shown no sympathy for Charlie, his own poor motherless son.

She was the one who had held everything together since her mother had died, yet her efforts had been unappreciated and undermined at every turn. The money she'd so carefully saved being stolen was the last straw. How in the name of God were they going to manage if the strike did come to pass?

'No,' she said softly to herself. 'I'm no' going to let them get away with it.'

* * *

'Where's the tea?' growled Arthur Collins. 'And why the hell is the table no' set?'

Billy and Arthur hadn't even noticed that. They were too busy arguing about the strike, the former for coming out, the latter against it. Josie took a deep breath and walked over to stand on the opposite side of the table from her stepfather. Rachel and Charlie were already fed and were now sitting quietly on the box bed, legs dangling over the side. Rachel was hearing her wee brother's reading.

'The tea's in those pots and pans,' Josie said, indicating the range with a lift of her chin. 'I've cooked it. Like I cook it every night.'

'That's what women are for, wee Josie,' young Arthur said, joining his father at the table. 'D'ye no' know that, hen?' He looked her up and down, lascivious eyes lingering on the curves of her body. 'That and one other thing.'

Billy guffawed and sat down too. Josie tapped her foot and waited for thirty seconds, savouring the incomprehension on their faces. Extracting the tin from her apron pocket, she opened it and laid both pieces flat in the centre of the table. 'You'll get your tea when I find out which one of you lot pinched the money that was in here.'

She could tell from the boys' faces that they had no idea what she was talking about. Billy at least was too stupid to put that on, so she turned to her stepfather. 'You took it then, did you?' she asked. Her voice was dangerously calm.

'What if I did?'

'It was my money. I was saving it up to take Rachel and Charlie on a day out. Or to help keep us all going if the strike comes off.'

Arthur Collins shrugged his shoulders. 'Where's our tea, girl?'

'You're not getting it until I get an explanation, an apology and my money back.'

Her stepfather stiffened, his powerful hands gripping the corners of the table as he gazed up at Josie from under dark and heavy eyebrows. Billy and young Arthur looked at their father. Then they looked at Josie. An expression of keen interest settled on their features as Arthur Collins senior rose slowly to his feet.

Josie had to dampen down panic when he came round the table towards her. He was a big man, both tall and broad. When he thrust his head close to hers, he had to stoop quite a long way. 'What-did-you-say?'

'You heard.' Her heart was pounding with such a loud and insistent beat she was convinced he must be able to hear it. Slipping an arm around her shoulders in a parody of a kindly touch, he put his mouth close to her ear.

'What if I did take your wee bit money? I'm your father, am I no'?'

'No, you're not actually.' Damn it, she wasn't going to put up with him touching her. She tried to move away but his hand came down on her shoulder, clamping it as strongly as though it were held in a vice. She twisted round, the contempt she felt for him filling her eyes and her voice. 'Thank God.'

He took the back of his free hand to the side of her head, maintaining his grip so she couldn't reel back from the blow. He did it twice more before he released her. 'Now,' he hissed softly into her face, 'put the tea on the table.'

He was already walking away from her, satisfied that he had resolved the problem. Ears ringing and pain echoing through her skull, Josie stared at his retreating back with eyes that burned. 'Do it yourself.'

He wheeled round. This time the blow sent her flying. She fetched up in front of the box bed. Winded and shocked, she struggled to sit up, aware of Rachel and

Charlie above her head. Her stepfather came after her, administered a punch to the side of her mouth.

'Oh!' she yelled as the impact juddered through her jaw. She felt Charlie's skinny little legs beside her as he slithered out of the bed. He ran at his father and started pummelling him with his tiny fists.

'You leave Josie alone!'

The little boy yelped as his father gripped him roughly by the upper arms, then threw him back on to the bed as though he were a sack of potatoes, leaving him wailing and crying. Shaking with fear, Rachel slid a trembling arm about Charlie's shoulders.

Arthur Collins dug his hand painfully into Josie's hair and dragged her to her feet. 'Now, ye bloody wee bitch,' he said. 'Put the fucking tea on the table. And open these bottles of beer for me and my boys.'

The drinking went on all weekend. Her stepfather didn't hit her again but the threat of it was never very far away, hanging viciously in the atmosphere. It made Josie's body tense up with fear and set her nerves a-jangling. That in turn made her clumsy, dropping pots and knocking plates together as she prepared the food she hoped would pacify him. Taking their cue from their father, Arthur and Billy's language grew ever coarser as they miscalled her for the noise she was making.

She discovered they themselves could be quiet enough when they wanted to. Standing at the stove stirring soup on Sunday morning she was unaware young Arthur was behind her until she felt his hands go round her waist. She froze in horror when they slid up to cup her breasts. When he pressed himself hard up against her back, forcing her to feel his arousal, revulsion rose in her throat like bile.

'Fancy a real man, wee Josie?' he murmured in her ear. 'You could have some o' this any time ye like. Better than all that canoodlin' ye dae out in the close wi' Tam Paterson.'

Outrage gave her strength. She whirled round in his arms, thrusting him away from her. He took one more voluntary step backwards and perched himself on the corner of the table, gesturing towards her right hand. 'Gonnae hit me wi' your wee wooden spoon, hen?' he inquired. 'Go on, then. Ah just *love* it when a lassie tries to fight me off. Makes me even keener,' he said softly, laying a hand on the front of his trousers. 'If you catch my drift.'

She adjusted her hold on the spoon. Her hands were slick with sweat. 'Try anything like that again and I'll pour the soup all over you!'

One stride brought him back up to her, his hand shooting out to grip her face. 'And if you try anything like that I'll give ye some more of what my daddy gave you yesterday. Plus this, ye wee trollop.'

She tried to twist her face away, but his grip was too strong. He squeezed her cheeks, forcing her mouth open and pushing his tongue between her teeth.

'Josie?' It was Rachel, just woken up and calling anxiously from behind the curtains of the box bed. The interruption was enough. Arthur released her, although his hand lingered on her face. 'Don't think we've finished here. That wee taste's just whetted ma appetite.'

He rubbed his thumb hard over her lips, distorting their shape. She winced as he pressed on the bruise which had come up at the side of her mouth. He laughed and threw himself down at the table. 'Nothing like a smack in the mouth to keep a woman in order, eh? I want ma breakfast,' he said. 'Now.'

Josie swallowed hard. She needed to swill her mouth out with water to get rid of the taste of him. 'After I've got Rachel and Charlie up.'

Arthur locked eyes with her. 'Now,' he repeated. Very

deliberately, he transferred his gaze to the box bed. Then he looked back at Josie. 'Ye're fond o'the wee brats, eh?'

She got him his breakfast. She had no idea whether he would really be prepared to hit the children. She couldn't afford to take the risk. Shaken as she was by her encounter with him, dizzy with terrified apprehension at the thought of what else he might try, it was fear for Rachel and Charlie which kept her indoors all Sunday. When Tam tapped on the front door in the late evening, she spoke to him through the letter box.

'I'm fine,' she whispered, careful not to let him see her discoloured mouth. Her hair was covering the rest of her bruises.

'They've been boozing, though?' he asked anxiously.

'Aye but they're away to bed now.' She'd been keeping the beer coming all evening, realising it was her best hope of getting any peace for herself and Rachel and Charlie. It was a galling thought that her own money had probably paid for the alcohol.

'Will ye no' come out for a wee minute then?' Tam pleaded. 'Please, Josie. I havenae seen you all weekend.'

'I'd better not. I'll see you tomorrow. Honest.'

'Are ye sure you're all right, Josie?'

It took her some time to convince him but at last he let go of the flap of the letter box. She stayed where she was, listening for his footsteps going up the stairs. She didn't hear them. He was still there, on the other side of the solid piece of wood which separated them. 'Josie?'

'Yes?'

His voice was as soft and warm as an April raindrop. 'I love you, by the way.'

It was the first time either of them had said it. They'd both been shy of uttering the actual words. Now, more than anything in the world, she wanted to tell him that she loved him too. She knew he would insist on her coming out if she did. He would see her bruise and then, sooner or later – but inevitably – he would get hurt too. She took a quick, shallow breath. 'Good night, Tam,' she said. 'Sleep tight.'

'Aye,' he said after a minute. She squeezed her eyes closed, sensing his disappointment. 'You too, lassie.'

She waited until she heard him pull his own front door behind him, the soft bang echoing down the stairwell. Then she relaxed back from a crouch to sit hunched up on the cold floor. The tiny lobby was too small for her to stretch her legs out. She wrapped her arms around her bent knees and let her head fall forward, curling up into a tight ball of misery.

She was so ashamed. Mild and browbeaten though her mother had seemed, her husband and stepsons would never have brought drink into the house while she had been alive. Nor would they have dared to use the sort of language Josie and the children had been subjected to over the weekend.

She lifted her head and laced her fingers through the thick waves of her hair, deliberately seeking out the sore points, smarting still from the blows inflicted on her. Tears of pain pricked her eyes as she pressed down on them. There must be something wrong with her that the Collins males now thought they could behave so badly. She released the pressure. It was too painful. Everything was too painful.

She slept fitfully, making her bleary-eyed and dozy when she got Rachel and Charlie up for school the following morning. They were both very subdued, although Charlie brought fresh tears to her eyes when he asked if he would kiss her sore mouth better. She crouched down and let him do it, touched also by the hug he bestowed on her before he and his sister left the house.

Rachel had dealt with the events of the weekend as she had dealt with her mother's death: by withdrawing into herself. This morning she seemed unwilling even to look her big sister in the eye. Josie dropped a kiss on top of her reluctant head anyway, glad they would both be out of the house all day, at school with their friends and teachers and doing normal things in the peaceful surroundings of a classroom.

Once she had waved them off she studied herself in the small mirror pinned up on the window frame to the side of the jawbox. She thought the bruising might be subsiding a little. Not enough for her to go into work, though. Although she could ill afford to lose a day's wages, people would ask what she'd done to herself and she wasn't in a fit enough state today to be able to lie convincingly about that.

There were no signs of anyone stirring through in the other room, so it looked as if none of them were going to work today either. More money lost.

The kitchen was a right mess, littered with empty beer bottles from the weekend's excess and the dirty plates from yesterday evening's meal. She hadn't had the heart to tackle them last night. She hadn't the heart to tackle them now. She leaned back against the sink and tried to summon up the energy to make herself a cup of tea and get dressed.

If she got this place really clean and tidy today, then read that lot the riot act when they finally surfaced . . . No more drink in the house, no more touching, no more foul language. Och, but she was so tired.

She stumbled over to the box bed, crawling in as she had crawled out an hour earlier. Her last conscious thought as she pulled the covers over herself was that she would just have a wee lie down. For half an hour, maybe. Then she would get up and get on with it.

She was woken by authoritative banging on the front door, three sharp raps being continuously repeated. She sat bolt upright. How long had she been asleep? The room was bright with sunlight, so the day must be well advanced. Hastily pulling on her mother's shabby old winter coat over her nightie, Josie hurried out into the lobby.

She opened the door a few cautious inches, peering round the edge to see who the persistent caller was. It was a man, tall and thin and wearing a dark suit and a bowler hat. He had a companion, identically dressed but comically different in shape, being short and broad. Josie frowned in puzzlement, wondering if they had come to the wrong house, but she asked them politely if she could help them.

'Would this be the Collins household?' asked the tall man. Still puzzled, Josie agreed that it was. Her questioner stepped aside and she stared in astonishment at the woman who'd been standing behind him.

'Miss Anderson? What on earth are you doing here?'

Chapter 14

Surprise gave way to alarm, her hand flying to her mouth in panic. 'Has something happened to Rachel or Charlie?'

'That's what we're here to establish,' said the short man.

Josie stared at him. The stern set of his features belied his homely appearance. His mouth was tight with disapproval.

'I don't understand,' she said. 'What's going on?'

Miss Anderson smiled superciliously. 'Don't pretend you don't know why we're here. Let us in, Josie Collins.'

Too dazed and confused to protest, she held the door open and pointed to the living room. Following them in there, she saw that they were all scrutinising their surroundings carefully. The room had looked bad enough when she had surveyed it herself this morning. Seeing it through their eyes was a hundred times worse, the dirty dishes and empty beer bottles all too evident.

Embarrassed and upset, Josie pulled her mother's coat more tightly about herself. Take all the mess away and the room would still be dingy and untidy. She hadn't washed the floor for several days and there were some cobwebs in the corners she'd been meaning to get round to for weeks.

The short man's face registered his disgust plainly. Seeing the tall man's eyes fixed on her own face, Josie's hand went up protectively to her bruised mouth. He kept staring at her but it was her former teacher to whom he spoke. 'I fancy you were absolutely right to recommend immediate action, Miss Anderson.'

156

Daphne Anderson nodded sagely. The comment was obviously a continuation of some discussion they'd been having before they got here. He turned to Josie, enunciating his words slowly and carefully, as though she were stupid or lacking in understanding in some other way. 'I'm sorry, young woman, but I'm afraid we're going to have to do something about this.'

'Do something?' Josie repeated blankly. 'About what?'

'About what Rachel told her teacher when she found her crying in the girls' lavatories at playtime this morning,' said Daphne Anderson. Must be a family trait, Josie thought crazily. Sneaking off to the lavvy to have a greet.

'What?' she said again. She sounded stupid. Maybe she was. Perhaps her stepfather's blows had knocked all the brains out of her head.

'She gave her teacher an account of the drunken and debauched violence which has occurred in this house over the last two days.'

Miss Anderson had affected a sombre voice, speaking more in sorrow than in anger. She didn't quite manage to pull it off. Condemnation had coated every syllable and there was a gleam in the woman's eyes which spoke of something going on behind them which Josie couldn't begin to work out.

What she did know was that there was no point in attempting to deny Miss Anderson's statement. The evidence was too damning. It was all around her. It was on her own face. She looked at the tall man. What had he meant by his comment about *immediate action*? What did he mean by *doing* something?

'I'll see tae it that it willnae happen again,' she said, her normal concern with speaking nicely swamped by mounting anxiety. 'And my brother and sister werenae hurt. I made sure o' it.'

She scanned the faces of her accusers. Surely they would give her some credit for that? She thought she saw a glimmer of sympathy in the tall man's face but his colleague responded sternly to what she had said.

'Do you have any idea how much damage it can do to a young mind simply to witness violence?' He took a small black notebook from the inside pocket of his jacket and flicked it open. 'According to our information there are three adult males living here. How can a young girl such as yourself possibly guarantee the children's safety in the future?'

He snapped the notebook shut and returned it to his pocket. There was a finality about the action, a sense he neither needed nor wanted an answer to the question he had just posed.

Josie was beginning to feel really panicky now. Her breathing was growing shallow and coming far too fast. She needed help. She looked towards the tall man.

'I'm sorry,' he said again, 'but we're going to have to take the children away. We would be failing in our duty if we did not. They're clearly not being looked after properly and it's obvious they're in both physical and moral danger here.'

Only three words of his little speech penetrated. *Take them away.*

'You cannae take them away!' she shouted. 'This is their home!'

'It's a squalid hovel, not worthy of the name,' Daphne Anderson said contemptuously.

'What in buggery is going on here?' It was Arthur junior, unkempt, unshaven and still wearing the clothes he'd fallen asleep in yesterday evening. He pushed his way through the visitors, placing a heavy arm around Josie's shoulders before she had time to resist. He lurched forward, swinging round and peering back up into her face. 'Aw, wee Josie's got a sore mouth. That's a crying shame.'

'Get off!' She gave him a shove which sent him reeling.

Somehow he managed to propel himself into the rocking chair by the fire. 'Hey, that was quite clever, eh?' He looked up, blinking. 'Who are all these bloody people, hen?'

'They want to take Rachel and Charlie away! Do something!'

'Take them away? Why would they want to dae that? You're talking shite, Josie. Tell them to fuck off.'

Miss Anderson's intake of breath must have been audible on the other side of the cathedral. Arthur smiled at her. Then he sank back into the rocking chair, his head rolling to one side. Josie ran forward and shook him. 'Wake up! Wake up!'

Her frantic efforts to rouse him were in vain. He was dead to the world. Josie spun round, her grey eyes wild. 'I don't know what to do!' she cried pathetically. 'I don't know what to do!'

The room was moving around her. She began to go with it. The only fixed points were the three people who stood watching her so intently. The tall man came forward and took her by the elbow, steering her towards the table and sitting her down at it. He was saying something, speaking over the top of her head, his words a soft murmur.

'Perhaps we could fetch a female neighbour. Or take her to one.'

She was in Mrs Fitzgerald's kitchen, neat as a new pin as her own was not, and she had the universal panacea in front of her. Despite Bridget's coaxing, the cup of tea remained untouched. Josie was too upset to do anything but sit there. All the fight had gone out of her now. Listening to her neighbour trying to reason with the men in the bowler hats she had realised that even her Irish eloquence wasn't going to sway them. Standing behind Josie, her arms on the girl's slim shoulders, Bridget had fixed unerringly on the tall man as being the one with the real authority.

'I hope you know what you're doing, sir. I really do. You may well have the power to take the children away, but do you have the right?'

He started citing laws and bye-laws, informed her he had a statutory duty to protect the welfare of all those children who fell within the jurisdiction of the corporation of the City of Glasgow.

'What about this child?' Bridget demanded, indicating Josie. 'What about *her* welfare if you take the little ones away from her?'

'She's over sixteen,' he said. 'Our concern is only with those below that age.'

'Mother of God,' said Bridget softly. 'Have you people no hearts at all? And you can quote all the laws and bye-laws you like at me but what I'm speaking of here is your moral right. One day we must all answer to a higher authority. I hope your conscience will be clear when that day comes!'

He inclined his head gracefully. He'd removed his hat in Bridget's house, a politeness Josie dully noticed hadn't been accorded to her. 'I believe it will be, Mrs Fitzgerald. One reason for that is the faith I have in the job I'm doing.' He addressed himself to Josie. 'I know you're distressed now, Miss Collins—'

Bridget moved her hands gently over Josie's shoulders. 'She's more than distressed, sir. She's distraught!'

He acknowledged the interruption but didn't let it put him off his stroke. 'Miss Collins, when you've had time to think about it, you'll see that this is for the best. As I explained earlier, your brother and sister will be boarded out with some kind people in the country who'll care for them as if they were their own. They'll have lots of fresh air and good food. Surely that's much better than what they've had here?'

Josie was staring fixedly at the cooling cup of tea. 'Can they come back if I get things sorted out?'

'It's a pretty big *if*, Miss Collins.' He sounded genuinely regretful.

'I could take them,' Bridget said suddenly. Josie twisted round in her chair and raised her hand to her. Bridget took it and gave it an encouraging squeeze.

'A very generous offer, Mrs Fitzgerald, but it wouldn't really remove the children from an unsuitable home, would it? We need to take them more than a few yards, I'm afraid. And,' he continued, choosing his words with care, 'judging by what we know about Mr Collins and his sons, such an arrangement might well have repercussions for you and your husband which would not be very pleasant. The children might once again be placed in a position where they would be at risk of witnessing or even experiencing violence.'

Hopes raised and dashed in less than a minute. Josie faced forward again. The man sitting opposite her wasn't unkind. She could tell that from his voice and his face, and from the time he had taken to explain all this to her. She could also tell that his mind was made up and that nothing was going to change it.

'Will I be able to visit them sometimes?' she asked, her eyes dropping once more to the cup of tea. It would be as cold as charity now.

'We generally find that it's best to make a clean break.'

'Can I say goodbye to them?'

The silence that question provoked made her look up. 'We've already removed them from the area,' he said. 'Over the years we've found that farewells can be very painful.' He stood up and lifted his hat. 'Goodbye, Miss Collins. Please try not to upset yourself too much. This really is for the best.'

When Bridget came back from seeing him out Josie

went wordlessly into her arms. 'I want Tam,' she sobbed. 'I want Tam.'

'Well then,' Bridget said, 'let's be taking you down to the lad.'

Josie sat on a bench in a corner of the stables with Tam's arms about her while Bridget told him and Mick what had happened. Not long back from their daily rounds, both men fell to discussing what they could do about the situation and how they might fit it in with their duties the next day.

'The relevant office will be closed now, I'm thinking,' Mick said. 'It'll be somewhere in the City Chambers, no doubt.'

Since he was due to be in that area in the middle of the following morning, it was decided he would go there and do his utmost to find out where Rachel and Charlie were. He leaned forward and patted Josie's knee. 'We'll get this sorted out and those children back where they belong or my name's not Michael Francis Fitzgerald.'

'Right then,' his wife said briskly, 'there's nothing more we can do at the moment and we'd all be the better for a good hot meal. You'll be staying with us tonight, Josie. It's not seemly for you to be on your own with your stepfather and the boys.'

A wave of relief swept through her. 'Thanks, Mrs Fitzgerald,' she murmured. 'But would you mind if Tam and me maybe stayed down here for a wee while?'

Bridget stood up, giving her husband a discreet wink. 'Stay as long as you like. I'll keep a meal warm for the both of you and I'll tell your ma what's happened and where you are, Tam.'

After the Fitzgeralds had gone and the other carters had settled their horses for the night and taken themselves off it grew very quiet, the warmth and peace of the stables punctuated only by the munching and snuffling of the horses in the stalls around them. Exhausted and wrung-out by all that had happened, Josie's eyelids began to flutter shut. She felt Tam move.

Placing his hands on her shoulders, he pushed her away from him a little. She made an inarticulate sound of protest, stopped in its tracks when he lifted one large hand and gently traced the bruise at the side of her mouth with his index finger. 'Would you like to tell me how you came by this, lassie?'

'Tam,' she said earnestly, all at once wide awake, 'it doesn't matter now. Nothing does except getting Rachel and Charlie back.'

'Was it your stepfather or one of the boys who did it?' he persisted.

She touched his chin with her fingers, causing him to briefly close his eyes.

Then he took her hand and kissed the tip of each one in turn. 'Answer my question.'

'No,' she said and put her mouth to his, giving him a succession of the little nuzzling kisses which she knew drove him wild.

He let out a soft moan but pushed her gently away once more. 'I've got to know, Josie.'

'So you can fight them?'

'So I can teach them a lesson they'll never forget,' he agreed.

'Tam, I don't want them to hurt you. They'd all go for you – the three of them together. You know that.'

'But it's all right for them to hurt you?' He shook his head. 'I don't think so, Josie.'

She searched his face, saw the love he felt for her written all over it. She saw his stubbornness too and had a sudden vision of where that combination might lead him. It was sickeningly vivid: her stepfather and stepbrothers smashing their fists into his face, putting the boot in mercilessly once they had wrested him to the ground.

'Oh, Tam!' she burst out. 'Please don't make me have to worry about you too. Please, Tam.' She started to cry, hot salty tears coursing down her smooth cheeks. 'I love you, Tam. I don't want to lose you as well. I couldn't bear it!'

The hand cupping one of her shoulders tightened convulsively. 'What did you just say?'

She stopped weeping as abruptly as she had started, wiping the wetness away with her fingers. 'I said that I loved you, Tam.'

A kind of solemn joy was spreading out over his handsome features. 'Och, Josie!' He snatched her into his arms, began raining kisses on to her face: her damp eyes, her bruised mouth, her nose, her cheeks. Back to her mouth again, his tongue flicked delicately along her parted lips. She groaned, and he lifted his head immediately. 'Is it sore, hen?'

'No,' she murmured, and coiled her arms around his neck. 'Don't stop. Don't stop, Tam.'

He took her at her word.

They were lying in an empty stall, on a tartan blanket he had spread out on top of the straw before he had laid her down there. He was propped up on one elbow so he could look at her and his blue eyes were sparkling. He thought he had never seen anything so lovely as his girl lying there with her hair tousled and her clothes in disarray.

Josie's usually pale complexion was delicately flushed with pink, both from what they had just done and the embarrassment of the unabashed and practical way Tam had helped her clean herself up afterwards. Flat on her back with her hands behind her head, she did her best to look stern. 'Got a bit carried away there, didn't we?'

He leaned over and kissed her lightly on the mouth. 'Ye could say that.'

'What if someone had come in?'

'Nobody did.' He kissed her again. 'Tell me something. Did ye like it?'

She brought one hand out from under her head and reached up to touch his face. 'Aye, Mr Paterson. I did.'

Tam took her hand and pressed his mouth softly against her palm. 'It hurt a wee bit, though? At the beginning?'

'You were very gentle,' she assured him. 'At the beginning.'

They smiled at each other. Then Josie frowned. 'I forgot Rachel and Charlie. Just for a few minutes. While we were . . .'

'Making love,' he supplied. 'That's what it's called.' He traced the lines creasing her forehead with the tips of two of his fingers. 'I suppose that must be one of the reasons people like it so much. Because it makes you forget everything.'

She gazed up at him, her eyes troubled.

'We'll get them back.'

'Will we?'

He slid down beside her and threw his warm arm about her waist. 'Of course we will, lassie,' he said reassuringly. 'Of course we will.'

Something else had occurred to Josie. 'What if I'm . . .'

'In foal?' he suggested, laughing when she tutted and pretended to be offended. He kept it going. Anything to lift that worried expression from her face and take the pain out of her bonnie grey eyes. 'I'd be as proud as a stallion. What would you prefer for our first wean – a wee filly or a wee colt?'

'Och, you!'

'We're too close together for you to elbow me in the ribs,' he said. 'So don't bother your shirt trying. Tell me you love me again instead.'

Her expression softened. 'I love you, Tam Paterson.'

'And I love you, Josie Collins.'

She turned her head to one side, listening to the straw under the blanket crackle with the pressure of the movement. The rafters above her head were growing shadowy. Tam would need to light some lamps soon.

Josie Collins. No, she wasn't going to bear that name any longer. She allowed her head to roll back. 'Josie Shaw,' she corrected.

'Not for long,' he said. 'I'm thinking of changing it to Josie Paterson.'

'Oh you are, are you?' She struggled up on to her elbows and gave him another stern look.

He stayed where he was, gazing up at her out of one eye. 'I thought so.' His bravado cracked. As did his voice. 'If you'll have me, Josie.'

'Och, Tam,' she breathed. He sounded so humble, so sincere.

He coughed and recovered his usual strong tones. 'Once we get Rachel and Charlie back we'll have them to live wi' us. Bring them up as our own.'

She adjusted her position so that she was sitting up properly, twisting round to look back down at him. 'What about your mother and your own brothers and sisters, Tam? How would you support us all? Where would we live?'

'I'd find a way,' he said decisively, 'if you'd only say yes. Please Josie. Say yes. Please.'

He sat up too, turning so that he was kneeling in front of her. He seized her hands, holding one in each of his. The words came tumbling out. There might be a house going in the tenement owned by the brewery. She knew that was a really nice building, well-maintained and not a high rent either. A room and kitchen, big enough for her and him and Rachel and Charlie. His wee brother Malcolm would be out at work after the summer holidays. He wouldn't be earning much, of course. Tam would have to continue giving his mother some money each week. It would be a struggle, but they could do it. With her beside him, he could do anything he set his mind to.

It was the longest speech Josie had ever heard him make. When it was finished and he was catching his breath she came up on to her knees too, cupping his face between her hands. His chin was bristly, soft and rough at the same time.

'I love you.'

'So you'll say yes?' he asked eagerly.

She studied his face. It was handsome, yes, but it was a lot more than that. It was solid and dependable, true and honest. It was full of love for her. Like the sun in a child's drawing, that love shone out of him, warming everything it touched. 'I'll say yes,' she said softly.

'Och, Josie, I feel like I'm gonnae burst with joy!'

Her mouth quirked. 'Don't do that. You'll scare the cuddies.'

'They're fine,' he said, swinging round automatically to check on the horses. 'So am I.' He seized her hands again. 'A lot more than fine.'

They smiled into each other's eyes. 'Give me a hug,' Tam said, his voice husky again. They held each other for a long time, while their surroundings grew ever darker and the animals around them ever quieter. Only the occasional soft whinny broke the warm silence.

'I love you,' Josie said at last, 'but my knees are beginning to get sore!'

He laughed and released her and the two of them sank back on to the blanket-covered straw. 'Listen,' Tam said, 'I've had another thought about Rachel and Charlie. Would the folk you work wi' at the paper no' be able to help? From what you say, they're all clever people. What about yon Sally you talk about – Miss Fleming, is it?'

'You're right,' she said, excitement bubbling up inside her. 'It should have occurred to me before. Sally would love to get her teeth into something like this. It could even make a story.'

'There ye go then,' he said enthusiastically.

If she enlisted Sally's help she'd have to tell her an awful lot of things she didn't want to tell anybody to explain why Glasgow Corporation had seen fit to remove her wee brother and sister from their home.

Tam was studying her thoughtful face. 'We cannae do any more about it tonight, lassie, that's for sure.'

'No,' she agreed. 'I suppose we'd better be getting up the road.'

'Eh,' he said innocently, 'do you think we need to go right now? Mrs Fitzgerald said she would keep our tea warm. There's no great rush, is there?'

'What are you up to, Tam Paterson?'

'I only thought you might be tired. Needin' another wee lie down, like.'

'Aye,' Josie said. 'Right.' But she was smiling at him. 'Should you not be thinking about putting some lights on in here?'

'Not yet,' he said, and pulled her into his arms.

Chapter 15

It was a relief to leave the Drygate on Tuesday morning. Arthur Collins had banged on the Fitzgeralds' door at nine o'clock the previous evening, demanding to know if they knew where the hell that useless lassie was. He and his boys were needing something to eat. Mick had a short, sharp altercation with him on the doorstep which didn't escalate into a fight only because the Irishman didn't allow it to.

From the sound of his voice, Josie's stepfather had been very much the worse for wear. Sitting in the kitchen with Bridget and Ella Paterson, who'd come downstairs to express her sympathy for what had happened, and listening closely to the conversation taking place a few feet away, Josie had wondered if Arthur Collins had even noticed that Rachel and Charlie were missing, and how much he would care when he did.

She herself had been battling with a terrible feeling of embarrassment, convinced Bridget and Ella would guess what had taken place between Tam and herself. There had been no indication of that, which didn't stop Josie from feeling acutely self-conscious. Surely a change like that must be evident to the people around you. Something in your face perhaps, or a difference in the way you moved.

Had Tam really proposed to her and had she really said yes? They'd had very little chance to talk privately after they came home from the stables, only a few moments' whispered conversation in the Fitzgeralds' lobby. She had extracted a promise from him that he wouldn't think about tackling the men still sobering up on the other side of the close without discussing it with her first. She had every intention of talking him out of it completely.

Life would be so much easier if they could get the room and kitchen in the tenement owned by the brewery. It would put some distance between her and the Collins men and allow her to give Rachel and Charlie a decent and peaceful home. The burden it would place on Tam would be considerable. Yet he was prepared to shoulder it – because he loved her, and because he was a good man.

She loved him unreservedly. She knew that now, although her regret that getting married would mean giving up her job on the *Dispatch* cut deep. It would make a lot of sense for them not to get wed too soon. If they postponed it for a few months she could save some money from her pay and refill her war chest. She'd have to pay Mrs Fitzgerald for her keep, naturally, and for Rachel and Charlie's when they came home.

Making her way down the Bell o' the Brae, Josie frowned. Was it assuming an awful lot to think Bridget would take them all in until she and Tam got married? Whether they could put that off for a wee while was also dependent on another factor, one which was now in the lap of the gods. Och, but it had been so beautiful . . . She sent a longing glance in the direction of the brewery stables before she turned the corner into George Street.

Tam had been so tender and loving, kissing and caressing her, introducing them both to unimagined pleasures. When they were married they would be able to enjoy those whenever they wanted, but even when they were warm and cosy in their own respectable bed they would always share a private smile when they remembered their first time on a bed of straw in a horse's stall.

Josie blushed and tucked a stray strand of hair behind her ear. Their first two times. Or should that be twice?

Twice is nice. Twice had been very nice, she thought, and blushed all the harder.

She was almost at George Square before she realised something was wrong. She paused after she crossed Montrose Street, trying to work out what it was. Then it came to her. The city was far too quiet.

She looked around at the offices and workshops and warehouses. She thought of the fruit and vegetable wholesalers she had passed a street or two back. They had been shuttered and deserted. Early starters they might be but they weren't usually finished with their business quite this promptly.

Spinning round on the balls of her feet, Josie scanned the length of the street, first towards High Street where she had come from and then the other way, towards George Square and the Tron Kirk. There wasn't a single tram in sight and precious little of any other kind of traffic either.

She walked on. When she reached the square she saw that Queen Street railway station was also unusually quiet. Suddenly she realised. The strike had been called.

Tam had heard that news an hour earlier when he arrived at the stables. To his immense relief, an emotion he saw reflected in full measure on Mick's face, there had been no picket line waiting to greet them.

'Sure, it would have put me in a terrible quandary,' Mick said, 'but if we're all agreed?' he queried, looking around at the other carters.

They were. They might as well carry on with their work as normal. The horses needed their exercise, after all. Not only that, the cargo they were transporting would be welcomed by folk of every political persuasion and standpoint on the strike.

'They'll all have a drouth on them,' one man said cheerfully. 'We shouldn't see any trouble.'

171

Dray loaded, Tam went to fetch Jimmy. As he made sure the Clydesdale was fed and watered for the day ahead his eyes kept drifting to the stall where he and Josie had lain yesterday evening. He smiled, remembering every minute of it. Every second of it.

He murmured gently to the horse as he tacked him up. 'I'm a very lucky man, son. The most beautiful lassie in the world is in love wi' me. You know that already, because you were here last night. You'll keep our secret, won't you now?'

He laughed as Jimmy turned his massive head and regarded him solemnly out of dark and intelligent eyes.

If Josie needed confirmation the strike was on it was waiting for her in Buchanan Street. There was a picket line strung out across the entrance to the *Dispatch*, eight people standing with linked hands across the bottom of the steps. It came as no surprise to see that two of them were Sally and Ben.

The small crowd of people standing in front of the pickets were largely other members of staff and it was clear from their troubled expressions that they were wrestling with indecision, their consciences, or both. She wondered how everyone had made it into the town. Like herself, they must have used Shanks's pony.

She walked a little further, stepping up behind Deirdre Smith and Alan Dewar. Arguing quietly with one another, they didn't notice her at first. Deirdre was in favour of going into work, Alan was refusing to cross the picket line. Josie heard him say the printers were already out, so what was the point of anyone else going in? Tossing her head in exasperation, Deirdre turned and spotted Josie.

'Hallo there, pet. Where were you yesterday?' Her eyes widened. 'What have you done to your face?'

'I walked into a door.' It was a lame excuse but both Deirdre and Alan seemed to accept it, too concerned with the drama unfolding in front of the *Dispatch* office to have much interest left over for anything else.

'Look,' Alan said, indicating the entrance portico. A handful of people were gathered together at the top of the steps. 'There are the scabs.' His deep voice grew sarcastic. 'Robert the Bruce is one of them, I see. What a surprise.'

'I don't think you should call them by that insulting name,' Deirdre said sharply. 'Are we not all scared we're going to lose our jobs over this?'

He tilted his head back and looked down his long nose at her. 'Ever thought your principles might be worth standing up for, Deirdre?'

She held his disdainful gaze for thirty seconds. 'I can't afford principles,' she said. 'I'm not sure that you can either, Alan.' She started walking towards the picket line, ignoring his pleas for her to come back. Deirdre chose not to reply to Sally's remonstrances too, passing through the line to join the people standing under the portico.

Alan exhaled a long and dismayed breath. He started saying something to Josie but she interrupted him, pointing out that Roderick and his father were now coming out on to the steps. Press baron and filthy capitalist or not, Josie felt a quick stab of sympathy. Mr Cunningham senior was an energetic and strong man but he looked each and every one of his mature years this morning. When he began to speak his words were drowned out by jeers from some of the people on the picket line.

'That's disgraceful,' muttered Alan. 'We've got to allow both sides to say their piece. Especially considering what our business is. Everybody's entitled to exercise their right to free speech.' He shouted out, his height carrying his words about the heads of the crowd, 'Let Mr Cunningham speak! Please!'

'Yes,' came Sally's voice. 'That's only fair.'

Josie saw Roddy give them both a little nod of acknowledgement. He turned to his father and laid an encouraging hand on the older man's shoulders. She read the words he said next from the movement of his lips. 'Shall I do it, Dad?'

Casually dressed as usual, he walked forward and began to address the workforce. 'Yesterday we worked together, as we do every day, to get the paper out. Today it looks as if we're going to have a few little difficulties in that regard.'

A ripple of amusement ran through the crowd. 'Aye, printing a newspaper wi' naebody to operate the presses might just be a wee touch problematic,' called out one male voice.

Roddy accorded that comment a grave smile. 'Not if we pull together. As all of the cities' newspapers plan to. We've agreed to put out a joint news-sheet for the duration of the crisis. We're calling it the *Emergency Press*.'

'The bosses learning the lessons of solidarity at last?' shouted Ben. 'That's a good one.'

Josie jumped as, beside her, Alan raised his voice once more. 'You're not suggesting other trades operate the printing presses, are you?'

'If necessary,' said Roddy, looking across the heads between himself and Alan. 'How else are we to put out the news and let people know the truth about what's going on?'

'The truth?' called Ben. 'Or what the bosses see as the truth?'

'You don't think we might all be on the same side when it comes to honestly reporting whatever's going to happen over the next few days?'

'No,' Ben replied. 'I don't.' His uncompromising reply drew a round of applause from some.

Roddy gave him a level look but hesitated only very briefly before he spoke again. 'All right. I suppose it's time to draw a line in the sand. Will everybody who is prepared to keep working please make his or her way into the building? I appeal to those of you on the picket line to allow your colleagues to go about their lawful business without any further intimidation.'

His use of that word caused some muttering but the pickets did make a gap in their line wide enough for two or three people to pass through at a time. Several people took advantage of it, earning themselves boos from one side and cheers from the other. Alan Dewar looked down at Josie, his face sombre. 'What about you?' he asked. 'Which side are you on?'

Tam was heading west. He had some deliveries to make around Charing Cross and after that in Finnieston and Partick. Passing the Grand Hotel and the famous fountain which stood in front of it, he surveyed the long straight stretch of Sauchiehall Street he and Jimmy were now entering.

It looked so odd without the trams. The absence of their whirring and clanking also made for an eerie silence, the clip-clop of the horse's hooves unusually loud and echoing. At the junction with University Avenue he turned left. A little knot of men standing outside a factory turned their heads at the sound of his approach, staring reproachfully at him as he bowled past.

Alan Dewar was waiting for Josie's answer. When she walked slowly towards the picket line he went with her. Sensing her uncertainty, she supposed. Ben Gold undoubtedly did. She could tell by the way he lowered his voice and spoke directly to her, trying to convince her by making his words for her ears only. 'This is about injustice, Josie.'

Standing at Ben's shoulder, Sally added her contribution. 'About supporting people like that miner's wife we interviewed,' she said. 'About trying to achieve fairness and equality. Not allowing one class in society to hold all the cards and all the power. So which side are you on, Josie? Are you with us or against us?'

Josie looked at her. She looked at Ben and up at the people standing under the portico. Her eyes travelled over Miss Clarke's face and then Roddy's. He gave her a faint smile.

Not allowing one class in society to hold all the cards and all the power. Wasn't that what had happened yesterday? Miss Anderson and the men in the bowler hats belonged to that class. They could take your wee brother and sister away from you and there was nothing you could do to stop them. Josie knew now that nobody here was going to be able to help her get them back. Especially not with all this uproar going on.

She thought about the question posed by the doctor who had attended Dorothy Collins in her last moments on this earth. *Why do women persist in putting themselves at the mercy of such butchers?* The answer was obvious. Because they had no other choice. Because the way the world works means everything is weighted against them.

'I'm with you,' she said and a small cheer went up. She moved to the back of the crowd, waiting while everyone else decided which side of the line they were on. Most of them chose to support the strike. Those who didn't shuffled into the building and the door swung shut behind them.

'Well, my fellow revolutionaries,' Ben said dramatically, 'shall we go and get ourselves a cup of tea somewhere?'

'Wouldn't it be strike-breaking if we found someone prepared to serve it to us, though?'

Several members of the group began arguing the toss about that and other issues. One girl wanted to know whether it would be legitimate to travel home on a tram being driven by a volunteer. She'd walked all the way in from Maryhill and her feet were killing her. Alan Dewar answered her definitely and in the negative. It wasn't on to use transport driven by blacklegs – probably, he added contemptuously, overprivileged young university students who thought it a bit of a lark to help try and break the strike.

The girl came up with some complicated counter argument which Josie couldn't follow. Caught up in the discussion, none of them noticed when she walked quietly away.

She didn't know if she had made the right decision. Depending on how long the strike lasted, that could be her finished with the *Dispatch*. Confused and dispirited, she trudged home. There looked to be some trouble brewing outside the City Chambers, putting paid to her idea of pre-empting Mr Fitzgerald's visit there later on this morning.

She was almost home when she decided that she would go and wait for Tam. He wouldn't be there for hours yet but she liked it in the stables. It was peaceful. If one or two of the horses weren't out she could put her arms about them and lay her head against their silky necks and just not think for a while. She double backed on herself, cutting through a lane which skirted the high prison wall and led down to Duke Street.

The wall of the building on the other side was also high and windowless but it was a bright day and the rising morning sun was funnelling into the narrow passageway, so dazzling Josie had to lower her head against the glare. She was nearly through when the sunlight was abruptly blotted out. Looking up, she saw her stepbrother Billy standing a few feet in front of her, blocking her exit from the lane.

'Hallo there, Josie. Have ye joined the strike? Up the workers, eh?'

He leered at her, the unmistakable smell of alcohol wafting towards her as he opened his mouth. The weekend bender hadn't finished yet, then.

'Get out of my way,' she said. 'I'm going somewhere.'

He stretched out his arms, placing one hand on either side of the lane, barring her way forward. She wasn't scared. Not then. The stupid drunken sot wanted to play silly games, that was all. He needn't think she was going to join in.

She turned, intending to go back along the lane and take the long way round to Duke Street but her way was blocked in that direction too. Young Arthur was standing behind her, casually putting a cigarette to his lips.

'Let me past,' she said. Her breathing had quickened and her breasts were beginning to rise and fall in response. Arthur's eyes dropped to them. He laughed and took a long drag of nicotine. Josie repeated her demand.

'Let me past. Now.'

Arthur allowed the cigarette to fall from his fingers on to the cobbles. He ground it out with the toe of his boot, his eyes never once leaving her face. He opened his mouth and allowed some smoke rings to float out. Then he laughed again. 'Not this time, wee Josie. Not this time.'

Chapter 16

Tam was having a difficult time of it. He'd run the gauntlet of a few pickets, been on the receiving end of some shouted insults. He was growing increasingly uncomfortable about whether or not he should be working today. Perhaps he ought to be joining in with the strike.

One man he met halfway through the morning had a gentler approach and was persuasive with it. He asked Tam to listen to him for five minutes and proceeded to provide him with a succinct summing up of why it was so important for working people to stick together to defend each other's pay and standard of living. 'Such as that is,' he added with a sour laugh.

'Aye,' sighed Tam, 'you're right there.' When the man asked if he would join the strike, he said he would think about it. He did, turning over all the issues in his mind as he went on with his deliveries. He could withdraw his labour but still look after the horses, take them round the local streets to exercise them. If his bosses agreed. As the man had said to Josie about getting the weans back, that was probably a gey big *if*.

Yet on the other hand, was the strike going to solve anything? Weren't both sides simply going to dig their heels in, moving further and further away from any chance of agreement or compromise?

There was also the small matter of money. As soon as he stopped working he would stop earning. How the hell could he do that? There were too many people dependent on him as it was, and he was about to take on three more.

Despite his worries about how he and his wee brother were going to manage to keep everybody housed and fed, Tam smiled happily at the thought. It wasn't going to be easy, but he'd have Josie to come home to each night. That would make everything worthwhile.

Throughout the morning more and more people had been coming out on to the streets, trying to get folk like himself to stop working and join them. He didn't doubt that the vast majority of them were sincere, like the man who'd tried to persuade him by reasoned argument. However, he had noticed some folk – usually men stravaiging about in small groups – whom he doubted very much were motivated by political principles. They were out looking for trouble and he had a cart which still had a substantial amount of alcohol on it.

It was time he was heading back anyway. A delivery to a pub opposite the Art Galleries in Dumbarton Road and his morning round was almost over, just one last commission in the city centre to fulfil. On his way back to the brewery he would call past the *Dispatch* office, see if Josie was still there.

She was so unhappy about Rachel and Charlie. He had to get them back for her. That might not be so easy, especially with all this kerfuffle going on, but Mick would help and Mick had the gift of the gab which he himself didn't. It was that talent God had given the Irish, the silver tongue which allowed them to speak on equal terms to everybody from a tramp to an emperor.

Both of the Fitzgeralds had been towers of strength through all this. Tam was deeply grateful to them and immensely relieved that Josie was now in their care. It was high time she was away from the Collins' household. They had treated her like a skivvy and shown her no respect. She still hadn't told him which one of them had struck her but he suspected it had been her stepfather.

Tam flicked the reins and gave Jimmy the command to

move off. How any man could hit a woman was beyond him. How a powerful brute like Arthur Collins could lay into a wee thing like Josie flummoxed him completely. A striker standing on the edge of the pavement was watching Tam drive past. He considered shouting at him, then thought better of it. The lad had a real fierce expression on his face.

Tam Paterson was no fighter and never had been but he longed to pay Arthur Collins back in kind for what he had done to Josie. It made his blood boil to think of what that bastard had subjected her to, and with himself only yards away at the time. She had sent him away, not allowed him to help her.

Tam's grim expression relaxed. That was because she loved him and didn't want to see him hurt. Oh, and he loved her so much! He was going to make sure she never suffered again. He was going to take care of her for the rest of her life. He thought of all the years to come when they would be together, loving and cherishing each other.

A smile lit up his handsome face. Maybe they would get that wee house by a loch sometime. A bit of land. A horse or two. 'You and a couple of Highland ponies,' he said aloud to Jimmy. 'What would you think o' that, son? Whoa, boy! We're here.'

He was still thinking about Josie when he secured the reins and carried in the first crate. Still thinking about her while he exchanged a few words with the landlady and she and her son helped him with the rest of the delivery.

Tam came out to find that the men looking for trouble had found it.

Something warm-blooded and smooth-skinned slithered over Josie's ankles. Even that failed to rouse her. She was lying where they had left her, the cobblestones of the lane digging into her back as she stared up at the sky. It was a cloudless azure blue.

They had taken it in turns.

Billy went first, having his way with her while Arthur knelt behind her head and pinioned her arms above it.

'Open your eyes, ye wee bitch,' he said, his breath on her face sour with beer and tobacco. 'Ma brother wants tae see that you're enjoying yourself.'

It didn't last long. Billy was too excited, collapsing heavily on top of her within a matter of seconds. Josie was praying. *Not Arthur too, please God, not Arthur too.*

Billy raised himself up on his arms and leered down at her. Arthur's eyes were also skimming down her body. 'Well, well, well,' he said. 'D'ye see whit ah see, Billy? Or whit ah don't see, mair like? Looks like Tam Paterson's beat us tae it. So the wee hure shouldnae mind if I have a go too. Spin her round, brother. Spin the wee hure round.'

They laughed as they did that, positioning her so that she was facing in the other direction. Then Billy held her down for his brother. Arthur was strong and powerful and she thought he was never going to stop. He drove himself into her, each brutal thrust accompanied by a terrible name picked from a small and obscene litany. The awful words were swirling still around her head.

The rat scampered up the side of her body. Josie turned her head to look at it. It was looking right back at her, its eyes bright and curious. Odd that it wasn't scared of her. Odd that she wasn't scared of it. Maybe that was because she belonged in its world now. Down in the gutter.

The creature moved on but Josie stayed where she was. She had no idea how long she lay there. At last, when the cobblestones became too uncomfortable, she struggled to her feet. She needed to wash herself and clean the dirt off her clothes. She would go to the stables. There was water there.

When she had cleaned herself up she sat down on a bale of hay to wait for Tam. She had no idea what she was going to tell him. She only knew that she needed his comfort and his presence more than she had ever needed anything in her whole life.

They had led the horse and dray over the deserted thoroughfare, on to the other side of the broad street, and they were helping themselves to what was left of his load.

'Here!' he cried. 'Stop that!'

'Or what, pal?' shouted one man, walking out into the road. He had an open bottle in his hand. Smashing it against the side of the cart, he raised it and allowed the beer to run out. He walked up the side of the cart. Watching in horrified disbelief, Tam saw him stretch his hand out towards Jimmy's hindquarters.

'No!' he yelled.

His ears were filled with the animal's cries. His big laddie was whinnying in pain and terror and all Tam wanted to do was get across there and kick in the teeth of the man who had hurt him. He ran out into the road. There had been practically no traffic on it all morning. Why should he expect any now?

The university student driving the tram clanking over the River Kelvin had been one of the first to respond to the government's call for volunteers to man the essential industries Britain needed to keep going. He believed in what he was doing. He was also having a whale of a time. It wasn't as difficult to drive this thing as he had thought.

He and his best friend who was acting as conductor had just dropped three girls off at the university gate. They'd boarded the tram at the top of Byres Road and had been flirting happily with the two charming young men all the way down it and along Church Street.

Blinded by rage and deafened by anxiety, Tam was aware of nothing but the need to reach Jimmy. The student threw a laughing comment over his shoulder to his friend, sharing a joke about the three jolly girls. Then the friend's face drained completely of colour.

'Look out!' he shouted. But it was too late. Tam wheeled round, saw what was bearing down on him a split second too late. Josie, he thought. *Josie . . .*

The young man at the controls of the tram found that while driving it might be easy, stopping it took time and distance. He was to remember the sickening thud of the impact for the rest of his life.

Chapter 17

So much pain. So much sorrow. So much loss. Heedless of the rain running down her cheeks and throat, Josie stood in the Necropolis gazing up at the beautiful white angel who reminded her so much of her mother.

She had failed the person who had brought her into the world, broken a promise made to a dying woman. If she had looked after Rachel and Charlie and the house properly, maybe those people wouldn't have taken them away.

After the strike had ended, nine days of turmoil which didn't resolve the dispute which had provoked it, Mick Fitzgerald had done his best to find out what had happened to the children. He had come up against a brick wall at every turn. Her wee brother and sister would be far away by now.

Over the hills and far away. Where Tam had wanted to take her.

She had failed him too. If she'd been paying more attention that day two months ago, or if she hadn't taken the shortcut through the lane . . . Arthur and Billy hadn't only violated her body, they had tainted what she and Tam had shared, soiling it for ever.

When she lowered her eyelids at night she ached to see his handsome and loving features in her mind's eye, hear his gentle voice murmuring soft endearments. Instead, she was tormented by the leering faces of Arthur and Billy and by the memory of what they had done to her. It was Arthur's foul words which echoed in her ears, not Tam's loving ones.

Her stepbrothers had taken off somewhere, dropped out of sight. Their father seemed determined on drinking himself to death. She would shed no tears over that. Why should he and his sons still be on this earth when one of the best men who had ever walked the face of it was gone? Ella Paterson was inconsolable, Tam's wee brothers and sisters lost and bewildered.

Josie wasn't prepared to bring any more pain on them, so she was going away. Knowing when her old home would be empty, she had gone in there and gathered her meagre belongings: her few clothes and her shorthand and typing certificates and medal.

She couldn't take the print of *The Cottar's Saturday Night*. It was too big and the glass might break. She studied it, fixing the picture in her mind and committing the verse to memory.

> *From scenes like these old Scotia's grandeur springs,*
> *That makes her loved at home, revered abroad:*
> *Princes and lords are but the breath of kings,*
> *An honest man's the noblest work of God.*

Tam Paterson had been an honest man. So had her father Andrew Shaw. Now the two of them would forever be intertwined, occupying a special place in her head and in her heart.

She had left a note for the Fitzgeralds. *Don't worry about me. I've gone away somewhere and I'll be all right. Thank you for everything. Say goodbye to Mrs Paterson for me.* She had gone down to the stables and said her farewells to Jimmy. Mick said the horse, recovering now from his injury, was grieving too. Josie didn't doubt it. When she reached up to put her arms about his neck the beast had bent forward, lowering his huge head to make it easier for her.

Now she was standing in the Necropolis with everything she owned in the world wrapped up in a bundle, an old sheet off the bed because she had nothing else to put her things in. She turned her back on the statue. It was time to go. She and the child she was carrying.

She had considered for thirty seconds the possibility of getting rid of it. Old Ma Robertson's face had swum in front of her eyes. It was neither lack of money nor the memory of what had happened to her mother which had stopped her from following that course of action. It was the possibility of the child being Tam's.

Even if the child growing inside her wasn't his, it was still an innocent. The sins of the fathers should not be visited upon the children. Like herself, her baby was one of Saint Mungo's bairns. So they would go to Saint Mungo for help.

She walked sedately down the hill. There would be no girlish fancies of trying to emulate the birds today. There would never be any dreams of flight again. Slowly, leaving her childhood and all of its ambitions behind, Josie went across the Bridge of Sighs and into the great cathedral.

Half an hour later the minister found her sitting hunched on the steps in front of the Saint's tomb. She was very pale as she looked up at the Reverend, her hair a dark cloud around her face and the marks of her tears staining her cheeks.

'Please, sir,' she said, 'I need your help.'

Chapter 18

Josie spent the long months of her pregnancy in a home run by the Kirk up on Partickhill, a big old mansion set in its own grounds. It was divided into two wings. The larger housed the girls before they had given birth, the smaller was set aside for them and their babies afterwards. Since all of the children were put up for adoption, given over to their new parents when they were six weeks old, there was no need for a lot of space on that side of the house.

Having her baby adopted wasn't presented as a choice but Josie knew that she had none. She had no money or resources. So she listened silently when she was told that her child would be brought up in a nice respectable family and that she ought to be grateful. She listened silently when she was told she herself would be found a position in domestic service. Another respectable household would take her in and give her a job and a roof over her head. Apparently she was supposed to be grateful for that too.

She was grateful that her basic physical needs were attended to. She had a bed, three square meals a day and the security of knowing she and her child would not end up on the streets. It all came at a price.

She and her fellow sinners, for such was the attitude of the staff towards them, were required to spend several hours each day cleaning their shared bedrooms and the public rooms of the house. They dusted and polished furniture, swept and mopped hard linoleum floors, got down on their hands and knees to wipe skirting boards. Only in the final weeks of their pregnancies were they excused the last activity.

Since the smallest speck of dirt never got a chance to settle, the too frequent cleaning by too many pairs of hands swiftly became pointless. Josie saw it clearly for what it was: a punishment, both physical and symbolic. They were washing away their sin.

At the same time, it was made clear to them that this was impossible. Having given in to the vile lusts of the body, they were forever sullied. No decent man would want to marry them after they had borne a child out of wedlock.

One girl, less cowed than the rest, had asked pertly how on earth he would know as long as you made sure the lights were out and weren't stupid enough to tell him. She was locked in a tiny room by herself for a week, her meals delivered by a stony-faced and silent member of staff.

Cleaning round the door on the fourth day of the girl's imprisonment, Josie heard muffled sobbing coming from inside. The sound made the hairs on the back of her neck stand up. The lassie had seemed such a hard nut. Crouching down with some difficulty – she was in her eighth month now – Josie managed a few whispered words of encouragement through the keyhole. She repeated the procedure until the week was up and was wildly pleased to see the culprit emerge at the end of it looking pale and wan but dry-eyed and with her head held high. That evening she gave Josie a surreptitious squeeze of the hand and a mouthed *thank you*.

When Josie's contractions started she was whisked off to the other wing of the house. There had been no instruction on what to expect, no forewarning of the stages of labour, no chance of moral support from the girls she'd spent the past months with either. Visits between the two different parts of the house were strictly forbidden.

So Josie gave birth in loneliness and fear and ignorance, crying quietly for her mother and for Tam and supervised by two disapproving nurses who gave her the bare minimum of information about what her body was going through.

A few days after the birth she lay in her narrow metal-framed bed listening to the panes of glass in the tall window next to her rattling in the February wind. There were three other beds in the high-ceilinged and draughty room but at the moment she was the only occupant. Turning her head listlessly to the left, she gazed out of the window. There was nothing flowering out there that she could see, only a few bare and forlorn trees and bushes. They stuck out of the hard and frosty earth like the spokes of a broken umbrella.

Weary and sore, she turned her head the other way so she could see the baby boy lying in a small crib beside her bed. She willed herself to feel something for him. Nothing came. The only sensation she was aware of at the moment was a paralysing numbness. At least she didn't hate him, as she had feared she might. It simply wasn't in her to feel such an emotion towards a wee helpless baby.

She had studied him hard for resemblances and found none – or at least none about which she could be definite. He was too young. She had come to the conclusion that he looked like himself.

The door opened. It was the girl she had helped, pressing a finger to her lips in a gesture demanding silence. She tiptoed over to the crib, speaking in a low voice. 'I just wanted tae see the wean. A wee laddie or a wee lassie?' She looked inquiringly at Josie.

'A boy,' she whispered.

The other girl bent over the crib, stroked the tiny cheek with a delicate finger. 'Och, he's so bonnie.'

'D'you think so?' Josie took another squint at him herself. Having examined his features so closely in detail she hadn't really thought much about the overall effect. She supposed he was nice-looking. He didn't have much hair yet but he did have lovely clear eyes and skin.

'I think he's just gorgeous.' Her clandestine visitor sat down on the narrow bed. She dug into the pocket of her pinafore dress, a shapeless sack made out of nondescript brown cotton which all the girls were required to wear, and brought out something which flashed briefly in the wintry light coming grudgingly through the window.

Leaning forward, she extended it to the baby, pressing it gently into his tiny palm so that he had touched it. She handed it to Josie. 'A lucky piece for him.'

'No,' Josie protested, glancing at the silver florin now resting in her own palm, 'you'll maybe need this yourself when you get out.'

The girl closed her fingers over the coin. 'You helped me when I really needed it,' she said. 'Take this for your boy. To bring him luck.'

Their eyes met in an identical expression of ruefulness, resignation and regret. 'To bring us all luck,' Josie said.

'Aye. What was the birth like?'

'Och, not too bad,' she replied, unwittingly joining in the conspiracy of all new mothers not to frighten those coming after them.

The other girl stood up. 'I'd better scarper. I'm no' wanting to get put on bread and water or clapped in irons. Here, I think this wee one needs feeding. Will I hand him to ye?'

Suppressing the loneliness she felt the minute the door closed, Josie concentrated on nursing the baby. He took his milk noisily, one of his little hands stuck up into the air as he suckled. That made her smile. She lifted the two-shilling piece and put it once more into his hand. His tiny fingers gripped it. That made her laugh.

He looked up, startled by the sound, his whole body reacting to it.

'Sorry, wee man,' she said softly, 'did Mammy give you a fright?'

His eyes were trying to focus on her. Not knowing exactly what he would be able to see at this tender age, she smiled at him. He settled again, turning once more to her breast for the sustenance he needed. He was four days' old and he knew who his mother was.

That was the moment when a terrible thing happened to Josie. That was the moment she fell in love with her son.

One morning two weeks later she was instructed to get up and dressed and proceed to the office of the home's superintendent. There was to be a meeting about her and the baby's future. Someone would care for him whilst she was attending it. Stiff after the long period in bed, her breasts heavy and tender with milk, she made her way gingerly along the corridor.

Apart from the superintendent, there were four other people waiting to see her, two women and two men, one of the latter wearing a minister's dog collar. They sat lined up in a row of upright chairs as if they were members of a tribunal. Sinking down thankfully into the single chair opposite them, a consideration her months here had not led her to expect, an irreverent thought flashed through Josie's head. *Prisoner at the bar, have you anything to say in your defence?*

She realised very swiftly that no defence was to be allowed. To these people there were no shades of grey, only black and white. They knew nothing of the chain of events which had led her here and she wasn't going to enlighten them. She could have blamed her stepbrothers for her predicament but that would sully Tam's memory and was therefore unthinkable.

Studying her judges, she saw plenty of condemnation and very little compassion. She wondered if none of them had ever been young, felt hot blood coursing through their veins, taken and given love, comfort and affection. Perhaps it was simply that she and the other girls in this place had broken the Eleventh Commandment: *thou shalt not get found out*.

Whatever this tribunal's own secrets, she was in front of them today because they considered her guilty of some sort of crime against respectable society and thought it was their duty to make her pay for it. With crushing clarity, it came to Josie what this interview was really about. She had not only to be punished but also humiliated. That was why she was sitting here now – stiff, bleeding and sore. There were no choices. They wanted to be absolutely sure that she knew that.

Perhaps they were right to expect her to be ashamed of herself. She didn't know. As she listened to them she realised they wanted her to be ashamed of her baby too, of his very existence in this harsh, cold and judgemental world.

That she would not and could not be. She lifted her head, squared her shoulders in the hideous brown cotton smock and looked straight at them as they told her once again what the future held.

That future arrived all too soon, the first few weeks of her baby's life passing in the blink of an eye. The day of separation came as she had known it must. She begged for another half-hour. They granted her twenty minutes.

Twenty minutes. It wasn't very long to pack in a lifetime of love, to gaze at his little face and try to fix it in her mind's eye so that it would always be there. Whenever she had the courage to look.

She looked down at him as he lay in the crook of her arm. Her son. In this place they didn't allow you to be a mother. They were always referred to as *the girls*. They were fallen women, wicked and immoral, not worthy of the honourable designation of mother.

She pressed her lips against his downy head. 'I love you, my son. Your mammy loves you. Don't ever forget that.'

Her voice cracked, her throat aching with the pain of it. She would remember this moment for the rest of her life, as she would remember him. He would have no recollection of her. How could he? He was too young, a tiny scrap of humanity soon to be handed over to another woman whom he would know as his mother.

She wondered if the couple who were adopting him would ever tell him that he wasn't their natural child. Nobody had seen fit to discuss that with her. Nobody had told her anything about them, where they lived, what they were like. She had no rights and no say in the matter.

She glanced up at the clock on the wall. Ten minutes to go. How could time pass so quickly when sometimes it passed so slowly? There was no logic to it. She looked at the clock again. The minute hand was like an evil figure in a long black coat, marching her inexorably towards the moment of parting. She tightened her grip on the baby.

It was all she could do not to hold him too tight, almost crushing him in her desire to hold his small yet solid body close to her own. If only he were still inside her. Under her heart. Nobody had been able to separate them then.

She lowered her mouth to his head once more. 'I kept you safe then, my son,' she said softly. 'But now you're going to good people. People who'll love you and take care of you and give you the kind of life I'd never be able to.'

How, she asked herself silently, do I know that they're good people? She just had to believe that the kind of people who adopted a baby did so because they were heartbroken at not being able to have children themselves.

They would have lots of love to give her son. Her son who would soon be their son.

The baby's head was wet. She smoothed it dry but a minute later she saw glistening drops of moisture settling once more on his fine hair. It was so damp it was forming curls. Was there rain coming in through the window?

She slid carefully forward on the bed, moving them away from the source of the moisture. He was still getting wet. Then Josie realised what was happening. Her tears were falling unchecked on his head.

My baptism of you, Thomas Paterson Shaw, she thought sadly, and felt her heart splinter into a thousand pieces.

When the time came they had to wrest him out of her arms. The nurse spoke, softer than Josie had ever heard her. 'You'll hurt him, lass.'

She released her grip immediately and let them take him away.

PART III

Chapter 19

1931

'Ah, Shaw.' Like a mole emerging out of the dark earth into the brightness of day, Professor Gardiner blinked as he looked up and spotted Josie standing in the doorway. 'We need some more coal on the fire. See to it, would you?'

By the time she had closed the door and taken the few steps necessary to bring her to the hearth, his head was once more bent over his book. Well, at least he had acknowledged her existence, which was more than could be said for the other occupants of the drawing room.

The professor's three children, a girl and two boys ranging in age from sixteen to twenty-one, were sitting at the small square table which stood in the bay window playing a boisterous game of Snakes and Ladders with some friends. The three young men visiting the house this crisp Saturday afternoon were students at Glasgow University, classmates of the two older Gardiner children. The board game was the latest craze among their set.

Opposite their father at the fire but with her armchair angled so she could cast an indulgent eye over the young people sat Mrs Gardiner's mother. Shortly after Josie had started working here, the cook-housekeeper had told her that the old lady belonged to quite an aristocratic family.

'Most definitely out o' the top drawer. Which is probably why she can seem a wee touch snooty now and again.'

Josie had realised the explanation was being proffered

in an attempt to mollify her. The professor's mother-in-law had clearly never lifted a duster nor wielded a sweeping brush in her life. That didn't stop her from having strong opinions on exactly how each and every household chore should be performed. According to her the new girl did none of them right.

At that stage Josie hadn't cared very much what anyone said to her, but she hadn't been long in her post before she appreciated the reason for Cook's anxiety. She had been scared that Josie, like several girls who had come and gone in a matter of weeks, would take umbrage at the old lady's attitude and hand in her notice, as the one remaining parlourmaid was always threatening to do.

The Gardiner home was set in the middle of a Victorian terrace in one of the streets running off Highburgh Road, tucked in behind Byres Road and handy for the professor's work at Glasgow University. Compact enough when viewed from the outside, appearances were deceptive. Counting the attic and the basement, the house rambled over five floors. It and the family which occupied it took some looking after. A staff of three – four if you counted Cook's husband the chauffeur – simply wasn't enough.

It wasn't that the Gardiners were short of money. Unlike several of their friends, even the stock market crash in the autumn of 1929 hadn't seemed to affect them too much. Josie presumed the professor's salary from the uni had also bolstered the family finances. Their staff problem was one which many well-off families were encountering.

Throughout Britain, hundreds of people just like the Gardiners were writing outraged letters to the newspapers complaining about young working-class women's reluctance to enter domestic service. The Great War got a lot of the blame. Called upon then to work in offices, shops and factories to free fighting men for the front, women's horizons had inevitably broadened.

Some people responded to that with a resounding *and quite right too*, pointing to the drudgery and sheer hard labour of domestic work, not to mention the antiquated attitudes employers demonstrated towards the people they invariably referred to as their servants. Afternoons off were grudgingly given and liable to be changed at a moment's notice. If those few free hours fell on a dismal Sunday afternoon in the middle of winter, it was a rare master or mistress who would tolerate a girl entertaining a friend to a cup of tea in the kitchen. Male friends, sniffily dismissed as *followers*, were completely banned. The pay was rotten too, half of what could be earned elsewhere.

The argument that board and lodgings were provided rang a bit hollow. Josie's case was a good example. Shown to a room in the attic on her first day, chilled after the half-mile walk down the hill from the mother and baby home, she had been deeply thankful to find she had the privacy of a room to herself. However, in contrast to the comfort enjoyed by the Gardiners on the floors below, it was as basic as a nun's cell. It had a bed, an upright chair, a deal washstand with a plain white ewer and basin on it and a hook on the back of the door to hang her clothes. Stark and cheerless, there wasn't even a wee rug on the sludgy-brown linoleum floor to brighten the place up a bit.

Crouching down to examine the drawing-room fire – drat, they had let it get too low – it occurred to Josie that it was a long time since Cook had felt the need to apologise to her for the old lady's high-handedness. She'd accepted it, as she had accepted pretty much everything which had happened to her over the past four years.

At first her distress at parting from her child had been so acute she had thought she would be unable to bear it. Barely functioning, she had simply allowed herself to be handed over to the Gardiners. There had been a short interview in which Mrs Gardiner had told her that as long as she conducted herself modestly from now on and did her work conscientiously, she was sure they would get along fine. 'The unfortunate event which you must now put behind you need never be mentioned to anyone else in the household, family members or staff.' *The unfortunate event*. The words rankled still.

There had followed the weeks and months when Josie had worn herself out spending every waking hour making fruitless plans to get her baby back. She could go back home to the Drygate. Mr and Mrs Fitzgerald would surely take her in. She would tell them and Ella Paterson that the baby was Tam's, cross her fingers and trust to luck that it was true.

Then she had remembered her stepbrothers and for a few terrifying nights she had woken shaken and shivering from repeated nightmares in which she relived every detail of what they had done to her. She couldn't go home. She had no home to go to. The tears had come like a flood then.

No one could grieve at such an intensity for long. Mother Nature must have known that, coating Josie in a blessed numbness which at least allowed her to put one foot in front of the other and get through the day. Now, gradually emerging from that protective cocoon, she permitted herself the few minutes before she went to sleep each night to think about her baby, remembering him in her prayers as she did Charlie and Rachel. *Please God, let them all be with good, kind families*. She always added a wee extra prayer to Saint Mungo, asking him to watch over all of them.

Giving the glowing coals in front of her a cautious rake so as not to run the risk of extinguishing them completely, Josie adjusted the air intake to improve the draught. Checking the ash pan, she saw that it didn't need emptying quite yet. She could leave it until dinner-time when the drawing room would be briefly empty again.

She reached for the gleaming brass tongs hanging from the companion set which stood on the dark green tiles of the hearth. Like all the implements, they were kept that way by small amounts of metal polish and hefty dollops of her own elbow grease. Lifting a few coals from the scuttle she positioned them carefully into a small pyramid. She moved from a crouch to a kneeling position, waiting for them to catch before putting any more on.

One day she and Charlie and Rachel and wee Tam would be reunited. She was sure of it. She had to be. It was the only thing which was keeping her going.

'Are you asleep, girl?'

Josie's head snapped up. The old lady was looking down her aristocratic nose at her. Mrs Gardiner herself was out today, at one of the charity dos she was forever attending: meetings of like-minded ladies who raised funds for local hospitals and other charitable institutions. Funny how women like her did so much of that kind of thing but could be blind to suffering much closer to home.

It must have been obvious throughout those long months of Josie's first year in this house how distressed she often was. Yet Mrs Gardiner had never once commented on her red-rimmed eyes, or asked how she was coping. Josie would have been pathetically grateful for one kind word.

Presumably her employer thought she'd done enough by taking a fallen woman into her home. Josie often wondered if that decision had been based on charitable or economic considerations. Brought low both by their experiences and the humiliation inflicted by the mother and baby home, girls like herself were unlikely to make strident demands for better wages and conditions.

'I'm waiting for it to come up a bit, ma'am,' she said in response to the old lady's question.

'I'll ring for you, girl.' She always addressed Josie in

that way, seemingly incapable of remembering her name. 'I'm sure there's something else you could be getting on with in the meantime instead of kneeling there gawping into the fire like a halfwit.'

Josie rose to her feet. There was always something she could be getting on with. Nor was it her place to point out that she would no sooner have returned to the basement kitchen than the bell would be ringing for her again. Either that or they would let the fire go out completely, which would give her even more work.

The old lady was frowning at her. 'Why aren't you wearing your white hat and apron and afternoon frock? The one my daughter bought specially for you?'

'I'm in the middle of polishing the silverware, ma'am,' Josie said evenly, forbearing to point out that the money for the dress had actually been docked from her wages.

Pacifying the parlourmaid by allowing her not one but two regular weekly afternoons off meant that Josie had been called upon to perform some of the other girl's duties as well as her own. It was important to the Gardiners that she should look the part when she did so, hence the purchase of the afternoon frock. All the same, she was hardly going to wear anything other than her normal drab overall and the matching hat into which she tucked her luxuriant hair while she was cleaning the cutlery. The fact that she'd been in the middle of a dirty job didn't wash with the old lady.

'That's no excuse,' she snapped, putting one bony hand over the other on top of the elegant ebony and silver walking stick she was never without. Josie privately thought it was more a badge of office than an aid to locomotion. The old dear was as healthy as a horse and had the appetite to match. She raised the walking stick and brandished it at Josie, who took a hasty step back.

'What if somebody comes to the door? Are you going to answer them looking like that? On the afternoons the other girl's off you dress like a parlourmaid. See you mind that in future, girl.'

Back down in the kitchen, Cook was looking harassed. 'You're back at last, Josie. Finish up the cutlery quickly now and get on with peeling the potatoes for me, there's a good lass.'

The woman and her husband were kind enough, as the parlourmaid was friendly in a distant sort of a way, but Josie was well aware that they all looked down on her. At first, despite Mrs Gardiner's assurances that no one else in the household need ever know about what she delicately referred to as *your history*, Josie thought it must be precisely because of that. However, she soon realised it was because of her position in the hierarchy of domestic service.

Despite the shortage of staff – or perhaps because of it – the other three had their defined roles and adhered strictly to them. Josie was required to do whatever anyone in the household asked of her. She was a skivvy, and that made her the lowest of the low. Once she had dared to dream of a quite different sort of a life. That had been foolish. What more could a wee lassie from the Drygate expect?

Less than ten minutes after she'd returned to the kitchen, the drawing-room bell, one of several fixed to the board above the kitchen door, jangled impatiently. She caught the fire just in time.

On Monday morning she got up at five-thirty as usual and hurriedly pulled on her clothes against the chill before padding softly downstairs. First she cleaned out and replenished the range in the kitchen. Then she filled the big black kettle and put it and the oatmeal which had been steeping overnight on to the heat.

Cook and her husband appeared at six-fifteen, followed shortly thereafter by the parlourmaid, yawning hugely. Throwing back the quick cup of tea Cook poured out for her, Josie left the now warm kitchen for the cold morning room. The fire in there had to be cleaned out, re-laid and lit immediately. That was where the family took breakfast at eight o'clock, so there was no time to lose if they were to have a nice warm room to sit in while the parlourmaid brought them the mail and the morning papers and served them breakfast.

Josie moved on to the dining room and the drawing room, cleaning out and re-laying their fires, ready for a match to be put to them an hour or so before the rooms were needed later on in the day. After that she returned to the kitchen and sat down to eat her porridge.

Obviously not feeling quite so harassed as usual this morning – it was only the mistress and her mother for luncheon – Cook poured her another cup of tea. Josie wrapped her stiff white fingers around it, glad of its comforting warmth after a succession of trips to the chilly outdoors with ash pans and coal scuttles. There was a sharp frost this morning.

'You know,' she mused, relishing the brief pause before she tackled the rest of her day's work, 'it would make a lot more sense if Mrs Gardiner and her mother ate their lunch in the morning room on days like today when they don't have company. It would save coal too. And work,' she added feelingly.

While the parlourmaid did the daily dusting and polishing, it fell to Josie to do the heavy duties: cleaning the windows, lifting the rugs and mopping the floors. She had tried to establish a routine but it was often thrown out of kilter by the two elder Gardiner children, who seemed to come and go at all hours of the day and evening. Their parents prided themselves on allowing them a considerable amount of liberty.

That liberty made life a lot more complicated for Josie. She couldn't clean a room if they or their friends were in it and whatever other work she was doing she always had to break off from it now and again to check on the fires. That was more of a nuisance on a day like today when she had the washing to do.

Several hours of transferring hot steaming bundles of clothes and bed linen between the boiler and the deep rinsing sinks lay before her, not to mention turning the great heavy mangle to squeeze the water out of all of them. Her arms would be aching by the end of the day. At least she never had any trouble sleeping on a Monday night. She was always exhausted.

Cook answered her question. 'You know what the trouble is here, don't you? Delusions of grandeur. Before the war this house had almost three times the number of servants but Mrs Gardiner doesn't want to drop her standards from what they were then. Things have to be done the proper way.'

Josie thought about it. 'The parlourmaid answers the door, meals are eaten in the dining room and Mrs Gardiner travels to her engagements driven by her own uniformed chauffeur.'

'Aye,' Cook agreed, nodding sagely. 'The staff they've got now doesn't really justify employing my better half just to do that. Not that I'm complaining, mind. It gives us both a job and a home.' She and her husband lived in their own flat in the mews behind the houses.

'So why don't they do things differently?' Josie asked. 'Live a bit more simply?'

Cook plucked the teacup out of her hand. 'Ours not to reason why,' she said blithely. 'Come on, lass, time we were kneiping on. The work won't do itself.'

Josie pondered Cook's comments as she lay in bed that night, huddled under the blankets with her coat on top of them to add an extra layer of heat. Ironic that. She spent so much time attending to fires, yet her own room didn't have one.

She had tried to create the illusion of warmth by buying

an old blue jug in a junk shop and filling it with dried flowers in shades of red and orange, placing it on the upright chair which she had positioned in the middle of the wall opposite her bed. It didn't really do much for the temperature in the room but at least her wee mock fireplace was nice to look at. Which was more than could be said for the afternoon frock, suspended on its hanger from the hook on the back of her door.

She'd had no say in its purchase. Mrs Gardiner and her eldest daughter had simply brought it back from a shopping trip one day. The material was a fussy print, tiny pink and green flowers on a shiny black background. Josie presumed the fabric was intended to resemble silk, an endeavour in which it failed miserably. Adding insult to injury, the dress was two sizes too big for her and in a style no longer in fashion. Drop waists were out, as were the very short skirts of the previous decade.

She surveyed it with narrowed and mutinous eyes. Short of ripping it up for dusters, was there any way she could possibly improve the gruesome thing?

She could belt it to achieve a more natural waistline. That would shorten it even further, of course, but she could let the hem down. Hang on a wee minute . . . maybe a big Puritan collar would do something for it. With her dark hair, she would probably suit white near her face.

She reached under the bed for the shoebox which held her few treasures. The box which contained her shorthand medal now also held the florin the girl at the home had given her, tucked in on the other side of the little velvet cushion. She would never part with the coin. Not unless and until she got the chance to give it to the person for whom it had been originally intended.

A notebook and some pencils had been bought the same day she'd treated herself to the jug and dried flowers. She'd had some half-formed idea of writing a diary, committing to paper all that had happened to her in the absence of having someone to confide in. The pages remained untouched. She hadn't been able to bring herself to write a word. The only other thing in the shoebox was the tin which had held wee Jamie's lucky money.

Josie was paid only five shillings a week – the parlour-maid was forever telling her she should ask for more – but since she spent very little of it, she had quite a bit of money in there, more than she'd realised. She could easily afford to buy a piece of material and some pins and needles and thread.

On her next afternoon off she covered the few hundred yards to Byres Road at a purposeful march. She surprised herself by thoroughly enjoying not only the choosing and purchasing of the required haberdashery but also by succumbing to some window-shopping, seriously tempted by a lovely pair of shoes which she realised she could also afford.

The ones she possessed were serviceable but not exactly in the height of fashion. These were smart little black leather shoes with red toecaps and heels and a two-piece strap across the instep secured by red laces. She'd think about them. She'd definitely think about them.

Since her room was almost as cold during the day as it was at night, Josie fetched the dress down to the kitchen and began the measuring and pinning necessary to cut out and sew the collar. Lost in the pleasure of the activity, she barely heard the summons of the drawing-room bell.

'That'll be for you,' said the cook, glancing at the parlourmaid. Deep in *Red Letter* magazine, the girl tutted before she stood up, smoothed her skirt and went upstairs. She was back two minutes later. 'The mistress wants some more coal put on the fire,' she said, before picking up her magazine and settling herself down again.

Josie removed the pins she was holding in her mouth. 'Well, couldn't you have done it?' she asked in exasperation. 'This *is* my afternoon off, you know.'

The girl stared at her, genuinely horrified. 'It's not my job.'

Irritated but knowing there was no point in arguing about it, Josie shrugged into her overall and cap. She didn't want to get any coal dust on her clothes which might transfer to the white collar.

She found the whole family in the drawing room, plus the guests they were entertaining this afternoon. Since they had already seen that the household did contain at least one proper parlourmaid, hopefully the old lady wasn't going to bawl Josie out for not having the afternoon frock on.

'More coal please, Shaw,' said Mrs Gardiner briefly, turning her attention immediately back to her visitors, a woman in her thirties and a young man who was unmistakably making eyes at Miss Gardiner.

It suddenly struck Josie as the height of absurdity that a perfectly fit and active woman couldn't lean forward and pick up a pair of beautifully clean brass coal tongs and put a few lumps of coal on the fire. Not only that, there were four healthy males in the room. Were they all so useless they were incapable of keeping themselves warm? None of them would have lasted very long in the days of the cavemen.

She lowered her eyes to hide the amusement in them and moved forward to perform the task. Servants weren't supposed to have thoughts and feelings and emotions. Nor were they supposed to betray by the slightest flicker that they were listening to the conversation going on above their heads, something Josie was currently finding quite difficult.

'I mean,' Miss Gardiner was saying, 'how are intelligent and educated women who hope to pursue a career before and perhaps even after marriage going to manage if they have to face the prospect of running a house without adequate help? The choice is going to be between living in a neglected home or spending all one's spare time getting down on one's knees oneself. Like Shaw there,' she said in accents of horror.

Josie's irritation surfaced again. It was bad enough when Mr and Mrs Gardiner addressed her by her surname but this girl was the same age as herself.

'Perish the thought that your beautiful hands should ever have to perform such lowly labour,' said her swain. 'They're so smooth and soft and white.'

Unlike my own, Josie thought, surveying them as she swept up the coal dust from the hearth. They're rough and hard and red from spending so much time in hot water and washing soda. She would have to scrub them again before she went back to her sewing.

'I mean,' Miss Gardiner continued, 'I wouldn't even know how to begin to make a meal or wash clothes!' She laughed, charmingly. As everyone else joined in, Josie pondered why being so totally unable to look after yourself or anybody else was considered attractive and desirable, not to mention a sign of social superiority.

Replacing the fireside implements, she rose to her feet. As she began to ask Mrs Gardiner if there would be anything else, another voice spoke over her own.

'I don't know what these girls want,' it said petulantly. 'For one thing, wouldn't you think they would be grateful to live in nice houses? Especially when you consider the hovels some of them come out of.'

Josie couldn't help it. She raised her head and met the woman's gaze full on. Blonde, chic and fashionably dressed, she was very beautiful. She was also discontented, the sort of person who would never be happy with her lot. You could see that in her face. At the moment it bore a startled expression. Presumably she was taken aback that a mere skivvy was having the audacity to look her in the eye. The woman frowned. 'Do we know each other?'

Fighting the urge to inform her that a cat may look at a king, Josie realised that they did. She was staring at Mrs Charles Campbell: Old Father Time's daughter and Roderick Cunningham's sister.

'I don't think so, ma'am,' she said, and dropped her eyes.

'No,' said Shona Campbell. 'How could we, after all?'

That raised more laughter. Mrs Gardiner murmured a dismissal and Josie left the room.

The memory of the encounter stayed with her throughout the next few days, provoking recollections of her time at the *Dispatch*. It seemed so long ago she sometimes felt that that life had belonged to a different person entirely. Now it all came flooding back, her focus as clear as crystal. She was recalling lots of things.

There was the heady excitement of dashing upstairs with some urgent copy, everybody working together to beat the deadline and have the story out before the competitors. Then there had been the camaraderie of the office; the friendship which Sally Fleming and Ben Gold had proffered so easily and so generously, as had Roddy Cunningham. It was strange how different he and his sister were.

She heard the petulant voice in her head again. *What do these girls want?* Somebody ought to tell her – and all those other people who droned on incessantly about the servant problem. Better wages would be a start, plus a bit of respect and recognition that the people who cooked and cleaned for them were human beings too.

What do these girls want? That would make a good title for an article, challenging and provoking. Before she knew where she was, Josie was beginning to compose it in her head. It developed further over the course of the following morning, while she was mopping floors and beating rugs.

That night, she dug her notebook out of the shoebox and wrote up a first draft. Sent out to Byres Road to fetch some butcher meat the following day, she bought a small packet of quarto paper and a pen. She wished she could type it, but as Miss French had said so long ago, she did have neat handwriting. She also purchased a copy of the *Evening Dispatch* so as to refresh her memory on how many words a features article ought to contain.

She took two evenings to edit the piece. Once she was satisfied it was as good as she could make it she copied it out neatly, stated the word count at the top and wrote a covering letter addressed to the Features Editor of the *Glasgow Evening Dispatch*. She could only hope that whoever occupied that position now would be liberal enough to publish an article examining the servant problem from the other side of the fence. She signed herself *J. Shaw (Miss)*. Nobody at the paper would connect her with the wee Josie Collins they had known.

Her resolve to then forget all about it was doomed to failure. Excited and alive in a way she hadn't been for a long time, she could think of little else. She lay in wait for the postie each morning, her hopes soaring when two days later the mail included a letter for her. She secreted it inside her pinafore and endured an agonising wait before she got the chance to sneak up to her room halfway through the morning to read it.

Dear Miss Shaw,
We were very excited by the piece you recently sent us. We should like to commission you to write two more on the same theme and to the same word count, and I am empowered to offer you a fee of half a guinea for each one. Please let me know as soon as possible if this is acceptable to you.
Yours sincerely,
Roderick Cunningham,
Features Editor

'Oh Roddy,' she yelled out loud. 'You wonderful, wonderful person!' She kissed the letter and danced around the room clutching it to her bosom. '*Excited by the piece*,' she chanted softly. 'They were *excited* by what I wrote.' As for ten shillings and sixpence being acceptable to her ... to someone earning less than half of that per week it was a small fortune.

She glided through her work that afternoon, bubbling over with ideas for her next two articles. She had to structure them carefully, making sure they weren't simply a list of complaints. She recalled something the fearsome Miss Clarke had once told her. 'Balance, my dear. A journalist should always strive for balance.' Bearing that in mind, she tried as hard as she could to see things from the employers' point of view, considering also Miss Gardiner's comments about the special difficulties facing the new breed of career women. Josie knew only too well how hard it was to go out to work and run a house too.

Housework was a skill which had to be learned, both an art and a science. There was little use in being able to tastefully arrange a bowl of flowers or knowing which furnishing colours went well together if you didn't get the basics right: cleaning and tidying and putting tasty meals on the table each day.

If employers had to do some of that themselves they might be more interested in these newfangled machines which were coming on to the market: electric ovens and washing machines and carpet sweepers and the like. They must enable you to get through the work in half the time.

Josie suggested that a change in attitudes was needed too, whether the lady of the house was working outside the home, immersed in charity work or had a crowded social calendar. Compromises had to be made. Was it really such an awful thing to occasionally open your own front door to your own friends?

Lightly and humorously, she wondered if men of all

classes might like to consider the pathetic dependency of being unable to cook themselves a simple meal. Perhaps it was time they learned. They might even discover cooking could be a satisfying and enjoyable occupation.

She came up with some conclusions, suggesting in her final article that the future for domestic service might be to put it on a more professional basis. *An army of well-trained domestic operatives coming to work on a daily basis and having the independence of living outside the home they care for. Even, one might dare to suggest, a contract between two equals, one providing a much-needed service and one willing not only to pay for that, but to respect the person providing it.* She was rather proud of that last sentence.

She received a second letter from Roddy informing her that he was very happy with the articles and that the *Evening Dispatch* proposed to run all three in successive editions of the paper. If she preferred, she needn't be named. The articles might indeed have more impact that way.

Josie permitted herself a wry smile. Not naming her would imply she was fearful of losing her position because she had spoken out. It would all add to the drama and controversy which helped sell newspapers.

However, Roddy wrote, they would be delighted to see more of her work on this or any other topic. Would she care to call at the *Dispatch* office on a date and time convenient to herself to discuss possible future projects?

Standing in her bare little room reading those words, Josephine Shaw permitted herself for the first time in a long time to think about the future. Holding Roddy's letter between her fingers, she raised her head and studied her reflection in the glass of her window. It was the only mirror she had.

Turning, she surveyed her bleak surroundings. She had put up with them for a long time, four joyless and lonely years. At first that had been because she was in no fit state to do anything else. Subsequently she hadn't seen what other option she had. She had no family home to return to, nowhere she might have used as a base to build a different kind of life for herself.

She had built a cocoon here, a safe if not particularly comfortable little niche where she had curled up and licked her wounds and hoped that the world would leave her alone. Yet even when she had been lost completely in the Slough of Despond, she had promised herself that one day she would find Rachel and Charlie and wee Tam.

Her son would be four now. If his adoptive parents planned to tell him the truth about his origins there might come a time when he would feel the need to come looking for the frightened girl who had brought him into the world. Did she want him to discover a worn-out skivvy living by grace and favour in the attic of someone else's house?

She folded Roddy's letter and put it carefully back in its envelope. Her old ambition – and her talent – were offering her an escape route from this apology for a life. She could write her way out of here.

Chapter 20

Josie experienced a quick pang of regret as the hairdresser made the first cut. Soon it was too late to worry. The floor around her was covered with great hanks of her hair. 'Athough you've still got an awful lot left,' the woman reassured her. 'Your hair's lovely and thick.'

Wielding her scissors and comb with alarming speed, she darted round the chair. 'The weight was pulling it down when it was so long. It'll be much nicer if we cut it about level with your chin. Trust me,' she added with a grin. She snapped her fingers to attract the attention of the apprentice, who approached brandishing a sweeping brush.

'I don't seem to have much choice now,' murmured Josie, watching mournfully as the young girl swept up her shorn locks. Having decided a bit of smartening up was called for before she went to her meeting with Roddy, she had succumbed to the hairdresser's blandishments. What she needed was a completely new hairstyle. Off with the old and on with the new. It had seemed like quite a good idea ten minutes ago. Now she wasn't so sure, scarcely daring to direct even the swiftest of glances at the large mirror in front of her.

However, when the time came to give her verdict she was amazed. Could that attractive young woman gazing so bemusedly back at her really be herself? She turned her head first one way and then the other to admire the end result.

'See?' the hairdresser said triumphantly, recognising a

satisfied customer when she saw one. 'It frames your face.'

'Aye,' agreed the apprentice. 'You look dead good. That style's real up-to-the-minute too.'

'Head forward,' instructed the hairdresser, 'and I'll brush any loose hairs off the back of your neck. Is your new look in honour of some special occasion?'

'I'm going for a sort of job interview,' Josie replied, her voice muffled by her posture. She supposed that was the best way of putting it.

The girl put her hands on her shoulders and pulled her gently upright. She studied their joint reflections and made one or two final adjustments to Josie's hair. 'You'll walk it,' she said confidently. 'How could they possibly turn you down?'

Pursued out of the salon by good luck wishes from both the stylist and the apprentice, Josie headed for the subway, chuckling inwardly when she noticed how often she was glancing over at shop windows in the hope of catching a glimpse of herself. A large clock in a jeweller's display window caught her eye. Her transformation hadn't taken nearly so long as she had anticipated.

Her appointment with Roddy wasn't for another two hours yet and the subway trip to Buchanan Street was only going to take her twenty minutes or so. That would mean hanging around for a long time before she went into the *Dispatch* office. Maybe she'd be better to do her waiting here, have a cup of tea or something. Undecided, she slowed her pace. She was outside the shoe shop. The little black shoes with the red trim were still in the window.

Ten minutes later she was walking smartly back up Highburgh Road with her old shoes in a box under her arm. The new ones might not match her dress very well but she hadn't been able to resist them. Maybe they would bring her luck too.

Not wanting to waste time by taking the extra minutes needed to walk round the terrace of houses to get to the back door, she marched up the garden path and rang the bell. Secure in the knowledge that the parlourmaid would open up to her, she still felt quite daring. She had never used the front entrance to the house before.

'Thank heavens you're here,' muttered the parlourmaid under her breath, reaching out and pulling Josie into the house. The large hall was full of young men and women, all chattering away brightly.

'What's going on?'

Before the other girl could answer Josie saw that Mrs Gardiner was bearing down on her. The old lady was right behind her daughter. As usual, she was making remarkably speedy progress for someone who claimed to be unable to walk more than a few feet without the aid of a stick. 'Coming in at the front door now, is it?'

Her daughter patted her arm soothingly. 'Don't bother about that now, mother. Shaw's got here in the nick of time.' Turning her attention from the old lady to Josephine, she registered the latter's changed appearance. 'What *have* you done to your hair?'

'I've had it cut, ma'am,' said Josie calmly, thinking that must be a prime example of stating the obvious.

'You've altered that dress too,' grumbled the old lady.

'Yes, ma'am. I've made it more fashionable.' Considering her lack of experience in needlework she was quite pleased with the way it had turned out.

Both of them were frowning at her.

'Shaw . . .' Mrs Gardiner began, 'don't you think you should have asked us before you made these changes to yourself?'

Josie stared at her. She was joking, wasn't she? Her employer gazed back at her, an expression of puzzled incomprehension on her well-bred face. No, she wasn't joking. She honestly couldn't understand why the little mouse hadn't come and humbly asked for permission before she went to the hairdresser's or altered this awful dress.

Josie was suddenly consumed by blinding anger – pure, red-hot and cleansing. They really thought they owned her, and all for a few shillings a week.

'We'll discuss what you've done to yourself later.' Mrs Gardiner's voice was crisp. Then it softened. 'For the moment, as you can see, my children have brought home a few unexpected guests.' She smiled benevolently at her offspring and their friends. 'We'll need you to help serve tea, Shaw.'

'This is my afternoon off,' Josie said quietly.

'Well, you'll have to take it another time,' snapped the old lady. 'Half of it, that is. You've already had some of it.'

Josie ignored the interruption. 'I'm very sorry, Mrs Gardiner,' she said, 'but I have an appointment in town this afternoon.'

'An appointment?' queried the old lady in incredulous tones.

'I'm sorry too, Shaw,' said Mrs Gardiner sharply, 'but your responsibilities to us come first. Your appointment will have to wait.'

'You think so?' Josie tilted her chin. Her voice had sharpened too. One or two of the young visitors were looking curiously at their hostess and the attractive young woman with the short dark hair framed by a big white collar with whom she was so deep in conversation. Quite deliberately, Josie raised her voice a little further.

'My appointment will have to wait,' she repeated, 'because your selfish and spoiled little children have to be indulged, no matter the inconvenience to anybody else? Do you really think the five bob you pay me each week and the freezing and poky wee room under your eaves entitles you to that kind of loyalty?'

Now she had the attention of everyone in the hallway. One or two mouths had even, quite literally, dropped open. Miss Gardiner was looking daggers at her. If looks could kill . . . Josie knew exactly what she was going to say next but she made them wait for it, savouring the moment.

'I resign,' she said. 'You'll have to put your own coal on the fire from now on.' Her cool grey gaze swept contemptuously over them. 'You're all intelligent and well-educated people. It's really not so difficult.' She looked at Miss Gardiner and then pointed to the parlourmaid, currently staring at Josie with frankly envious eyes. 'Get her to show you how to make tea. That's no' very difficult either. With a bit o' practice I'm sure you'll be able to master it.'

As she made her way towards the staircase people fell back to allow her through, like the Red Sea parting before the Israelites. Drunk with the sheer power of it, Josie paused at the foot of the stairs and swung round to survey her captive audience. She saw shock, incredulity and amazement. It was hard not to burst out laughing.

'You might like to read the *Glasgow Evening Dispatch* next week,' she said pleasantly. 'I hear they're going to be running a series of very interesting articles on the current crisis in domestic service.'

The words had winged their way into her head. Like a flock of brightly coloured and tuneful little birds, more followed. As Josie stood there with one small hand resting lightly on the bannister which she'd polished more times than she cared to remember, they fell eloquently from her lips.

'Whilst recognising that women's entrance into the wider labour market during the war may well have been the catalyst for the current shortage of domestic workers, the writer suggests that the difficulties being experienced

221

by many households like this one may necessitate a fundamental shift in attitudes amongst the middle classes.' She stopped to take a breath. No one attempted to interrupt her.

'People like yourselves may indeed have to forge a dramatically different relationship with those you have been pleased to refer to as the servant classes. Look on it as a challenge,' she said in encouraging tones. 'I'll just away and get my wee bits and pieces now. Do excuse me.' Smiling benignly at them all, she placed her foot on the first step.

'SHAW!'

The old lady would burst a blood vessel if she wasn't careful. Her face was purple with rage, her tone venomous.

'So you do know my name,' Josie observed.

'You'll regret this, Shaw.'

'Oh, I don't think so. I should have done it a long time ago. A very long time ago.' She walked up the stairs with her head held high, as proud and as graceful as a queen. On the half-landing she stopped and turned, speaking directly to the old woman who had done her best to make her life a misery over the past four years.

'Oh, and by the way, it's *Miss* Shaw to you.'

The elation bore her aloft for the next hour. It lasted while she packed her things, said goodbye to a bemused Cook and returned to Byres Road, buying a cheap suitcase on her way to the subway and piling her possessions into it there and then, transferring them from the bundle in which she had transported them from the Gardiners' house.

She plunged down into the underground thinking that she was actually soaring in the other direction. The earthbound bird had found its wings at last.

I resign. Those must be the two most beautiful words in

the English language. Apart from *And it's* Miss *Shaw to you*. Remembering the thunderstruck expression on the old lady's face, Josie giggled. Then she began to howl with laughter. It was a good job the subway carriage was completely empty.

Her face was glowing with pleasure when she emerged at Buchanan Street, prompting some admiring glances from male passers-by. To her considerable surprise, Josie found herself enjoying those. This must be the new Josephine Shaw, she thought, the confident woman who's going to take the future by the throat and win.

When she reached the *Dispatch* building she paused briefly, allowing herself a moment or two to deal with the memories. Not too long, though. That was then and this was now and she didn't have any time to waste. She didn't recognise anybody on duty at the front desk but the girl who dealt with her was friendly, volunteering to keep her suitcase before she phoned upstairs to let Mr Cunningham know that his 3.30 appointment had arrived. Josie noted that he wasn't *Mr Roderick* any more. He always had hated that.

Politely declining the offer of a seat, she walked over to gaze out of one of the arched windows which flanked the door. Roddy was going to get a surprise when he found out who *J. Shaw* was. She was really looking forward to seeing him again. Please God, let him have a job to offer her! For the first time since she had left the Gardiners, her buoyant mood began to be edged around with coils of apprehension.

Brisk masculine footsteps were crossing the entrance hall behind her. 'Miss Shaw? I'm Roderick Cunningham.'

She turned to face him, extending her hand with a smile. 'I know. How are you, Roddy?'

Physically he was more or less exactly as she remembered him. A lot might have happened to her over the five years since they had last met, but it really wasn't such a very long time. What age was he now, anyway – twenty-six, twenty-seven? The dark trousers and double-breasted waistcoat he wore obviously belonged to a formal three-piece suit, but the waistcoat was unbuttoned and the sleeves of his white shirt were rolled up to the elbows. With his thick fair hair tousled and windswept, he looked his usual attractively rumpled self.

He had matured, naturally. His shoulders were broader and his features more manly and less boyish. That was only to be expected. There was, however, a tightness about his generous mouth which hadn't been there before and when he spoke, his voice was cool and detached.

'Well, well, well. I might have guessed from the subject-matter. Still fighting the class war, Jo?'

'I don't know that I ever was,' she said lightly.

Roderick raised one sceptical eyebrow. That was when Josie realised that as far as he was concerned, she had walked out on him, his father and the *Evening Dispatch*. He knew nothing of all the other things which had been going on in her life at the time. He couldn't know why she had never been able to bring herself to write to the paper to explain why she hadn't come back after the strike.

At first she had been too distressed. Then she had been too ashamed. She still was. Which meant she had no explanation to offer Roderick Cunningham for why she had apparently deserted the *Dispatch* without so much as a backward glance.

That was when Josie realised how decisively she had cooked her goose with the Gardiners.

That was when she realised that it was half past three on a Thursday afternoon and she had neither a job nor a place to lay her head tonight.

Chapter 21

She had absolutely nothing to lose by being bold. 'I'm looking for a job,' she said, lifting her chin and her voice in the manner of someone making an announcement. 'A proper one, I mean, not just writing the occasional article. Would you have one to give me?'

Did her directness cause the ghost of a smile to hover about his lips? Josie wasn't sure. That cool eyebrow was still raised and he was looking her over in a very appraising way.

'I might have.' He thrust his hands into his pockets. Almost immediately, as though he had suddenly remembered his manners, he removed them and indicated the doorway which led to the upper reaches of the building. 'Why don't you come upstairs and we'll discuss it?'

'What happened to *Collins*?' he asked once they were seated on opposite sides of the large desk which occupied most of the space within his compact office. She'd forgotten what a rabbit warren the *Dispatch* building was.

'Belonged to my stepfather,' she said briefly, hoping he wasn't going to ask her too many questions about her personal circumstances. 'I decided to revert to my real father's name.'

Roddy sat back in his chair, placed one ankle on the opposite knee and settled down to the interview. His relaxed posture reminded her that he was on home territory. She was an interloper. She might have belonged here once but she couldn't expect that to count for anything now.

'Well, *Miss Shaw*,' he began, a trace of his old charm evident as he emphasised the name, 'what have you been doing since we last met? Working for these people?' He flipped open the buff folder which lay in front of him and she saw that it contained her articles. She was suddenly embarrassed by her own handwriting. It was amateurish not to have been able to type her submissions.

'Judging by what you've written here, they don't treat you very well.'

'No,' she agreed. She reminded herself once more that she had nothing to lose. He had accepted her pieces. Therefore he must think her writing was good enough. 'Which is perhaps why I handed my notice in just over an hour ago.'

Roddy leaned forward over the desk, his face sharp with interest. 'Care to share the details with me?'

Josie gave him a succinct but comprehensive summary of the events of the early afternoon. She thought she saw his lips twitch on a couple of occasions but when she had finished he made no direct reference to what had been said. 'I presume you don't want your old copytaking job back. You want to write.'

'Yes.'

'On the basis of the three articles we're about to publish?' His long fingers beat out a quick tattoo on her manuscripts.

'I thought you liked them.' Her heart was sinking towards the floor.

Roddy shot her a keen look. 'They're among the best pieces we've received in the past year and they're exactly the sort of thing we need to beef up the features. Sally thought they were manna from heaven.'

'Oh,' she cried excitedly, feeling her cheeks grow pink at the praise, 'Sally came back after the strike?'

'She did. You haven't been in touch with her since then?'

Josie shook her head.

'She'll be delighted to see you,' he murmured, eyes downcast as he closed the folder and slid it to one side.

'Does that mean you do have a job for me?' she asked bluntly. 'Because if you don't, I really need to go looking elsewhere.'

He looked up, and their eyes met. She was reminded of the first time they had spoken to each other down on the portico and of how dashing and light-hearted he had been in his Arab sheikh's headdress and robes. Merry and laughing eyes, that had been her impression then. They weren't laughing now, as the man sitting across the desk from her was no longer the carefree youth he had been back then. You've changed, she thought sadly, and felt her spirits sink even further.

He leaned forward again and another memory surfaced – of his father looming at her when she had last come to this building to be interviewed. Unlike Old Father Time, however, Roddy's voice was low and quiet. 'Burnt all the boats in your fleet, Jo?'

She had to force herself to continue to meet his penetrating green gaze. This man knew she had nowhere to go tonight, that she was homeless as well as out of work. She swallowed hard. 'I don't want you to give me a job out of sympathy.'

'Good,' Roderick said, flinging himself back into his chair. 'Because I wouldn't give anybody a job on that basis. I care too much about the standard of writing on this newspaper. Three months' trial,' he said. 'If we satisfy each other's requirements by the end of that period, then the job becomes permanent. Can you start tomorrow?'

'I c-could s-start now.'

He smiled. 'We'd better see if we can get you sorted out with some accommodation first. Maybe Sally will be able to come up with something. The pay's rotten to start with,' he said cheerfully. 'Fifteen shillings a week. If everything works out after the three months it goes up to one pound ten, with yearly rises to follow.'

'Th-that's f-fine,' she said, still stammering with excitement and relief. Thirty bob a week? She'd be as rich as Croesus. 'There really is a job vacancy?'

'We've been looking for someone suitable for the last wee while. Since Miss Clarke retired a few months ago and everyone else moved up the ladder.'

'Including yourself,' she said, indicating the triangular piece of wood at the front of his desk which confirmed his status as Features Editor.

'For my sins,' he said drily. 'I'd rather be a foot soldier on the news desk.'

'Can't you ask your father to move you?'

His face clouded over. 'You don't know?' When Josie shook her head he explained it to her. 'The *Dispatch* no longer belongs to the Cunningham family. I'm merely an employee here now.'

'The Crash?'

'How did you guess?' He had drawled the words, as though the loss of the family business was a minor inconvenience. 'My father's passed on,' he said in a softer voice. 'Took a stroke when we had to sell the business and never really recovered, I'm afraid.'

'Oh, I'm sorry,' Josie said impulsively. 'He was a good man.'

Roderick acknowledged that with a formal nod of his fair head. 'It's good of you to say so.' He stood up and came round the big desk. 'Come on, I'll take you to Sally.'

Miss Fleming was shocked into uncharacteristic speechlessness when Roddy stepped politely back to allow Josie to precede him into the room. In a few terse sentences he explained what was going on, asked Sally if Josie might stay with her for a few days and if she knew of any suitable long-term lodgings, told the two girls they could leave early if they wanted to and then took himself off. Josie wondered if he would have stayed longer if Ben Gold hadn't been in the room. It was obvious that there was still very little love lost between the two young men.

Ben was smiling broadly enough at Josie, coming forward to enfold her in a great bear hug. That felt lovely. It was such a long time since anyone had held her . . .

She stood in the shelter of Ben's strong arms and felt herself begin to relax. She had a job. She had somewhere to sleep tonight. She was with friends again.

Then the questions started to tumble out of Sally's mouth. 'But where have you been, Josie? You seemed to disappear off the face of the earth. And you wrote these articles about domestic service? They're terrific Josie, they really are. But Good Lord, you weren't really working for such horrible people all this time, were you? Why on earth didn't you come back to the paper?'

'Give the girl a chance, Sally,' Ben said mildly, slanting Josie down a smile. She gave him a rather uncertain one back and tried to think of the best way of diverting Sally's reporter's instinct.

'I didn't think people would get their jobs back,' she said, wondering if her response sounded very lame. 'I thought there would have been victimisation.'

Sally looked sombre. 'There was at some of the other papers but even Ben had to admit that Roddy's father was very fair about reinstating people.'

'Only if we were all prepared to eat humble pie,' Ben said darkly. 'Formally reapply for our own jobs and agree that the *Dispatch* should employ non-union labour from then on.'

'But you didn't even make inquiries about coming back, Josie,' Sally said with a puzzled frown. 'Why was that?'

'Asks too many questions, doesn't she?' Ben pulled Josie to him in another swift hug. Over her head, he mouthed a silent instruction to Sally. *Let it go for now.*

When Josie emerged for the second time from Ben's

embrace, she found herself being subjected to an exaggerated visual inspection.

'Mmm,' Sally said thoughtfully.

Ben went to stand beside her. 'She's made not a bad job of it considering, Miss Fleming.'

'Considering it was completely hideous to start off with, Mr Gold?'

'Precisely. Maybe she could save the collar.'

'Or buy herself a nice new outfit and give the whole thing to the poor.'

Ben shuddered theatrically. 'Don't the poor have enough to contend with, Miss Fleming? The material that frock's made of is irredeemably vile. Although her shoes are just the ticket.'

'And her hair looks great,' Sally said, patting her own fashionable Marcel wave.

'Thanks very much,' said Josie, relieved that Sally had stopped asking questions and making a very creditable attempt at pretending to be offended. 'I'm glad there are some aspects of my appearance which don't positively repel the two of you. Unfortunately, until I get paid for my three articles my financial resources are somewhat depleted,' she said, happily slipping into the exaggerated manner of speech so beloved of those who toiled under the roof of the *Glasgow Evening Dispatch*. 'I'd better keep what I've got until I fix myself up with somewhere to stay.' She frowned, wondering how difficult that was going to be. 'Do landladies usually ask you to put down a deposit?'

'Not our landlady,' Ben said airily. 'Especially not if we graciously agree to vouch for your trustworthiness.'

'You two are living together?' The question, not to mention the incredulity in her voice, was out before Josie could stop herself.

'Not in the Biblical sense,' Ben said.

Sally pulled a face. 'But since our parents think we are,

we thought we might as well be hung for sheep as for lambs.'

Ben mimed a punch to her chin. 'That's my girl.'

'I wish I was,' Sally said, looking at him out of soft eyes. When he moved his hand from her chin to gently squeeze her shoulder her expression grew more rueful still. This complex and complicated relationship clearly hadn't got any simpler.

Josie coughed to clear her throat. 'Does your landlady have a room available?'

'We've just helped her fit it out,' Sally said brightly. 'It was full of boxes up until last week. Now she's looking for a third lodger. And I think we've just found her. But,' she asked with a smile, 'do you think you could stand living with the two of us, Josie?'

'I think I'd love it,' she said swiftly, hardly able to believe her luck. 'If you two wouldn't object to me.'

'Oh, I think we could probably tolerate your presence,' Ben said cheerfully. He adopted a pained look, as if an elephant were standing on his foot. 'But only if we get you into some decent clothes. I'm not sure I could bring myself to walk down the street with you wearing that apology for a garment.' He snapped his fingers. 'Miss Fleming? I believe you may be able to come to the rescue here.'

Sally danced over to a cupboard in the corner of the room and pulled it open with an extravagant gesture. The clothes inside were, she explained, outfits supplied to the *Dispatch* by some of the big stores to be sketched for fashion articles.

'Don't they want them back?'

'Sometimes they do but they said we could keep these. It's good advertising for them, I suppose.' Sally was rummaging through the hangers. 'Right, these are all your size.'

Josie repaired to the ladies' lavatory to try each outfit

on in turn. There was a soft black woollen skirt teamed with a powder blue lacy jumper with a neat little collar and puff sleeves. Then she emerged wearing a smart and businesslike navy polka dot shirtwaister with crisp white revers, belt and cuffs. Finally she tried a red and black checked woollen dress with a black Peter Pan collar and a short boxy red jacket designed to be worn on top of it. Everything was the new fashionable length, covering the knees to the middle of the calf.

'All of those,' Sally said. Nodding his curly head in enthusiastic agreement, Ben suggested that a beret in red or black would set the last outfit off perfectly.

Delighted with herself, Josie opted to wear the black skirt and pale blue jumper immediately, folding up the afternoon frock and putting it in a bag Sally found for her. It *was* worth saving the collar. Her fashion advisers grudgingly permitted that but after she had put the dress away she looked up to find them once more gazing disapprovingly at her.

To be specific, they were scrutinising her chest. Josie was about to demand what they thought they were playing at when they looked sagely at each other and nodded. Sally spoke first.

'Girls only this time, Ben.'

'All right,' he agreed. 'I'll see you back at the house this evening.'

Twenty minutes later Josie was in the lingerie department of Wylie & Lochhead, blushing like a beetroot as a saleslady measured her naked bosom and then handed her an undergarment she didn't quite recognise.

'Is it a bust girdle?' she asked, puzzled by its brevity. The two of those she owned, purchased when the style was for flat chests and now washed and worn to an embarrassing greyness, were much more substantial pieces of underwear.

'It's called a *brassière*,' explained the saleslady. 'It's

designed to enhance your natural assets instead of flattening them. If Madam would like to slip her jumper back on?' She held back the curtain of the changing room so Josie could walk out and show Sally the effect of her new foundation garment.

'Now we're talking,' said Miss Fleming. 'She'll have two of those, please.'

It would have been very hard to tell whether Sally and Ben's landlady was wearing one of the new style bust bodices. Mrs Beaton wasn't so much dressed as draped. Several layers of tweedy and knitted garments were surmounted by a voluminous hand-woven shawl, each and every item of apparel in a multiplicity of hues and textures.

She welcomed Josie warmly, holding on to her hand for what seemed like several minutes. 'Aye, lassie,' she sighed. 'Ye've had a hard time of it, I'm thinking.'

As she took Josie by the elbow and steered her through to see the room, Sally muttered a character description. 'She's a bit of an eccentric, but an absolute gem. Thinks she can talk to the spirits of those who have passed through the veil between this world and the next.'

Sally had adopted the appropriate voice for the last few words. Now she reverted to her usual brisk tones. 'Including the late Mr Beaton. Apparently he puts in an appearance from time to time.'

'Like the ghostly editor at Buchanan Street?' Josie asked, a little discomfited by the landlady's welcome to her.

'Yes, but Mr B usually has a message or two for whichever motley selection of people his widow's got gathered round her parlour table. Right,' she said, flicking on a light switch. 'What do you think? It's not quite as big as the rooms Ben and I have but it does open out into the back garden, which is really nice in the summer. You've got a table and chairs in here although we usually eat together. We have our own sitting room with a wee kitchenette off and sometimes Mrs B invites us to spend an hour or so with her of an evening. When she's not communing with the departed.'

Sally walked over to the French windows. 'Don't worry,' she said over her shoulder, 'she doesn't try to ram it down our throats. I'll just pull these curtains. It's a bit cold. The fire in here hasn't been lit for ages. I'll go and fetch some coal and kindling in a minute. Mrs B feels the cold herself, so she's always very generous about that sort of thing.'

'Not very big?' Josie repeated, looking around her in amazement. The room was four times the size of the one she'd occupied at the Gardiners' house. There was the table and chairs Sally had mentioned, a double bed with a colourful patchwork quilt on top, a wardrobe with a mirrored door, a matching chest of drawers and a white porcelain sink in one corner with another good-sized mirror above. The small cast-iron fireplace was painted white and two elderly but comfortable-looking armchairs faced each other on either side of it. They sat on top of a large rug whose colours were as bright and as varied as Mrs Beaton's clothes.

'Once you get some bits and pieces of your own it'll be nice and homey,' said Sally cheerfully, her back now to the dark blue velvet curtains she had closed. Josie walked over to one of the armchairs and turned, gazing around her. Then she sat down very abruptly and covered her face with her hands. After a short pause, she heard Sally's voice. 'I didn't think the room was *that* bad.'

Josie spoke through her fingers. 'It's a lovely room. Really lovely.'

She heard Sally move, felt her crouch in front of her. 'Long day, Josie?'

'A very strange day.'

234

Sally patted her knee and waited. Eventually Josie took her hands from her face. 'I've been so lonely, Sally.'

The pretty face so close to her own was full of sympathy and concern. 'Want to talk about it, petal?'

Josie shook her glossy head. 'N-not yet. M-maybe sometime. Is that all right?' she asked anxiously.

'Of course it is.' Sally gave her a final pat on the knee and reached for her hand, rising to her feet and pulling Josie with her. 'Come and help me get our dinner. Oh,' she said, catching herself on as they headed for the door, 'I forgot about your fire. I'd better do that first so the room will be nice and warm when you come to bed.'

'Show me where the stuff is and I'll do it.'

'Sure you can manage?'

Josie smiled. 'Aye. I'm no' bad at lighting fires.'

She woke with a start the next morning, panicking that she had overslept. Oh Lord, she was going to be in trouble if the morning room was cold when the family went in for their breakfast! There was a smart rap on her door.

'Are you decent, sweetie?'

'What?' Confused, she sat up and pushed the hair out of her eyes. It was Ben, in pyjamas and dressing gown and carrying a tea tray.

'Oh,' she said shyly, 'this is very nice. Thank you.'

'All part of the service, madam,' he said, placing the tray carefully over her legs. 'I can't guarantee you'll get it every morning but Sally and I reckon you could probably be doing with a bit of pampering in the meantime.' He smiled down at her and she rolled her bottom lip under her top one so she wouldn't embarrass both of them by bursting into tears.

Ben stretched out a hand to gently tweak her nose. 'Enjoy while it lasts, wee one.' He glanced over at the wardrobe. 'Do you know,' he observed, 'I believe the clothes are actually supposed to go *inside*.'

'I wanted to see them as soon as I woke up,' Josie said, following his gaze to where her new outfits hung on the outside of the wardrobe. 'So I could admire them.'

Ben smiled at her again. 'Which one are you wearing today?'

'Which one would you recommend?'

He took the question seriously, cupping his chin in his fingers as he considered. 'The checked dress with the wee red jacket,' he pronounced at last. 'Because your new shoes go so well with it and it's the most dressy, appropriate to this being the first day of your new life. Now,' he said, 'drink your tea. Breakfast will be served in half an hour.' He rolled his eyes. 'If Miss Fleming has managed to complete her exacting *toilette* by then.'

The first day of your new life. Ben's words stayed with Josie while she sipped the tea, washed and completed her own toilette. Once she was dressed she put the other two outfits away in the wardrobe and studied herself in the mirror.

Only yesterday, less than twenty-four hours ago, she'd been a skivvy in someone else's house, dressed in a dowdy overall or an ill-fitting frock and at everyone's beck and call. Now she was an independent woman with a job and a home of her own. And she looked nae bad either.

Give her a few months to catch her breath and regain some self-confidence and she'd be ready to take on the world. She was determined to come through Roddy's trial period with flying colours. She was going to knuckle down and work as hard as she could, learning everything there was to know about the job and applying herself to her writing, striving always to make it as good as it could possibly be.

If she did all that she'd soon be a well-paid and professional woman: a career girl. That would suit her just fine. Love? That was in the past. That was where it could stay. Love equalled pain, anyway. Look at Sally and Ben.

There was only one other thing Josie needed in her life and that was to be reunited with her lost children. That's how she thought of them now: Rachel, Charlie and wee Tam. It wasn't going to be easy to find them. She knew that. She also knew that she could never stop trying to do so.

Without them she might become the best journalist in the world and her success would be hollow. Her need for them was like a physical ache which never went away. It would only be assuaged if she could once more feel Charlie's arms about her neck or coax a smile out of Rachel or hold her baby close.

They would all be older, of course. Next year, unbelievably, Rachel would be sixteen. Sixteen. No longer under the jurisdiction of Glasgow Corporation.

Rachel's big sister smiled at the smart young woman in the mirror.

Chapter 22

'Sally,' Josie asked as they lingered over their meal one evening a few weeks later, 'what's happened to Roddy?'

Sally grimaced as she offered her the bread plate. 'You noticed, then?'

'It would be hard not to.' Josie took one of the two buttered slices remaining and chewed it thoughtfully. Although several older members of staff had retired, she'd caught up with many of the people she had known before her departure from the *Dispatch*. She'd been delighted to find Alan Dewar back in his copytaker's cubbyhole, as acerbic and anarchic as ever. Looking around in vain for Deirdre Smith, Josie had found him regarding her with a devilish twinkle in his eye.

'Wondering whether the two of us ever made it up?'

Grinning hugely, he had then informed her that Deirdre was now Mrs Dewar and the mother of their small daughter. At home looking after the wee girl, she sometimes visited the office when she got up the courage to tackle the city centre with a pushchair. Josie had made the proud husband and father promise to let her know the next time his little family called past.

At first she had thought Roddy had acquired the same sort of sharp tongue as Alan, a necessary defence and natural progression of having spent several years working in the hectic and highly charged atmosphere of a busy newspaper office. However, while Mr Dewar's utterances always had an underlying tinge of good humour, it seemed to her that Roddy had developed a hard and sarcastic edge to his personality – or at least that part of it which he allowed other people to see.

She hadn't yet been the object of his scorn herself but she suspected that was only a matter of time. She wasn't looking forward to it. If a piece of work didn't come up to his exacting standards he didn't mince his words. Being told off because you had made a mistake was one thing. Being on the receiving end of Roddy's masterly but often wounding command of the English language was quite another.

Josie had also been dismayed to notice that he seemed to drink rather a lot, not popping out for a cocktail as his younger self had done but joining the hardened drinkers who repaired all too frequently to the pub next door to the *Dispatch*.

'Was it the Crash?' she asked. 'Does he feel bad because he couldn't save the family business?'

'That's part of it.' Sally finished eating and pushed herself back from the table. 'Quite a large part of it. I think Roddy believes all of that hastened Old Father Time to his grave.'

'Mr Cunningham was quite old, though.'

'Yes, but I don't suppose that makes Roddy feel any better.'

'His gruesome big sister gave him a hard time too,' put in Ben, rising from the table and gathering up the dinner plates. 'Had hysterics in the front hall the day the paper was sold. Ranting and raving at her father and brother in front of everybody. Old Mr C went as white as a sheet.'

He gathered all three sets of cutlery on to the topmost plate and stood for a moment, obviously remembering the scene. 'He kind of crumpled, you know? Like a piece of paper someone had crushed and tossed into the waste-paper basket. I may have had my reservations about the old man but that wasn't a nice thing to witness, whoever it was happening to. Young Master Roderick had to sort everything out. Calm his sister down and attend to his father too.'

As he carried the plates through to the kitchenette, Sally leaned forward. 'Ben felt sorry for Roddy that day the same as everyone did,' she whispered. 'Although he'd die rather than admit it.'

'Do you think it bothers Roddy that he's now just an employee of the paper?' Josie asked.

'An employee of Incorporated News Limited,' Sally corrected with a grimace. 'Sounds so anonymous, doesn't it? I think it probably does bother Roddy. Something like that would bother most people, I suppose.'

'Wouldn't he be better trying to get a job elsewhere? Doesn't Incorporated News own other titles?'

'Lots of 'em. Including a London morning daily. I suspect Roddy would love to try his hand there. Although I also think he still really cares about the *Dispatch*, feels a strong loyalty towards it.'

'Tied up with loyalty to his father?'

'That would be the psychology of it,' Sally agreed. 'He does have a good position here, of course, especially for someone of his age.'

'Quite a bit of freedom of action too,' Josie said. 'I noticed he took me on without having to refer to the editor.'

'I gather that freedom was part of the deal when he agreed to take charge of the Features Desk. He's very good at it but it's not what he really wants to do.' She sighed. 'He did have another major upset. There was this girl, one he was really serious about.'

'How could you tell?'

Roddy obviously wasn't the only person who could imbue a few words with layers of sarcasm. Eyebrows raised in exaggerated inquiry, Ben set down a cork mat in front of Sally and placed a large brown teapot on top of it. 'There have been so many girls in young Mr Cunningham's life. Now he seems to prefer to love 'em and leave 'em. Will you be mother, sweetie?'

'Sure,' Sally responded absently. She turned to Josie. 'I went to a couple of newspaper dinners he took this girl to. It was the way he looked at her, when he thought nobody else was looking. You know how he always tries to hide his feelings?'

'Aye,' Josie said. 'I know exactly what you mean.'

Ben groaned. 'If you two are going to do the female intuition thing, I'm off to bed with a good book.'

Sally smiled up at him. 'I'll bring you a cup of tea in a minute.'

'Good night, Ben,' Josie said. 'We'll do the dishes.'

'That you will,' he replied cheerfully. 'Good night, Josie. Sweet dreams.'

Elbows on the table and her chin propped on her fists, she gazed after him as he closed the door. 'Ben's such a nice person, isn't he?'

'I would say so,' Sally said.

Josie swung back round to look at her. Simple words, quietly spoken. Yet there were oceans of meaning and emotion lying beneath them. 'I'm sorry,' she said impulsively. 'It can't be easy for you.'

Sally gave her a very level look. 'Don't be sorry for me. He and I are soulmates. Except for one little thing. I reckon it's Mother Nature's little joke, making him the way he is.' Her mouth twisted wryly. 'And me not a man.'

'Oh, Sally,' Josie breathed, reaching out a sympathetic hand.

Sally took it, threading her own fingers through Josie's. 'It's ironic, you know. He always credits me with having helped him come to terms with the way he is. Working against my own best interests there, wasn't I? Especially as we were actually boyfriend and girlfriend at the time.'

'You and he were at school together, weren't you?'

Sally nodded, and a sad little smile stole across her face. 'All of the other girls envied me. Benjamin Goldmann was considered quite a catch. Handsome and funny and more considerate than any of the other boys. Being Jewish made him seem exotic. That was attractive too. A bit dangerous.' The nostalgic smile gave way to something more serious: something a lot more painful.

'I began to realise things weren't quite right,' she said softly. 'I was busy engineering opportunities for us to be alone together. Not an easy task with a father as strict as mine, who also couldn't believe I was having the temerity to disobey his orders by continuing to see a Jewish boy.'

Sally dropped her gaze to the table, studying her own and Josie's intertwined fingers. 'The only thing was that Ben never really seemed to want to take advantage of those opportunities in the ways I hoped he might.' She glanced up again. 'Sorry. I'm maybe not explaining this very well.'

'You're explaining it beautifully,' Josie said.

Sally flashed her a grateful look. 'I confronted Ben about it. Told him I thought he loved me as much as I loved him, pointed out how well we got on together in every other way and asked him just what the problem was. It took a while but eventually I managed to extract it from him. He got really upset, kept going on about how much he wanted to be *normal*.' Sally had given the word a mocking emphasis. Now her voice grew husky. 'He told me that he loved me very much. In every way but one. Which meant that I deserved better.' She stopped, clearly unable to go on.

'And,' Josie suggested, 'you told him that he was the best there was as far as you were concerned. Always had been and always would be?'

Sally withdrew her hand from Josie's grasp and sniffed

loudly. 'Correct,' she managed. 'How did you guess?'

Josie responded to that rueful question with a gentle one of her own. 'What does Ben think now?'

Sally let out a long sigh. 'Oh, that I should go out and find myself somebody else. *A real man*, as he puts it. We have this agreement, you see. About seeing other people.'

'Romantically, you mean?'

'That's the general idea.' Her mouth tightened. 'Although it wouldn't be very romantic if he got himself arrested, would it now? He could go to prison, you know. Not to mention losing his job. Just for being what he is.'

Pondering that and thinking how much Sally must worry about such an eventuality, Josie was silent for a while. 'I wish I could help you in some way,' she said at last.

Sally sat up straight in her chair and reached for the teapot. 'It's helped talking about it. It's not exactly a subject you can broach with many people. Come on,' she said briskly. 'This tea will be getting cold.' She poured them both a cup and firmly changed the subject.

'I was telling you about Roddy and this girl. They got as far as getting engaged and then she broke it off. Precisely one week after the *Dispatch* was sold to Incorporated News.'

'No,' Josie breathed.

'There's more,' Sally said with grim satisfaction. 'She then promptly upped and married a friend of his. They invited him to the wedding.'

'They never did . . . Oh, poor Roddy.'

'He didn't go, thank goodness. He bought them a hugely extravagant present which by that time he could barely afford, and then went off on one of the longest pub crawls in history.' She registered Josie's frown. 'Lots of men drink, Josie. Especially in our business and especially in this city.'

'I know they do,' she said bleakly. 'I just don't ever remember Roddy as having been like that.'

Sally shrugged. 'He wasn't.'

'And this thing about loving and leaving them?'

'I think he's determined not to be hurt again. Plus I think the girls he's going out with at the moment know very well what the deal is. I get the impression it's pretty superficial on both sides. Right,' she said, 'I'm going to take his lordship a cup of tea.'

Josie did experience the sharp edge of Roddy's tongue on two or three occasions during her trial period but he gave her some praise too, telling her several weeks before the end of it that she could now consider herself a permanent member of staff. Her pay went up immediately. Despite his acidity, she had already noted that like his father before him he was always scrupulously fair.

It was clear too that his views on the ethics of journalism were as firm as ever, something which caused Josie to have a brief tussle with her own conscience. Waiting until the year had turned so as to be absolutely certain that her job was secure, she began to make inquiries of Glasgow Corporation as to their policy regarding children removed from their families and taken into the city's care.

As Miss Josephine Shaw of the *Glasgow Evening Dispatch* the relevant information fell into her lap. An invitation to make an appointment with the appropriate office should she wish to take the matter any further was proffered. The problem for her conscience to solve was whether she was going to let them know that far from being a disinterested journalist she was actually someone who had a very personal interest indeed in the fate of two children in particular.

Reasoning that they might refuse her an interview if they knew who she was, she made the appointment without telling them, shelving the decision until she got there. While she was waiting to go she started making plans.

Mrs Beaton's house was on the borders of Kelvinbridge and Hillhead, an area where many people let rooms. The next-door neighbour had one going at the moment. Josie duly inspected it. It corresponded to her own, on the ground floor and opening out into the garden. That, she thought, would be ideal for Charlie. He was coming up for twelve now and wouldn't want to share a bedroom with his sisters but it would be easy enough for him to hop over the wall and join them. Rachel would come in with Josie herself, of course. She had a double bed so there was no problem there. The neighbour, one of Mrs Beaton's spiritualist friends, agreed to hold the room for a week.

Josie hadn't yet broached the topic with her own landlady – or with Ben and Sally. Would they object to having a couple of boisterous children around the place? She shelved that question too, along with the uncomfortable thought of how much Rachel and Charlie might have changed in the last five and a half years. That was a long time in a child's life.

She resolved to cross those bridges when she came to them. What mattered at the moment was that she had a clean and comfortable home to offer her brother and sister. While Rachel was about to leave the city's jurisdiction, Charlie would be subject to it for another four years. She was going to have to convince the powers-that-be that his big sister was now an eminently suitable person to have charge of him.

She wondered if they would cavil about her being out at work all day. Surely not. Her job was respectable and well paid, and crucial to her having the wherewithal to take the children back. Charlie at least would be at school most of the time anyway. That thought sent Josie out investigating the local seats of learning. There was one well within striking distance.

She stood for a moment or two peering through the iron railings which enclosed its large playground, imagining what it would look like during the week when all of the children were in there. The girls would be skipping and bouncing balls off the school wall in the elaborate games she remembered from her own childhood. No doubt most of the boys would be emulating their footballing heroes while the bolder spirits of both sexes used their feet to make a slide: taking a run at any frozen puddles they found and polishing them to a terrifying smoothness.

Her own son would be starting school before next winter came. How odd that seemed. In her mind he remained that baby she had held in her arms for those few short weeks but he would be growing all the time, of course he would. She gripped the railings in front of her, caught by a bolt of blind panic.

Wee ones faced so many dangers once they were out and about in the world. There were all the illnesses to which they might succumb, not to mention school itself. If you got a good teacher you were fine. The wrong one could make your life a misery. Then there were the hazards of the playground: older children being too rough and boisterous and all those perilous and icy slides.

The fear swept through Josie with an intensity which left her cold and shivering. She couldn't protect her boy. That right and privilege had been taken away from her, as surely as he had been snatched out of her arms. Oh God, what chance did she really have of ever seeing him again?

The moment of despair didn't last long. She couldn't allow it to. She might not be strong enough yet to fight her way through all of the obstacles which she knew lay between her and her baby, but she could do something about getting Rachel and Charlie back. Josie released her grip on the railings and determinedly straightened her shoulders.

Thinking it all over carefully, she decided she had to come clean as soon as possible into the interview. It wouldn't help her case if they thought she was trying to pull the wool over their eyes as to her own identity. When she got there, she realised she had no choice about that. The man standing up and coming round from behind his desk to greet the smartly dressed and attractive young reporter was the man who had taken Rachel and Charlie away.

He was the tall one, the clever one who had been in charge that day. Not an unkind man, she remembered. He had been genuinely touched by her distress.

'Miss Shaw?' His eyes were already narrowing thoughtfully. He knew her from somewhere.

Josie took his hand. 'You might remember me better as Collins. I used to live in the Drygate.'

Realisation dawned. 'Good grief! So you did. Let me see . . . about four years ago?'

'Almost six now,' she corrected.

'Well,' he said, smiling broadly and shaking her hand with great enthusiasm, 'you have done well for yourself, haven't you?'

No thanks to you. The words were on the tip of her tongue but she managed to restrain herself. She had to be diplomatic.

'Please,' he said, indicating the chair in front of his desk. 'Take a seat.' He moved back to his own, sat down and put his hands together in front of him as though he were praying. 'Now then, what can I do for you?'

'Isn't it obvious?' she asked, startled out of her planned diplomacy.

'Ah,' he said, and tapped his fingertips against his lips. His eyes surveyed her shrewdly.

One tiny little word, Josie thought, yet it speaks

volumes. The cloud of anticipation and joy which had been sustaining her for the past few months began to plunge with sickening speed towards the earth.

Chapter 23

Not an unkind man. But an immovable one. Yes, Rachel would soon be beyond his jurisdiction, but what if the family with whom she had been boarded-out now thought of her as their daughter? What if Rachel returned their affection? He refused to be drawn as to whether or not that had actually happened, but told Josie it certainly wasn't unknown in these cases. Was she really proposing to go in and disrupt a happy family situation?

'But *I'm* their family,' she protested. 'Rachel and Charlie both.'

'The same thing might have happened with your brother.' The welfare officer adjusted the blotter in the middle of his desk, positioning it so that it was exactly central. 'I can't quite recall if they were placed with the same family . . .'

Josie stared at him in horror. Over all these years that possibility had never occurred to her. 'Surely a brother and sister wouldn't have been separated?'

He looked up from his blotter, sounding for the first time a little testy. 'Put yourself in our shoes, Miss Coll—, I beg your pardon, Miss Shaw. Sometimes we find it hard enough to get people who are willing to take one child in.' He shook his head in apparent incomprehension. 'Despite the money we pay towards their keep. Despite the fact that the children are a useful extra pair of hands around their new homes.'

Josie was still staring at him but now she was travelling back in time, to the previous occasion on which this man and she had conversed with each other. *Some kind people in the country. Lots of fresh air and good food.* That was what he had promised her. She had envisaged a farm somewhere, a motherly woman serving up three square meals a day, animals to play with, fields and woods to play in. The words he had just uttered were painting a different picture in her mind.

'Who are these people who take the children in?' she asked. 'Where are they?'

'All over the place,' he said, as though it were the most natural thing in the world to uproot small Glaswegians from their homes and disperse them to the four corners of Scotland. 'Aberdeenshire and Banffshire, The Highlands and Islands, Perthshire.'

'Where are my brother and sister? Specifically, I mean.'

He smiled. 'Now Miss Shaw, if I told you that you'd only head for the hills looking for them, I suspect.'

'And you really don't understand why I would want to do that?' she asked incredulously. 'Don't you have a family of your own?'

The smile slid off his face. 'My dear young woman,' he said, 'that's neither here nor there. What you must understand is the importance which we attach to the welfare of the children in our care. We remove them from undesirable situations – rescue them, if you like – and once we've done that we consider it our bounden duty to prevent them from being sucked back into those. We have to keep their whereabouts confidential. It's a fundamental tenet of our work.'

'But I'm their sister! I was suffering in that undesirable situation too!'

He sent her a look from under his heavy black brows. 'I know you were.'

The words silenced her, reminding her that this man had seen her when she had been bruised and battered. She felt obscurely ashamed and embarrassed. It was as if he had once seen her naked. Seeing her discomfiture, he pressed his advantage.

'Look,' he said, and if his tone was a little patronising, it was also gentle. 'Judging from your appearance and the profession you're now in, it's clear to me that you've made enormous efforts to rise above your background. You're making a good life for yourself, Miss Shaw. My advice to you is to get on with that life and forget the past.'

'You want me to forget my family,' she said dully.

'Sometimes it's for the best. Believe me. We often find that the children don't want to examine their original roots too closely. Especially if they've been living with a kind and loving foster family.' His voice grew sympathetic again. 'The vast majority of them are, Miss Shaw. I can assure you of that.'

'What if my sister comes looking for me?'

'I don't think she will, you know.'

'If she does,' Josie persisted. 'My brother too when he's old enough.'

'Don't give up easily, do you?' He sighed heavily and studied her for a few moments. 'Write me a letter,' he said at last. 'State that you would be more than happy for them to contact you. I'll keep it on file and make sure they see it if they ever ask.'

It was the best she was going to get. She raised her eyes to his face. 'Do you give me your solemn promise that they'll see it?'

'I give you my word of honour,' he said gravely.

'You all right, Josie?'

'I'm fine.' She was seated by the fire in the sitting room, gazing into the flames.

'You're very quiet.'

'Is there some law that says I have to chatter all the time?'

Sally and Ben's eyes met over her bowed head. 'Well,' he said brightly, clapping his hands together, 'I think I might pop out for an hour. That all right with you girls?'

'Cup of tea, Josie?' Sally asked after he had gone.

Josie answered without looking up. 'If you want one.'

'I'll go and make it now, then.'

'Fine.'

'Then I'll go and cut off my head.'

'Fine.'

Sally chuckled. 'I'm glad you approve.'

Having just registered her previous comment, Josie had at last raised her own head. 'What?'

Sally's smile faded as she studied her pale and serious face. 'Josie,' she said slowly, 'this might be as good a time as any for me to tell you something I should have told you several months ago. Would that be all right with you?'

Josie shrugged listlessly. 'Go ahead.'

Sally sat down in the chair on the other side of the fireplace and plunged in. 'I felt really bad when you didn't come back to the *Dispatch* after the strike. Apart from anything else, I was worried that Ben and I had maybe persuaded you to come out against your own better judgement. It took me ages to decide what I should do for the best. Eventually I checked your address in the files and went looking for you.'

'Oh. You went to the Drygate?'

The first emotion she was aware of was embarrassment, that Sally should have seen the poor circumstances in which she had been raised. The realisation lifted her out of her absorption. She adjusted her position in the armchair and focused properly on Sally and on what she was saying.

'I did. I met this lovely Irish lady.'

'Mrs Fitzgerald,' Josie said slowly.

This afternoon that man who had the power to keep Rachel and Charlie from her had praised her for *rising above her background*. Why would anyone want to rise above people like Bridget and Mick Fitzgerald? They were the salt of the earth. *The salt of the earth, Michael Francis Fitzgerald, and don't you forget it!* A wave of longing for them swept through Josie. They had been so kind to her.

'Yes,' Sally was saying, 'Mrs Fitzgerald. There was another lady too. A Mrs Paterson?'

It was a long time since she had heard that name said out loud. Josie stared at the girl sitting opposite her and saw only Tam. He was there in perfect detail: the chestnut-brown waves of his hair blowing around his smiling face, his clear eyes lighting up with love as he looked at her. She could see Jimmy the Clydesdale too. Impossible to think of Tam Paterson without thinking of horses.

'Josie?' Sally ducked her head, checking that the younger girl was still listening to her. 'The two ladies I met were really worried about you. You'd gone off about a week before I got there. They showed me the note you'd left.'

'Oh,' Josie said again. Now she was in her old home, gathering together that pathetic bundle of belongings, climbing up the path at the Necropolis, saying her sad farewells. If she'd waited another week Sally would have helped her. She gave herself a little shake. It was useless to think that way. That road led nowhere.

'They made me promise I'd let them know if I ever found out anything about where you'd gone. You could do that yourself now.'

'Sally . . .' Josie stopped. She had reproached herself many times for not getting in touch with the Fitzgeralds or Tam's mother. She didn't think she would ever be able to face going back to the Drygate in person, but she could have written, let them at least know that she was alive and well: alive and well and the mother of a child who might or might not be Ella Paterson's grandson.

Trying hard to hold on to the mental image of Tam, Josie found that his face was being replaced by other images, ones she had fought hard to suppress. The recollection wasn't simply visual. She could feel it. Taste, smell it and hear it.

The cobbles of the lane were digging into her back. As her body was invaded she was being pushed hard and rhythmically against them. A greedy mouth was blowing stale alcohol and tobacco fumes into her face. Another one was calling her obscene and disgusting names. Repeating them with a terrible vicious pleasure. Using those awful and ugly words about her over and over again.

She could hear them laughing. They had laughed as they had used her and then they had left her lying there like some worthless piece of rubbish. Down in the gutter with the rats.

'Josie. Come back.'

'What?' She gazed uncomprehendingly into Sally's concerned face.

'You were miles away.'

'Not anywhere I wanted to be,' she whispered. She forced herself to concentrate, to return to the here and now. She was sitting at the fireside with Sally. She was safe. All of that had happened a long time ago. She was safe. She was with friends. She was safe . . .

'A deep breath might be a good idea.'

Josie took it. Then she took another one. Sally had moved, dragged a chair over from the table so that she could sit down next to her. She took Josie's two hands between her own. 'You're cold,' she said. 'Shall I see if I can scrounge some whisky off Mrs B? She always has some in the house, you know. Just in case her late husband should float in through the window and fancy a wee dram.'

Josie tried to smile. 'I think I'm all right now.'

Sally released her hands. 'Back in the land of the living?'
'Aye.'

'And you don't want to talk about it. Whatever *it* is.'

Josie shook her head, her hair swinging like a velvet hood around her face. 'I want to forget about it.' Maybe the tall man was right. Maybe she should put the past behind her and get on with her life. It was all jumbled up together, the bad irretrievably linked to the good. She couldn't think of the latter without recollections of the former intruding, tramping all over the happy memories.

'But there are some things you don't want to forget about it,' Sally said quietly. 'Or maybe that should be some people. The ladies asked me if I knew anything about your brother and sister, Josie. Would you like to talk about them?'

Josie stared at her for a few seconds. Then the floodgates opened. 'Oh yes,' she said brokenly, 'I would!'

It poured out. She spoke of how the children had been taken away in the first place. Confessing to the beating her stepfather had given her, she felt Sally's hands tightening on her own in outrage. Recounting her plans for getting Rachel and Charlie back, she berated herself for having been such a naïve idiot as to think it would all be so easy. She repeated what had been said at the interview earlier in the day, voicing her concerns that the children might not be with people who really cared about them.

'You can't know if that's the case,' Sally said, doing her best to offer comfort.

'I can't know that it isn't.' Josie wiped her eyes, beginning to calm down a little. 'It's like there's this great high wall between the children and me. There's no way I can climb over it. The people in charge won't allow it.'

'Do you want me to go and speak to this man?'

Josie smiled. This time it was genuine. Sally looked so

belligerent, ready to ride out like Joan of Arc and do battle on her behalf. 'I would appreciate it if you tried,' Josie said, 'but I really don't think you'll get anywhere.' She sniffed. 'Maybe he does have a point. It could be upsetting for Rachel and Charlie if I suddenly breenged back into their lives. I have to consider that.'

If it would be upsetting for Rachel and Charlie, how much more so would it be for someone who had been adopted at birth? Someone who was probably completely unaware that the people he thought of as his parents weren't the man and woman who had actually given him life. Josie wished she could bring herself to tell Sally about him too. But if she did she would have to return to that alleyway she had just clawed her way out of . . .

'I can't imagine you breenging in anywhere, Josie. You always seem to approach things very gently.' Sally stood up, ready to head for the kitchen and the kettle. 'It's a great asset, you know. Especially for a journalist. People talk to you when they wouldn't open up to somebody more aggressive. Because they know you genuinely care about them and their story.'

Josie sniffed again, touched by Sally's words. 'So what do I do now?'

'You take up the idea of the letter. You send a fresh one in every year so that it's clear your commitment to your brother and sister is still as strong as ever it was. You give the paper's address to emphasise that you're a professional woman and also in case you ever move out of this place. It'll be simpler than people having different addresses for you in their files.'

'And then I sit around and wait for Rachel and Charlie to get in touch with me?'

Sally shook her head. 'Then you get on with your life. You take the cards you've been dealt and you make the best of them. You live life to the full.' Her voice grew much less brisk. 'Only you never give up hope that the thing you want most in the world will come to pass.' She paused, smiling wistfully. 'Even if you know that to be completely impossible.'

Chapter 24

'*The world's press has decamped to the beautiful yet brooding shores of Loch Ness, and your own* Glasgow Evening Dispatch *is here too. On behalf of our readers, we have joined our colleagues, both national and international, on the hunt for the Loch Ness Monster.*

'*The search is concentrated around the picturesque ruins of Castle Urquhart, on the western shore of the loch and hard by the new road through the wild and romantic Great Glen. Since this link between Inverness and Fort William was opened last year there have been numerous sightings of the mysterious beast. The legend of her existence is however an ancient one, shrouded in the mists of time and antiquity.*

'*Should she once again decide to emerge from her hiding place in some dark fastness deep below the black waters of this most awe-inspiring of Scotland's lochs, our readers can rest assured that Glasgow's favourite evening paper will be on hand to capture the moment.*'

Roderick stopped reading aloud from the previous evening's edition of the *Dispatch* and sent Ben and Josie a pained look across the breakfast table of the hotel in Inverness where the three of them were staying. They'd had to pay well over the usual asking price for their rooms. The possible existence of a monster in Loch Ness was having a decidedly beneficial effect on the local economy.

To save money on travelling costs – journalists' expenses being a perennial bone of contention between themselves and their employers – they had all travelled north in Roddy's car. Despite the narrow and twisting

258

roads, Josie had enjoyed every minute of the journey up from Glasgow. Even her companions apparently finding it difficult to exchange a civil word with one another had failed to dampen her enjoyment.

'Who wrote this flummery?' Roderick demanded now.

'I did,' Josie said calmly, responding to Ben's request for her to pass the milk jug. 'Acting under instructions. Our esteemed editor suggested a bit of purple prose might be called for.'

'He would,' said Roddy darkly, folding the paper and tossing it on to the spare chair, already occupied by Ben's camera equipment, of the square table at which the three of them were sitting.

The new editor of the *Dispatch*, appointed by Incorporated News Limited, had been introduced to a nervous workforce as a new broom. Their anxiety had been occasioned by the manner of his predecessor's departure. Somebody else acting under instructions, the proprietors' representative in Glasgow, had simply marched into the building one morning and told the old editor to clear his desk and go. He was out on Buchanan Street in less than fifteen minutes, leaving several dropped jaws behind him.

His crime had been to preside over a period of falling circulation. Competition between newspapers was intense, hence the decision to send two journalists and a photographer to cover this summer's alleged resurfacing of the Loch Ness monster. It might be a prime example of what the ladies and gentlemen of the press referred to as a silly season story, the ones which filled their pages in the summer when the politicians were on holiday and international and domestic crises alike were briefly forgotten. It was however one in which the public was keenly interested, hence the reluctant participation of the Features Editor himself.

Everyone knew Roddy was desperate to get back to the news desk, but the new boss had insisted he stay where he was, making him the first of several casualties of the man's abrasive style. There were many at the *Dispatch* who were fully expecting Roddy to be slamming his resignation down on the editor's desk any day now.

'Och, aye,' interjected Ben, pouring milk lavishly over his porridge. He batted his luxuriant dark eyelashes at Josie. 'And aren't the lassie's words as purple as the bonnie heather?'

Josie winced, not at his music hall Highland accent, but because he was now sprinkling sugar on his porridge. 'Call yourself a Scotsman?' she muttered.

He grinned at her. 'There's no law that says you *must* have salt on it.'

'*Ancient legend*,' Roddy scoffed. 'About as ancient as last April. Or whenever the new road was officially opened.'

'Maybe not,' said Josie, lifting her knife and fork and applying herself to her scrambled eggs on toast. There was something about the air here which was giving her an extremely hearty appetite. 'I was talking to this wee woman at the public library yesterday. She says there are lots of really old stories about Nessie.'

'*Nessie*, God help us.' Roderick rolled his eyes in despair, but Josie ploughed on regardless. She'd grown accustomed to his sharp tongue. She still didn't like it, but she had learned to let his sarcasm wash over her.

'No,' she insisted. 'Apparently there are tales of odd things happening in the loch and the river,' using her knife as a pointer, she indicated the Ness, flowing confidently past outside the breakfast-room window on its short journey to the Moray Firth and the open sea beyond, 'which go back to the time of Saint Columba. I thought I might call in at the library again this morning, see what I can dig up. Seemingly one of the librarians is a bit of an expert on the subject. He was off yesterday but he's back on duty today.'

'Do you think it would make a piece?' Roderick stopped scoffing, as he usually did when there was a possibility of a good article emerging from a particular line of inquiry.

Josie stopped eating and surveyed him over the breakfast table. 'I'm sure I could get a thousand words out of it.'

'Make it seven hundred and fifty and go to it. We've got to interview and photograph that hotelier out at Beauly who claims to have made a sighting,' he pronounced gloomily, clearly less than entranced by the prospect. 'We'll meet you at twelve o'clock and head off down the loch again. All right?' he asked coolly, looking across the table at Ben. Ben gave him as cool a nod back.

All three of them set off together, walking the few steps to where Roddy's car was parked before Josie headed off for the library. Spotting something in the window of an art shop next door to the hotel, she walked over to look at it. Ben was beside her in an instant, interested to see what had caught her attention. 'Robert Burns?' he asked, surveying the display of framed prints.

'That one,' she said, pointing to it with one hand while she rested the other flat against the glass. The illustration of *The Cottar's Saturday Night* was identical to the one which had graced the kitchen in the Drygate.

Ben began to read the verse out loud. '*From scenes like these old Scotia's grandeur springs, That makes her loved at home, revered abroad—*'

'*Princes and lords are but the breath of kings, An honest man's the noblest work of God.*' As she completed it, speaking in the softest of voices, Ben gave her a curious look.

'Sentimental claptrap,' came a voice from behind their heads. Josie went very still, her palm and fingers flattening against the glass.

'Can we please get on?' Roddy asked impatiently. 'This is our last day here and we've a lot of ground to cover.'

She turned, a tight little smile on her face. 'Oh aye, of

course. Do please let us get on.' She was off, her heels tapping angrily on the pavement. Roderick stood staring at her rigid and retreating back.

'What did I say?' he murmured.

'You really don't know?'

Roddy stiffened visibly, looking down his long nose at Ben. 'I beg your pardon?'

'You know what I'm talking about. Being snooty about that print she likes.' They had moved away from the art shop but Ben waved an angry hand back in the direction of its window. 'Couldn't you see that it obviously holds memories for her? She may put on that tough wee Glasgow keelie act, but underneath she's very vulnerable. That girl hasn't had it easy.'

Roderick shot him an alert glance from under his fair brows. 'You think I don't know that?'

Ben looked him straight in the eye. 'Well, if you do, and you still treat her like that, you're an even bigger *schmuck* than I always thought you were.'

Roddy was still looking at him as though he possessed several legs and had crawled out from under a particularly nasty stone. 'I take it the word you've just used isn't a complimentary one.'

'Damn right it isn't. And I don't care if you are the Features Editor. You're still an insensitive shit.'

Roderick raised his eyebrows.

The public library was cool, dark and pervaded by an atmosphere of hushed scholarship. Josie made her initial inquiry in whispers. The librarian was at first inclined to be suspicious of any journalist but thawed under her gentle questioning and honest admission that she really didn't know very much about the story. She soon had what she wanted: an account of Saint Columba meeting the monster whilst on a trip to Inverness to convert King Brude of the Picts to Christianity.

The holy man's mission had been much assisted by an incident involving a man swimming across the River Ness to retrieve a boat. Menaced by the monster whilst he was midstream, he had been saved by dint of Saint Columba making the sign of the cross and commanding the creature to depart in the name of God. The beast duly did so, thus saving the man's life and proving the power of Columba's religion. From that day to this, Nessie had never been spotted in the river again. Josie had the story written up and phoned in by a quarter past eleven.

'Although I think we're saving everything for a big splash the day after tomorrow,' she told Alan Dewar after he'd taken the copy down from her.

'A big splash,' he repeated with a chuckle, 'that's very good. How's life up among the teuchters, Josie?'

'Don't be nasty. They're lovely people.'

'I'm sure they are. Have Ben and Roddy come to blows yet?'

'Not so far,' she said ruefully, 'but I'm thinking it might only be a matter of time.'

'You need to knock their heads together, flower.'

'I wish I could, Alan,' she sighed. 'I really wish I could.'

With time to spare before she met up with the two sparring partners, she went for a quick stroll around the town. In front of the castle she stood and studied the statue of Flora MacDonald, thinking that her story might also make a good feature article. She'd ask Ben to take a photograph before they left the Highland capital the following morning.

On the way up to Inverness they had stopped a few miles outside the town to view the site of the Battle of Culloden. Roddy had been surprisingly knowledgeable about Bonnie Prince Charlie and his doings, and whilst highly critical of the man himself and scathing about the romantic myths which surrounded him, he had spoken eloquently about his followers and their sufferings. Josie could have sworn his voice had grown husky when he had described what they had endured on the battlefield and in the bloody aftermath of that defeat.

She was pretty sure Ben had noticed that too. Interested in history, he had certainly been listening very attentively to what Roddy was saying. It was a real pity the two of them couldn't manage to get on with each other a bit better.

'Oh, look! Over there!'

Josie thrust her arm through the open window of the car. At the wheel, Roderick sat up straight and glanced quickly over at the loch. 'What?' he demanded. Despite his best efforts, he couldn't help sounding excited.

She turned towards him and smiled sweetly. 'Lots of water,' she said.

In the back seat with his camera at the ready, Ben laughed. 'You have to admit she got you there. Even the most cynical of us are susceptible to the attraction of spotting the Loch Ness monster.'

Roddy gave Josie a dirty look. 'Very funny,' he said sourly. 'Extremely droll.'

They stopped at Drumnadrochit for a sandwich lunch and then drove the short distance to Castle Urquhart. Roddy and Josie stood by the side of the road and watched Ben plunge down the grassy slope.

'Happy as a sandboy,' she murmured. 'Something interesting and beautiful to take pictures of.'

'Mmm,' said Roddy, head bent over a guidebook he'd bought at Drumnadrochit. He began reading out statistics. 'Twenty-four miles long, up to a mile wide, nine hundred feet deep in places.' He glanced up at Josie. 'That's deeper than the North Sea.'

'Which might lend credence to the fact that there is a beastie,' she observed, her eyes still fixed on Ben.

'Perhaps,' Roddy allowed grudgingly. 'It's more likely

the local hotel owners made the whole thing up to bring more visitors to the area.'

'Quite clever if they did. People have to make a living. But aren't you just about to interview one of the monks at the abbey in Fort Augustus? He can't have that sort of axe to grind. If there really is anything to it,' she went on, 'there would have to be a family of monsters. Some sort of relics of ancient times which have somehow managed to survive until today.' She turned questioningly to Roderick. 'Surely that's a possibility?'

'I remain to be convinced. None of the people we've spoken to has impressed me terribly much.'

She had to agree with him on that one. The stories they'd heard so far had been too pat and too well-rehearsed. What they needed was an eyewitness whose account sounded fresh and original and, above all, genuine.

At Fort Augustus, they agreed that Roddy and Ben should go into the abbey by themselves. 'A woman might shock the good brothers,' said Ben, smiling down at her. 'Mind you, I'm probably a bit of a shock myself. Do you think they've ever met anyone Jewish before?'

Josie stood by the progression of lock gates rising like a staircase where the Caledonian Canal opened out into Loch Ness and watched Ben and Roddy walk over the swing bridge towards the abbey. They paused in the middle, both of them looking down with interest and exchanging a few words with the skipper of one of the fishing boats going through. For the second time that day Josie wished that they could try to be friends. They might find they had quite a lot in common if they did.

She looked around her, enjoying the hustle and bustle. There were lots of people about, helping with the locks and the boats or simply watching the world go by. She spotted an old man sitting on the end of one of the catwalks. There was just something about him . . .

She walked over and engaged him in conversation. Within minutes she was taking her shorthand notebook out of her bag, telling him she worked for the *Glasgow Evening Dispatch* and asking if he minded if she took a few notes. He didn't mind at all, but he was diffident about being able to give her any information which might be useful to her. He fished on the loch and had indeed seen something out there on one occasion last year but wasn't at all convinced in his own mind exactly what he had seen.

Josie told him warmly that his story was just what she was looking for. She got the quote she was seeking when she exercised the power of the pause and let him sum up what he had been telling her. He said it in a beautiful Highland lilt.

'I saw something in the loch which I have never seen before, which I cannot explain and which I hope never to see again. It put the fear of God into me and I rowed as quickly as I could to shore.'

It was perfect, his admission of having been terrified adding a much sharper edge to the story than anything else they had gathered. Roddy ought to be pleased about that.

Half an hour later he and Ben walked out of the abbey grounds. When the young man sitting astride a motorbike on the road outside saw them he raised a hand in greeting, his face lighting up with unmistakable pleasure.

'Friend of yours?'

'We met at a pub in Inverness last night. He offered to meet me here, take me round the other side of the loch. You never know,' Ben said lightly, 'I might get a sighting of the monster. We are finished for the day, I take it?'

Roddy glanced at the young man on the motorbike. The smile he was now sending in their direction was warm and intimate. Roddy's own gaze came back to Ben's face. 'You do know what you're doing?'

Ben's voice was silky. 'I'm sorry if you disapprove, Mr Cunningham.'

'I don't give a damn what you do in your private life as long as you don't do it in the street and frighten the horses,' Roddy said dismissively, 'but I'd be grateful if you'd at least be discreet.'

'Don't want a scandal to affect the *Dispatch*?'

'Believe that if you like,' Roddy said in clipped tones. 'I'm more concerned that Sally Fleming shouldn't be upset. I should have thought you might have cared about that too.'

'You don't want Sally to be upset?' Ben's studied incredulity gave way to anger. 'Coming from you, don't you think that's a little bit rich?' He glared at Roddy, who stared just as haughtily back at him.

It was the young man with the motorbike who defused the situation, strolling over and laying a hand on Ben's shoulder. 'Going to introduce me to your colleague, Benjamin?'

Duly performed, the introduction was rather stiff. The one which followed to Josie was more relaxed although after Ben had taken some pictures of the old man whom she had interviewed she followed the departure of the motorbike with troubled eyes. It was one thing to know he and Sally had agreed they were going to see other people. It was quite another to witness that happening – especially knowing the risks which were being run here.

'Not entirely the maidenly innocent you appear, then?'

Startled, she looked up at Roddy, surveying her with those cool green eyes which always saw far too much – although he had missed one thing. Maidenly? If only he knew.

'Well,' she said as they walked to the car, deliberately changing the subject, 'I think we've done pretty well today, don't you?'

'As long as your old chap doesn't give a second

exclusive to someone else before we get your interview with him into the paper.'

'He promised he wouldn't.'

Roderick had unlocked the passenger door, was holding it open for her. 'How touching,' he said, standing with his fingers curved round the top of the car window. 'The girl reporter still believes in the essential goodness of human nature.'

On the point of getting in, she stopped dead. 'Do you have to sneer at absolutely everything?' she asked quietly.

Roddy shrugged. 'Probably.'

Josie tried to hold on to her temper. She failed. Seizing the car door, she slammed it shut. 'Honestly, Roderick Cunningham, sometimes you make me so angry! Do you ever stop to think how lucky you are?'

'Lucky not to have had my fingers crushed in the door?' he inquired archly.

'Stop it!' she cried, infuriated by his attitude. 'Why do you think people are so interested in this story we're covering right now, the one you consider to be so beneath your dignity? Because it's a bit of light relief from everything else that's going on, that's why. Do you know how many people are out of work in this country?'

'As a matter of fact, I do—'

'So you bloody well should! You wrote that brilliant article about the unemployed shipyard workers in Clydebank and how the stop on the building of the new liner was affecting them and their families.'

'I'm so glad you liked it,' he murmured.

'Did you learn anything from talking to those people?' she demanded. 'What it's like to really be on your uppers, for instance? Not know where the next penny's coming from? There's no need to look at me like that. I know you lost the business in the crash but you're not exactly out on the streets, are you?'

She tossed her dark head contemptuously. This had

been a long time coming and she had no intention of stopping until she'd said her piece – all of it.

'I don't suppose it ever occurs to you that you're a lot more fortunate than millions of other people simply because you have a job. It's a bloody good one too, varied and well-paid and interesting. How many people get to be features editors at your age?'

'It's not what I want to do,' he said tightly.

Josie's hands went to her hips. 'Not what you want to do? Och, you poor wee soul! My heart bleeds for you! How many people get to do what they want to in this life? And you're still young. You could be working out some sensible plan for getting back into hard news if you weren't so busy feeling sorry for yourself.'

Roddy drew his breath in sharply. She had rattled him. Good. He needed a shaking up. He got himself under control again almost immediately, his voice carefully light. 'Any other words of wisdom?'

She was almost sure he had been on the point of yelling back at her. Instead, he had chosen to retreat behind the mask. 'Aye,' she said, angry with him for that, 'you should stop racketing about so much.'

'Racketing about so much?' he inquired.

'You know what I mean. All those girls you go out with.'

He smiled smoothly at her. 'Some of them I stay in with.'

Josie tutted in disgust. 'Have you decided to dislike all women because one spoilt little rich girl jilted you?'

Roddy stiffened. 'That's a step too far, Miss Shaw.'

She ignored both the interruption and the warning note in his voice. 'Do you really think someone who loved your money more than she loved you is worth shedding any tears over? Why don't you put it behind you and get on with your life?'

'And that's so easy, is it?'

269

'No. It's extremely hard, but you can do it if you try. If you're determined enough not to let your past govern your future.'

He affected a pained expression and looked down his nose at her. 'Spare me the wayside pulpit homilies.'

'Oh, for God's sake,' Josie burst out, exasperated beyond endurance. 'You really think you know it all, don't you?'

'No,' he snapped. 'Despite what you seem to think, I'm not that arrogant. But I am wondering what makes our little Miss Shaw such an expert on life.'

'Don't patronise me,' she said quietly.

There was something in her voice which brought him up short. He took a step back and a deep breath and she saw his shoulders relax. 'Anything else wrong with the way I run my life?'

'You drink too much.' Passion spent, she too was beginning to calm down.

He gave another of his nonchalant little shrugs. 'Everybody drinks too much in our business. It's expected.'

'It's a matter of choice,' she insisted. 'I knew a man once who worked in an industry where people drank a lot. He didn't drink at all. He was strong-minded enough to be able to turn it down without any of his colleagues thinking the worse of him.'

She turned her head away, eyes fixed on a group of gnarled old Scots pines on the edge of the car park. Och Tam, she thought sadly, you were such a nice man. You wouldn't have known how to be sneering and sarcastic.

'Are you quite finished?' Roddy's face bore an aloof and distant expression, with faint traces of the sort of distaste you might exhibit if there was a bad smell under your nose. 'Can I take it the lecture is over?'

'Yes,' she said, 'I'm finished.' She pulled open the door and got into the car.

They drove back to Inverness in spiky silence. Having

resolved there was no way on earth she was going to spend the evening with him, Josie was hurrying towards the hotel door when she heard a woman's voice calling his name. Caught up in the greeting, she found herself being introduced to 'my old friends Pamela and Douglas MacPherson'.

'A colleague of Roddy's,' the girl said, shaking her vigorously by the hand. 'You're on the hunt for Nessie, I take it. Isn't it the most marvellous story?' Josie couldn't help but warm to her enthusiasm and friendly smile.

'Look,' her husband said, 'Pam and I are about to have a bite to eat before heading back to Kingussie on the train. Do say you'll join us – both of you. Very naughty of you not to have called in on us on the way up, Roderick.'

Josie caught Roddy's eye and saw that he expected her to refuse. 'Thank you,' she said to Douglas. 'Some pleasant company over dinner would be lovely.' She noted with considerable satisfaction that Mr Cunningham hadn't missed that faint emphasis on *pleasant*.

As she walked into the dining room with Pamela an old memory surfaced. 'Kingussie,' she said. 'Was it you Roddy was visiting when he broke his nose?'

'Yes, Douglas and I were newlyweds then.' Pamela chuckled. 'Oh, it wasn't a laughing matter at the time.' She swung round to the men. 'Although I seem to remember you still managing to crack jokes with blood pouring out of your nose, Roddy darling. He's such fun to be with. You must find that too, Miss Shaw.'

'Oh aye,' Josie said, 'he's a real bundle of laughs. Keeps us all in stitches at the *Dispatch*.'

Roddy coughed and politely pulled out Pamela's chair while her husband did the same for Josie before ordering some white wine. After the waiter had let him taste it, he instructed the man to fill Josie's glass first.

Roddy's voice was cool and detached. 'Miss Shaw disapproves of alcohol.'

'No, I don't,' she said sharply. 'I think it's daft when people drink it to excess, that's all.' She smiled up at the wine waiter. 'Thank you. I'd love a glass.'

Conversation flowed smoothly over dinner, the MacPhersons interested in hearing all the details of the news-gathering operation and contributing their own anecdotes about the monster fever currently gripping the Inverness area. When Josie excused herself to visit the ladies' room before the coffee arrived, Pamela MacPherson stood up too. 'I'll come with you, Miss Shaw.'

Douglas affected the puzzled expression of the bemused male. 'Why do women do that, Roddy old man? Go to the lavatory in pairs?'

His wife leaned over and patted his cheek. 'So we can talk about you fellows, my darling. What else?'

She was as good as her word, looking speculatively at Josie as they stood together in front of the mirrors washing their hands. 'I know this is frightfully nosy of me, Miss Shaw . . .'

'Go on,' Josie said rashly, curious as to what was coming next. She liked this woman. There was something very open and honest about her.

Her interrogator took the plunge. 'Are you and Roddy more than colleagues?'

'I wouldn't have him in a gift,' Josie said firmly.

Pamela smiled, but her voice had a wistful note to it. 'Pity,' she said, 'he could do with finding someone like you. He's had a bit of a rough time over the past couple of years.'

Josie dried her hands on one of the squares of linen provided. 'So have a lot of us but we don't go around looking down our long noses at anyone who has the misfortune to bore us in any way.'

Pamela's face lit up with genuine amusement. 'Oh yes, you'd definitely be good for him. He can do the disdainful thing rather too well when he wants to, can't he? He likes you, though.'

Josie looked at her in disbelief. 'I don't think so.'

'He keeps glancing at you,' Pamela insisted. 'When he thinks nobody is noticing. That's always a dead give-away with Roddy.'

Josie shook her head. 'No, if he keeps looking at me it's because he's contemplating feeding me to Nessie. He's wondering if I would fit in the boot of his car so he could transport me unobtrusively to the lochside.'

Pamela laughed out loud. 'Oh, Miss Shaw, I do hope we'll meet again!'

She insisted on Josie accompanying them to the railway station, cheerfully linking arms with her and planting a swift and impulsive kiss on her cheek before she and Douglas boarded the train, hanging out of the window to say their final farewells.

'May I look you up the next time we're in Glasgow? Perhaps we could have lunch or tea together.'

'I'd love to,' Josie called, waving as the train pulled out of the station and puffed steam into the evening sky. 'I like your friends,' she said warmly, mellowed and relaxed by the two hours spent in the MacPhersons' company. 'They're really nice people.'

There was an odd look on Roddy's face. 'Don't bear a grudge, do you?'

'Life's too short.' She had decided some time ago that there were two things you could do with anger and bitterness and a longing for what might have been. You could allow it to consume you totally, eating away at you like acid. Or you could put it all in a box and get on with your life, hoping perhaps that one day you might be able to do something about what had raised those negative emotions in your breast in the first place.

'It's a nice night.' He was standing with his head tilted back, looking up at the darkling sky.

'It is that,' she agreed. A few days' residence and she was beginning to sound like an Invernesian. People did say that having learned it originally as a foreign language the residents of the Highland capital spoke the purest English in the British Isles.

'I don't suppose you'd fancy a stroll by the river?'

Mr Disdainful sounded surprisingly diffident. Josie decided to take him up on the offer.

They walked over the suspension bridge and along Huntly Street, sauntering down towards the cathedral. When they got there they stopped, leaning on the guard rail which protected the unwary from the steep banks and powerful currents of the river. Inverness Castle crowned the hill on the opposite bank. As the long day faded into evening, the statue of Flora MacDonald was silhouetted against the sky.

'Why does she have a dog with her? Does a hound come into the story of her rescuing Bonnie Prince Charlie from the Redcoats?'

'Not that I've ever heard,' Roddy replied, extracting a silver cigarette case from the inside pocket of his jacket. 'I suspect the Victorian worthies who had the statue erected thought one of our four-legged friends would add yet another layer of choking sentimentality to the legend.'

'You hate all that romanticising, don't you?'

'It's so dishonest,' he said. 'I like honesty. In all things.'

Apart from your own feelings, Josie thought. No, that wasn't fair. He was the kind of man who would probably be rigorously honest with himself. He just would never allow anybody else to see how he really felt about anything.

He held out the cigarette case, then realised his mistake. 'Sorry, I forgot. You don't, do you?'

'I don't like the smell,' she said neutrally.

'Then I won't smoke till later,' he said, replacing the cigarette he'd already removed from the case. 'Sudden attack of good manners,' he offered, looking up to find her watching him. 'I bring them out on special occasions. I'm sorry if they weren't very much in evidence today.'

'That's all right.' She was at peace with the world now, a combination of the sense of satisfaction and achievement caused by a productive day's work and the pleasant dinner and conversation with the MacPhersons.

'No, it's not. I apologise. I said some unforgivable things.'

'I forgive you for them anyway,' she said easily. 'Apology accepted.'

'Shake on it?' His hand was warm, his grasp firm. 'Pax, then?'

'I don't know what that means.'

He smiled. It was the first genuine smile she'd seen on his face in a long time. 'You're never afraid to admit that, are you? That you don't understand something.'

'It's the only way I'm going to learn,' she said, puzzled by the observation.

'Pax is Latin for peace,' he explained. 'It means we're calling a truce.'

'Pax, then,' Josie agreed. She grinned impishly. 'Until the next time we fall out.' She looked back across the Ness at Flora MacDonald. 'I thought her story might make a good feature, especially if we try to come at it from a different angle.' She threw him another smile. 'Not the sentimental one.'

'Always thinking up new things to write about, aren't you?'

'Isn't that our job?'

'It was a compliment,' Roddy assured her. 'Tell me something. What do you want out of life?'

She didn't hesitate. 'I'm after your job.'

'Well, you might have to throw Sally in front of a train first but otherwise you're welcome to it.'

'Unlike you,' Josie said, raising her eyebrows just to show him that she could do it too, 'I happen to think features are very valid. If they're done properly they don't have to be all fluff and flummery. Not that newspapers don't need a wee bit of that,' she informed him severely. 'To leaven the bread.'

'Och, but you're fierce, little Miss Shaw.'

'Don't call me that. I'm not *that* little.'

'Not in personality, certainly,' he murmured. 'That was some telling-off you gave me this afternoon.' His lips twitched. 'My second of the day, as it happens.'

Before she could inquire more closely into that statement, he moved swiftly on. 'Will you tell me something else, Jo? While you were bawling me out today, you mentioned a strong-minded man.'

'What about him?' she responded cautiously.

'You spoke of him in the past tense.'

She studied the Ness, flowing smoothly to the sea. 'He's dead,' she said. 'He was killed in an accident. During the strike.'

'So that's what happened to you.'

She raised her head from the water, reluctantly meeting his eyes. Such a languid exterior. Such sharp powers of observation lurking beneath it.

'There are times when you look so sad,' he said softly. 'I've often wondered what it is that ails you. I thought you might be remembering a special somebody.'

Several of them, she thought sadly, several of them.

'Are you still in love with your strong-minded man?'

Josie took her hands off the guard rail and straightened up. 'Good night Roddy,' she said brightly. 'I think I'll go back to the hotel now.'

'Oh,' he said, folding his arms across his chest and adopting an extremely arch expression. 'I see. You're allowed to poke your very attractive nose into my private life but I'm not permitted to retaliate.'

'That's about it,' she agreed evenly.

He laughed. 'They broke the mould after they made

you, didn't they? Come on then, we'll walk back together.'

'No more questions?'

'Scout's honour,' he replied.

When they got back to Glasgow the following day, he waited until Ben had disappeared through Mrs Beaton's open front door before handing her a parcel wrapped up in brown paper and string. 'It's that print of *The Cottar's Saturday Night*. I knocked them up before we left Inverness this morning and bought it for you. I thought you might like it,' he said, watching as she put her bag down on the pavement so she could take the picture from him.

'Oh,' she said. 'Thank you. Thank you very much.'

Roddy got back into his car, closed the door and wound down the window. He pulled the sunglasses he was wearing down on to the end of his nose. 'I thought I ought to thank you for all the good work you did up there. I also thought I owed you an apology for . . . Well, you know what for.'

Josie grimaced as she looked down at him. 'Maybe I should apologise too. For not minding my own business.'

'You had provocation. Quite a lot of it.'

She readjusted her grip on the print. It was heavy. She could do with setting it down somewhere. 'Well,' she said, 'I suppose I'd better be getting in.'

'I love Burns,' Roddy said abruptly. 'I don't like sentimentality but there's nothing wrong with genuine emotion. Nothing at all.'

She smiled at him. 'I know you love Burns. You and I used to discuss poetry, remember?'

'Yes,' he said. 'I do. Are you still interested in that sort of thing? Haven't grown out of it?'

Josie laughed. 'No, I'm still interested.'

'Good,' he said. 'Good.'

She waited for him to start the car up again and go.

'Maybe we could do that sometime,' he said. 'Discuss poetry, I mean.'

'That would be nice.' If she didn't lay her burden down very soon the circulation of blood to her fingers was going to be completely cut off.

'Good,' Roddy said for the third time. 'I'll see you tomorrow, then.'

As he drove off Josie lowered the print gently to the ground, allowing it to rest against her legs. Following the departure of his car until it turned the corner at the top of the road and disappeared out of sight, she was aware of a feeling of bemusement. Had Roderick Cunningham just asked her out?

The weight pressing against her legs was suddenly removed. It was Ben, effortlessly hoisting the parcel aloft. 'Gifts from the boss, is it? He has taken a shine to you!'

'We fell out yesterday,' Josie said. 'It's an apology.'

'I fell out with him too,' Ben pointed out. 'But he didn't buy me a present.' He threw a teasing smile over his shoulder as he led the way to the front door.

Josie made the required face back. Of course Roddy hadn't been asking her out. She had seen the sort of girls he went out with. Or stayed in with, she thought, stepping into Mrs Beaton's hallway and wondering why that comment had made her feel so embarrassed. It was him who should have been ashamed of himself for coming out with it.

Roderick Cunningham favoured tall and willowy blondes. Usually the social butterfly type, they were invariably immaculately groomed and coiffed and had figures like fashion models. He might have told Josie that she had a very attractive nose but she knew very well that shapely but undeniably short dark-haired women dedicated to their work weren't his type at all.

He'd merely been trying to smooth her ruffled feathers, that was all. That was fine by her. Absolutely fine by her.

Chapter 25

'Listen to this.' Sally's voice was dripping with disgust. *'Marcia Clifford lay back on the soft lace-edged pillows of her bed in the exquisitely appointed bedroom in her luxurious flat in Mayfair, and sipped daintily at the cup of tea which had just been brought her by her maid.* Why do we have to print this rubbish?'

'You think the sentence is too long?' Josie asked mischievously, looking up from watering the plants which lined the windowsill. She knew exactly what Sally's beef was. The new editor, so tough in many ways, had some very old-fashioned ideas when it came to catering for his female readership. Despite vociferous and repeated representations from Sally that the syndicated serials of which he was so fond were unlikely to appeal to the intelligent and discerning cross-section of women of all social classes who read the *Dispatch*, he continued to buy them in.

This caused considerable irritation to everyone in the features department. It also deprived them of column inches for what they considered to be much more interesting pieces. 'Like Roddy's Clydebank article,' Sally said. 'We got a great reaction to that.'

'Genuine human interest pieces are always popular,' Josie agreed. 'Where is he today, by the way?'

'Interviewing somebody in Stirling. He said he'd be back later this afternoon.'

'What does he have to say about that serial?'

'It's unrepeatable.' Sally heaved a weary sigh,

prompting a query from Ben, who had just walked into the room. She told him what the problem was, further depressing them all by raising the editor's liking for pictures and stories dealing with the lives of aristocratic ladies. 'We're back to the doings of The Honourable Miss Double-Barrelled again,' she finished gloomily, 'when what we need is a real story.'

'A nice juicy murder,' Ben suggested.

'Don't be horrible,' Josie said, gently brushing back the leaves of a luxuriant trailing geranium so she could get the water to its roots.

He looked cynical. 'Come off it. You know the reading public love that sort of thing. Especially if there's some sort of sex-crime element to it as well.' He strolled over to join her at the window. 'There are people out there who'd happily go along to public hangings if we still had them.'

'You're right, I suppose. The trouble is, it's still the silly season. Nothing much seems to be happening. I suppose the occasional serial isn't a bad idea in principle.' She felt the earth in the next plant pot with the tips of her fingers. It was still pretty moist. 'Not Marcia Clifford and her adventures, though. That really is the most complete and utter tripe.'

She got no response to that statement, unusual when the room contained two people more than capable of talking the hind legs off several donkeys. She looked up, saw the expression on Ben's face and turned slowly to face the undoubted music, the miniature watering can he had given her as a present earlier in the summer dangling from her hand.

'Busy, Miss Shaw?' asked the editor sarcastically.

'She's been working hard all morning,' Sally said stoutly. 'This is her lunch break.'

'This *was* her lunch break.' The editor looked grim. 'There's been an accident on a level crossing in Dumbarton. A goods train struck an excursion bus full of kiddies. One of them has been killed. A five-year-old boy named Charlie.'

'Dear God,' Josie breathed, sitting down very abruptly on the edge of the windowsill.

Not her Charlie, of course not. He was much older than that. Even her own baby would be older than that by now.

'We've had a reporter and snapper at the scene but they had to go on to another job. The news desk is under strength at the moment.' The editor neglected to mention that this was due to two of the reporters deciding last week that they couldn't stick his aggressive manner one moment longer. 'I'm told you're a very sympathetic interviewer, Miss Shaw. We've already got a picture of the mother and her other children. We need to know how they all feel and we also need a photo of the dead boy. Don't come back here without one.'

It was the mechanical way he said it, rattling out instructions as though he were ordering a consignment of goods to be uplifted. *How they all feel.* How in the name of God did he think they felt?

Josie stood up and walked slowly over to her desk to pick up her notebook and bag.

'Do you have any difficulty with this assignment, Miss Shaw?'

She lifted her chin. 'None. I'll get you what you need.'

'Good. I believe that is what we pay you for.'

Ben let out a very rude word after the editor had left the room. Sally looked anxiously at Josie. 'Are you sure you're all right about this? I could go instead.'

'No, you couldn't. With Roddy out of the office you have to be here as his second-in-command. I'm a journalist and my editor has asked me to do a job. I'll be fine. You have to take the rough with the smooth in this business.'

She wondered if she had fooled them. She certainly hadn't fooled herself. All the way down she was nervous.

The knowledge that she was about to intrude on a shocked and grieving family at the worst moment in their lives was simply awful.

In the end, it was all too easy. The mother wanted to talk about her boy and insisted on making Josie a cup of tea while she did so. His bewildered brothers and sisters were eager to help the sympathetic lady from the newspaper. When she tentatively mentioned a photograph one of the girls ran to get her one.

None of it made Josie feel any less like a vulture.

On the way back to the office she stared out at Clydebank's idle cranes and quiet shipyards. Hating herself for thinking of her own sorrows in the midst of someone else's loss, it occurred to her that the fate which had befallen the small boy whose family she had just left could happen to any one of her lost children. And she would never know about it.

'Tough day?'

At her desk with her head in her hands, she didn't look up when she heard Roddy's voice. Right now she could do without any cutting comments about unprofessional behaviour. She presumed that's how he would classify bursting into tears over a story. Oh, she had waited until she had it written, handing it over to a copyboy for transfer to the subs' office before she had broken down.

Ben had taken her in his arms and given her a hug. Now she was waiting to go home with him and Sally, both of them currently busy elsewhere in the building.

'I've just read your interview with the bereaved mother and her family,' came Roderick's voice again. 'It's excellent. Compassionate without being in the least sentimental.'

'You would approve of that.'

'I do. It's an honest piece of work. You should be proud of it.'

'Proud of it!' She had to give a big sniff and wipe her face with her hand before she could say anything else. 'It's exploitative and intrusive.'

'You think we ply a dirty trade?'

'Yes. Sometimes I wonder why I want so much to be a part of it.'

She heard him sit down, a few feet away from her at Sally's desk. It faced her own, no gap between them because of the chronic shortage of space within the *Dispatch* office. 'Oh dear,' Roddy said softly. 'Crisis of conscience?'

She raised her head, past caring now that he would be able to see she'd been crying. 'One of the girls got me a snapshot of her brother. She took it out of a frame for me. This cheap wee frame on a cheap wee sideboard in a poor wee house. I promised the mother she'd get it back.'

'She will. That's the kind of person you are. That's also why people talk to you so openly. I'll give you a run to her house with it tomorrow if you like.' Roderick's strong and broad face showed nothing but sympathy. 'Don't you think you maybe helped that family today, Jo?'

'I can't bring their wee brother back,' she said bitterly.

'No,' he agreed, 'but you've acknowledged his existence, his importance to his mother and his family and in the great scheme of things. I bet they'll keep your article, bring it out over the years, tell other family members about him. His brothers and sisters will probably show it to their children. Don't you think that might be something for them to hold on to in the future? In the fullness of time it might even bring them some consolation that his passing was marked.'

Josie gazed mournfully across the desks at him. 'You wouldn't be saying all this just to cheer me up, would you?'

'Does Mr Cunningham ever do anything with the intention of cheering anybody up?' came a voice from the doorway. It was Ben. Judging by the way he was leaning against the doorframe, he'd been there for some time.

Roddy looked over at him. 'As a matter of fact I'm thinking of taking this young lady out to dinner. That all right with you?'

Given their relationship, the question should have sounded sarcastic. It didn't. As Ben's response sounded almost friendly. 'Great idea,' he said. 'Sally and I'll see you later then, Josie.'

As Ben vanished as unobtrusively as he had materialised, Roddy turned back to Josie. 'Where d'you fancy then?' He leaned forward conspiratorially, trying to coax a smile out of her. 'Since your face is all blotchy from crying, I'd be inclined to suggest a nice dark restaurant.'

'I'm not fit to go anywhere.' She laced her fingers through her hair. 'I'm not really in the mood to go anywhere.'

'Then come and have something to eat at my place,' he said. 'I'll walk you home afterwards. I'm only at the other end of Woodlands Road from you. Go on,' he urged. 'Be a devil.'

He lived in Charing Cross Mansions towards the western end of Sauchiehall Street. His third-floor home in the impressive red sandstone building, whose architect had obviously been a lover of all things French, had a balcony running along outside it.

'Oh,' Josie cried as he threw up the window of his dining room so that they could step out. 'Isn't this lovely! What a marvellous view you've got!' She was looking out over the elegant Victorian terraces of Sauchiehall Street. The imposing dome of the Mitchell Library could be glimpsed over the rooftops to the left and in the distance the Gothic spire of Glasgow University reached up into the sky.

'I like it,' Roddy said smugly. 'Stay there and I'll bring you a glass of wine while I get on with our dinner.'

'Can I help?' she asked as he disappeared back inside.

'Nothing much to do. I'm afraid it's only last night's kedgeree heated up,' he said apologetically. 'I always seem to cook far too much.' When they sat down at the table twenty minutes later, Josie being not entirely sure what kedgeree was, she found that he had also set out salad and brown bread. Further down the long dark table a small marble slab held cheese and biscuits and grapes.

'This looks lovely.'

'All my own work,' he said, passing her a linen napkin.

'You don't have someone to cook for you?'

'No,' he said. 'There's a servant problem, didn't you know?'

Her head snapped up. Then she saw that he quite literally had his tongue in his cheek. He removed it and grinned at her. 'I don't have the money to lead that sort of life any more, Jo. Although,' he added, refilling her glass with white wine, 'I do have enough to send my dirty linen to the laundry and employ a lady who comes in twice a week to do the cleaning and dusting. As someone said to me not so long ago, I'm not exactly on the streets.'

Josie blushed. 'I'm sorry if I went a bit overboard that day.'

'I deserved it,' he said calmly. 'Let's eat before it gets cold.' He lifted one of the two plates in front of him and began doling her out a portion. Josie studied it carefully after he had handed it over to her. There were slices of boiled egg and smoked haddock and rice. 'Rice?' she queried, wrinkling her nose at him. 'In a savoury dish?'

He laughed. 'Most of the world eats rice in savoury dishes, Miss Culinary Ignoramus. It doesn't have to be baked with sugar and milk and sultanas and served up for pudding.'

'I can cook,' she said indignantly.

'Good homely fare?' he teased.

'There's nothing wrong with good homely fare.'

'Agreed.' He put a forkful of kedgeree into his mouth and dispatched it before he spoke again. 'Tell me what you can cook, then. After that I'll tell you what I can cook. Only we'll both eat some of this first. I don't know about you but I'm absolutely starving.'

So they ate together and he extracted the cautious admission that his kedgeree did seem to be rather tasty. Then they compared notes about what sort of food they liked and he waxed lyrical about how much he enjoyed cooking. It relaxed him after the stresses of the working day.

'You weren't brought up to it, though?'

'No, but I read this really good article once on how men maybe ought to give it a try.'

Tired after the emotion of the day, Josie was beginning to unwind. 'Away and boil your head and make soup with it,' she said equably. 'You must have been cooking before then.'

He grinned at her. 'It was still a great article.'

After dinner, he made coffee and carried it to the sitting room, firmly refusing her offer of help with the washing up. Following him through, she came to an abrupt halt in the doorway.

'Oh, look at all your books!' Apart from the wall where the window and balcony were, the room was lined with bookcases crammed full of them.

Roddy put the tray he was carrying on a low table set between two long sofas. 'There used to be a lot more of them. We had a proper library in the old house.'

Already examining the volumes, Josie turned at the note of regret in his voice. 'It's hard leaving the place you've grown up in, isn't it?'

'Yes,' he agreed. He began pouring the coffee. 'Yet in a funny sort of way there was something positive about it.' He paused, cup and saucer in one hand and coffee jug in the other. 'Liberating. As though I'd been set free from something.'

'Like a bird finding its wings?' she suggested.

'Exactly like that.' Eyes narrowing, he regarded her thoughtfully.

She extended her hand. 'Is that my cup?'

He walked her home as promised. As they turned into Woodlands Road he recalled their teacher at the commercial college and her collapsing coiffure. They chatted easily about that, swapping memories of how they had suffered together to master shorthand and typing. Only when that topic was exhausted and they were almost at Mrs Beaton's house did he stray on to dangerous ground.

'You're very sensitive about anything to do with children, aren't you?'

'Isn't everyone?' She was more alert now, ready as ever to divert anyone who got anywhere near this topic.

'Perhaps,' he allowed, 'but you more than most, I think.'

She mumbled something noncommittal and he dropped the subject. When they reached the front door, she delved in her bag for her key and asked him if he'd like to come in for a wee while.

'Better not. It's quite late. And your fellow lodger of the masculine variety might not be too pleased to see me.'

They were standing together in the porch of the house, a small passageway between the storm door and the internal one. That was wooden at the bottom and glazed at the top, adorned by a beautiful and jewel-bright stained glass panel of an old-fashioned ship with billowing sails.

Glancing up at Roddy, Josie was aware of an awkwardness she didn't really think had anything to do with the possibility of Ben Gold giving him a hostile reception. That was daft. It wasn't as if the two of them had spent the evening together in a boyfriend and girlfriend sort of a way. 'Well,' she said, fighting an absurd urge to shake hands with him, 'thank you for a lovely evening.'

'It's been a pleasure. Shall we do it again sometime? Maybe you could cook for me.' He leaned forward as though to give her a peck on the cheek. Whether he changed direction at the last minute or she turned her head the wrong way, their lips met in a brief kiss.

'Oh,' he murmured, 'that was nice.' His mouth was still very close to hers and his voice was as soft as velvet. 'Is it something else we should do again . . . right now, perhaps?'

'No,' she said and took a step back, as far as that was possible in such a small space.

Roddy stayed where he was. 'Really no?' he inquired. 'Not playing hard to get no?'

'You're only doing it because you think it's expected of you,' Josie said in a reasoned and kindly tone of voice. 'And I'd much rather be your friend than one of your many conquests.'

It took him several minutes to stop laughing.

She reached the safety of the hall to find a reception committee waiting for her. Ben and Sally were standing on either side of the door into their joint sitting room, arms folded and feet tapping. Their identical facial expressions could only be described as smirks.

Josie unbuttoned her jacket. 'Snooping's a very un-attractive trait, you know.'

'Well, Miss Shaw,' Ben said, 'if two people are walking across the hallway after spending an hour or two with their landlady . . .'

'And they happen to see two different figures on the other side of the front door . . .' put in Sally.

'One male and one female . . .'

'And if the two heads of those two figures seem to be awfully close together . . .'

'And if the male person then laughs in an uninhibited

288

fashion for a good half hour ... well then, the two other people can hardly be blamed for taking a healthy interest in what's going on, can they?'

'Snooping,' Josie repeated. 'It's sad, really.' She shrugged out of her jacket and headed for her room. 'Good night, all. See you in the morning. I must get my beauty sleep.'

'Of course you must,' Ben said, giving her an outrageous wink. 'Especially since all your youth and beauty is now dedicated to dear Roderick. Och, it's so romantic! See what a glow the lassie has, Miss Fleming.'

Sally turned her eyes heavenwards, clasped her hands together in front of her breast and pretended to swoon, Ben catching her as she slumped prettily against him.

'Daft gowks,' Josie said, and firmly closed her door on them.

Once she was in her room, she walked over to the wardrobe. After she had hung up her jacket she looked at herself in the mirror. She was a little flushed this evening, a natural reaction to that unexpected meeting of mouths. It didn't mean anything.

The glow lasting while she undressed and got into bed was also a perfectly understandable phenomenon. The kiss had been very pleasant. Roddy Cunningham had kissed a lot of girls. That would be why he was so good at it. And it was an awful long time since a man had kissed her.

Josie smiled in the darkness, remembering all those nights with Tam in the darkness of the close at the Drygate. She fell asleep with the smile still on her face.

Chapter 26

Casting a brief glance at the grey December day on the other side of the office window – with a bit of luck she might actually get out of this place on time tonight – Josephine gave her profile of the new Queen a final read through. Destined for tomorrow's centre page spread, the pen portrait was a comprehensive one, giving as much information as possible about the personality and life so far of the lady known as the Smiling Duchess.

The Duke of York's wife had always been a favourite with the reading public, but the abdication of her brother-in-law Edward VIII exactly one week ago today had catapulted her and her husband into the very centre of the stage. 1936 had certainly been an eventful year: especially the latter half of it.

Back in August, Adolf Hitler had used the Olympic Games in Berlin to demonstrate the stranglehold he and his Nazi Party now had on Germany. It was becoming horribly clear that all resistance within the country was being ruthlessly crushed. The race laws which had been introduced in 1935 were enough to make any decent person's blood run cold. Despite that, optimists insisted it was still possible to contain and control him and laughingly dismissed Benito Mussolini, his Italian counterpart and ally, as all pomp and bombast.

The laughter had begun to ring a little hollow when both of the Fascist dictators sent large numbers of men and machines to the assistance of General Francisco Franco, leader of the the military uprising in Spain.

Launched from Morocco in July, that uprising had now blown up into a full-scale civil war.

Incensed by the cautious non-intervention of their own governments, communists and socialists in France, Britain, the United States and beyond had taken themselves off to Spain as volunteers. Now formed into brigades based on their respective nationalities, they had just seen action at the Siege of Madrid, successfully holding the Spanish capital for the Republican government.

Josie sighed. Since the story of the King's romance with the twice-divorced Mrs Wallis Simpson had broken, Spain had been pushed off the front pages. She supposed it was understandable enough. Journalists had known of the rumours of the royal affair much earlier than the general public, but the reality of the abdication was no less of a drama for that.

Having voluntarily agreed to suppress the story for as long as possible, British newspapers were now in a quandary as to what they should print and what position they should take. Many of those in the know suspected that King Edward VIII's enforced abdication had more to do with his flirtation with Hitler and Mussolini than his love affair with the American lady. On the other hand, the now former King had a high personal popularity. There was a fine line to be trod.

What *was* certain was that the public appetite for information on the new Queen and her two little daughters was voracious. Satisfied that her own piece was rounded, lively and informative, Josie tugged the last page out of her typewriter and put it with the others. In the process of neatening up the small sheaf, she had them plucked from her hand by Roddy, who strode into the room, took the article and strode out again.

'Perfect timing,' he threw back over his shoulder. 'We're on the point of choosing the pix to illustrate this.' Twenty minutes later he swept back into the room and narrowly avoided colliding with Sally. When she rattled a collecting tin under his nose he raised his hands in a gesture of surrender. 'What is it now? Orphans of the Spanish Civil War or Jewish refugees from the Nazis?'

'The former,' she said, 'so stop being so sarcastic and put some money in, you filthy capitalist.'

'Me?' he queried, striking his chest with his hand and going for the look of injured innocence. 'I'm a member of the proletariat. *All those who toil by hand or brain.* Isn't that what Keir Hardie said?'

'Even the Devil can quote Scripture to suit his own ends,' said Sally loftily. Her expression changed. 'You know the Spanish Civil War isn't getting the coverage it deserves.'

'Which was the case even before the Abdication story broke,' Roddy responded, nodding in agreement. 'I've tried convincing our esteemed editor of that but he insists *Dispatch* readers aren't interested in what's happening to, and I quote – "a bunch of bloody foreigners". He's wrong, of course,' he continued gloomily. 'People are passionately interested.'

Despite Sally's reference to filthy capitalists, in reality Roddy's interest in politics had sharpened and taken a sidestep to the left, a direct result of his visit to Berlin to cover the Olympics in August. Ben had gone with him as photographer, a professional partnership only possible because both men had individually and quietly decided to at least be civil to each other for Josie's sake.

If they hadn't exactly come back from Berlin friends, their relationship had acquired a tinge of genuine warmth. Outraged by Adolf Hitler's refusal to shake the hand of Jesse Owens, the black American athlete, they had both been appalled by more personal encounters with the philosophy of the master race. Witnessing the way Nazi officialdom had dealt with his Jewish photographer –

contemptuous didn't begin to describe it – had inspired Roddy to defend Ben at the time and subsequently to write a passionate yet thoughtful essay which both Josie and Sally considered a minor masterpiece.

The editor had refused to print it. The *Glasgow Evening Dispatch*, its proprietors and the other newspapers within the Incorporated News group were firmly behind the policy of Appeasement. Mr Cunningham's masterly dissection of the ideology of National Socialism and his warnings that its outward manifestations were going to become uglier than anyone could imagine might cause offence to Herr Hitler and his government.

The furore which then erupted was all the more ironic because sending Roddy to Berlin had been a sop to keep him at the *Dispatch*. It had only come about because of the financial backing of the proprietors and the clout of the London daily which they also owned. Prepared to do a lot to keep an excellent Features Editor where he was, they had nevertheless baulked at publishing that particular article.

'Do you think Incorporated News is part of a right-wing conspiracy?' Sally asked darkly. 'Deliberately trying to suppress the news coming out of Spain?'

Roddy looked deeply cynical. 'I think they're too inept for anything as organised as that. I'd put it down to rank stupidity. Apart from the fact that anyone with a modicum of intelligence might consider that Spain could just be a dress rehearsal for a bigger show, how many towns and cities throughout Britain have men serving in the Inter-national Brigades?'

'Lots,' Josie chipped in. 'I did read the figures some-where. There's a couple of hundred gone from Glasgow alone.'

Roddy glanced over at her. 'I expect it's the same story in Liverpool and Manchester and London and a dozen other places besides, Jo. Apart from our moral duty to cover the conflict, we should do it if only out of self-interest. Those men are the husbands and fathers and sons of our readers.'

'There's women gone too.' Sally's eyes shone with enthusiasm. 'That would be something to tell your grandchildren, wouldn't it? That you'd actually stood up and been counted: been prepared to fight for your beliefs.'

'It takes a special sort of courage,' Roddy agreed. 'I have to say that I admire them enormously.'

'You know,' Sally remarked after he had left the room, 'he's a much nicer person since the two of you started going out together. More relaxed. Drinking a lot less too.'

'We are *not* going out together,' Josie said in the exasperated tones of a woman who had uttered the same denial more times than she could count. And, she thought, despite Roddy having made his feelings about that issue abundantly clear over the past couple of years, we're certainly not staying in together.

Sally raised her beautifully plucked eyebrows. 'No? So the fact that the two of you cook each other a meal at least once a week means nothing, does it? Or that you're planning to spend most of Christmas together?'

'Not a thing,' Josie said, feeding a fresh sheet of paper into her typewriter and flipping open her notebook.

'How about that German night class the two of you go to every Thursday evening?'

'Roddy thinks it would be a good idea if we were able to speak nicely to them when they invade us. I agree with him.' Josie lifted her notebook and pretended to peer at an indecipherable shorthand outline. She knew exactly what the word was.

'And your regular and joint visits to the restaurants of Glasgow?'

'All in the interests of culinary research. It's a hobby we both enjoy.'

'Hah!' said Sally, who had temporarily run out of ammunition.

Josie smiled sweetly over her notebook at her. 'Roderick Cunningham and I are just good friends. That's all.'

A look of triumph spread across Sally's face. 'That's what Eddie and Wallis used to say.'

It was lunchtime on Christmas Eve and Roderick was waiting for Josie to finish up. He had decreed an early closure of the Features Department today, an unusual treat which Sally and Ben were unfortunately not in a position to enjoy. Following an edict issued by the editor to which Roddy had grudgingly acceded, they had been packed off to Gretna Green yesterday to secure some pictures and sentimental stories of romantic winter weddings. Those would come in useful for brightening the pages of the *Dispatch* between Christmas and New Year, a time which was often a miniature version of summer's silly season.

Bored with waiting, Josie's immediate boss was driving her mad by wandering aimlessly about the office picking things up and laying them down again. Eventually he sauntered across to the windows and stood gazing out at the snow. Obviously getting into the mood, he began to sing Christmas carols.

'Roddy,' Josie said, head still bent over her typewriter, 'you're a man of many talents but I'm afraid the ability to sing is not one of them.'

Pausing briefly in his undoubtedly rather off-key rendition of 'Good King Wenceslas', Roderick flashed her a brilliant smile and kept right on going. His second offering was 'I Saw Three Ships Come Sailing In'.

'Roddy!' she yelled. 'Shut up! Please!' She only had a few more lines to compose. If she got some peace and quiet she could rattle them off in as many minutes.

Mr Cunningham struck a quizzical pose. 'Didn't you

tell me last year when I dragged you to that carol concert that this was one of your favourites?'

'Exactly! You're murdering it!'

'Where's your Christmas spirit, Jo?'

'At the end of this piece I'm trying to finish,' she said smartly, giving him a dirty look. He came and stood behind her, then laughed out loud.

'About how to introduce your little darlings to the joys of Christmas and make sure they understand its true meaning. While you yourself are doing an excellent impersonation of Ebenezer Scrooge. Still too Presbyterian to throw yourself into the celebrations, Miss Shaw? Yuletide must have been great fun in your family.'

Josie raised her head abruptly from her article. Roddy's seemingly innocuous comment had sent her hurtling back into the past, to the memory of another Christmas Eve when snow had been falling softly on Buchanan Street. She stared at the flakes drifting past outside the windows, remembering it all so clearly.

That had been the night she had found out about the shorthand and typing classes, when she had hugged Ben, and Tam had been so jealous. She had managed to reassure him on the journey home, riding through the snow with Jimmy the Clydesdale pulling them safely back to Duke Street.

She could hear her mother's voice. *I'm feeling fine. Blooming, you might say*. At the time, she hadn't understood what Dorothy had meant by that. Now it seemed so obvious. She must have just found out that she was pregnant again.

'Jo?' Roderick's voice was deep and gentle. He came round beside her, put his hand on her shoulder. 'Are you all right?'

She snapped back to reality, looking up at him with a smile. 'I'm fine,' she said. 'Give me two minutes and I'll be right with you.'

They had lunch in one of their favourite restaurants and then spent an hour or so doing some last-minute Christmas shopping. When she saw his eyes begin to glaze over she took pity on him and suggested an early house at a cinema near Charing Cross Mansions. It was his turn to cook tonight.

'Although I prepared our meal yesterday evening,' he informed her. 'To allow the flavours to develop properly and integrate with each other in a fusion of savoury delight.' He bunched his fingertips together, put them to his lips and blew them open with a kiss.

'Aye,' Josie said, looking askance at the extravagant gesture. 'Right.'

As he set the dish between them she peered at it suspiciously. It bore a certain resemblance to beef stew but it had a reddish hue and the aroma indicated that it was flavoured with some kind of spice. Mr Cunningham was inordinately fond of spicy food.

'It's not curry, is it?' she asked.

'No, it's Hungarian Goulash. Not nearly as hot as curry. Anyway,' he said defensively, 'I really think you should give curry another try. My hand slipped when I was putting in the spices last time. I told you that. Give me your plate.'

'I'll say your hand slipped. I seem to recall we considered calling out the fire brigade to extinguish the conflagration raging in my mouth.'

'Och, Jo-se-phine,' he said, putting on an exaggerated Glasgow accent. 'You're gey fond o' thae big words since you started going to your English night class.'

He had encouraged her to sign up for that as well as the German one, following a long conversation in which he had listened sympathetically to her regret that she wasn't as well-educated as she would have liked to be. However, he had also told her sternly that she was much more intelligent than she gave herself credit for and that her main problem as he saw it was lack of self-esteem.

Searching for the roots of that, he had tried some gentle probing into her past. Politely but firmly rebuffed, he had declared another characteristic to be an inherent part of her personality: stubbornness.

Josie took an experimental mouthful of goulash. 'Mmm,' she said. 'This is nice.'

'Don't sound so surprised.' He let them both eat for a while before he spoke again. 'Christmas Dinner with Sally and Mr Gold tomorrow?'

Knowing very well that it was rude to speak with your mouth full, Josie nodded. Despite Roddy and Ben's rapprochement, this was going to be a first. She and Sally had discussed it at some length and had come to the conclusion that both young men could be trusted to be on their best behaviour when it was a special occasion meal, even if that occasion wasn't one which was part of Ben's own tradition.

Roddy posed a second question. 'And you will come with me for drinks at my sister's on Boxing Day?'

Josie swallowed. His goulash really was very good. 'I promised, didn't I? You know she doesn't approve of me, of course.'

Roddy didn't bother to deny the charge. Shona Campbell's frosty attitude was too overt. It stemmed from her unshakeable belief that Josie had been a viper in the bosom of the Gardiners. Despite the fact that she hadn't named them in her articles about the servant problem and despite all the other evidence to the contrary, Roddy's sister refused to believe Josie hadn't gone to work there with the express intention of writing about the experience.

She had also made it quite clear that Josie was not of the required social status to have a close personal friendship with a member of the Cunningham family. She had been a servant, she obviously came from a humble background and – something which Shona found absolutely beyond the pale – she continued to speak with a warm Glasgow accent.

Both Roddy and Josie were well aware that his sister was consumed with curiosity as to how close their friendship actually was. In mischievous moods, neither of them could resist playing up to that. In most moods, Roddy was unable to resist annoying Shona by coming out with some of the more colourful Glaswegian turns of phrase he had picked up from young Miss Shaw.

On one occasion he had blithely told his nephew Matthew that Sir Oswald Mosley talked a load of mince. Matt should away and boil his head and make soup with it if he thought the leader of the British Union of Fascists was preaching a message which would find much support among the people of the British Isles. Terrified that she herself was about to burst into hysterical giggles, Josie had watched in horrified fascination as he lurched onwards, caught up in the momentum of it all.

Seeing his sister shudder at his language, he patted her on the shoulder and told her not to look so black affronted. He could understand Matt's politics were an embarrassment but the big daft laddie would grow out of them soon enough.

Roddy had spoken pure Oxford English when he had issued his sister with an ultimatum of which Josie remained blissfully unaware. If Shona didn't accept Miss Shaw as his friend then he himself would find it extremely difficult to visit the Campbell household with any degree of frequency. Close though he liked to think he still was to his nephew Matthew, he often thought he continued to remain so for the sake of the people he mentioned next. 'Come for Caroline's sake,' he urged Josie now. 'You like her and wee Archie.'

Matthew Campbell had married a bright and bouncy redhead whose recently deceased father had been the stationmaster at Partick. Young though she was, Mrs

Campbell junior already had a baby son. Josie had felt for the girl when she had suffered a second bereavement, losing her mother on the very day young Archie was born.

'I do like Carrie,' Josie agreed. 'She's had an awful lot to cope with in the past year but she seems determined to look on the bright side. Although,' she said, putting her empty plate into Roddy's outstretched hand, 'I think she finds it quite a strain having to live with her parents-in-law.'

'I don't blame her,' he said feelingly. 'I can't understand why Matt doesn't do something about getting them a home of their own.' He stood up and carried their plates through to the kitchen. They had got into the habit of eating there but in honour of its being Christmas Eve they were in the dining room tonight.

Josie privately thought Matthew was far too comfortable where he was. The archetypal tall dark handsome stranger, there was something about Roddy's nephew which disturbed her. Unlike his mother, he had always been charming to her. He seemed to be very loving and attentive towards his young wife. All the same, Josie could never quite rid herself of the uneasy feelings she had about him.

'Oh!' she exclaimed when Roddy returned to the table, clapping her hands together in a gesture of joy. 'Cheese and biscuits and grapes. How very novel!' It was what he served for dessert nine times out of ten.

'Don't be so bloody cheeky,' he murmured. 'I'll happily admit you're much better at puddings than I am. If they were hanging me at dawn, I would request your lemon meringue pie for my last meal.'

Josie batted her eyelashes at him.

Cheeseboard in hand, Roddy stood and looked down at her. 'I keep hoping you'll do that for real.'

'Stop right there,' she said automatically.

Roddy heaved a sigh and put the dessert on the table. Then he threw himself down into his chair and changed tack. 'Like to tell me which particular memory of yours I trod all over in my size elevens before we left the salt mines today?' He pulled a grape off the bunch on the marble slab and tossed it into his mouth.

'No,' she said, just as automatically.

'Stubborn as a mule,' he said and cut them both a slice of cheese.

'You seem to be holding my hand, Roderick.'

'Gosh. Really? Why, so I do.' Seen in the light of a Woodlands Road lamp-post, his smile was almost angelic.

'Why are you holding my hand, Roderick?'

'Because it feels nice?' he suggested. 'A kiss would feel nice too, don't you think?' He tugged on the hand he held, pulling her round to face him. 'Go on, seeing as how it's Christmas. There's no one else about.'

'No one else is daft enough to be trudging through the snow at this time of night on Christmas Eve.'

'Och,' he grumbled, 'you're so unromantic.'

'That's what you always say when I tell you I'm not interested in having an affair with you.'

'Is your reluctance on moral grounds or because you find me repellent? In the sexual attractiveness sense, I mean.'

'Surely the number of young ladies who have succumbed to your manly charms over the years must give you a wee inkling that you're not exactly ugly. Or lacking in sex appeal.'

'I bet you say that to all the boys.'

'I don't say it to any of them. I'm not interested in that sort of thing and you know it.' That was a well-rehearsed response. They'd had this conversation – or variations on it – many times over the past couple of years.

'Would you be interested in the fact that no young lady

has succumbed to my manly charms for quite some time now?' Roddy looked momentarily horrified. 'Years rather than months, now I come to think about it.'

'Lost your touch with the fair sex?'

'Now, there's an unfortunate turn of phrase,' he said smoothly, chuckling when he saw her blush. 'No, as a matter of fact I've been voluntarily denying myself the pleasures of the flesh. I've been trying to prove that I can live a pure life.'

Josie made a rude noise. 'You want a medal?'

'No. I want you. You're the person to whom I'm trying to prove my purity.'

'Roddy,' she said, speaking in a tone of sweet reason, 'I've explained all this to you a hundred times. It's only because you can't understand how you can be seeing a woman so regularly on a purely Platonic basis. It conflicts with this image you have of yourself as some sort of Lothario.'

He did his eyebrow-raising trick. 'Platonic? Lothario? Did you get those from your English evening class?'

She extracted her hand from his grip and used it to poke him in the chest. 'I got the second one from observing you, Mr Cunningham.'

'I'm a reformed character. Ever since I fell for you.'

'And you want to convince me of your purity so we can then go to bed together? Very reformed.'

He seized her hand again, using his own to hold it flat against the collar of his heavy overcoat. 'We could always get married,' he said lightly.

'Forgive me if I don't swoon at the romantic nature of your proposal. You don't want to get married anyway.'

'Don't I?'

'No. You want to go off and prove yourself as a war correspondent or something. I don't want to get married either. I'd have to give up my job if I did.'

'Your job being the most important thing in your life?'

302

'Correct,' she said crisply. 'Look, can we keep moving? My feet are freezing.'

'Only if you let me hold your hand.'

'All right. We're nearly there anyway.'

'You're so gracious. Couldn't we go the long way round?'

'No, we could not. I told you, my feet are turning blue as it is.'

'You could always let me warm them up for you,' he said hopefully.

Josie laughed and slanted him a sideways look. 'Never give up, do you?'

He tilted his head back and looked down his nose at her. 'One day I'll wear down your resistance, Josephine Shaw. Oh, dammit, we're here already.'

Before Josie could even extract her key from her bag, Mrs Beaton flung open the door to them. Dressed in her usual array of colours and textures, it was the expression on her face which caught their attention. She was beaming with joy.

'We've been waiting ages for you two,' she complained. 'Wait till you hear our news!' Leaning forward, she pulled both Josie and Roderick into the hall.

Sally and Ben were standing very close together in the middle of it. Like Mrs Beaton, they were smiling all over their faces. Sally was holding a bouquet of winter roses and the little scraps of white sprinkled through Ben's dark curls weren't snowflakes. Looking as if she was about to burst with happiness, Sally stepped forward and made an announcement. 'We've just got married!'

Chapter 27

Josie was struck dumb, hating herself for that reaction when she saw Sally's smile dim. The new bride recovered quickly, handing her bouquet to Mrs Beaton and answering the questions which hadn't yet been asked.

'Right,' she said briskly, 'you'll want the what, where, when, why and how. The what you know. We're married. The rest is Gretna Green, this morning, because we love each other and over the anvil.'

'No,' Roddy breathed. 'Really? Is it still legal? Oh, you mad impulsive fools!' He at least reacted properly to the momentous news, striding forward to shake Ben's hand and kiss Sally on both cheeks.

'Isn't it romantic?' sighed Mrs Beaton. 'You can make your Christmas dinner the wedding breakfast, celebrate it properly.'

'Let's celebrate it tonight,' Roddy said. 'Shall I run back to my place and fetch a bottle of champagne?'

'We've got one cooling,' Ben said. 'Will the two of you share it with us and Mrs B?'

Sally walked over to Josie, still standing dumbfounded by the door. 'Be happy for us,' she said in a low voice.

Josie searched her friend's face. 'Are you happy, Sally?'

Sally smiled. 'I love him, Josie. Now I'm his wife. Of course I'm happy.' Linking arms with her, she turned them both around. 'Come on,' she said, 'if Roddy can kiss the bride, I don't see why you shouldn't kiss the groom.'

Ben did more than kiss her, he gave her one of his huge bear hugs. Before he released her again he whispered a few words into her hair. 'Don't worry, sweetie. It's going to work out. I know it is.' He raised his voice, sending a loving glance towards his new wife before he spoke. 'Should we get all the shocks out of the way at once, Mrs Gold?'

Wondering what on earth was coming now, Josie gazed up at him. He still had his arm loosely about her waist but his words were directed at Roddy. 'We're going to Spain,' he said calmly, 'to cover the war. As freelances, of course – but we'll need friends here to make sure Sally's dispatches and my photographs have half a chance of getting into print.'

Mrs Beaton looked troubled. Stunned, Josie wasn't sure how to respond. Once more it fell to Roddy to do the right thing, walking over to Ben and shaking hands with him for the second time in five minutes. 'You can count on me to do as much as possible at this end. You're a better man than any of us, Ben.' He raised his free hand to clap him on the shoulder.

Clearly moved, Ben returned the firm handshake. 'I appreciate that,' he said. 'Thanks, Roddy. Thank you very much.'

Some time later, in the wee small hours of Christmas morning, Sally sat on the end of Josie's bed hugging a cushion and quietly discussing practical arrangements. She and Ben were going to move all their stuff into her room and Mrs Beaton had agreed to charge them a reduced rent for the next six months.

'Is that how long you're intending to go for?' Josie asked, doing her best to keep her questions on a practical footing. Six months. That wouldn't be so bad.

'Who knows? We'll have to see what happens when we get there.'

Josie studied her friend's face. Always lively and animated, now it held a special glow. 'You're really looking forward to it, aren't you?'

Dressed in pyjamas, silk kimono and dainty slippers, Sally drew her legs up and laid them along the edge of the bed. 'It's like this, Josie. Ben and I have always been so interested in politics and we share the same strong beliefs.'

'You don't say.' Josie opened her mouth in mock amazement. Sally grinned and tossed the cushion at her.

'Seriously, though. We've always supported all these causes but we've never really *done* anything. Not put our money where our mouth is.'

'You'll be doing something now, all right,' Josie said. Despite trying her utmost not to betray any anxiety, she couldn't help asking the question. 'Are you not scared, Sally?'

'Only of not being able to buy silk stockings or the right shade of nail polish.' She struck the appropriate pose, extending her arm and regarding her beautifully manicured nails.

'Oh Sally, I'm really going to miss you! And Ben!'

Sally lowered her legs to the floor and slid up the bed. 'We'll be back sooner than you know,' she said, her voice muffled because her head was against Josie's shoulder. 'Driving you mad by teasing you about Roddy. Oh,' she said, pulling back, 'I'm getting my hair mussed up. And this my wedding night too.'

Their eyes met. The expression on Sally's face was wry and brave and it broke Josie's heart.

'I'll take whatever he's able to give me, Josie,' she said softly. 'And be happy with it. Isn't that what love means?' she queried. 'Accepting the other person totally? The things you don't like about them along with those that you do.'

'Aye,' Josie said slowly. 'I suppose that's as good a definition as any. I wish you both well,' she said earnestly. 'A long and happy life together.'

Sally got up from the bed. 'A long life with him as my husband will do me just fine.'

'He's a lucky man,' Josie said.
Sally smiled down at her. 'I'm a lucky woman.'

Chapter 28

The first result of Ben and Sally's departure in early January 1937 was Josie's promotion to Deputy Features Editor. Ready to doubt her own ability to do the job, she discovered Roddy had no such qualms. She had the brains, there was no question about that. Since she'd been working closely with Sally and himself for the last six years she also knew exactly what was required. He wasn't taking no for an answer.

His determination led to her reluctant agreement, although she made the proviso that her elevation was temporary. Sally and Ben would be back in six months and then everything would return to normal.

The second consequence of Mr and Mrs Gold taking themselves off to Spain, one which Josie had foreseen, was that Roderick's dissatisfaction with his own position rose sharply. She knew he admired Sally and Ben tremendously for what they were doing. Measured against them, he found himself wanting. Once he began having regular fights with the editor over the publishing of the copy and the pictures they were filing from Spain – and the freelance payments due for supplying those – the situation became increasingly fraught.

Josie succeeded in easing it after a discussion with Alan Dewar. In phone contact with Sally as often as conditions permitted, his own sympathies very much with the beleaguered Spanish government, he too felt that coverage of the war in the British press was woefully inadequate.

Perhaps the editor could be convinced to regularly

publish Sally and Ben's work if it were pointed out that it could be syndicated throughout the rest of the newspapers in the group and seen all over the British Isles. The reporter and photographer being former members of his staff would surely be a feather in his cap. Everybody knew the man intended to stay at the *Dispatch* only long enough to make a name for himself.

'Maybe we can kill two birds with one stone, Josie,' Alan said. 'Help Sally and Ben and get the great dictator off our own backs sooner rather than later.'

Casually mentioned by Josie at an editorial meeting as though she had just that moment plucked the idea out of the air, Alan's suggestion found immediate favour. Not only that, Sally and Ben were put back on to the payroll. That delighted both Josie and Roddy. It didn't, however, do much to alleviate his frustration. That was both personal and professional, and as spring gave way to summer it began to manifest itself in an increasing irritability: even with her. Maybe especially with her.

One morning in early June, tired after yet another sleepless night spent worrying about Ben and Sally, Josie broached a topic which had been preying on her mind since their departure. It was all very well getting married and taking off for Spain in a blaze of adventure, but what was going to happen when they came home and settled down in Glasgow?

Standing reading some copy which he'd spread out along the tops of the bank of filing cabinets in the Features Department, Roddy turned and peered at her. 'What's going to happen?' he repeated. 'I don't understand what you mean.'

'Well,' she began cautiously, 'at the moment they're all buoyed up by being in Spain and covering the war, but once they're back and life's not so exciting . . . well, I'm just wondering what's going to happen to their marriage then . . .'

Embarrassed, and discomfited by finding herself on the receiving end of one of Roddy's best haughty looks, she broke off.

'Why should anything happen to it?'

'Och Roddy,' she burst out, 'you know what I'm trying to say! You know what the problem is.'

'Maybe they think love will conquer all.' He gathered together his sheets of paper and spoke quietly into the overflowing wire filing basket which lived permanently on top of the filing cabinets. 'Maybe they're right.'

'Isn't that a bit naïve?'

The disdainful look was firmly in place again. 'Always count the cost of everything you do, Jo? Never thought of taking a chance on anything? How dull your life must be.'

He swept out of the room – infuriatingly – before she had the chance to retaliate.

Shortly after lunch Josie was fetched by a breathless copyboy with the information that Sally was on the line in the copytakers' room. She clattered down the stairs at breakneck speed only to find that the connection had been broken thirty seconds before she got there. Alan tried several of the numbers which Sally had given him over the past few months, but to no avail.

When Roddy rushed in hot on her heels also hoping to talk to Sally, Josie took her disappointment out on him, biting his head off when he unreasonably demanded to know why she and Alan hadn't been able to maintain the link with Spain. Later, he asked stiffly if she could still be bothered to cook tonight.

'Of course,' she snapped. 'Why wouldn't I be?'

She was finding entertaining less pleasant than it had been, a development largely due to Mrs Beaton's new lodger. The junior lecturer at Glasgow University was nice enough but Josie found her and her friends a little immature.

Presumably all intelligent people, they seemed to her

to go out of their way to be silly. If any serious topic did manage to fight its way through the general frivolity of their conversation it was immediately dismissed, the girls emphasising their disdain with shrieks of horror. High-pitched shrieks of horror. Josie wasn't sure how much longer she was going to be able to stand it.

While Mr Cunningham might once have fitted in perfectly with such a group, he had matured considerably over the years. Observing his disdain for the determined silliness and fearful of the sarcastic comments he might come out with if the new girl and her friends succeeded in irritating him enough, Josie now used the table in her own room when he came round, smiling tightly at the suggestive comments and exaggerated winks that arrangement provoked.

Twenty minutes after they sat down to eat this evening, there was a knock on the bedroom door. 'Yoo-hoo! Josephine!'

'Come in,' she called brusquely.

'We don't know if we should. We wouldn't want to catch you doing anything naughty!' The door was solid but the giggling which followed this sally was all too audible.

Roddy looked up from his meal, muttering, 'Would any court in the land convict me if I strangled that woman?'

'You'd have to fight me for her,' murmured Josie in a rare meeting of minds with him on this bad-tempered evening. She stood up and walked over to the door, swinging it wide open. 'Something I can do for you?'

'We're going out. We just wanted to let you know.'

'Thank you,' Josie said, already closing the door again.

'Be good, you two,' called the girl cheerfully.

'And if you can't be good, be careful!' chipped in a young male voice.

Another girl capped his comment. 'And if you can't be

careful we know someone who wants to sell a pram!'

As Mrs Beaton's front door crashed shut behind them Roddy laid his knife and fork down in disgust. 'This is intolerable. It's time you moved somewhere more private. There's something going in my building. Three rooms and the usual offices. Shall I make inquiries about it?'

'I can't afford something that size. Especially not in your building.'

'You can if I get you another pay rise.'

'And what will people say about that?' Josie demanded, her temper flaring. 'They're gossiping about us already, you know. At the *Dispatch*, I mean, since you promoted me. There are some people who find it hard to believe that a woman can get anywhere on merit. Especially a wee mouse like me.'

Roderick gave her a level look. 'Nobody who knows you could ever think you were that.' He picked up his cutlery and applied himself once more to his meal. 'Who cares what people say, anyway?'

'I do,' she said sharply. 'I can't afford not to. It's always the woman's reputation that suffers.'

'It shouldn't be that way. There's an unjustifiable double standard.'

'Well, it is that way,' she snapped. 'Do please let us be realistic, Roddy.'

He laid his knife and fork down again, stretched a hand across the table to her. 'Jo,' he said softly. 'Do please let us calm down.'

She had moved her hand out of his reach. He extended his own a little further. 'Pax?' he queried with a tentative smile.

She threw her own cutlery on to her plate. 'I'm not in the mood to play games.' Upset and depressed, and worried about Ben and Sally, she lowered her head and shaded her eyes with the hand she wasn't allowing him to hold.

'You know,' Roddy said, a hard edge to his voice, 'it's

ironic. Everyone thinks we're having this wild and passionate affair.' He gestured towards the door. 'That lot think
I've just thrown you on to the bed over there and am
currently in the middle of ravishing you. Little do they
know that you'll hardly even let me touch you.'

Josie didn't raise her head. She knew what she
would see. During unguarded moments, the ones they
spent alone together, the look was always there. She
was no longer able to convince herself that the hunger
and longing which filled his eyes was merely a matter
of sexual attraction. He certainly wanted her that way.
She was coming to believe that he wanted an awful
lot more, and she was coming to believe there was something about that which scared him as much as it scared
her.

'I delude myself that you're fond of me.' He gave a
bitter little laugh. 'Up until this evening I haven't had any
inkling that you actively *dislike* my company.'

'I don't dislike your company,' she said quietly.

'Damned with faint praise, Jo?' His voice had lost its
harshness. 'Haven't you even got any curiosity about the
act itself? Don't you ever wonder what it would feel like?'

Josie looked up at last. She took a quick little breath.
'What makes you think I don't know already?'

If she'd been hoping to shock him, she hadn't succeeded. 'Ah,' he said calmly, tapping one long finger
against his lips. 'The strong-minded man?'

Their conversation had always been wide-ranging.
When they weren't setting the world to rights they
discussed books they had read and concerts they
had attended or chatted about mutual friends and
acquaintances. One subject area had always been taboo:
her past. Maybe it was time she shared some of it with
him.

'His name was Tam,' she said. 'Tam Paterson.'

'What was he like?'

She thought about it. 'Gentle. Courteous. A straight-forward sort of a person.'

'Nothing at all like me, then,' Roderick said wryly.

He lifted her plate, slid it on top of his own and put them both to one side. He reached for her hand again. This time she let him take it. 'You and he made love to each other once?'

'Twice,' she said, with a sad little reminiscent smile.

Roddy was rubbing her knuckles with his thumb. 'And you were going to get married but he was killed. And no one else has ever been able to match up to him.'

Was that how she felt about Tam now? She didn't know. She watched Roddy's thumb caressing her knuckles and she didn't know. 'There are other complications,' she said slowly. 'Loose ends in my life.'

'Like your brother and sister?'

Her eyes flew to his face and her hand stiffened in his grasp.

'That's all I know, Jo,' he said apologetically. 'That you have a brother and sister somewhere. Sally told me before she went off. In case she didn't get the chance again, she said.' He paused while they both stared at the tablecloth and considered exactly what Sally had meant by that.

The news coming out of Spain was terrible, and the bloody conflict had just seen the birth of a new and dreadful weapon of war. The German Condor Legion had started to bomb civilians from the air, a development which had shocked the world.

Roddy raised his eyes once more to Josie's face. 'She said it was a story I ought to hear. But do you want to tell me?'

Some time later she stood in his arms in the porch of the house, her back to the stained-glass sailing ship. 'A chaste embrace,' he said. 'But none the less enjoyable for that.'

'Thank you for listening.'

'Thank you for telling me your guilty secret,' he responded lightly, dropping a kiss on her forehead.

Josie laid her head against his shoulder. Oh no, she thought, I could never tell you either of those . . .

He was moving his chin gently backwards and forwards over her hair. 'Jo,' he said, 'maybe I can never measure up to your Tam. But would you consider allowing me to try?'

It was odd hearing Tam's name on his lips. 'I don't know,' she said. 'Right at this moment, I'm a wee bit confused.'

'You're human, then,' Roddy said. 'That's a relief. I thought you might be some beautiful Venusian, sent to torment Earthling men by proving impervious to their advances.'

Josie laughed softly into the collar of his raincoat. 'You're daft,' she said.

'What I am is very fond of you,' he said quietly. 'Extremely fond of you,' he corrected. When she gave him no answer he spoke again, his voice filled with wry self-mockery. 'I'm too frightened to say the words. Pathetic, eh?'

She raised her head and put her fingers to his mouth. 'The last person you said them to was unworthy of them. No wonder you're frightened.'

He gazed fondly at her. 'How did you know that?'

'Elementary, my dear Watson. You're not the only one with powers of perception, you know.' She sighed. 'This is all a bit complicated, isn't it?'

His arms tightened around her. 'Isn't it just. I'm scared and you're scared and you don't even know how you feel about me.'

She sighed again. 'Why don't you go and find yourself some nice uncomplicated girl?'

Roddy's lips twitched. 'The species doesn't exist. Even if it did I wouldn't be interested. I'm only interested in you, Miss Shaw.'

'I'll give you an answer,' she said suddenly. 'For yea or nay. Friends or lovers. Either one or the other. Will you accept it?'

He lifted his hands to cup her face. 'When will you give me an answer?'

'One week from today.'

'Significant date?'

She grimaced. 'Something like that.'

'Sealed with a kiss,' he said and bent his head forward to touch his lips lightly to hers.

Back in her own room, Josie closed the door and stood leaning against it for a few minutes. It wasn't fair on him to go on like this. She owed him a definite answer. She thought, perhaps, that she already knew what it was. Her gaze drifted over the debris of their meal and on to her bed.

Given her personal history, she should have been scared when he had spoken bitterly of throwing her on to it. Instead, she had been aware of excitement. Of that curiosity of which he had spoken. Of wanting him to touch her in the most intimate of ways and of her blood rushing and tumbling through her veins at the prospect. She hadn't experienced those feelings since she had felt them for Tam Paterson.

It was time for her to confront the ghosts of her past.

Chapter 29

Her heart was pounding as she turned the corner into the High Street. She would be passing the end of the lane after she had gone another few yards. In a conscious effort to calm herself down, she glanced along Duke Street in the direction of her old school. Miss French, at least, was an unreservedly happy memory.

No, she couldn't say that. With the perspective of hindsight she saw that Irene French's life had contained its share of unhappiness. What was it she had said to her once? *Work, Josephine, that's the thing. Satisfying work is a great blessing.* Although the adult Josie knew that to be true, she wondered if that satisfaction might have been painfully won, born perhaps out of necessity and loss. Had Miss French sacrificed the love of her life to Flanders Fields, like so many women of her generation?

Josie would probably never know. She would love to think that one day she might meet up again with her old teacher and have the opportunity of thanking her properly for everything she had done for her. Unfortunately, she knew only too well that life didn't neatly tie up its loose ends simply because you wanted it to.

She had chosen to walk up the pavement on the opposite side of the Bell o' the Brae from the lane opening and the wall of the prison. Now level with it, she stopped and looked across. It had happened exactly eleven years ago today. It had been the start of the General Strike of May 1926, the first day of the stoppage. The weather had been as fine then as it was now, sunshine and blue skies.

The girl who had walked through that lane with her head down against the glare of the sun had been lost and confused, battered and bruised and bewildered by what had happened to her brother and sister. Yet she had just experienced great happiness too. Josie allowed her thoughts to drift back to that evening in the stables with Tam.

She could recall every aspect of it. She could see it. Feel it. Taste, smell and hear it. There was Tam's face above her as he moved gently inside her, the silky feel of his hair under her fingertips. His lips were on hers, his tongue flicking delicately against her teeth. All around them had been the warm smell of hay and horses, the great beasts whinnying softly as they settled down for the night.

Josie let the memories wash over her for a moment. Then she smiled and went on her way.

As she skirted the prison wall and entered the Drygate she was aware of some trepidation. Eleven years. It was a long time to leave those people who had really cared for her in ignorance. Would the Fitzgeralds and Tam's mother be angry with her? It was too late to worry about that now. She walked into the close and knocked smartly on the door.

'Can I help you, miss?'

To Josie's eyes she looked exactly the same. Maybe there were a few grey hairs among the brown ones. Frowning in puzzlement at the smartly dressed young lady in her neat little costume and beret, she repeated her question.

'Do you not know me, Mrs Fitzgerald? Have I changed that much?'

Bridget clapped a hand to her bosom. 'Holy Mother of God,' she breathed. 'Jesus, Mary and Saint Joseph . . .' A smile breaking out all over her face, she threw a less sacred set of names over her shoulder. 'Michael Francis

Fitzgerald, will you get up off your bahookey and come and see who's standing at your own front door!'

'Sure,' Bridget kept saying, 'it's a miracle, nothing short of a miracle.' Having dispatched Mick to fetch Ella Paterson, she was bustling around making tea and bemoaning the fact she had so little to offer her unexpected visitor in the way of home-baking. In the meanwhile, Josie sat and watched the table fill up with soda bread and tattie scones and gingerbread.

Preceding Mick into the room, Ella Paterson was initially overcome with emotion. Her face working painfully, she silently opened her arms. Josie leaped up from her chair and went into them. 'Och hen,' Ella said at last, 'we thought ye were gone forever.'

'Well, she's back,' Mick said exuberantly. 'By the looks of it she's not done too badly for herself either. So let the girl sit down again and give us her *craic*. Will ye do that for us, Josephine? Tell us about your life now?'

Josie curled her fingers round the back of a chair and studied Mick Fitzgerald's wise and craggy features. She should have known there would be no reproaches or prying into the past in this man's house.

'I'd be glad to,' she said, 'but there's one question I have to get out of the way first.' She took her hands off the chair and squared her shoulders. 'Who's living across the way?'

Bridget's eyes softened. 'You've no need to worry on that account, my dear. There's a new family there. Your stepfather's gone.'

'Gone?' Josie asked, watching Bridget set the teapot down and cover it with a knitted cosy. 'You mean dead and gone?'

Bridget crossed herself. 'May his soul rest in heaven and his body rot in hell,' she said blithely. 'It was the drink that got him in the end – which came as no surprise to anybody. Will you all sit down?' she requested.

Ella Paterson took her place but Josie had one more question to ask. 'And the boys – my stepbrothers – did they ever come back?'

'Aye,' Mick said slowly, 'although in a manner of speaking you could say that the drink got them too. They got their jobs back and then lost them again through it. Billy wandered off again. God knows where he is now.'

'Probably lying drunk in a ditch somewhere,' Bridget said.

'And Arthur?' Josie asked, hoping her voice didn't sound as faint to her hosts as it did to her own ears.

'Married on to one o' Ma Robertson's daughters,' Ella Paterson said. 'He's a bit of a poor soul now, though. He lifted his hand to her one night and her brothers did the same to him the next one.'

'More than their hands,' Mick said soberly. 'Seemingly they gave him a hell of a kicking. I can't say I ever had much time for either of those lads but it's pitiful to see young Arthur now. He shuffles about like a man twice his age.'

'Oh,' Josie said, and sat down rather abruptly. She was aware of no sense of triumph, no feeling that revenge had been exacted. There was only relief, even a little pity . . . and perhaps that was the best triumph of all.

They talked for an hour, Mick's eyes lighting up with joy when he discovered that Josie was a journalist. He fired hundreds of questions at her about that. When his wife scolded him for not allowing the girl to eat, they all took turns at filling her in on the local gossip. Could she believe that Alan Thomson was now not only the proud father of four little girls but also a lay preacher? Having forsworn the demon drink, he now railed against it with all of the energy and enthusiasm he had once applied to consuming it.

Quite easily and naturally, they spoke of Tam. Mick

recalled with laughter the occasion when the two of them had transported the very same Alan Thomson back to his mother's house when he'd had a lot more than one over the eight. Ella told Josie proudly that her second son Malcolm was now a carter at the brewery, training under Mick as his brother had done before him.

'Working with Jimmy too,' Mick interjected. 'You'll remember the big handsome horse, Josephine?'

'Of course I do,' she said warmly. 'Oh, that's lovely! I'm really pleased about that.'

'Shall I take you down to the stables next time you visit?' he asked eagerly. Seconds later he stifled an exclamation and looked accusingly at his wife. Bridget had obviously kicked him under the table.

It was a manoeuvre with which Josie was well acquainted. She'd often had to resort to it whilst in company with Mr Cunningham, usually when she knew he was either bored or angry and was about to alleviate his feelings by coming out with a few sarcastic comments. She guessed that Bridget's warning to her husband had to do with the dangers of assuming too much. Well, she was happy to set everybody's mind at rest about that.

'I'd love to see Jimmy again,' she said firmly. 'As I'd love to visit you all again. If you'll have me,' she added.

Bridget tutted. 'If we'll have her, the girl says. Of course we will.'

'It's more a case of whether you've grown too grand for the Drygate,' Ella remarked – sadly, as though that were a foregone conclusion.

Josie turned to her with a gentle smile. 'Never, Mrs Paterson. This is where I come from and I don't ever want to forget that.'

She left an hour later, swimming in tea and stuffed full of gingerbread and insisting they also had to come and visit her. When she asked Mick if she could interest him in a tour of the *Dispatch* office sometime soon, he was so overcome she thought he was going to cry. He pressed her hand silently in farewell and allowed the womenfolk to see her out.

'You're not married then, Josie?' Bridget asked as they emerged from the close mouth.

Josie shook her head.

'But there'll be a special someone in your life?'

That was Ella Paterson. Josie looked into her eyes, bright with kindly curiosity. 'You wouldn't think it was disloyal of me, Mrs Paterson?'

Ella answered her with simple eloquence. 'My Tam was a good man and he loved you dearly. He would have been the last person in the world to have wanted you to spend the rest of your life alone.'

'Oh, Mrs Paterson!' Once more she found herself wrapped in Tam's mother's arms.

Bridget patted them both on the shoulder. 'Ella and Bridget from now on, my dear. You're a grown woman now. Bring your young man with you the next time.'

Josie astonished herself by thinking that she probably would. She extracted herself from Ella's embrace and looked around her, her gaze resting in turn on the Drygate, the Royal Infirmary, the cathedral and the Necropolis.

Everything she was today had been formed by what had happened to her in this small patch of Glasgow. There had been pain and sadness in plenty but there were happy memories too. She could separate them all out now. Her eyes returned to the cathedral. 'I think I'll away in there for a wee while before I leave.'

'For a Protestant church it's not a bad place at all,' Bridget allowed. 'Especially if you're wanting to do a wee bit of thinking and remembering.'

Josie took her leave of her and Ella. Walking past the entrance to the Bridge of Sighs she glanced up at the Necropolis. She'd save that for another time. Maybe

Roddy would walk there with her. As she negotiated the entrance to the cathedral and entered the cool and lofty building she was aware of a great sense of calmness and serenity. It settled itself upon her shoulders like the folds of a warm cloak.

She walked up the centre of the nave and down the steps to the Laigh Kirk, not an underground crypt because its external walls followed the drop of the slope which rose from the valley of the Molendinar. That meant there was some daylight in here, enough for Josie to be able to appreciate the multitude of graceful stone pillars and sweeping mediaeval curves of the vaulted ceiling which they supported. She went first to stand in front of the tomb of Saint Mungo.

Eleven years ago a weeping girl fearful of what the future might hold had huddled there seeking help and comfort. Now that girl was a poised young woman, her future bright and full of promise – and the hope would never die that one day she would be reunited with her lost children.

Josie thought of all those children who were lost and could never be found. In her own family there was wee Jamie and her mother's other babies – including the one who had died with her. Dorothy would never have contemplated the awful and terrible step she had taken if she hadn't been completely desperate. She must have been in such torment of mind. Josie laid a hand on the cool stone of the Saint's tomb and prayed that her mother was now at peace.

'Look after them,' she whispered. 'Please God and Saint Mungo, look after my mother and all of her children.' Pity this wasn't a Catholic church any more. She would have liked to light candles for all of them, the living and the dead, but she kept a little light burning permanently in her own heart for them and surely that was just as good.

Josie walked slowly around the lower church, her footsteps echoing softly in this forest of stone. Pausing at one of the old chapels set into bays against the end wall, she read a small plaque which informed her that this particular one had in former times been dedicated to Saint Nicholas, patron saint of seafarers and children.

That seemed appropriate, so she sank down on to the ledge which ran along the side wall. *The weak shall go to the wall.* Only she wasn't weak any more. She was strong. The people who had hurt her so much eleven years ago had no power to harm her now.

The weak would have needed long legs. The ledge was quite high, although Josie was comfortable enough as she perched there. Clasping her hands together, she closed her eyes and bent her head. She was neither thinking nor praying. She was simply being, allowing the peace and tranquillity of this ancient and hallowed place to wash over her.

She wasn't sure exactly when she became aware of a presence, the sense of others having joined her within the confines of the tiny chapel. There seemed to be a small group of them, two of whom detached themselves and came to sit next to her on the stone ledge, one on either side. She knew she mustn't open her eyes or they would go away.

She felt a hand being laid on her left shoulder. It was a strong and masculine one, used to hard work yet capable of great tenderness too. The well-remembered touch filled her with a bubbling joy. On her other side a woman placed her hand on Josie's bowed head. The thin fingers rested gently on her hair. Now there was deep peace to accompany the joy.

She didn't know how long she sat there. It seemed like a long time. Then, having given her their blessing and their valediction, they were gone. Josie opened her eyes and raised her head, aware of a profound and abiding gratitude. 'Thank you,' she said softly. 'Thank you.'

She spared the lane the briefest of glances as she walked back down the High Street, too busy thinking about the stables further along Duke Street. She would go there on her next visit and she would give Jimmy the Clydesdale a hug and share memories of Tam with his wee brother.

Not one particular memory, of course. There was only one person in the world who would ever learn the details of that. How odd that seemed. Josie smiled. How entirely appropriate that seemed.

At ten o'clock the following morning, returning to the Features Department after a discussion with the picture editor, Josie found Roderick waiting for her. He was standing leaning against her desk, arms folded and eyes downcast.

'Roddy?' she inquired anxiously, thinking he looked rather depressed. When he raised his head she saw that the emotions he was experiencing were far more complex than that.

'Jo . . .' He exhaled a long breath. 'Will you come into my office for a minute?'

He didn't even give her time to sit down. 'I've just had a phone call from London. They'd like me to go and work there. As a senior news reporter.' His cautious smile didn't fool her for one minute. He was bursting with excitement about this. She walked over to the window and stood looking out, her back to him.

'Jo?' he queried. When he got no immediate response, he gave her another piece of information. 'I said I'd phone them back with my answer as soon as possible.'

She took another few seconds. Then she was ready to face him, turning with a smile. 'You must go. It's a great opportunity and you've been wanting to do something like this for years. We all know the international situation is hotting up.' She grimaced. 'There's going to be a lot of news about in the next few years. You'd be mad not to go, Roddy.'

She hoped her enthusiasm didn't sound forced. He had to do this. She knew that he desperately wanted to.

He looked her straight in the eye. 'I'd pass it up if you gave me a different type of opportunity.'

'And you'd hate me for it,' she said ruefully.

'Come with me, then,' he said. 'We'll go together.'

'What would I do in London?'

'Work,' he said. 'I'm sure there could be a job for you too.'

Josie shook her head. 'You'd be asking them to create a job for me. I don't want that. Plus you don't need encumbrances at this stage in your career. What happens if the balloon does go up in Europe?' she demanded. 'You'll want to be out there in the thick of it. In any case,' she said firmly, 'I belong here. This is where *my* work is.'

They didn't have time to skirt around the issues. Roddy straightened his shoulders and came to stand in front of her. 'I need to know if I'm going as your friend or as your lover.'

'Go as my friend,' she said. 'Come back as my friend.' She smiled at him. 'No more and certainly no less.'

He was searching her face, trying to work out if she was telling him what she really thought. She'd spent too much time with him, that was the trouble. She had learned at the feet of a master all there was to know about hiding her feelings.

'You said last week you'd give me a decision about us. Is that it?'

She laid her hand on the lapel of his jacket: the affectionate gesture of a friend, not the tender touch of a lover. 'That's it,' she said brightly. 'Now go, Dick Whittington. Go and seek your fortune. Come back and see me sometimes, though.' Damn, her voice had gone husky—

There were young footsteps running along the corridor outside the room. Urgent knocking was followed by panicky shouting. 'Miss Shaw! Mr Cunningham! Spain on the line! Mr Dewar says you've both to come straightaway.'

They knew immediately that something was wrong. Every copytaker in the room was on his or her feet, clustered around Alan Dewar's cubbyhole. It was their unusual silence which struck Josie.

'Hold on a minute,' Alan said into his mouthpiece. He peeled the headphones off and stood up, ushering her into his chair before he spoke further. 'Josie,' he said, 'you're going to have to brace yourself.'

'Bad news?' asked Roddy, moving to stand behind her.

'The worst.'

Alan put the headphones on her. As Roddy placed his hands firmly on her shoulders, Josie took a deep breath and prepared to talk to Sally.

Not Ben. Oh please God, don't let something have happened to Ben. Oh please God— But it was Ben's voice she heard on the other end of the crackly line. That was odd. As the person filing the written reports, it was usually always Sally who phoned.

All the same, the relief threatened to overwhelm Josie. Ben was all right. She began to tune in to what he was telling her, half-sobbing as he said the words.

And as she listened to them, her face turned the colour of marble.

Chapter 30

It was the shock and disbelief which kept Josie going over the next twenty-four hours, sustaining her while she and Roddy co-wrote Sally's obituary. Only when that appeared in the paper the following day, under the heading of *Spanish Conflict Claims Life of Dispatch Journalist*, did she break down, going blindly into the arms which were waiting for her.

'Obituaries are for old people,' she sobbed against his shoulder. Seeing the words in black and white had made it real, bringing it home with the most brutal of impacts. 'Folk who've had years and years of life. Tell me it's not true, Roddy,' she begged. 'Tell me we've all made some terrible mistake!'

'Oh Jo,' he murmured, pressing his lips against her soft dark hair. 'If only I could . . .'

During the painful and difficult days which followed he was never very far from her side, comforting her when the letter she wrote to Ben's parents received only the most formal of acknowledgements and no offer to take their bereaved son in when he came home. They went together to visit Sally's parents.

While Josie silently held hands with a woman she had never met before in her life, Roddy managed to carry on some sort of a conversation with Mr Fleming, politely but firmly responding to a query about his daughter's possessions with the information that what became of those was surely up to Mr Gold. Perhaps Mr and Mrs Fleming might care to call at Mrs Beaton's

328

when their son-in-law returned from Spain.

Something flared in Sally's mother's eyes at that description of Ben. Josie felt sure it was the hope that her stiff and unyielding spouse would agree to them establishing some sort of relationship with the man their daughter had loved. She wished fervently that it might be so.

After a garbled telephone call from London, Ben himself stumbled off the train at Glasgow Central one sunlit evening two weeks later. As Josie hugged him and Roddy laid a sympathetic hand on his back, it was clear that their friend was helpless with grief, barely coherent or able to function. God only knew how he had managed to travel halfway across Europe by himself. It made Josie think of a wounded animal, using sheer instinct to crawl back home and find a safe, dark place in which to lick its wounds.

Once they got to Mrs Beaton's, Roddy watched as Josie and the landlady coaxed Ben into taking a few spoonfuls of soup. Then he helped the two women undress him and get him into bed. It was like dealing with a very large child, one too young to be able to do anything for himself.

'Would I perhaps ask the doctor to call?' Mrs Beaton asked anxiously as they sat in her sitting room discussing the situation.

'Might be as well to get him checked over,' Roddy said, stretching his long legs out on the hearth rug. Even although it was the middle of summer, there was still a small fire burning in the grate. 'Although I suspect we'll only be told what we already know: that he needs food and sleep and comforting.'

His hand went to the inside pocket of his jacket. It withdrew before it got there but Mrs Beaton, correctly interpreting the gesture, was already on her feet to fetch him an ashtray. Roddy looked up at Josie, standing on the other side of the fireplace. 'Sorry, Jo. Would you mind?'

She waved a hand in permission. Knowing that she disliked the smell, he rarely smoked in her company. She reckoned he had more than deserved this particular cigarette. 'Ben's going to need someone with him all the time,' she said, thinking gratefully that at least her fellow lodger was away at the moment, it being the university vacation. 'I know you would volunteer, Mrs B, but you've got your housework and everything else that you do. You'll be here if I need you?'

'Of course, lass,' Mrs Beaton said, and went off in search of the whisky bottle to give Roddy a small nightcap before he went home. Josie looked down at him.

'I'm just assuming I can take those holidays that are due to me, Roddy. Is that all right?'

'Of course. You've accumulated a fortnight, haven't you? I'll come every evening, give you a bit of a break. If we don't see any improvement at the end of two weeks, I'll take some time off and we can swap over.'

She nodded, knowing both of them couldn't be away from the *Dispatch* at the same time. Roddy would be covering her work as well as his own over the next two weeks. That thought brought back something which recent events had pushed completely out of her head. 'What about London?'

'What about it?' he asked blankly.

'Well, I presume they're not very pleased about you postponing your transfer.'

He shrugged. 'It can't be helped. I can hardly leave you to cope with Ben by yourself, can I?' He took a draw on his cigarette and turned his head to stare into the fire.

Mentally preparing herself for Ben to start talking about Sally, Josie grew more and more uneasy as the week wore on. He had said very little, coming out with only a few jerky half sentences which she pieced together and transmitted to Roddy one evening as they sat in her room.

'Apparently they'd been working solidly for weeks and they got to the stage where they had to decide whether they were going to stay on longer or come home. I think they'd fallen in love with Spain,' she said thoughtfully. 'Despite all the horrors of the war.'

Her eyes were fixed on the two figures visible through the open French windows of her room. Having cajoled Ben into taking a turn around the garden with her, Mrs Beaton had obviously just invited him to smell some of the flowers in her herbaceous border. He was bending over obediently to do so. He did everything that way: went to bed and got up when Josie told him to and sat down meekly at the table at mealtimes.

She knew very well that he lay awake for most of the night. As she could see that he ate practically nothing, merely pushed the food about the plate. Painfully thin already, the doctor had warned that if he didn't start sleeping and eating properly very soon he was going to make himself physically ill.

'Anyway,' she continued, 'they realised they needed a break, so they went to a pension in this small town up the coast from Barcelona for a few days: as far away from the front line as they could get.' She paused, a lump in her throat.

Roddy's voice was very gentle. 'Only it wasn't far enough?'

Josie nodded, and found her own voice again. 'They'd been having a long lie one morning, laughing and joking and teasing each other about whose turn it was to go to the baker's in the town square and buy some bread for their breakfast. Sally told Ben he was a lazy lump and that she would go. He'd better have organised some coffee by the time she came back.'

She stopped to take a hasty little breath, and Roddy leaned forward and took her hands in his. 'There was just the one plane,' she managed. 'According to what the survivors said it would appear to have been a stray member of the Condor Legion.'

'Offloading from a bigger bombing raid somewhere else before he went back to his base?' Roddy suggested softly.

Josie nodded again. Her too-vivid imagination was painting a picture of a devastated market square in that small Spanish town, death and destruction swooping down out of a clear blue sky.

Roddy's voice grew softer still. 'And Ben thinks it should have been him.'

'Yes. That's what he keeps saying. *It should have been me.* I asked him today what Sally would have said about him not eating and he just gave me this odd wee smile and said he was sorry he was being such a nuisance to everybody but that we wouldn't have to bother about him for much longer. Oh, Roddy,' she said, raising anguished eyes to his face, 'what are we going to do? I can't work out how to help him!'

Roddy took a firmer grip on her hands. 'I don't know,' he said grimly, 'but we will think of something—' He broke off. 'Did he bring his camera stuff back?'

The seeming irrelevance of the question caused Josie to wrinkle her forehead in puzzlement. 'Aye, it's all in his room. Why?'

He pulled her to her feet. 'Quick,' he said. 'Before he comes back in.'

Sally was smiling at them, a big beaming grin on her lovely face. Sitting on a large flat rock on a sunny beach with her head tilted back and her arms gracefully outstretched, the former Miss Fleming was adopting a model-like pose. It was comically at odds with her tumbling auburn tresses – longer and more tousled than Josie had ever seen them – and her uncharacteristically casual clothes. Black canvas trousers and a blue fisherman's jersey were topped by a checked shirt of Ben's, its ends knotted around her trim waist.

Biting her lip and furiously trying not to weep, Josie lifted her eyes from the picture, one of several on the undeveloped spools which had been in Ben's camera bag and which Roddy had got the *Dispatch* photo lab to print and enlarge. The three of them had been sitting around the small table set in the bay window of Roddy's sitting room for the last twenty minutes looking at them. Josie dared a quick glance at Ben's face. It was completely impassive.

Following Roddy's lead, she had done her best to comment on the photographs, chatting as naturally as she could about what Sally was wearing or speculating on where the different shots had been taken. That hadn't been easy. Especially when Ben had passed no comment at all on any of the photos.

Josie felt a great wave of despair break over her. The picture of Sally sitting on the big rock was the last one, and the most striking. If he wasn't going to react to it, he wasn't going to react at all. She looked at Roddy and couldn't quite interpret the discreet gesture she got in return. Did he agree that his idea hadn't worked out, or did he think they should keep trying?

Ben was looking at the picture, giving it more attention than he had accorded some of the others. Then he raised his head and fixed his gaze on the dining-room window. After such a long silence, the sound of his voice came as a shock. 'Please take the pix away. I don't want to look at them any more.'

Josie reached out to sweep up the photos but Roddy's hands came over her own, preventing her from doing so.

'Why do you want us to take them away, Ben?'

'I just do.'

'I'm afraid that's not good enough,' Roddy said lightly. 'We're journalists, you know, we always need an answer to our questions. In fact, we'd like you to examine this picture in some detail, tell us what you see in it.' He released Josie's hands and picked up the last photograph, raising it in an attempt to force Ben to look at it again.

'Roddy, I'm not sure we should—'

He continued as though she hadn't spoken. 'You know what I see in this, Ben? I see a woman in love. Wouldn't you agree, Jo?'

Not at all sure they were doing the right thing, Josie nevertheless took her cue. He was right. Face glowing and eyes merry, Sally was looking directly into the camera. The viewer could be in absolutely no doubt that she was in love with the man operating it.

'Look at it, Ben.' Roddy's voice was no longer light. Hard and steely, it was the voice of a man who wasn't prepared to take no for an answer. Perhaps Ben hoped that if he did as Roddy asked, they would leave him alone. Perhaps he was simply too tired to resist any more. He transferred his gaze to the picture.

'What do you see?'

It came out all in a rush. 'I see a beautiful girl who died three days after that shot was taken. Because some stupid bastard wanted to go adventuring in Spain.'

'That beautiful girl loved you,' Roddy said. 'That beautiful girl wanted to go on the adventure just as much as you did.'

Ben had begun to shake his head. 'I didn't deserve her love. I wasn't worthy of it.'

'Och Ben,' Josie burst out, unable to contain herself, 'of course you were!'

He turned to her, his dark eyes full of pain. 'I wasn't good enough for her, Josie. Not the husband she deserved.' He gave her a smile which threatened to break her heart. 'Not a real man, you see. You know that.'

She reached out to him but he stood up, pushing his chair away so violently that it crashed to the floor. 'I tried to be a proper husband to her, Josie. Oh God, how I tried! But I couldn't be what I'm not.' As he stepped away from the table Roddy was already on his feet.

'Not a real man,' Ben repeated. 'Not the husband she deserved.' He was still walking backwards, Roddy quietly closing in on him. Josie stood up and went to join them.

'A woman like Sally could have had any man she wanted. Why did she pick a useless specimen like me?' Now up against the wall, he was shaking his head again, moving it angrily from side to side. If they didn't put a stop to this soon, he was going to really hurt himself.

'I'll hold him,' Roddy murmured. Taking Ben by surprise, he grabbed him and spun him round, pinioning his arms so that he couldn't move. Weakened as he was by his refusal to eat, he was no match for anybody: not even Josie, who reached up and cupped his face between her hands.

'Listen to me, Ben. *Listen to me!*' She couldn't bear it. He looked like a trapped animal. Obeying a sudden instinct, she lowered her voice to a whisper. 'Please listen to me, Ben. Please. Ben, come on. Please.'

Was it working? He had quietened a little, although he obviously wasn't prepared to look her in the eye.

'It made Sally so happy to be your wife. It really did. Do you know what she once told me? That love means accepting the other person wholeheartedly, the things you don't like about them as much as those that you do. Sally loved so many things about you, Ben. You made her very happy. You really did.'

She repeated it all, over and over again, trying to soothe him both with the meaning of the words and the softness of her voice. Just when she thought she wasn't going to be able to keep it up any longer, the dark eyes focused on her face. '*Did* I make her happy, Josie?'

'Oh, yes. You did.' Sending up a silent prayer of thankfulness, she pressed her advantage. 'But Sally wouldn't be happy to see you like this, Ben. She'd want you to sleep and eat and do your best to get well again.'

'Would she?'

'You know she would. You know how much she loved you.'

He stared at her for a long moment. Then, still held fast in Roddy's grip, he slumped, buckling at the knees. Together they got him over to one of the two sofas in the room and while Josie slipped off his shoes, Roddy fetched a blanket to cover him with. Once they were sure he was asleep, they made their way quietly through to the kitchen.

'Oh, Roddy,' she said. He stretched out one long finger and tilted her chin up, planting a light kiss on her lips. He might have prolonged it if she hadn't pulled away. She felt completely drained, drowning in emotion.

Roddy didn't comment. Pulling out one of the chairs set round the kitchen table he sank heavily down into it. Josie followed suit and for a good quarter of an hour neither of them said a word.

'It's a hell of a powerful thing,' he observed at last. 'Love, that is.'

'Aye.' She glanced across at him. 'Want a drink?'

'I'll get us something in a minute,' he responded, but it was some time before he rose to his feet and fetched a corkscrew and a bottle of red wine. As he placed them on the table, the voice from the open doorway of the kitchen made them both jump.

'Could I maybe have something to eat?'

Roddy placed a quelling hand on Josie's shoulder and went to meet Ben, ushering him towards the table. 'Of course you can, old chap. Come and sit down here. Jo can pour out the wine while I cook us all a meal.'

Doing her best to emulate Roddy's matter-of-fact approach, Josie handed Ben his glass and tried not to watch as he began to sip from it.

He was following Roddy's movements as he strode

around the kitchen gathering up cooking utensils and ingredients. 'He's a dab hand at the cooking, eh?' He was smiling at her. Or trying to, at least.

Recognising with deep thankfulness that they had turned a corner, she smiled back. 'He's no' bad. I'll miss him when he goes to London.'

Copper pan in one hand and a large onion in the other, Roddy swung round. 'I am going to London then, am I?'

'Of course you are.'

Roddy looked at her for a second or two, then glanced at Ben, including him in the conversation. 'She just wants me out of the way, you know.'

Josie gazed up at him uncomprehendingly.

'It achieves an ambition for you too,' he pointed out. 'You'll be Features Editor once I go.'

'Oh yes,' she said, with a weary smile. 'So I will.'

PART IV

Chapter 31

1941

'So this is the *Dispatch* in wartime!' Smart in her WVS uniform, Pamela MacPherson looked around her with interest. In Glasgow for a conference of the women's organisation formed the year before war had broken out – one of many domestic responses to the long-running international crisis which had preceded that event – Pamela was spending the night with Josie before driving home to Kingussie the following morning. Having volunteered to bring some government bigwig visiting one of the several mysterious establishments now dotting the Highlands down to Glasgow, she'd been granted a precious few extra gallons of petrol.

'Only a shadow of our former selves, I'm afraid,' Josie said in response to her comment. 'You're not seeing us at our best.'

'On the contrary,' Pamela said vehemently. 'I'm most impressed. Turning out a newspaper every day with only a skeleton staff can't be easy.'

'It's certainly a challenge. Especially since a large proportion of that staff is either very young or completely inexperienced. Although,' she said, ushering Pamela through from her own office into the Features Department proper, 'several of our pensioners have rallied round, come out of retirement to lend a hand. The legendary Miss Clarke gives us three days a week. She spent years on the News Desk here and she's still as sharp as a tack. Then there's the doyen of copytakers, Robert Bruce. He's

341

back with us every weekday morning.'

'Wonderful name,' Pamela murmured. 'I take it your own role is no longer confined to simply being the Features Editor.'

'I'm doing a bit of everything: News Desk, sub-editing, even copytaking if everyone else is busy.' Josie grinned. 'Making the tea, manning the front desk and a spot of fire-watching as well. It's all hands to the pumps at the moment.'

'And you're without an overall editor now, I believe. Does that make life more difficult?'

'Not a bit of it. We were all glad to see the back of that man. He seemed to have the gift of setting people against each other. Now we're all co-operating. We have to. There's always a new problem to contend with. For example, our allocation of newsprint has been cut again. I fear another cut in the number of pages is looming.'

'An unforeseen consequence of the fall of Norway,' Pamela observed. 'The shortage of newsprint, I mean.'

'I don't think it was necessarily unforeseen, I think it was simply too late to do anything about it. We couldn't grow forests overnight, that was the trouble.'

'You mentioned fire-watching. Glasgow's had quite a few air raids, then?'

'Aye. Nothing like London, though. I don't know how they cope, I really don't.'

'You worry about Roddy.'

Josie met Pamela's sympathetic eyes. 'Of course,' she said simply. 'I almost feel it'll be a relief when he gets accredited as a war correspondent and starts travelling about. Although he'll only be out of the frying pan into the fire: where the bullets are flying rather than where the bombs are dropping.' She gave Pamela a wry smile. 'That's exactly what he wants, of course. Quite a lot of us had a tough job convincing him he shouldn't just join up as an ordinary foot soldier.'

'Because this war needs goods journalists too,' Pamela said. 'What's Roddy doing while he's waiting to go?'

'A stint at the Mystery of Information. The journalists on all the big newspapers and newspaper groups take their turn. It means that the rest of us have a contact there, allows us to submit our pieces to the censors and get them back much more quickly. Speed is of the essence in our business. It took a wee while for the government to realise that but it works quite smoothly now.'

Pamela nodded thoughtfully. Then she gave Josie an odd look. 'Don't you mean the *Ministry* of Information?'

'No,' Josie said darkly, 'I got it right the first time.'

Pamela laughed. 'It does all get a bit cloak and dagger sometimes, doesn't it?' Her eyes went to a large framed photograph on the wall. 'Who is that most attractive young woman?' She walked across to examine the picture more closely. 'Oh,' she said, 'I'm sorry. This is your friend who died in Spain, isn't it?'

'It's all right. I like to talk about her.'

She joined Pamela in front of the photo. 'Her husband took that a few days before she was killed.'

Stopping short, Josie lifted the back of her hand to her mouth. Four years on, the realisation that all of that love and life and generosity of spirit which had been Sally had been snuffed out in a few seconds could still catch her unawares, lacerating her emotions with a strength and power which recalled the shock and disbelief she had felt on first hearing the news.

Locked in behind the Pyrenees, the Spaniards were now under the heel of a Fascist dictatorship as ruthless as those operating in Germany and Italy. Having indeed used Spain's tragedy as an awful dress rehearsal, the Axis powers were now throwing all the knowledge and experience they had gained there against Britain and her allies.

Pamela patted Josie's shoulder until she had recovered. 'So tragic for her husband to become a widower after only a few months of marriage. What's he doing now?'

'He joined up as soon as he could. He's got more reasons than most to want to fight the Nazis. It was a German bomb which killed Sally, and he's Jewish, of course. He also thought he'd have a better chance of plying his trade within the army than outside it. Censorship's even more difficult for photographers than it is for journalists.' She indicated the door. 'Would you like to see our fire-watching station on the roof?' she asked. 'The moon's out, providing us both with enough light to see by and a suitable atmosphere for the tale of a former editor's room where things are said to go bump in the night.'

'Oh goody,' Pamela said. 'I do love a ghost story.'

They found Alan Dewar on the top of the building, ensconced in a steamer chair with a blanket over him and a sleeping bag ready to slip into when the crisp March night grew colder still. It had been a fine day, unseasonably warm for the time of year. He was surrounded by a motley selection of fire-fighting equipment, including a stirrup pump and several buckets of sand and water.

'The only able-bodied man we have left,' Josie called cheerfully as they approached him through the moonlight.

'Not through my choice,' he grumbled. Considerably frustrated at being a mere two years outwith the age range for the call-up, he did everything else he could for the war effort. Like Pamela's husband Douglas, Alan was one of the leading lights of his local Home Guard troop.

'When I'm not keeping an eye on this tinder-box,' he told Pamela after he had said hello to her. The two of them had met on several previous occasions. 'We wouldn't want any of Miss Shaw's deathless prose to go up in flames, would we now?'

'And your own,' Josie reminded him.

'You're writing too, now?' Pamela asked.

'Gamekeeper turned poacher. A sad comedown.'

'Come off it,' Josie said. 'It'll be good practice for the

great Scottish novel you've been going to write for the past fifteen years.'

'Don't think I'll ever get round to it now, flower,' he said sadly.

'Of course you will,' she said. 'Once all this lot is over. You could be composing it in your head while you're sitting up here.'

'I'm doing a wee bit more than that,' he said, looking just a little guilty. He slipped a hand into the sleeping bag and brought out a notebook and pencil.

'Aha!' Pamela said. 'So you haven't given up on your dream. Well done, you.'

The night was suddenly rent by the banshee wail of the air-raid siren. As it whooped and shrieked its warning the three people on the roof looked questioningly at each other. Wisely deciding not to compete with the racket reverberating and bouncing off the buildings around them, Pamela mouthed a question. 'False alarm?' Those were so common as to almost be routine.

Alan shook his head. Pulling on his earlobe with one hand, he pointed skywards with the other. Listening intently, trying to hear other sounds currently being masked by the siren, Josie could at first detect nothing. Then she got it. The drone of aeroplane engines in the distance was unmistakeable.

'Not ours,' she mouthed.

Alan shook his head again. As the siren finally stopped, he repeated Josie's words. 'Not ours,' he confirmed. 'Not very far off either. I think we could hazard a guess as to where they're heading.' Turning, he set his face towards the west: to Clydebank, a few miles downriver from where they stood on the roof. 'You could say this is long overdue,' he said grimly. 'They were bound to want to hit it.'

The two women followed his gaze. Josie caught a glimpse of the Clyde, gleaming like a white ribbon in the moonlight. Oh God, she thought, that's going to make it even easier for them. Alan was right, of course he was. With its shipyards working at full tilt, its oil depots, power station and factories – including the giant Singer sewing machine complex which had been turned over to munitions for the duration – Clydebank had always been going to be a target for German bombs.

The engine noise was building now, beginning to surround them on all sides. They must be coming in from more than one direction, probably some from France and undoubtedly some from Norway, flying into a deadly rendezvous over Clydebank. A town full of shipyards and factories. A town full of people – fifty thousand men, women and children.

Mesmerised by what was happening – the bombers were now dropping flares to illuminate their target even further – it didn't occur to Josie, Pamela or Alan that they should seek shelter. They jumped when the sound of the first impacts reached them. The sight of the first flames shooting up into the air made them gasp.

'Those'll be from incendiaries,' Alan muttered. 'More light for the bastards to see by.' He didn't apologise for the swearword. He didn't need to. A spasm of an emotion she couldn't quite define flashed through Josie's throat and chest. There was fear in there, anger too. There was also resolution. She looked up at Alan.

'Are we going to stand here watching Clydebank burn or are we going to do what people like you and me are supposed to do on occasions like this?'

'You want to go down there?' He studied her face thoughtfully. Whatever he saw in it obviously satisfied him. 'All right,' he said. 'Let me get a replacement fire-watcher up here and then we'll work out how the hell we're going to get to Clydebank with all of this going on.'

'I've got a car,' came a bright voice. 'It's even got some petrol in it.'

They turned together to look at Pamela. She shrugged

like a Frenchwoman. 'I'm wearing a uniform,' she pointed out. 'There are things people like me are supposed to do on occasions like this too.'

It was much worse than any of them could have imagined – like a hideous parody of Guy Fawkes's night. Noise. Smoke. Flames. Sparks. They were driving into the most terrible danger.

Pamela took them as far as she could. A crater in the road stopped them. They looked at each other and solemnly asked if everyone wanted to proceed. When all three of them said yes, they got out of the car. They would have to cover the rest of the distance on foot.

With Pamela at their side, Josie and Alan then followed the noblest precepts of their much maligned profession. Instead of running away from the burning buildings, they headed straight for them.

Chapter 32

'*The baby is dead, but the mother who cradles her so tenderly in her arms isn't ready to accept that yet. For the sake of the wide-eyed and bandaged toddler sitting more quietly than a child ever should on the camp bed beside her, she must be persuaded to relinquish her precious burden. A young woman dressed in the uniform of an auxiliary nurse does this with a tender firmness which is beautiful to observe.*

'*While the bombs were dropping on this Clydeside town last night, she and a group of medical student friends from Glasgow's Western Infirmary made their way through those bombs to do what they could for the injured and the dying. One of them tells me quietly not to make them out to be heroes. "We just wanted to help," he says. "We're doing what anybody would".*'

'It's terrific, Jo,' came Roddy's voice over the phone line, 'but let me stop you for a moment. They won't pass that mention of a dead baby. I can tell you that right now.'

'I was afraid of that,' Josie said, her tone one of glum resignation. 'It really weakens the piece to take it out, though.'

'I know,' he said consolingly, 'but you'll manage it. Come at it obliquely. Suggest the horrors the nurse and the medical students were having to deal with. Do you want to re-jig it and phone me back as quickly as possible? That way you can get it into the paper for tonight.'

'All right,' she said. 'I suppose we do have to put "*a Clydeside town*"? We can't mention Clydebank by name?'

'I'm afraid not. The censors might not even allow that

reference to the Western, at least not until the powers-that-be are sure the Germans do know where they hit.'

'Roddy,' she said in exasperation, 'this was a planned raid. Those *Luftwaffe* pilots knew exactly where they were.'

'It's daft,' he agreed, 'but you know what this lot are like. Leave the hospital's name in and we'll see what they say. Right, speak to you shortly.'

Twenty minutes later she phoned him down the amended article. Half an hour after that he called back to let her know it had been passed. Josie yelled for a copyboy, handed over the typescript and asked the lad to close the door on his way out. Now that the business part of their conversation was out of the way Roddy posed a personal question, his voice low and concerned. 'Are you all right, Jo? It sounds as if things got pretty rough last night.'

Perched on the corner of her desk, Josie raised her head and looked out of the window of her office. She saw what she always saw when she did that, the building on the opposite side of Buchanan Street. There were other pictures intruding this morning, sharp and horribly vivid in her mind's eye.

The bombers had pounded Clydebank for hour after hour, almost until first light. Once the all-clear had sounded at half past six she and Alan had walked out into the town, leaving Pamela at the first-aid station where they had spent most of the night. Mrs MacPherson had still been going strong, getting ready with other WVS colleagues to serve tea to the rescue squads hurrying towards Clydebank from all over the west of Scotland and beyond.

It hadn't taken Alan and Josie long to realise the magnitude of the task which confronted those squads. Picking their way through ripped-up tramlines and over the water pouring like rivers out of burst mains, it quickly became clear that the devastation was horrendous. The awe-inspiring scale and extent of it was given added weight by the eerie silence which hung over the town.

Whole tenement blocks had crumpled into heaps of stone and rubble. Roof beams and wooden spars stuck out of the impromptu hillocks at crazy angles. Other buildings which still stood no longer had any front or side walls. Ripped off by the force of a nearby blast, the homes inside them were pitifully exposed. The pathetic remains of kitchens and living rooms where people had been quietly listening to the nine o'clock news on the wireless, all unaware of what was heading their way, was a poignant metaphor for the hundreds of lives which had been wrecked.

Josie wondered what the final death toll was going to be. She also wondered if the newspapers were going to be permitted to report it.

They had seen several bodies. Alan reckoned some people must have been caught in the street while they were trying to get home or to a shelter, and that others had been blown out of buildings by the force of a particular explosion. The idea of flying helplessly through the night air to your death had upset Josie more than anything. When they had come upon a young boy lying in the middle of the road she had crouched beside his lifeless form for a long, long time.

'Jo?' came Roddy's voice. 'Speak to me, Jo.'

She turned away from the window. The image of that boy's face was one of the many pictures she couldn't seem to get out of her head. 'It was terrible. Absolutely dreadful. But I'm fine. I'm all right.'

'Josephine.' The reproach in Roddy's voice was coming through loud and clear, all the way along the four hundred miles of telephone line which both linked and separated them. 'Remember who you're talking to. Don't tell me you're fine. Tell me how you really feel.'

'Och Roddy, I'm feeling all sorts of things!'

'Elucidate,' he commanded gently. 'I'm not going anywhere for a while.'

She gave him all of it, feeling immediate relief at being able to share the shock and anger and distress with someone who knew exactly what she was talking about. Roddy had experienced the London Blitz, night after night of it. 'I understand your *Letter from London* much better now,' Josie told him.

That was a column he filed as a weekly diary. During the very worst of the prolonged bombing of the capital it had taken a deliberately light-hearted view of the whole thing, mirroring the stubborn determination of London's population. Roddy had repeated the rude jokes going the rounds against the Nazi leadership – those that were printable, at any rate – and highlighted individual acts of defiance like the shops with their windows blown in which bore notices informing their customers that they were *More Open Than Usual*.

Josie quoted that story back at him, telling him of similar sights she had seen in Clydebank this morning. 'It was like yesterday evening,' she said, 'with the nurse and the medical students. Everybody kept cracking these really awful jokes.'

'Human nature at its best,' he said. 'Human nature at its worst. You see both under these sorts of circumstances.'

'Roddy,' she said hesitantly, 'I've got all these really conflicting emotions as well . . .'

'Go on.'

'Have you got time? Other folk are probably trying to get through to you.'

'Let 'em wait,' he said blithely. 'Tell me about your conflicting emotions.'

'Well, I'm sad and upset of course. Desperately sorry for the people who were killed and injured. Angry at Hitler and the Nazis for starting all of this. Och Roddy, I'm also really glad to be alive. Almost exhilarated that I survived it,' she confessed. 'Is that a terrible thing to feel when so many people have died?'

'It's a natural thing to feel and I know exactly what you mean. I've felt it too. You just want to go and do something to prove to yourself that you *are* still alive.'

'Is it natural to be callous? I looked at that mother with the dead baby last night and observed her. I watched quite coolly how the nurse dealt with her.'

'That's not callous,' he chided softly. 'That's being detached. How much use do you think your nurse would have been if she hadn't been able to maintain some detachment? It's a very necessary quality in both her profession and our own.'

'D'you really think so, Roddy? I thought I must be getting as hard as nails.'

'You're not hard,' he said, the words expelled on an affectionate laugh. 'If you haven't already done it, you'll cry for that baby soon enough. And the boy in the street and all the other things you saw. Last night and this morning you were a professional journalist and therefore couldn't allow your feelings to get the better of you.'

'I'm not sure how professional I was. Both Alan and I ended up helping. We mucked in with Pamela.'

'Jo,' he said firmly, 'that's called being human.'

Josie slid off her desk. 'You're a very comforting person to talk to, you know.'

'I've helped then, have I?'

'You certainly have. I suppose we'd both better get back to work. As your father used to say, time and tide wait for no man.'

There was a smile in his voice. 'Aye,' he said. His accent was always more Scottish at the end of a phone call to her than at the beginning of it. 'Listen, Jo. Phone me whenever you like if you're feeling the need of someone to talk to. Here or at the flat. Any hour of the day or night.'

'You never sleep?' she queried, amused at the typically extravagant invitation.

'Something like that. Speak to you soon, darling.'

After she had replaced the receiver Josie stood where she was for a minute or two, staring at the solid black telephone. Their friendship was as strong as ever, cemented by the frequency with which they spoke to each other. Run off their feet as they both were, their working calls invariably ended with a few moments of personal chit-chat, punctuated on his side by the usual casual endearments: the ones he used with everybody.

She had no idea whether he still harboured romantic feelings towards her. The two of them seemed to have taken a step back from all of that. When he returned to Glasgow at Christmas or for a week or two each summer they did spend a lot of time together. Then again, since Josie had agreed to his suggestion of moving to Charing Cross Mansions, that was natural enough.

She had rejected the offer of simply taking over his own home on the grounds that it would give rise to gossip at the *Dispatch*, but over the four years of his absence she had become very familiar with it, running upstairs frequently to check all was well and to pick up any letters for sending on.

Sometimes she lingered there for an hour or so. Curled up in the corner of one of his big sofas with a selection of his poetry books scattered around her, she could imagine he was simply out in the kitchen concocting some exotic meal for them both. She missed him, and she didn't mind admitting it. That was natural enough too. He was her friend.

She was glad he still called Glasgow home – he described his flat in London as *bijou*, translating that for her as *a wee bit on the poky side* – but it was really just as well their relationship had not developed into a romantic one. Sometimes she wondered if they'd both got a bit carried away when Sally and Ben had married, swept up in the romance of it all.

She was convinced now that getting involved with Roddy in that way would only have made life unnecessarily complicated. Remaining good friends was a much more sensible option.

They were good enough friends for her not to hesitate too much before phoning him early one morning two weeks after the Clydebank Blitz, when the pictures roaming about her head hadn't diminished or grown any less disturbing. She'd had a sleepless night with them, eventually admitting defeat at five o'clock and getting up to make herself some tea. At six o'clock she picked up the phone and put a call through to Roddy's flat.

Unlike herself, the woman who answered the phone had obviously slept well the night before. The sophisticated voice was slow, heavy and relaxed. Hideously embarrassed, Josie muttered something about a wrong number and hastily hung up.

Well, had she really been so naïve as to think Roderick Cunningham had spent four years in London without female company? He'd never mentioned any woman as occupying a special place in his life, but then again, he was a gentleman. He'd always been discreet about his affairs.

As she washed and dressed for the day ahead, Josie told herself again that she'd been absolutely right to make the decision she had four years ago. The man clearly wasn't cut out for settling down with one woman for the rest of his life.

Two months after the bombing of Clydebank the port of Greenock was subjected to the same treatment. Shortly after that another airborne German caused something of a stir in the west of Scotland.

The man who parachuted into a field near Eaglesham

and was taken into custody by the local Home Guard turned out to be Rudolf Hess, second-in-command to Adolf Hitler himself. The censors allowed the news of his arrival to be passed on to the public remarkably quickly, within a matter of days. Josie presumed their reasoning was that this was the first sign of a crack within the leadership of the Third Reich.

Some believed Hess had come to sue for peace. He himself claimed he wanted to persuade the British of the wisdom of accepting a negotiated one with his master. He had landed where he did because he hoped to meet up with the Duke of Hamilton. Another theory was that Hess had made the flight because he was mentally unbalanced and had been very much on a one-man mission when he had taken off from the Messerschmitt works in Augsburg in Bavaria.

The speculation kept the rumour mills grinding for months. The Ministry of Information saw to it that very few of those rumours ever reached the newspapers. Whilst reluctantly seeing the need for the continuing censorship, some of the restrictions imposed continued to irk Josie and her colleagues within the fourth estate.

After the Americans entered the war at the end of 1941 their servicemen began flooding into Britain. Thousands of them disembarked at a recovering Greenock. Its docks had been more than busy since the very beginning of hostilities but it could only ever be referred to as a 'northern port' – which could have been almost anywhere. Since the enemy could hardly fail to notice such large troop movements, Josie thought it was a pity the place didn't get the credit for everything it was doing towards the war effort.

By that time Roddy had ceased to be her conduit to the people wielding the blue pencils. Having gained his coveted accreditation as a war correspondent, he started making trips he couldn't tell her about until he was safely home from them and the resultant articles had appeared in the papers.

His first, shortly after the New Year, was to visit the fleet at Scapa Flow. When he phoned her afterwards he informed her grandly that he had very probably flown over her head on his way back to London. Then he made her laugh with a dramatic description of the terrors of the choppy Pentland Firth – especially on a cold and inhospitable January day – and his own blind terror that he might make a fool of himself in front of 'all those rufty-tufty matelots' by being seasick.

'And me in a dead smart uniform too,' he said, treating her to his best Glasgow accent.

'A uniform?' Josie said in reply, responding to his teasing tone. 'Gosh, I'm impressed. I hope it's got a great big flash on it saying you're a reporter. I wouldn't want the other side to shoot at you.'

'Darling, some of our own side wouldn't be averse to taking a pot shot at a reporter or two.'

'Do they give you a gun so you can shoot back?' she asked. A prolonged silence greeted her question. 'Roddy?' she said again.

'I'm pondering what the right answer is,' came the voice from the other end of the phone. 'If I tell you I don't have a gun you'll probably worry about someone shooting me. If I tell you that I do – and/or that I've received some basic combat training – you'll probably worry about me doing someone else a mischief.'

He was perfectly correct. Whether he was armed or not, she worried more or less constantly about him. She was also very proud of him. Reading between the lines of what he wrote and what he told her, she deduced that he frequently ended up in some tight corners in his keenness to bring home the news. As a journalist he was a non-combatant but she had a strong suspicion there were occasions when he put himself at risk to help the fighting men to whom he became close over a series of assignments.

She was proud of his writing, too. That was appearing in several newspapers. Understandably enough, the Army, Air Force and Navy were often only willing to look after one nuisance of a reporter at a time. When that happened, a single journalist covered the event for everyone. Josie bought all the papers in which Roddy's dispatches appeared and pasted them up into a scrapbook. She often took it with her when she went visiting.

Mick Fitzgerald took a keen interest in Roddy's exploits. Alan and Deirdre and their growing family also liked to hear what Mr Cunningham had been up to, as did Carrie Campbell and her son. One wintry Sunday afternoon in March, Archie was sitting at his mother's kitchen table solemnly turning over the pages which contained his young great-uncle's articles while Carrie told Josephine the tale of her visit to the local Labour Exchange.

Determined to do her bit towards the war effort, the young mother had known from the outset that she wanted to work on the railways, more specifically at Partick where her father had been for many years the well-respected stationmaster. The station itself was minutes away from her present home in Dumbarton Road, she and her husband Matt having finally managed to break away from his parents.

The railway companies were desperately short of staff at the moment, many clerks and porters and signalmen having been called-up due to a shortage of manpower in the forces. Matthew Campbell was one of them. He had gone off to join the Argyll and Sutherland Highlanders a few weeks previously.

Since the gaps now left could largely only be filled by women volunteering to do the work, Carrie had been a little put out to discover she had to jump through several bureaucratic hoops before a position could be assigned to her. The interviewer she had encountered at the women's section of the Labour Exchange had obviously raised her hackles. It was the first time Josie had seen any evidence of the fiery temperament popularly supposed to go with red hair.

Tucking a strand of those beautiful glossy locks behind her ear, Carrie leaned forward and scooped her small daughter April up on to her lap. 'Och,' she said, 'the girl was just so snooty. You'll know the type.'

'Only too well. They think they're doing us all a favour.'

Carrie nodded vigorously. 'They also think they know it all but in fact they often don't know very much.' She frowned, thinking about it. 'Some of these people seem to me to have led very narrow lives.'

'Blinded by the walls around their own social circles,' Josie agreed, remembering the Gardiners. 'They're not even aware of how blinkered they are yet they feel qualified to pontificate about everyone and everything.'

'Yes,' Carrie said. 'That about sums up this girl. She had a really silly hat too,' she added scornfully.

Josie laughed. 'She did rub you up the wrong way, didn't she? What kind of questions did she ask?'

'Oh, she wondered if I realised I had an exemption from war work because I've got young children. I ask you,' Carrie said, rolling her eyes in outrage. 'Did she think I had porridge in my head instead of brains?'

It was good to see Roddy's niece-in-law like this, lively and animated and telling her story with gusto. This was how she remembered Carrie when she had first met her as a newlywed. Over the years the young woman had changed, becoming much quieter, almost subdued. Observing the interplay between her and her strikingly handsome husband, Josie had often wondered what was going on behind closed doors.

Matthew Campbell struck Josie as being a strange

mixture of a man. Sometimes he came over as charming, at others as arrogant and overly sure of himself. Roddy always said he was the sort of person you would want with you in an emergency: good in a crisis. Carrie herself had proudly told Josie how brave Matthew had been during the Blitz last year, making sure everyone in their tenement building got safely into the shelter in the back court and keeping everyone's spirits up during the terrifying hours they had spent there.

It was clear too that he loved Carrie and their children very deeply. It was also obvious that he was very possessive of his attractive young wife. On one or two occasions Josie had caught glimpses of the temper he might have on him if he was roused. Coupling those two characteristics with the quietening down of Carrie's personality had given rise to some terrible suspicions in her mind.

Those had hardened recently. Since Matthew had joined up and was away from home, Carrie seemed an awful lot happier. She and the children were certainly more relaxed, the tension Josie had so often noticed in the atmosphere pervading the Campbell household now completely absent.

'Do you know what else she had the gall to say?' Carrie asked. 'She wondered if going out to work wouldn't be too demanding for me.' She mimicked her interviewer's well-bred tones. ' ". . . Especially if you've been merely a housewife for the past few years, and not working at all". I had to stop myself from asking her to pick a window.'

Josie laughed again and held out her arms to April, who had just squirmed down from her mother's lap. 'Obviously your posh young lady has never done a washing. Or beaten a rug.'

'Or black-leaded a range,' Carrie contributed feelingly, looking with a mixture of love and hate at her own.

'Listen,' Josie said, bearing up womanfully as April practised her mountaineering skills, 'you've just given me an idea for an article. Ow!' she yelped as a small knee dug into her thigh. She glanced down at the little girl, a redhead like her mother. 'Have you got ants in your pants this afternoon, wee woman? Sit still or I'll tickle your feet.' She looked up at Carrie again. 'Maybe I should turn the tables on your interviewer. Do a piece on women like yourself who volunteer to do war work and the sort of difficulties they face trying to get work which suits them. She's based at the local Labour Exchange, you said?'

'Yes. Her name's Miss Simpson. I only know that because I pointed out to her that she hadn't even had the good manners to introduce herself to me. I can't remember her Christian name. Probably doesn't have one.'

'D'you think she'd agree to talk to me?'

'I don't see why not. Doubtless you'll have to go through the proper channels. April Campbell, what do you think you're doing?'

For April had peeled off her slippers and socks and was now presenting the sole of her foot to Josie. 'Tickle me,' she commanded.

'You asked for it, Miss C,' Josie said cheerfully.

Seven weeks later – Carrie had been dead right about having to go through the proper channels – Josephine knocked confidently on the door of the small office at the back of the Labour Exchange to which she'd been directed, and walked in without waiting to be summoned. She'd got out of that habit a long time ago.

Her interviewee was playing that game favoured by people who like everyone else to know how terribly important they are. Sat behind a desk with her eyes glued to the papers in front of her, she was clearly far too busy to be able to look up immediately. While she waited for her to tire of the play-acting, Josie studied her bowed head.

She saw brown hair as dark as her own and the elegant

clothes on which Carrie had commented. The claret-coloured costume and white blouse might be in approved Utility style, designed to avoid any wasteful frills and furbelows, but the material of which they were made was of the highest quality. Josie wondered if the extravagant hat which lay on the desk in front of Miss Simpson's papers was the one which had so offended Carrie.

It was a bit much, the size of a side-plate and adorned with net and a huge artificial lily. Hats were one of the few items of apparel not subject to the strictures of the Utility scheme and this one must have cost a fortune. Miss Simpson was obviously rather well-off although the overall effect was a little stiff for Josie's own taste. A bit too perjink, perhaps.

Even people who play silly games are curious to see who's come to visit them. Miss Simpson looked up at last. Josie studied a pale and pretty face and judged the girl to be in her mid-twenties. That was odd. She not only had hair the same colour as herself, her eyes were also exactly the same shade of grey.

Dark brown hair. Grey eyes. Perjink. The hairs on the back of Josie's neck stood up. She knew what Miss Simpson's first name was.

Chapter 33

'Rachel?'

The girl was staring at her. She's wondering why I'm using her first name, Josie thought, confused as to how I even know it. She took a few cautious steps forward. 'Don't you know me, Rachel? It's Josephine. Your sister Josie.'

Rachel continued to stare at her for a few seconds. Then the expression on her face changed.

'Aye,' Josie said eagerly. 'It's me. Do you recognise me now?' She started forward but Rachel stood up before she could get anywhere near her. There was something in her face now which halted Josie in her tracks.

'Rachel,' she said, her voice as gentle as she could possibly make it. 'There's nothing to worry about. It's all right, Rachel.'

Her sister spoke at last. 'There's a park round the corner. Can we go there?'

Josie had dreamed of this moment so many times. In those imaginings she and Rachel had run to each other, hugged and held each other, poured out everything that had happened to them over the years of separation. Never in a million years had she thought their reunion would be characterised by the kind of rigid silence being exhibited by the girl walking alongside her.

Even when they sat down on a bench in the small swing park Rachel seemed disinclined to speak. Thinking perhaps she might be overcome with emotion, Josie reached for her hand. Rachel withdrew it – abruptly, as if she'd been burned. Then she turned her head away.

Josie felt a great wave of guilt break over her. Did her sister blame her for what had happened? Had she perhaps, God forbid, been treated cruelly by the people with whom she'd been boarded out?

'Rachel,' she pleaded. 'Talk to me. Tell me what's happened to you since you left the Drygate.'

A tremor passed through Rachel's fashionably clad shoulders at the mention of that name. Josie was suddenly transported back to the last awful weekend her sister and Charlie had spent there, recalling in vivid detail the treatment she herself had endured at the hands of their stepfather. Oh dear God, she thought brokenly, they had been forced to witness that, had seen the big sister who was their protector and defender beaten and humiliated. That must have had a terrible effect on both of them.

Once more she reached out towards Rachel. She didn't jump this time but she did edge away. Josie pulled her hand back. If her sister didn't want to be touched she would have to respect that. If she didn't want to talk she would have to accept that too. Maybe it was too painful for her. Just as Josie had the thought, Rachel opened her mouth.

'I don't know what happened to Charlie. We were separated. Quite early on.'

Damping down the crushing disappointment provoked by those terse statements, Josie bit her tongue, sensing she would get less and less out of Rachel the more she badgered. She'd never had to use her interviewing skills so acutely. Allowing the pause to lengthen gave her the reward of some more information. It was a doubled-edged sword, one which stabbed viciously at her heart.

'He was so upset.' Rachel still had her face turned away, apparently staring at some children playing on a seesaw. 'He was shouting the place down. Calling for

Mammy.' The familiar term sounded so odd in the refined accent with which she now spoke. 'Calling for you.'

The sword had metamorphosed into a hundred tiny daggers, all of them stabbing at the backs of Josie's eyes. Dear brave wee Charlie who had tried in his childish innocence to stop his father from hitting her, dear sweet wee Charlie who had kissed her sore mouth better. He was as lost to her as he had ever been.

She forced back the tears. If she succumbed to her emotions she wouldn't be able to help Rachel, who had turned at last to look at her.

'They couldn't calm him down. Neither could I. The people took him away. I don't know where to.' She stopped abruptly and swallowed, visibly moved.

'You mustn't blame yourself for that,' Josie said huskily, having to force herself not to offer physical comfort. She was the big sister. It was up to her to try to understand, not to be hurt by how Rachel was reacting. But, oh God, it was hard! Difficult too not to pour out questions about what had happened to Charlie, useless though those would be. Rachel had clearly told her everything she knew.

'And you, Rachel,' Josie queried after another long pause, 'did they take you to some nice people?' *Some kind people in the country*. Please God, she was thinking, please God let it be so.

For the first time in this whole tortured conversation a spark of animation lit Rachel's face. 'Yes,' she said. 'They took me to the Simpsons.'

'They were good to you?'

'They've been everything to me,' she said simply. 'Looked after me and loved me and brought me up as one of their own. I have four big brothers.' She smiled. 'A great bunch of boys.'

'That's good,' Josie said, trying not to think of the other big brothers Rachel had had. 'I'm really glad to hear that. Mr and Mrs Simpson gave you an education?'

'They put me through Edinburgh University.' A tinge of pride coloured her voice. 'I have an honours degree in History.'

'That's wonderful, Rachel. I'm so pleased.' When no more information seemed to be forthcoming, Josie posed a tentative question. 'Would you maybe tell me something about your life now?'

'I have a good life. I'm engaged to be married.'

'Congratulations.' Josie gave her sister the warmest smile she could muster. 'Tell me about your young man.'

Rachel shrugged. 'There's not much to tell. We studied together at Edinburgh. He's serving with the King's Own Scottish Borderers for the duration. We're hoping to be married next year.'

'What's his name?'

'Peter,' Rachel said. 'Peter MacDougall.'

'You must worry about him when he's away.'

Rachel chose not to respond to that sympathetic statement. Instead she asked a question of her own, the first intimation of interest she had shown in her sister's life. 'You're not married?'

Josie shook her head. 'No, I'm a career girl. A journalist.'

'With the *Evening Dispatch*?' Rachel inquired. 'You worked your way up, I suppose. I remember you worked there.'

'Aye . . .' Josie said, all at once realising how little Rachel knew about her. Another illusion she'd had about this moment of reunion was that it would be followed by days and nights of conversation during which she would recount what had happened between herself and Tam Paterson. Rachel would be the one person she could tell about her baby.

She had known Tam. Josie could remember her pretty little face lighting up with mischief and amusement as she had teased her about him. Looking at the fearsomely self-possessed young lady sitting on the bench next to her, she wondered sadly if the wee sister to whom she'd once been so close was still in there somewhere, buried deep under the prim and proper façade.

Seeing that she was desperate to leave, Josie plastered a smile on to her face and extracted one of her business cards from her handbag. 'Can we keep in touch, Rachel? Now that we've found each other again?'

Her sister took the card and spent far too much time looking at it. It didn't take that long to digest the information it contained. 'I suppose so,' she said at last.

Josie's face was growing sore with the effort of maintaining the smile. 'Maybe we could have afternoon tea together now and again. Perhaps you might like to bring your fiancé along when he next has leave.' It was, she thought bleakly, the kind of invitation you issued to casual acquaintances, not the sister whom you had found so unexpectedly after so many years of longing for her. Rachel had turned her head away again.

'Peter's family don't know about my background. They think the Simpsons are my real parents.'

There was another painful pause. Josie's voice was thin and tight, battling against the overwhelming sense of hurt and rejection. 'And you don't want them to know.'

'I think I'd prefer it that way, yes.'

'I won't show you up,' she said drily. 'If we meet anyone you know you can introduce me as a friend.'

'Thanks, Josie,' said the girl. It was the first time in the whole conversation that she had used her big sister's name.

Josie stormed out into the corridor. Unluckily for him, the lad she was looking for came panting up the stairs at exactly the same moment as she reached the top of the landing. 'Where have you been?' she demanded. 'Mr Dewar's just phoned me to ask where that article is.' She put her hands on her hips and loomed over the unfortunate boy in a manner which would have done credit to old Mr Cunningham himself.

The copyboy looked startled. The Features Editor didn't usually act like this. 'I'm awful s-sorry, M-miss S-shaw,' he stammered nervously. 'Miss Clarke and Mr Bruce both asked me to do something else while I was on my way. I'm taking the piece you gave me to Mr Dewar right now.'

'That's not good enough,' Josie snapped. 'He should have had it twenty minutes ago. If you want to keep this job you'd better buck up your ideas, young man. Don't stand staring at me like that! Get on with it!'

She retreated into her office, slammed the door shut, sank down behind her desk and buried her face in her hands. It wasn't fair of her to shout at the lad like that, and she had realised it the instant the harsh words were out of her mouth. At his age she had found it impossible to say no to Miss Clarke and Mr Bruce too.

Josie raised her head and stared into space. She'd been shouting at quite a few people over the past two weeks. She knew very well how unforgivable that was but she couldn't seem to stop herself. She'd hardly slept since her disastrous reunion with Rachel.

Sitting up late into the night, going over and over the past, Josie was berating herself anew for all the mistakes she had made after her mother had died. It was her fault the family had been split up and she had been foolish to think that any reunion with her lost children would go smoothly. Of course they would have bitterness. She had failed them.

Finding them had been her holy grail for so long, the very foundation on which her life was built. Now she was questioning everything about that life. She looked around her at her pleasant home and her successful career and for the first time in a long time wondered if it was enough.

Material achievements were all very well but it was the relationships you forged with other people which really fed your soul.

Last night, wandering aimlessly about the house, she had found herself staring at the print of *The Cottar's Saturday Night*. Tied up as it was with her memories of Tam Paterson and her father, it had always had great sentimental value for Josie. This particular copy of it had been a present from Roddy, of course.

Studying the picture, she had thought how odd it was that this treasured possession had a connection with three of the men who had mattered most in her life, three of the men she had . . . She had taken a step back, spoken two words out loud into the silence of her sitting room. 'Oh, no,' she had said. 'Oh, no.'

Someone was coming into her office. She looked up, in exactly the right mood to bawl someone else out. Alan Dewar closed the door behind him, strode into the room and plonked himself down in the chair on the other side of the desk.

'I've been deputed to tell you that you're behaving like a pain in the neck. Actually,' he said brightly, 'I've cleaned that up a bit. Some of your underlings mentioned a part of the anatomy somewhat lower down than the neck.' He leaned forward over the desk. 'Want to talk about it, Madam Features Editor?'

She propped her chin on her fists. 'Talk about what?'

'Josie,' Alan said patiently, 'you and I go back a long way. I've worked with a lot of prima donnas in here, both male and female, and you've never been one of them. I've also been married to Deirdre for fifteen years and I know when a woman's upset about something, so I'll repeat the question. Do you want to talk about whatever it is that's distressing you?'

When she had neither answered his question nor shouted at him, he sat back in his chair and delivered the punch-line, forcing her to confront what she'd been trying to deny for the past few hours. What she had been trying to deny for the past few years.

'Josie, tell me to mind my own business if you want, but has it ever occurred to you to let Roddy know how you feel about him?'

Chapter 34

'Mind your own business, Alan,' she said, too shaken to pretend. 'You're several years too late anyway.'

'I knew it,' he said, slapping her desk in satisfaction. 'You sent him off to London in one of those fits of self-sacrifice which seem to afflict females from time to time. They always make the male who's the object of such unselfish behaviour feel like a complete heel.'

Josie laid her hands flat in front of her. 'I don't think Roddy feels like a heel. I think he's enjoying himself in the way he always has done. With lots of different female companions.'

'Let me get this right,' Alan said archly. 'We are talking about Mr-If-I-pretend-I-don't-give-a-damn-about-any-thing-or -anyone-I'll-never-get-hurt-again-Cunningham, aren't we? Doubtless we can also assume you sent him off to find fame and fortune with the instruction that he shouldn't feel himself tied to you in any way. What sort of a message do you think he took out of that?'

He adopted the appropriate pose, flinging one arm out in a gesture of dismissal.

'*Get lost Roderick, I don't want or need you in my life.* You're the second woman who's told him that, you know. Have you any idea how hard one rejection makes it for a man to summon up his courage and try again?'

'He's seeing other women in London,' she said stubbornly. 'I know he is.'

'Only because the one he really wants told him to go

370

away and never gives him any encouragement to come back.'

'Do you really think there's a woman out there who could hold his interest longer than a couple of weeks?'

'I'm looking at her,' Alan said quietly. 'Why do you think he keeps coming back to Glasgow? And phoning you? And letting you know what's going on in his life?'

She raised her eyes to his face. 'You really think that?'

'I do. You know what else I think? That the two of you took cold feet five years ago. Because of Ben. All of that emotion terrified you, sent you running screaming back to the place where you both feel safest: immersed in your work.' He smiled. 'You and Roddy are very alike in many ways.'

'You've missed your vocation,' Josie said dolefully. 'You should be writing a column of advice to the lovelorn. One of those based on all the latest psychological theories.'

Alan's smile broadened. Then he grew serious again. 'I suppose it's occurred to you that our Roddy is by way of being in the line of fire these days?'

'It's occurred to me,' she agreed, her grey eyes full of the worry of that.

'Think about it, flower,' he said gently. 'How would you feel if anything were to happen to him and you had never told him how much you love him?'

She didn't attempt to deny what he had just said. She had always known that he was an observant man. 'Och Alan, I'd feel bloody awful!'

'Then tell him,' he said. 'Do it soon.' He placed his hands over hers, giving them a reassuring squeeze before pushing his chair back and standing up. 'Right then. Duty calls.' He smiled down at her. 'Advice to the lovelorn, eh? Now there's an idea. Let's scrap some of the more depressing news in favour of that.'

She managed a smile in return. 'Thanks for the advice you've just given me, oh wise one. I'll try to stop being such a pain. In whichever part of the anatomy.'

Bustling around making tea for them on the following Sunday afternoon, Carrie Campbell threw a casual question over her shoulder. 'How did you get on with little Miss Snooty at the Labour Exchange? It's ages since we talked about that, isn't it?' She swung round, tea caddy in hand. 'Did you get permission to speak to her?'

Josie was standing at the window looking into the back court. The Campbell children were down there with one of the neighbours, old Mrs Cooke from across the landing. Always a big help to Carrie, Josie knew both she and her widowed daughter-in-law had been indispensable since Archie and April's mother had started working in the booking office at Partick railway station.

'Jo? Have I said something I shouldn't have?'

Jo. Carrie was the only other person who addressed her by that version of her name. She turned and looked into the young woman's eyes. She saw three things there: concern, a willingness to help, and a capacity for understanding surprising in someone so young. 'Carrie,' she said, 'can I talk to you about something?'

'Of course you can,' the girl said sympathetically. 'Is it about Roddy?'

Was she surrounded by people who could give Sherlock Holmes a run for his money? 'In a way.'

Carrie set the tea caddy down. 'You're in love with him, aren't you?'

Suddenly unable to speak, Josie nodded. Carrie walked over to her, took her by the arm and led her to the table. 'There's nothing to be afraid of,' she said as they both sat down. 'He loves you too.'

'I don't know that any more.'

'I do,' Carrie said. 'I've seen the way he looks at you when he thinks you're not looking at him. I noticed it again last Christmas. Like I've noticed it every Christmas for the past however many years.'

Josie bit her lip, hardly daring to believe her. She dropped her gaze to the blue glass bowl and crocheted lace doily in the middle of Carrie's table. 'There are things I should tell him,' she said. 'Things about my past.'

'Surely,' Carrie said gently, 'there's nothing that would shock someone as sophisticated as Roddy?'

No, Josie thought, he was unlikely to be horrified by the fact that she'd borne a child out of wedlock. But what about the rest of it? If she was going to tell him the story she would have to tell him all of it.

That she couldn't know for certain who her child's father had been was a burning shame which never entirely left her. As the memory of the event which had given rise to that doubt never quite went away. Would Roddy be disgusted by all of that, perhaps find it unbearably sordid?

'There's quite a lot,' she said painfully. 'I'm not sure how I would go about telling him.'

'You're a writer,' Carrie pointed out.

'Do it as an article and send it to him, you mean?'

'Aye. Change the names. That way you won't be embarrassed thinking about the censors intercepting it. Roddy will still know it's about you.'

Josie thought about it. 'Maybe,' she said at last.

Carrie smiled. 'Good. Now, let's have a cup of tea and you can tell me about the young lady at the Labour Exchange. If you want to, that is.'

'I want to,' Josie said gratefully, watching as the other girl walked over to the range. 'Can I return the compliment at all?'

Carrie swung round to look at her. 'I'm not sure what you mean.'

'Is there anything *you'd* like to talk about?'

'Me?' Carrie said brightly. She turned her back on Josie and reached for the teapot. 'I'm fine.'

* * *

It was the hardest thing Josie had ever had to write. She worked on it in the evenings and it took her three weeks to complete. *The Unmarried Mother's Tale* was a somewhat abridged version of events, concentrating on what had happened to her after she became pregnant rather than before. It still took her a month to summon up the courage to send it to him.

In the end she took the coward's way out, posting it to arrive a couple of days before he left London on a prolonged journalistic assignment. That would give them both some breathing space, allowing him to absorb what she had told him before she had to meet him face to face and gauge what his reaction was. From the subtle hints he had dropped about getting himself a nice suntan, she suspected that he was off to North Africa.

He'd be on the phone as soon as he'd read it, of course. Not looking forward to that conversation, she was hurt and upset when it didn't come, neither during the working day nor at home that evening. She slept very little that night, wearing herself out with speculation as to why he hadn't been in touch.

Maybe he *was* shocked by her story. No, that was a daft idea. He might be hurt though, upset that she hadn't told him before. Or perhaps he was disgusted by what she had written about why Rachel and Charlie had been removed from the Drygate. She had rather glossed over the details of that when she had told him before.

She was tired and irritable at work the next day. Mindful of her promise to Alan Dewar, she forbore to take it out on the staff. Inanimate objects didn't have feelings, though. After a very unsatisfactory lunch break she stomped into her office and kicked the door shut behind her.

Then, turning to sit down at her desk, she shrieked. Arms folded across his broad and uniformed chest, Roddy was standing to one side of the slammed door. He looked pale and tired and fed-up. He was also glowering ferociously at her.

Chapter 35

'What are you doing here?'

'What the bloody hell do you think I'm doing here?' he snapped. 'You send me what you've just sent me and then ask what I'm doing here?' His voice rose on a note of mingled outrage and disbelief.

'Don't shout at me,' she yelled back, totally unaware that she was committing the same offence herself.

Roddy walked forward and gripped her by the upper arms, administering a vigorous shake. 'Listen to me, Josephine Shaw. I've been on a train for the past sixteen hours, starting and stopping and getting stuck in godforsaken places all of last night and half of this morning. I have to catch one back at half past six tomorrow night at the absolute latest. Which means we have a little over twenty-four hours, and in that space of time I want to hear the whole story. All of it,' he said grimly, shaking her again to emphasise his point.

'It's all in the article.'

'No, it damn well isn't. Do you think I'm stupid or something?' he demanded. 'There's a reason why you've decided to tell me this now and I want to know what it is. For God's sake, Jo! Did you really think I didn't know you'd had a baby to Tam Paterson?'

She went pale to the lips. 'How did you know?'

His face was a mixture of exasperation and affection. 'Och Jo,' he cried. 'I guessed! It was obvious!' He tugged on the arms he held, pulling her towards him. 'Jo,' he breathed, 'I can't not do this. I can't not say this. I love—'

'Don't say it! Please don't say it!' She put her two hands flat against his chest and tried her utmost to push him away. That was hard when she wanted more than anything else in the world to do the exact opposite.

'I have to say the words. I have to,' he repeated in a calmer tone of voice. His grip on her arms relaxed. 'I should have said them a long time ago.'

She raised one hand to his mouth, laid her fingers against his lips. 'Wait till you've heard it all,' she pleaded. 'Then decide whether you want to say them or not.'

'There's a lot, is there?' he asked lightly. 'A veritable *War and Peace*?'

Josie took a deep breath. 'There's a lot.'

'We'd better go home then. This place will have to manage without you for a while. I daresay Alan will be able to cope.'

They were standing on either side of his sitting-room window, looking out over the balcony towards the Mitchell Library on the corner of North Street and Sauchiehall Street. She had told him about the disastrous reunion with Rachel which had provoked her need to tell him her story. Going back to the beginning, she had then related how her mother had died and how her stepfather had beaten her, filling in the gaps which helped explain why Rachel and Charlie had been taken away. Now she had to tell him the most difficult story of all.

'Take your time,' he said softly. He hadn't attempted to touch her again. She knew he was waiting until it was all done. She hoped he would still want to touch her then.

She had always loved the dark green damask curtains in this room, still in place over the blackout blinds. She took a fold of them between her thumb and her index finger and began to gently stroke the fabric. When she had seen the anger in Roddy's face when he had heard what her stepfather had done to her, it had given her some courage. Now that courage was faltering. 'I'm scared this will make you think badly of me,' she said at last.

'Jo,' he said firmly. 'Nothing you do, or have done, or ever will do, could make me think badly of you.'

That definite and defiant statement brought a smile to her face. She glanced over at him, standing so still and watchful on the other side of the big window. 'Even if I was a mass murderer?'

'In your case I'm sure there were mitigating circumstances.'

'A master criminal or an international jewel thief?'

He flicked his elegant fingers in a gesture of dismissal. 'The dirty capitalists have too much wealth as it is. You'd obviously simply be redistributing it as a logical extension of your socialist principles.'

He loves me, she thought, he really does love me. Please God let him still feel the same way after he hears this. She took a deep breath. 'I had two stepbrothers,' she began.

It took some time to tell. There were false starts and half-completed sentences which told him more than she knew. About some things, like her inability to know for certain who had fathered her child, she was brutally frank. She was honest too about the reality of the rape. She saw Roddy wince when she carefully repeated the words her stepbrother had used, that obscene litany which had accompanied and been part of her violation. It was the first and only time she herself had ever said those words out loud.

'That's it,' she said at last. Whilst she had been recounting her terrible story she had been studying his face, searching for his reactions to what he was hearing. Now she found she could no longer bear to look him in the eye.

He reached her in one long stride, his fingers strong and cool as he forced her head up to meet his gaze and went unerringly for what was worrying her the most. 'You have absolutely nothing to be ashamed of, Jo,' he said in an impassioned whisper. 'Nothing at all. And I love you. I love you more than anything in the whole wide world.'

'They made me feel worthless,' she said, hearing his words but still too scared to accept them. 'Like a piece of rubbish left there among the rats.'

'You're the most precious thing in the world,' he assured her. 'Let me prove it to you. Like a knight of the round table I shall perform some valiant deed to show my lady her worth. And,' Roddy continued, his eyes soft and overflowing with love, 'to show my lady that I'm worthy of her. What can I do for you, my Guinevere?'

'Looks a bit like a prison,' he observed an hour later as they emerged from the mother and baby home on Partickhill.

'That's more or less what it was,' Josie agreed. 'A prison for fallen women. I've never had the courage to come back here. I always knew that one day I would have to.'

Roddy nodded. 'Because if he decides to come looking for you, his search may bring him here. Well, you've left your details now. He'll know where to find you.'

Josie's eyes were travelling up the walls of the house in which she had spent so many unhappy months. 'I suppose there are some other poor girls stuck in there right now.'

'You can't take them all home with you, Jo,' Roddy said gently as her gaze came back to his face. 'And attitudes are changing. The war's seeing to that. Probably the regime's not as harsh as it was in your day. You didn't get *such* a hostile reception, did you?' He pulled a wry face.

'You mean you noticed the subtle change of attitude when the superintendent realised I was a former inmate?'

Roddy's voice was an amused murmur. 'Your choice of that particular word was perhaps a trifle provocative.'

'Perhaps,' she allowed, flashing him a wicked glance, 'but I didn't half enjoy using it. I think that woman would have been hostile if I hadn't had you with me: a well-spoken man in uniform claiming to be my fiancé and telling her that no, he wasn't the father of the child I gave birth to here, he just wished he was.'

Roddy grinned. 'As you would say, that set her gas at a peep, didn't it?'

'She was fairly stunned,' Josie agreed, smiling back at him with a mixture of gratitude and mischief and something else Mr Roderick Cunningham was too scared to define.

He reached out and touched her cheek with his fingertips. 'Funny to think that you have a fifteen-year-old son. You don't look old enough.'

'Flatterer.' Catching hold of his wrist, she slipped her hand in his and took one last look at the house before they headed for the gate. 'Can I ask a question?'

'Ask away.'

'You said you knew that I'd had a baby. How did you know?'

His fingers intertwined themselves with hers. 'There were various clues. You've always been extremely sensitive about anything to do with children and there's always been something special about the way you get on with Archie and April Campbell.'

As they made their way towards the main road and a tram or a taxi to wherever she wanted to go next, he tightened his grip on her hand.

'I think it was when I saw you hold April for the first time that I really knew. It was the way your face softened as you looked at her.'

They were passing under the branches of a huge oak tree set on the very edge of the road. Judging by its girth and the way its roots were coming up through the pavement, it had been here long before the streets and houses around them had been built. Roddy stopped walking and edged Josie back towards its trunk. 'Do you know why else I thought there might have been a baby?'

She shook her head, feeling the rough bark of the oak grazing her hair. Roddy's hands were on her shoulders now, gently cupping them. The street was deserted. There was no one to see them.

'Because people who make love to each other also run the risk of making a baby, especially when they're very young like you and Tam were. I deduced that neither of you might have known how not to make a baby.'

'Oh,' Josie said faintly.

Smile though he did at her response, Roddy's voice was dry and regretful. 'It's a skill at which I'm afraid I must admit to having some expertise.'

'You've had affairs while you've been in London.'

'A few lapses,' he said. 'Nothing that lasted very long. I'm sorry.'

'You were a free man,' she pointed out. 'Did you love any of them?'

His smile grew a little bitter. 'Love doesn't come into it. On either side. Especially when all you really want to do is prove that the last German bomb didn't get you.' He frowned. 'Am I trying to justify the unjustifiable?'

Josie tilted her head back against the oak tree and looked up through its sparse autumnal branches to the sky. She thought back to how she had felt after the Clydebank Blitz. 'I think I can understand.'

'You're not jealous, then?'

She looked at him. 'I'd like to scratch their eyes out. Not to mention kicking you in the appropriate place.'

'Ooh,' he murmured. 'Don't do that. It makes my eyes water even thinking about it.' Then he realised what might lie underneath her frivolous words. 'What does that really mean?' he asked, peering intently at her. 'What you said just then?'

'Funny,' she muttered, her gaze dropping briefly to his mouth, 'you never used to be slow on the uptake.'

Something flared in his eyes then. It spoke of a love and a yearning and a desire which had been thwarted for too long. 'Jo . . .'

She took pity on him. 'I think it probably means that I love you. I think it probably means that I want you to take me home and make love to me.'

The hands caressing her shoulders stiffened and stopped moving. 'You're sure?'

Josie reached up to plant a kiss on his mouth. 'I'm sure.' She would have pulled back but his arms came around her, enfolding her in a tight embrace. He spoke softly into her hair.

'You don't want to see if we can jump the queue at the registry office tomorrow morning? Or head for Gretna Green right now?'

She pushed back against his arms, squinting up at him. 'Come down with a sudden fit of morality, have you?'

'No,' he said, relaxing his grip so he could use one hand to smooth her hair back from her face. 'I've come down with a sudden fit of love. Oh God, Jo. It's not that sudden, is it?'

'Not sudden at all,' she said fondly, revelling in the feel of his fingers on her brow and her hair. She was wearing one of her favourite berets. Set at a jaunty angle, it left much of her head uncovered. 'Unfortunately even the emergency regulations don't let you get married that quickly, and since last year a marriage over the anvil hasn't any legal validity.'

She laid her hands flat on his chest and explained with a quick smile how she knew that so exactly. 'I wrote an article about the very last one. Besides,' she informed him, growing serious, 'I'm not trading here. I don't need a handful of beads.'

'Marriage should never be that,' he said gravely.

'No,' she agreed. 'Marriage should be about love and friendship and companionship.'

'And passion,' he said softly. His deep voice grew softer still. 'You do love me, Jo?'

'I love you,' she said. 'Now take me home and do what I asked you to do.'

His eyes were full of tenderness. 'You're not scared?'

'Only that you'll be disappointed.'

'Why on earth would I be disappointed?' As his high and intelligent forehead creased in perplexity Josie lowered her eyes and studied the insignia on his uniform jacket.

'You've quite a lot to compare me with.' She allowed her gaze to drift to the side, watching as a single leaf fluttered gracefully down to join its fellows on the pavement.

'Look at me, Jo. *Look at me!*'

Her head snapped up. Look at him? They were completely concentrated on each other, staring deep into each other's eyes, deep into each other's souls.

'No one compares to you,' Roddy said fiercely. 'No one ever has done. No one ever will.'

'We're serious about this then, are we?'

'Forsaking all others,' he said. 'Till death us do part.'

Under the spreading branches of the oak tree, the kiss which followed was a solemn one, holding a promise at its centre. The giving and receiving of a mutual commitment. The plighting of a troth.

They went to Josie's home because, as she informed him on the journey back to Charing Cross, she had some food in her larder. His cupboards were empty. When had he last eaten anyway? She scolded him roundly when she told her. When they arrived at their destination the shyness which had propelled her into this discussion of practical matters threatened to overwhelm her.

'It's all right,' Roddy said. 'There's no rush. Let's stand at the window for a moment or two and I'll put my arm around you.'

383

They did that. After five minutes Josie spoke. '*Are* you hungry?'

He bent his head and planted a kiss on her earlobe. 'I'm famished.'

'I'll go and start cooking then.' She slid out from under his arm and started towards the kitchen.

'No, you won't.'

She turned, smiling a little uncertainly at him. 'I thought you were famished.'

'I am,' he said. Then he reached for her.

On the receiving end of a knowing and very affectionate smile from Alan Dewar, Josie retreated into her office to allow the blush to subside and silently willed the phone to ring. It did.

'Hallo, beautiful one. How are you this fine morning?'

'Wonderful,' she said softly into the receiver. 'If a little tender in certain rather interesting places.'

There was a low moan from the other end of the telephone line.

'Roddy?'

'I was just remembering how you got that way. I spent the whole train journey down last night thinking about how you got that way.' Mischief crept into the deep voice. 'I should really have been resting, you know. I don't seem to have had much sleep over the past couple of days. Do you know,' he continued, 'the night before last I didn't get so much as a wink!'

Josie's blush wasn't subsiding. 'It was rather ... repetitive.'

'Mmm,' he said. 'That it was.'

'There's no need to sound so smug.'

'Isn't there? I seem to recall you expressing some appreciation of my stamina. During one of your more coherent utterances, that is.'

'Are you implying that I was making incoherent ones?'

'Oh, yes,' he murmured. 'Lots of them. Did I tell you that I'm blissfully happy, by the way?'

'Me too. I've been spreading sweetness and light around this place since I got in this morning.'

'Oh dear,' he said. 'Do you think they'll be able to cope?' She could hear the smile in his voice, visualise his eyes crinkling at the corners. 'How will they manage when you and I get married next time I'm home?'

'You know,' she said. 'I would really like to have a proper proposal of marriage some time. Not just this series of assumptions.'

'Down on bended knee?'

'Naturally.'

'Will you help me back up again if I get stuck?'

She put on a ludicrously suggestive voice, a low and throaty murmur. 'A man as agile as I now know you to be? Come off it, Mr Cunningham.'

'Oh Jo,' he laughed in delight. 'I love you.'

'And I love you.'

'More than anything?'

'More than anything in the whole wide world.'

Concerned though she was that he would now be well on his way to whichever hazardous destination he was bound for, she was up in the clouds herself at four o'clock that afternoon, singing under her breath as she wandered out of the copytakers' room. One of the receptionists on duty in the front office came through the double doors into the inner lobby, laughing and pink.

'What's up?'

'You may well ask. We only have a very handsome and extremely charming young American soldier out here asking for you by name.'

Josie wrinkled her nose in puzzlement. 'I don't know any Americans. Apart from the ones I've interviewed.'

'Well, one of them has obviously taken a shine to you.

Wait till you get a load of this guy!'

'Overpaid, oversexed and over here. Not to mention ruining the English language.' She was laughing as she followed the receptionist out to the front desk. Nothing could dent her happiness this afternoon.

The young man in the uniform of an American GI was indeed quite a guy. Tall and broad-shouldered, he had short fair hair which promised to run to curls if it were allowed to grow a little. That would suit his boyishly handsome face, Josie thought, currently wearing the broadest of smiles as he surveyed her.

He was a bit young for her, though. She'd have been accused of cradle snatching. He could only be about twenty years old. She returned his smile. It would have been impossible not to. There was something so open and good-natured about him, a kind of childlike sweetness.

Josie drew her breath in sharply. It couldn't be . . . Could it? Blond curls. Inherently sweet and good-natured. Knowing her name and here at the *Dispatch* looking for her. But this young man was an American.

Watching her work it out, his smile grew mischievous. 'Got it yet?' he asked.

Yes, she had got it. 'Do you still keep mouldy biscuits and dead worms in your pocket?' she asked breathlessly. Absurdly. Or not so absurdly. It was her long-lost brother Charlie.

Chapter 36

They talked solidly for an hour, eagerly swapping information with each other. Josie's first question was how he had managed to end up in the United States. 'What did you do?' she asked. 'Stow away on a ship?'

Perched on the edge of his sister's desk while she sat on the windowsill, Charlie grinned at her. 'Nothing so adventurous. I was sent there. Well, to Canada.'

'Canada!'

'It happened to a lot of us, Josie – the ones they thought were too much of a handful. They put me to this farm in Ontario. The folks there . . . well, they weren't very nice people.'

'Oh, Charlie!' She gazed at him, her eyes soft with pain and regret. 'Did they beat you?'

His wide mouth set into a tight line. 'That. Never gave us enough to eat either.' He laughed mirthlessly. 'They were a Scottish family but there was precious little sentiment or Scottish hospitality about them. Me and this other wee guy were there just to do all the work.'

Josie suppressed a smile. The Scots words which peppered Charlie's speech sounded so funny when they were said with a North American accent.

'Their own kids weren't very nice to us either.' He leaned back against the desk and crossed his legs at the ankles, his head bent as he checked the disposition of his feet. GIs might wear much more stylish uniforms than their British counterparts but military boots were military boots, heavy and solid. He looked up again.

'But you don't need to hear about that.'

Josie couldn't speak. The wee brother who now towered over her was trying to protect her, as the tiny child he had once been had tried to protect her from his father's fists.

'It happened a long time ago,' he said softly, watching her face. 'It's all in the past now.'

'You got away from those people?' she managed.

'Sure did. Me and the other guy ran away when we were fourteen, over the border into the States. We thought we'd be safe there and they wouldn't be able to take us back.' He grinned again, sloughing off the bad memories. 'We were right. We got jobs in a hotel in Vermont – which also gave us somewhere to stay – and we've been there until we joined up a year ago and began training. We landed at Greenock last week.'

Smiling again at his accent – he had pronounced the port's name with a heavy emphasis on the second syllable – Josie shook her head in amazement.

'You were only a wee boy,' she said. 'How could they send you away from your own country like that?'

'I was a noisy wee boy,' Charlie said ruefully. 'I think I also had quite a mouth on me. I can remember all these shocked faces around me.' His expression was part amusement, part regret. 'I can't just recall what I said but I guess it probably included a few curses.'

She could hear him in her head, innocently mimicking the foul language used by his father and his stepbrothers. She was also remembering what Rachel had told her. *He was shouting the place down. Calling for Mammy. Calling for you.*

The adult Charlie leaned forward and wrapped his fingers around her wrist. 'Don't look so sad, sis. We've found each other again. Isn't that all that matters?'

Thrilled and moved by that casual *sis*, Josie lifted her free hand to her mouth, struggling to contain her emotions.

'Hey,' he said, rising to his feet. 'Less of this now. Otherwise I might kinda get the impression you're not glad to see me.'

'Charlie, I'm so happy to see you!'

Her brother's arms came round her. His deep voice was husky. 'I never forgot about you, Josie. My big sister who looked after me when Mammy died. I remember you and Rachel used to read to me. I always liked that.'

'I don't think I looked after you very well, Charlie,' she said sadly. 'I didn't manage to keep the family together.'

'You did everything you could,' he insisted, giving her a final squeeze and releasing her. 'It was my father who broke our family up. Him and my stepbrothers. I went looking for them earlier this afternoon.' Charlie's expression grew grim. 'I've never been a violent man but I have to confess I was thinking of punching their lights out. I was a mite disappointed when I discovered I was too late.'

'You've been to the Drygate?'

'How do you think I found you?'

'You remembered it?'

'Sure I did. I knew we had lived near a big cemetery and a big church.' He smiled at her. 'I didn't remember that the big church was Glasgow Cathedral but I could recall a funny little poem you used to recite about a bell and a fish and a tree and a bird. You also used to tell Rachel and me that we were all Saint Mungo's bairns. I got the train up from Greenock this morning and repeated all of that to a cab driver at the railway station. He looked at me as though I was nuts but he deposited me in the right place.'

'You met the Fitzgeralds and Mrs Paterson?' she asked.

'They told me where to find you. Now all we have to do is find Rachel.'

'Charlie . . .' Josie stopped, wondering exactly how she was going to explain to him that their sister was found but didn't seem very happy about it. She had seen her twice over the past six months, on both occasions because she herself had extended an invitation to afternoon tea in a city centre restaurant. Other warm invitations to visit her at home, perhaps spend a Sunday afternoon with her, had been politely turned down.

Josie had discovered that Rachel's adoptive parents lived in a large country house south of Perth. She returned there each alternate weekend, spending the week in Glasgow with the parents of her fiancé. No invitation had been issued to Josie to visit either location. She transmitted it all as diplomatically as she could to Charlie. Perhaps she was too diplomatic. She could see he was all enthusiasm for the three of them meeting up together as soon as possible.

'Although maybe not tonight,' he said, glancing up at the clock on the wall of Josie's office. 'I have to be back at the base by eight o'clock. Shall I see if I can get a pass in a couple of weeks' time?'

'Charlie,' she said cautiously, 'please don't get your hopes up too much. Rachel doesn't want to think or talk about the Drygate. I think she wants to pretend that it never happened. I think maybe,' she went on, being painfully honest with him, 'that she blames me for what happened.'

'I'm sure she doesn't,' Charlie said expansively. 'How could she? You were only a kid yourself, Josie.'

'Five years younger than you are now,' she said with a smile. 'How did you get to be so mature?'

'The university of life,' he said grandly. Suddenly they were grinning at each other like idiots.

'Och, Charlie!' she cried as he leaned forward to hug her again. 'It's so good to have found you.'

'Thanks to the Fitzgeralds,' he said. 'You've kept in touch with them, I hear.'

'I found them again,' she corrected. 'I've had some adventures of my own since we left the Drygate, Charlie.'

'You want to tell me about those?'

She looked into his fresh young face. 'I'll tell you about some of them,' she offered. 'The rest may have to wait a while. Is that all right?'

'Fine by me,' he said equably. 'You want to tell me about the man in your life too?'

'How do you know there is one?'

Charlie winked at her. 'People don't glow like you're glowing today if they're not in love, sis. That's something else I learned at the university of life!'

He phoned her two weeks later with the information that he had an overnight pass coming up halfway through the following week. 'Could I stay at your apartment?' he asked in his leisurely twang.

'Anytime you like. You don't need to ask.'

'Maybe we could get Rachel to come by for a bite to eat?'

'I'm not sure if she'll come, Charlie. She might prefer to meet us somewhere.'

'Whatever. What did she say about me turning up?' he asked eagerly.

She was troubled when she came off the phone to him. Never very good at telling lies, she had nevertheless told him that Rachel had been delighted to hear of his reappearance. In reality their sister had barely reacted to the news. Josie was terribly afraid Charlie was in for a huge and painful disappointment and she didn't see how she could shield him from it.

As she'd suspected, Rachel plumped for a drink in a hotel. Josie knew what her reasoning was. The meeting would be short and public places were safe, much less likely than a private home to be the scene of great displays of emotion or affection. Rachel hadn't counted on Charlie's exuberance. Beaming with delight, he enfolded her in an impulsive embrace.

She quite obviously hated it, extricating herself from her brother's arms as soon as she possibly could. Seeing Charlie's face fall, Josie had to suppress irritation at her sister's attitude. Of all of them, their wee brother had suffered the most, plucked away from his home, his family and his country and beaten regularly throughout his childhood. Yet he seemed determined to put all that to one side and get on with his life. Couldn't Rachel see how commendable that was and at least try to respond to it?

At first the awkwardness of the occasion was masked by Charlie telling Rachel much of what he had told Josie. She noticed again how he tended to skate over the unpleasant things. Rachel listened politely but said very little herself. Josie tried to draw her out but even the most innocuous of questions produced only a few words in reply.

Upset on Charlie's behalf, she couldn't help smiling inwardly at his perseverance and obvious determination to win Rachel over. When his attempt to share memories of their early life was firmly rebuffed he ordered a second round of cocktails and told outrageous and very funny stories about life working in a hotel. Josie laughed and enjoyed them, caught anew by the wonder of having her brother back. Rachel hardly smiled.

'So,' Charlie asked her eventually, 'you'll have met Josie's friend Roddy?'

'I didn't know she had a friend called Roddy.'

Having taken a sip of his drink after he had posed the question, Charlie replaced his glass carefully on the table. Then he looked straight and unsmiling at the younger of his two sisters. 'Why don't you know about Roddy? He's a very important person in our sister's life.'

'Is he?' Rachel's voice was brittle.

Charlie looked her straight in the eye. 'Could it be that you don't take much interest in her life? You do appreciate

392

that she's a highly successful newspaperwoman?'

Josie's amusement at that very North American description of herself was overlaid by anxiety. This had the potential to develop into a quarrel between her brother and sister. Here I go again, she thought ruefully, running towards the burning buildings instead of away from them. 'Rachel has her own life, Charlie—'

He raised a hand to stop her. 'That doesn't excuse her for not taking an interest in yours. I've been trying to make allowances for her for the past hour or so but I'm kinda running out of patience now.' There was an edge to his voice. 'Tell me, Rachel, have you ever given much thought to what Josie's been through over the years?'

Rachel turned her face away. Josie recognised the technique. See no evil, hear no evil. Charlie was having none of it. 'You do remember what my father did to her back in the Drygate, don't you?'

'Charlie,' Josie said again, damping down a great wave of shame and embarrassment and regret, 'I prefer to forget about that. Like you said to me, it's all in the past. Over and done with.'

Her brother laid his hand over hers. 'You were defending both of us,' he said gently. 'I think we should remember that and be grateful.' His voice hardened again. 'Don't you, Rachel? Or don't you have an opinion on that?' When she didn't reply, he fired another two questions at her. 'You do know how hard Josie tried to get us back, don't you? How she never gave up hope of finding us?'

Rachel stopped pretending to be transfixed by whatever was happening on the other side of the hotel lounge. There was something in those eyes so like her own which took Josie's breath away. 'You never told me that,' she said.

'You never asked,' Josie said lightly, hoping the whole subject might be glossed over there and then. Only Charlie had clearly had enough.

'Ever thought your attitude might be a mite selfish, Rachel?'

Josie waited for her sister to explode. Instead, white-faced, she rose abruptly from the table. 'I have to go.'

Charlie laid his hand on Josie's arm, preventing her from setting off in pursuit. 'Let her stew for a bit. I reckon that's what she needs. Come on,' he said, 'let's go dancing.'

Dragging her eyes off a rapidly retreating Rachel, Josie looked at him in astonishment. 'Dancing?'

'Sure,' he said easily. 'I have to teach you how to do some decent dances before they post me off somewhere. You guys over here don't seem to have progressed much beyond the minuet.' He smiled at her obvious confusion. 'Look, Josie,' he said, 'you think I'm not upset by what's just happened?' He grimaced, and the good-natured face became wry and regretful.

Josie looked into his eyes, saw the hidden depths behind the young and carefree exterior. 'You've learned to settle for less?' she suggested.

'Never that. But I have learned you can't make people act the way you want them to. However much you want 'em to.'

She thought about it, nodding slowly in agreement. 'You're right,' she said. 'Of course you're right.'

Charlie smiled. 'So, are you going to let me teach you how to dance the Jitterbug?'

Josie was giving Miss Clarke a description of her most recent trip to the American servicemen's club in Glasgow. Smiling, she glanced up at the photograph on the wall of the Features Department. 'Sally loved dancing, you know, but I think even she might have had some difficulty with the way they dance. It's more like acrobatics than the palais glide!'

'Sounds as though you were lucky not to slip a disc,' Miss Clarke said, her eyes twinkling.

'Och,' Josie laughed, 'my brother's very kind to his big sister. He's breaking me in gently.'

'Will he be getting his marching orders soon? Or are you trying not to think about that?'

Josie gave a resigned shrug. 'He's got to go sometime. I'm concentrating on appreciating him while he's here. We've been lucky. It's a good eight weeks now.' She glanced towards the window. The black-out blinds were down but they could hear the snow driving against the panes. 'It's a foul night,' she commented.

'Yes,' Miss Clarke said. 'I reckon that wind's blowing in straight from Siberia.' She patted Josie's hand. 'Almost makes you glad you're spending the night here, doesn't it?'

'I wouldn't go that far,' murmured Josie with a smile. The two women were sharing the night shift, manning the news desk in case of there being a breaking story over the hours of darkness. Alan Dewar had done it single-handedly far too many times and Josie had insisted he take a break from it.

'I'll go first,' Miss Clarke said. Approaching eighty, she showed no signs of allowing her accumulation of years to stop her from doing anything she wanted to do. 'Are you bedding down in here?'

Josie pointed to the camp bed in the corner. Remembering her last stint at overnight duty, she'd brought in a couple of thick blankets and an equally thick quilt and placed a Thermos of coffee within reach of her hand. 'All the comforts of home.'

'I'll come and fetch you at four o'clock to take over.'

Josie nodded. Lying down as she was, she pulled the covers snugly over herself and went out like a light. Miss Clarke came for her well before 4 a.m.

'Josephine,' she said, gently shaking her arm. 'Wake up, dear. I'm afraid I have some bad news.' She moved over to switch on one of the desk lights. 'Personal bad news,' she added.

Josie shot up in bed, fear clutching at her heart. 'Not Roddy?' she gasped.

The older woman hastened to reassure her. 'No, no. It's his nephew. Old Mr Cunningham's grandson.'

'Matthew Campbell?'

Miss Clarke nodded. 'There's been an accident on the railway. Late last night in all that terrible snow.'

'On the railway?' Josie repeated in incomprehension. 'But Matthew's away, serving with the Argyll and Sutherland Highlanders.'

Miss Clarke looked nonplussed. 'Well, he must have been helping out while he was home on leave.'

Josie sat up. 'Poor Carrie.' She swung her legs over the edge of the camp bed. 'Poor Matthew. Is he badly hurt?'

Miss Clarke stared at her. 'He's dead, Josephine. I'm afraid he's dead.'

Chapter 37

On the morning of Matthew Campbell's funeral, Josie met Roddy off the overnight train from London. He had made it home just in time, flying in from North Africa two days before. He looked tanned and fit but very sombre. After they had embraced he asked how Carrie was bearing up.

Josie let out a long sigh. 'Holding together for the sake of the children. Those neighbours of hers have been very good.'

'The two Mrs Cookes, you mean?' Roddy asked, walking down the platform carrying his bag in one hand while his other arm encircled Josie's waist. 'I think they've helped her out a lot over the years. What about Archie and April? How are they reacting?'

'Och,' Josie said sadly, 'the poor wee souls are very confused. Seemingly they didn't even know their father was on leave. He'd come home on a forty-eight hour pass and gone straight to the station to see Carrie. Not very long before the accident on Sunday night.'

Josie wasn't entirely sure that those last two statements were accurate. When she'd been round to visit Carrie yesterday the elder Mrs Cooke had let slip something about Matthew Campbell having arrived back on the morning of the day he had died. There had been one of those odd pauses when people's eyes meet furtively and then slide away to carefully look at nothing. Something was going on that Josie couldn't quite fathom, although she suspected it might have something to do with the person she mentioned next.

'There was this other man at the station before the accident happened, an old friend of Carrie's called Ewen Livingstone.'

'Where does he fit in?' Roddy asked as they joined the taxi queue outside the main entrance of the station.

'He's some sort of inspector from the LNER in Edinburgh. Apparently he used to work at Partick in Carrie's father's time and he's also an old friend of the Mrs Cookes. He's been staying with them for the past couple of weeks. Across the landing from Carrie,' she added, not sure why she had felt the need to transmit that particular piece of information.

Roddy had been gazing blankly at the hustle and bustle of Gordon Street. Now he slanted her down an odd look. 'You're not implying anything, are you? Carrie's not that sort of a person.'

'She's absolutely not that sort of a person,' Josie agreed. 'It's only that there seems to be some sort of . . .' She paused, searching for the right word. 'Some sort of *connection* between her and this Ewen Livingstone. Something more than a professional relationship.'

'Connection? What the hell does that mean?'

The odd look had metamorphosed into one with which Josie had long been familiar, although she couldn't remember when it had last been turned on her. She imagined this was exactly the pattern into which his features set when he was quizzing some politician or military commander whom he considered to be a fool or a charlatan or worse.

'I don't know,' she said, fervently wishing she hadn't led the conversation off at this particular tangent. 'I can't quite work it out, that's all.'

His words were clipped. 'I think you're letting your imagination run away with you. Don't you?'

She looked up at him in dismay. Desperately sorry for

Carrie and the children, and wanting to discuss something she found puzzling and unsettling, she had succeeded only in offending Roddy. He was very fond of Carrie. As he had been very fond of his nephew. The taxi queue shuffled along the pavement, gingerly avoiding half-melted patches of snow and ice.

'Shall I tell you about the accident?'

'If you like.'

That didn't sound very encouraging but she told him anyway, describing how empty coaches travelling at speed had run into the back of a passenger train halted at a red light between Partick and the next station along the line.

'There was a blizzard,' she explained, 'and they think the wind blew out the lamps on the back of the standing train. Visibility was extremely poor anyway and the weather had been disrupting services all day, so the empty coaches were going through at an unscheduled time. Everything just sort of horribly came together.'

'Both trains were derailed?' Roddy asked shortly.

'Aye, leaving the passenger train suspended over a drop. Apparently the ground falls away from the railway line quite steeply at that point. There were only two people on board: a mother and child in a carriage which had toppled on to its side and was rather precariously balanced. Matthew climbed up on to it and inched his way along.' She paused, thinking how painful it must be for Roddy listening to all of this.

'He got them out and handed them down to this Ewen Livingstone and Carrie. Then it seems he stayed where he was a bit longer than he should have.' She hesitated again.

'The carriage fell into the drop?'

'Yes. They say it must have been more or less instantaneous. As soon as it hit the ground.'

They had reached the top of the queue. Roddy said nothing until a taxi had arrived and they were inside it, heading up Hope Street. Darting a glance at his face, Josie saw that it was working painfully. She gave him a moment, turning to gaze out of the window on her own side of the vehicle.

'Matt demonstrated very great courage, then,' he said eventually.

Upset because he was so upset, Josie laid her hand over his. He wanted more than that. There was accusation in the cool green gaze. 'You'd allow him that?'

'Of course I would,' she said gently. 'He was very brave and he saved the lives of two people.'

'But you never liked him, did you?'

'That's neither here nor there,' she said awkwardly. 'Is it?'

Roddy slid his hand out from under hers. 'I want to go straight to the church,' he said, leaning forward to give the driver the instruction.

They were almost an hour early and the church was as cold as charity. Sitting beside a silent Roddy in one of the pews at the front, Josie couldn't decide whether to leave him be or rack her brains for some neutral topic of conversation which would bring them back on to an even keel on this sad and difficult day. He needed comforting. That much was obvious.

She laid her fingers tentatively on the back of his wrist. He didn't reject her touch but his own hand didn't come over hers either. Wondering if it was an inane thing to say, she observed that his skin was quite brown. 'Have you been lying out in the sun?'

'Do you think it's a picnic down there?' he asked brusquely, his eyes fixed on the communion table.

'No,' she said, 'of course not. I've read your articles. I know it's as serious in North Africa as anywhere.'

She could have quoted what he had written chapter and verse, especially his eye-witness account of the battle of El Alamein. General Montgomery's hard-fought victory over Field Marshal Rommel and the subsequent German retreat from Egypt had given the Allies such a boost that church bells throughout Britain silenced for the duration had rung out to celebrate the victory.

Everyone was hoping a major turning point had been reached. It had come, as all battles do, at a cost. British casualties had been dreadful. The man sitting beside her must have seen some terrible things. She moved her hand to his sleeve. 'Roddy . . .'

'Look,' he said, 'can we just be quiet for a while?'

She broke the contact, returning her hand to her lap. 'Of course. If that's what you want.'

It was a relief to Josie when the coffin was brought in and the funeral service began, although she ached with sympathy for a very pale Carrie and an obviously bewildered Archie and April. She would do what she could to help in the days and weeks to come. Perhaps she could volunteer to take the children out from time to time. Or simply be available if their mother wanted to talk.

The bereaved Campbell family would have plenty of people around them today. After the funeral breakfast was over Josie's own priority was Roddy. Once she got him home maybe he would be able to relax. She realised he hadn't said how long he was going to be able to stay. She hoped it would be over Christmas and New Year as usual.

He was saying something to her, bending to whisper in her ear. With the service about to start, she indicated silently that he should repeat whatever it was he had said. His words struck a chill into her heart. '*Where's my bloody sister?*'

Josie looked at the pew in front of them where Carrie and the children sat with Mr Campbell senior. As unobtrusively as possible, she glanced over her shoulder. First in one direction, then the other. Matthew's mother Shona was nowhere to be seen.

* * *

He was pacing the floor of Josie's sitting room saying the same thing over and over again. 'I simply can't believe it. Poor Matt. Oh, poor Matt.'

Josie couldn't believe it either. How could a mother not attend her own son's funeral? She had never seen Roddy like this. He was close to distraught. Casting around desperately for some way of softening it for him, she repeated what his brother-in-law had said. 'Charles said she felt she just wouldn't have been able to face it . . .'

Roddy stopped his restless marching and wheeled round to face her. 'You believe Shona's lying somewhere prostrate with grief? Somehow I don't think so. You of all people know that she's always been a cold bitch.'

Josie couldn't deny that without him heaping derision on whatever she said. He bent his head, pinching the bridge of his nose between his thumb and forefinger.

'Do you have a headache? Shall I get you something?'

He ignored those solicitous questions. 'That cold bitch was the only woman in my life after my mother died. People don't have to hit you to hurt you, you know.'

'I do know that,' Josie said gently. Obviously his grief over his nephew's death was bringing all sorts of things bubbling to the surface, thoughts and memories he'd suppressed for years. Should she try and get him to talk about some of them? He didn't give her the opportunity, turning his back on her to stand staring blindly out of the window. She saw his shoulders lift in a deep breath.

'I'm only glad Matt didn't turn out like either of his parents. At least he and Carrie had a few years of real happiness together. I'm hoping that will maybe sustain her.'

It was a good job he couldn't see the expression on Josie's face. Normally so perceptive, he had a real blind spot here. As they had taken their leave of Carrie at the

402

funeral breakfast, Roddy had sat down next to the young widow and taken her hand in the two of his, offering what comfort he could.

Carrie had turned to smile a little wanly up at Josie and in that instant her lovely red hair had swung back from her face. There had been an ugly bruise on the side of her head, the make-up with which she had attempted to cover it beginning to flake off. As the eyes of the two young women had met, Josie had known that all her suspicions about Matthew Campbell were justified.

Roddy had turned from the window. She wasn't going to share those thoughts with him. He was too distressed.

'It is a terrible thing for a mother to lose a child,' she said, still trying to soften the blow of his sister's absence from Matthew's funeral.

Roddy folded his arms and directed an unforgiving look at her. 'How can you think of yourself at a time like this?'

That wasn't fair. She hadn't been thinking of herself but of all the mothers who were losing sons and daughters to this war. Hardly knowing what she was saying, Josie raised her eyes to his face. 'Isn't it natural to think about family at a time like this – when you see another family going through the rituals of farewell?'

'And your reunion with your family has been so satisfying, has it? Your sister sounds as selfish a little bitch as Shona.'

She didn't want to hear him talking about her sister in the same breath as his own. 'Rachel's finding it difficult to come to terms—'

'Stop making excuses for her,' he snapped.

Telling herself he was too upset to know what he was saying, Josie forced a small smile. 'Could we maybe try and forget about all this for the rest of the day?'

'Carrie and the children can't forget about it.'

'No,' she said slowly, 'but I think the children are what

will sustain Carrie. Perhaps rather more than her years with Matt.'

'Is there something behind that comment?'

'Roddy,' she said carefully, 'there were a lot of problems between Carrie and Matt.'

'Problems? What kind of problems?'

'Forget it,' Josie said, waving a jerky hand in dismissal of the topic. 'Forget that I mentioned it.'

'No,' he said, his eyes narrowing. 'I want to know what you mean.'

Distressed by what Carrie's life must have been like and smarting from the fact he was taking his anger towards his sister out on her and her sister, Josie's temper flared. 'He *hit* her, Roddy. On more than one occasion. Probably several, now that I come to think about it. Shouldn't you and I have noticed that over the years and tried to do something to help?'

He stared at her for a full five seconds. Then, suppressing an expletive, he let rip. 'Don't be ridiculous, Jo. Matt hit Carrie? It's risible. *Jesus Christ!* It's an absolutely bloody ludicrous suggestion.'

'It's the truth,' she said stubbornly. 'I know it is.'

He unfolded his arms and inclined his head towards her, the investigative journalist at work. 'How do you know? Has Carrie told you? Do you have any other evidence?'

'No, but . . .'

'Then I think you're putting two and two together and making five, don't you? Equating Carrie's life to your own sordid upbringing.'

Josie drew her breath in on a hiss. 'How dare you say that! My upbringing was not sordid! My mother was—'

'A saint, I'm sure!' he flung at her. 'Just like the blessed Tam Paterson, the man to whom I can never match up. Well, it's pretty bloody easy to be perfect when you're dead, Jo.'

'That's a horrible thing to say!'

'Oh, spare me your working-class sensibilities about not speaking ill of the dead! Is there some reason why they don't apply to my nephew?' He looked so haughty. So dismissive. So condescending.

With a supreme effort of will, Josie forced herself to take a step back from him, and from the argument. 'I think you should go upstairs,' she said tightly. 'Otherwise we're both liable to say things we'll regret.'

'Maybe I should go further than that. Back to London, perhaps. I don't seem to be getting a very warm welcome here!'

That unforgiving response shattered Josie's precarious resolution not to retaliate. 'Go back to London, then!' she yelled. 'No doubt there are any number of well-spoken young ladies queuing up to give you that warm welcome you're looking for!'

The words hurtled through the charged air which shimmered between them and crashed into an edgy silence. When Roddy finally broke it, his voice was low and deceptively quiet. 'You really think I'd be unfaithful to you?' His voice grew dry, his expression sardonic. 'You don't understand me at all, do you, Jo?'

'Maybe I understand you only too well,' she said bitterly. 'Maybe I was daft to believe that the leopard could ever change his spots. Maybe I know Roderick Cunningham can resist everything except temptation and maybe I know there are too many women nowadays with the morals of alley cats who're all too willing to provide it.'

Anger flashed across his face. 'Don't you think that's a trifle judgemental coming from a woman who doesn't know who fathered her child? Who knows what it's like to lie on her back in an alleyway being called a slut and a wh—'

The damage had been done well before he stopped himself from saying any more.

You don't have to hit somebody to hurt them. No, you only had to take something they had told you in confidence – something they had disclosed to no other living soul but you, something which it had taken so much courage to tell you – and then throw it back in their face.

White-faced and trembling, Josie knew it was only a matter of time before she broke down. She had to get him out of here before she did.

'Go away,' she said. 'Just go away and leave me alone.'

'With pleasure!' he said savagely.

He slammed her front door behind him with such violence that the noise reverberated throughout the whole building.

When he got back to London he went out and got mindlessly, viciously drunk. Coming to in the wee small hours with a thumping head and a raging thirst, he padded through to the small bathroom of his flat and surveyed himself in the mirror. He didn't much care for what he saw.

The only reason he hadn't ended up in bed with the blonde he'd met last night – might as well live down to what was expected of him – was that he had drunk too much to be capable of anything. The girl had taken pity on him, poured him into a taxi. He had the vaguest of recollections of the driver asking for his key and opening the door for him.

Work, that was what he needed. Good, honest work. They were always looking for some poor sap willing to spend Christmas with the troops and send back heart-warming stories to keep up morale on the home front. After that he would volunteer for some other job nobody else wanted: preferably a prolonged one. But he had to speak to her before he went. He rang Glasgow in the early afternoon, when his headache had worn off a little.

'Are you all right?'

'Fine,' she said. Miss Cool, Calm and Collected of 1942. She wouldn't have gone out and got guttered last night. That wasn't the way she did things.

'I'm going away,' he said.

'On another assignment?'

'Yes. You won't be hearing from me for a while.'

'Right,' she said crisply. 'Thank you for letting me know.'

He waited for her to say something else. She didn't.

'We'll keep in touch?'

'We may have to professionally.'

'Yes,' he said dully. 'Goodbye, Jo.'

The phone went dead in her hand. Josie replaced the receiver, pushed her typewriter across the polished wood of her desk and sank her head forward on to her arms. She stayed like that for a very long time.

Chapter 38

Climbing the stairs at Kelvinbridge underground station on her way to pay one of her regular visits to Mrs Beaton, Josie was brought up short by the sight of a small poster stuck roughly to the wall. The drawing was a simple one, a white cross against a shadowy background. There was a printed sentence underneath it: *The forces of darkness halt before the forces of light*.

She had thought she was impervious to slogans. The Ministry of Information had been churning them out thick and fast over the past five and a half years. *Dig for Victory. Careless Talk Costs Lives. Make Do And Mend. Be Like Dad, Keep Mum*. The huge percentage of the female population currently working outside the home had been mightily offended by that one.

This poster seemed to be more of a home-made effort than a Ministry job. Someone had wanted to share the message. *The forces of darkness halt before the forces of light*. The words gave Josie an unexpected lift of the spirits. With the invasion force which had successfully landed in France last summer having fought its way almost to Berlin, it really did seem as if it was only a matter of time now before it was all over. Thank God.

She knew Roddy was with the Allied Army, making a name for himself by filing some terrific articles which were being syndicated throughout the Incorporated News group. Two weeks ago she had read, published and wept over a piece he had written about the liberation of Buchenwald concentration camp. So many people had commented on it she had felt obliged to write and tell him so.

It was the first communication between them since that bitter parting on the day of Matthew Campbell's funeral, two years ago now. It didn't exactly qualify as keeping in touch. Stravaiging about Europe as he was, she wasn't sure how much chance there was of him even receiving her letter.

Standing waiting for Mrs Beaton to answer the door, she looked at the stained-glass panel of the old sailing ship and allowed herself a wistful smile. This was where it had all begun, that night when they had accidentally kissed each other. Had it really been so accidental? The door flew open.

'Turn around!'

'Pardon?' Used as she was to Mrs B's eccentricities, it was a bit much being told to go when she had only just got there.

'Josephine, I know you're a sceptic but I have a message for you. From the other side.'

Although she knew that many people who'd lost loved ones took great comfort from spiritualism, Josie herself had always shied away from Mrs Beaton's alleged psychic abilities, faintly perturbed and slightly offended when her former landlady claimed to have received messages from Sally. Doing her best to keep an open mind about it, she nevertheless had a reprehensible tendency to mock. It was rising to the surface now.

'I have a message for you from a lady who died young,' Mrs Beaton declaimed.

Well. That narrows it down a lot.

'She's laughing.'

A happy spirit. That was good.

Then Mrs Beaton came out with some words which stopped the inclination to mockery dead in its tracks.

'She's laughing about a shoe. I'm to remind you about the single shoe.'

Josie's breath caught in her throat. 'What else does she say?'

'That she wants to see her two girls friends again. She says you'll know where to go.'

Why was she doing this? It was daft. Completely and utterly illogical. As she hopped off the tram she glanced over at the Drygate. Maybe she should just drop in on Bridget and Mick and Ella instead. But something impelled her to keep walking towards the cathedral.

She plunged out of the April sunshine into its shady interior and did a slow circuit of the whole building, progressing from the nave to the choir and back into the transept. Nothing. Simply the peace which she had always found here.

Still, she couldn't leave without going down to the Laigh Kirk to pay her respects to Saint Mungo. He had brought Charlie back to her. She'd been overjoyed to receive a letter from her brother last week. Currently in liberated Holland, he'd told her he was allowing himself to think about the future, trying to decide whether that would be in North America or Scotland. Hard though it was, Josie was determined not to influence Charlie in any way. He had to do what was best for him.

After a brief pause at Saint Mungo's tomb, she did a tour of the lower church too, lingering in Saint Nicholas's chapel – not that she expected anything to happen there. Her experience of eight years ago, which she had accepted as easily as she was usually sceptical, had been a precious and unique event: too precious and unique ever to be repeated. It was enough to sit for a while on the stone bench lining the wall, remembering.

She mounted one flight of stone steps and walked purposefully towards those which would take her back up to the main church. She had done as she had been asked but nothing had happened and now her duty was done. Just before she reached the stairs, she glanced over at the Saint's tomb. There was a girl sitting hunched on the steps in front of it. Josie peered at her through the dim light.

'Rachel? Is that you?'

It was like a vision of the past, herself when young. A cloud of dark hair. A pale and tear-stained face.

'I was here to make arrangements about the wedding. Once Peter comes home we're getting married here. Upstairs, I mean.' Rachel sniffed, and wiped the back of her hand over her nose and mouth.

Trying not to wonder if she herself would be on the guest list, Josie sat down beside her on the cold stone steps. They had last seen each other before Christmas, as usual only because she had pressed an invitation to afternoon tea on her reluctant sister.

'So what's the problem?' Since that first disastrous reunion, she had never tried to touch Rachel. Now, very gingerly, she placed a hand on her shoulder. 'Don't you want to marry Peter any more?'

The girl turned in to her like a small and frightened child. 'Yes, I do. I love him so much. But oh Josie, I'm so scared!'

Josie slid her arm properly about her. 'Scared of what, Rachel?'

'Of having children,' she blurted out. 'That's what killed Mammy, isn't it? She had all those babies who died, as well. That's why I've put the wedding off for so long. Peter wanted to get married ages ago and I wouldn't and I feel so selfish but I'm just so scared!'

Josie rubbed her chin gently over the hair which was so like her own. 'Rachel,' she said. 'I want you to come for a walk with me. I have some things to tell you.'

She led her sister over the Bridge of Sighs and up the hill between the tombs and monuments of the Necropolis. When they reached the mausoleum flanked by the two white angels she began to talk, starting with exactly how and why their mother had died and going on to speak about herself and Tam.

'So you see,' she finished up, 'it was all perfectly straightforward for me and my baby was fit and healthy. I don't see why it should be any different for you.'

Rachel was staring up at the angel on the right of the mausoleum, the one holding a baby in her arms. 'Is Mammy buried in here?'

'No, she's up at Sighthill. This place was only ever really for the toffs.'

'But we used to play in here, didn't we? I remember you telling us stories.'

'Telling *you* stories maybe,' Josie said, her mouth quirking with amusement. 'Charlie was usually busy trying to give himself any number of communicable diseases.'

Having turned her back on the white angel, Rachel's grey eyes were drifting over the monuments and obelisks which dotted the hillside. Her gaze lingered on the cathedral and the Royal Infirmary behind it. She glanced quickly in the other direction, towards the Drygate, before looking just as quickly away again. Watching her, Josie wondered just how deep the place was where her sister had buried the memories of her early life.

'Have you ever tried to find your baby?'

'He's almost a man now,' Josie said gravely. 'And I decided a long time ago that I wouldn't go searching for him.'

'Don't you long to know what kind of a person he is? What he looks like, even?'

'Both of those things,' Josie replied, thinking that there was only one person in the world who knew exactly why what her son looked like as a man was so important. 'But he may not even know that he's adopted. I don't want to risk disrupting his life by suddenly turning up out of the blue. I've left a trail,' she explained, 'with every place and organisation I can think of. If he wants to find me, I've made it easy for him.'

Now it was Josie whose eyes were drifting: seeing the present, remembering the past. 'I hope he will want to find me,' she said at last.

Rachel was looking at her. 'Thank you for telling me all this,' she said. 'It can't have been easy.'

Josie shrugged. 'I've been living with it for a long time.'

'I didn't mean that. I meant thank you for telling me when I've been so . . .' Rachel paused, searching for the right word with which to berate herself. She came up with three. 'Difficult. Selfish. Cold.'

'Good grief,' Josie said lightly, 'when you have a go at yourself you don't believe in half measures, do you?'

Rachel was studying the white angel again. 'Where's Charlie now?'

'Enjoying a free continental holiday with the rest of them. I could give you a forwarding address if you like. I'm sure he'd appreciate a letter.'

'Would he want to hear from me?' Her chin was trembling.

'Of course he would.'

Rachel turned her head and gave her sister a cautious little smile.

Four weeks later Josie made her curtsey at the end of an impromptu eightsome reel and smilingly extricated herself from the group of giggly girls and grinning sailors with whom she'd been dancing it. Going in the opposite direction to what seemed like the entire population of Glasgow and the west of Scotland, she fought her way back through towards St Vincent Place.

Celebrating the end of the war in Europe was all very well, but everyone who was letting their hair down in George Square this afternoon would expect to see their activities reported in the special victory edition of the

413

Glasgow Evening Dispatch. She had work to do.

The photographer from whom she'd been separated by the noisy and joyful crowd had got back to Buchanan Street ten minutes before her and was already processing the pictures. The girl was a hard worker, and talented too. Later, viewing what she had produced, Josie told her so. Tough with her staff when she had to be, she had never been one to deny praise where it was due.

'These are great,' she said. 'You've caught the atmosphere exactly. Well done.'

The girl flushed with pleasure. 'Miss Shaw,' she said impulsively, 'could I ask you something?'

'Make it quick,' Josie said, her mind already on other things. 'We're working against the clock even more than usual today.'

The girl took the instruction to heart, her question straightforward and to the point. 'When the men come back, am I out on my ear?'

'Not if I have anything to do it. You're an excellent photographer.'

'But the women were all sent home the last time. Or so my mother says.'

Josie dragged her thoughts back from page layouts. Obviously there was some reassurance needed here. She stole five minutes from her more than usually hectic schedule to supply it, assuring the anxious girl that while she was hoping many of those former members of the *Dispatch* workforce who'd been serving their country would come back to their old jobs, there was no way she was going to let a gifted and enthusiastic member of staff go simply because she was a female.

Thinking about it later, it occurred to Josie that a lot of women might have the same worry as the young photographer. Others, perhaps most obviously those who'd been working in the heavy industries, would find it a relief to cede their positions to the returning menfolk, gratefully going back to doing just one job instead of two: looking after their homes and families.

Some women had less of a choice, of course. Widows like Carrie Campbell had to work if they weren't to find themselves and their children on the breadline. Josie had seen the young woman who'd become her close friend blossom and grow over the past few years, enjoying her work and proud in the knowledge that she was providing for her fatherless children.

Discreet though Carrie always was about such things, Josie now knew something of what she had suffered at the hands of her late husband, knew too where Ewen Livingstone fitted into the story. For Carrie's sake, she wished she could think that story might have a happy ending. She was painfully aware that happy endings belonged in fairytales.

One of those former members of the *Dispatch* workforce who'd been serving his country turned up unannounced on Josie's doorstep on New Year's Day. Her eyes lighting up with delight, she began firing questions at him.

'Ben! Oh Ben, how lovely to see you! How long can you stay? How on earth did you manage to travel today? Why didn't you let me know you were coming? Are you hungry? Oh come in, come in!'

As he walked into the house, Josie frowned. 'Why are you walking with a limp?'

'Let me answer all that,' he said, grinning at her. 'As long as you'll have me. Two people who were as desperate to get back to Glasgow as I was gave me a lift in their car. Because I wanted to surprise you. Yes, I could eat a horse.' He dropped his kitbag on to the floor of the lobby and began unbuttoning his overcoat. 'Lastly, because I had a bit of a contretemps with a German sniper about seven or eight months ago. Considering the only weapon I was operating at the time was a camera, I do think his reaction was a wee touch extreme.'

'Oh Ben!' she said, looking up at him with concern. 'Are you all right?'

'I'm fine now,' he assured her. As she took his coat from him, he struck a pose. 'And it does give me the chance to say things like, "Why madam, 'tis naught but a scratch," and act all manly and heroic.' His dark eyes were full of laughter.

'Oh Ben,' Josie said, throwing his coat over a chair and her arms about his neck. 'It's so good to have you back!'

They spent the following evening at Alan and Deirdre's house and talked, as seemed only natural, about the future. Initially the other three quizzed Ben about his plans. Stretching out what he was pleased to refer to as his gammy leg, he nursed a malt whisky and told them.

'I'm torn two ways. Part of me quite fancies doing the sort of reportage Sally and I did in Spain.'

'In partnership with another journalist?' Deirdre asked, her face softening at the mention of Sally.

'No, by myself I think. Working as a photo-journalist. No doubt there'll be more wars to get involved with in the future.'

Alan grimaced. 'That's a happy thought. What's your other choice, Ben?'

'Fashion photography,' he said boldly. 'I've always had this hankering to do it.' He took a sip of his whisky and looked reflective. 'Maybe I could do a bit of both. Year about, or something. D'you think it would be possible?'

'Dunno,' Alan said, 'but it would certainly make for an interesting career path.'

'What about you, Deirdre?' Josie asked her hostess. 'Do you fancy going out to work again now that the children are a bit older?'

'Perhaps. Another piece of shortbread, Josie? Of course, I may decide my most important role in life is as helpmeet to the great white hope of Scottish post-war literature.'

Her husband gave her a dirty look. 'Your turn, Josie. Ever fancied a change from the *Dispatch*?'

'I've sometimes thought about going freelance,' she said consideringly, taking a petticoat tail from the plate Deirdre was proffering. It looked as if it might actually be the real thing, not the substitute they'd had to put up with over the war years. 'There are quite a few subjects I'd like to get my teeth into in a way you can't when you're putting a newspaper out every day.'

Ben's face bore a deceptively innocent look. 'How about your personal life, Josie? Do you envisage any changes taking place there?'

'Don't start,' she said, using the piece of shortbread to point accusingly at Alan. 'I get this from Mr Dewar every second Tuesday.'

'We just can't understand why you don't try to get in touch with him, Josie,' Deirdre said gently.

'I wrote. He didn't write back.' She forcibly changed the subject, asking Ben to tell Deirdre and Alan about the phone call he had made to Sally's mother earlier in the day.

'I'm taking her out for lunch the day after tomorrow,' he said with a smile. 'I expect we'll spend most of it talking about Sally.'

'Mr Fleming still isn't prepared to meet you?' Deirdre asked.

'Won't give me houseroom.'

'It's his loss,' Josie said stoutly. 'Isn't it terrible that he's so stiff and unforgiving after all these years? Hard to understand how anyone can be so stubborn.' She popped the last piece of petticoat tail into her mouth, looked up and almost choked on it. All three of them had turned towards her, identical expressions of exaggerated disbelief on their faces.

'Don't start,' she said again. 'Just don't start.'

★ ★ ★

'Would you like another dram, Ben? I've got a bottle of malt here somewhere. I think I might go straight to bed, if you don't mind.'

Following her into the sitting room, he reached forward, grabbed her wrist and pulled her on to the sofa. 'I do mind, as a matter of fact.' He didn't beat about the bush. 'Why haven't you written to him again, Josie?'

Sinking into the cushions because of the force with which he had yanked her down, Josie turned her head and gave him a deliberately vacuous smile. 'Because it's his turn to write?'

Ben frowned at her. 'Don't be flippant, sweetie. This is too serious.'

'I don't want to talk about it,' she said, trying and failing to remove her hand from his grasp.

'Well, that's just tough, Miss Shaw, because I do. Tell me one thing: do you still love him?'

She looked away, but Ben shook the hand he held and forced her to meet his eye. She couldn't lie to this man. He knew her too well.

'Yes,' she whispered.

'So it really is stubbornness that's stopping you getting in touch with him? That's pathetic, Josie. I'd have expected better from you.' He released his grip on her wrist.

Stung, she tried to defend herself. 'We had this quarrel—'

'I know. You mentioned it in a letter you wrote to me sometime after the event. Very much *en passant*,' Ben added, giving her a baleful look. 'I presumed you'd had a lovers' tiff.'

'Rather more than that,' she said sadly. 'We said some really dreadful things to each other that day.' She paused, thinking about those.

You really think I'd be unfaithful to you? At the time, she'd been too hurt and angry to register the pain behind

418

those quietly uttered words. Now she saw that she had drawn blood with the bitter statements which had provoked that answer. As badly wounded as herself, Roddy had simply and blindly reached for the first weapon which had come to hand in order to defend himself.

With the benefit of hindsight, Josie saw too that he must always have believed he came in a poor second to her golden memories of her first love. Tam Paterson had been just that and she would never forget him and what they had meant to each other, but Roderick Cunningham had been the love of her maturity: her best friend as well as her lover, the man with whom she had hoped to spend the rest of her life. Had hoped. Those were the operative words.

Watching the emotions chase themselves across her face, Ben's voice was gentle. 'You're admitting to being as much in the wrong as Roddy?'

'Yes,' she said, with painful honesty. 'I'm afraid I have to.'

'Yet you're still going to give up on him?'

'He seems to have given up on me. He never replied to my letter.'

'Josie,' Ben said reproachfully. 'You don't know that he even received it. Give me the real reason.'

She took a deep breath. 'I'm scared, Ben,' she said. 'How do I know that he still loves me?'

'You don't. You'll have to take a chance on it.'

When she looked doubtfully at him, he smiled and reached once more for her hand. Only this time it was to plant a kiss on the back of it before holding it lightly in his. 'Let me tell you a story, Josie. It's about two very dear friends of mine. They had another friend who experienced a tragedy from which he thought he'd never recover.'

Ben's smile grew grim. 'He thought he didn't even *want* to recover from it, but because his friends really cared about him they weren't prepared to allow that to happen. It wasn't easy, but they worked together and turned a piece of human wreckage back into a man.' His lips twitched. 'I use the word in its loosest sense, of course.'

Josie was still looking very doubtful. 'What's your point, Ben?'

'Call me an old romantic if you like, sweetie, but I've always thought those two friends of mine were made for each other. They complement each other beautifully. So much in common, you see. Not to mention the years of friendship they have behind them.' His voice grew gentler still. 'And you only have to watch them together for five minutes to be aware of the attraction between them. It's tangible.' He tugged gently on her hand. 'It would be a sin to let all of that go without a fight.'

'You think so?'

'I know so. Write to him, Josie. Send it to his flat in London. Then you'll be sure he'll get it eventually.'

'All right,' she said at last.

'Promise?'

'I promise.' She slid her hand out of his and stood up. 'I'll get you that whisky now.'

Ben sighed, leaned back and closed his eyes. 'After you've done that you can go to bed.'

Halfway towards the door, she turned and looked at him, sprawled out on her sofa. 'Thank you, oh great one,' she muttered. He opened his eyes and grinned at her. Josie smiled back. 'Do you really fancy fashion photography?'

He lifted one of the small cushions which dotted the settee and placed it behind his curly head. 'It would make a nice change from what I've been taking pictures of recently. Being surrounded by lovely women could have its attractions.' He gave Josie an outrageous wink. 'Not to mention the occasional lovely man.'

Chapter 39

He had seen devastation before. Lots of it. He'd been in the thick of that merciless pounding of London, night after night of bombs followed by day after day of blasted buildings and blasted lives. Still travelling through a ravaged Europe two years after he had dodged German bullets on a Normandy beach, he felt as if he'd experienced a lifetime's worth of watching men trying to inflict as much damage as possible on each other. War: diplomacy by other means.

Back in North Africa in '42, wondering why he was reporting on the struggle instead of adding his own strength to it, he had begun to question his manhood. A young Army Major with whom he'd become friendly quoted the old saying to him: the one about truth being the first casualty of war. Journalists were defending, preserving and transmitting it. Wasn't that one of the principles for which they were all fighting?

The next day a landmine blew the young Major to kingdom come. With the group of soldiers who found the wreckage, Roddy helped pick up what was left of a cultured, humorous and courageous man. He joined in with the terrible jokes. Less than a week after that experience he attended his nephew's funeral.

Somewhere deep inside himself he had known all was not right with Matthew or his marriage. He had shut his eyes to it, wanting to believe in the fairytale. Now, journeying through that part of defeated Germany rapidly being transformed into the Russian zone, he knew there were no fairytales. He was seeing a whole country laid waste. It was a sobering and profoundly depressing experience.

He commented on it to the American journalist with whom he was travelling. Somehow the man had managed to commandeer one of his own army's jeeps. Roddy didn't think the two of them actually liked each other very much but there was strength in numbers.

Although individual Russians were still friendly, it wouldn't be long before western newsmen were shown the door. After the initial euphoria of victory and expressions of brotherly love, the battle lines were beginning to be redrawn for a very different type of war. Roddy found that profoundly depressing too.

His travelling companion shrugged in response to his comment about the devastated towns and countryside through which they were passing. 'They started it. It's right that they should suffer for it. There's no such thing as a good German,' he insisted. 'You were at Buchenwald. You saw what those bastards did there. Think about that, Cunningham.'

He did. Long and hard. What he had seen in the beechwood on the Ettersberg Heights had been like falling into the abyss, a manifestation of evil so chilling it had left him asking where God had been while it had all been going on. Nor could he believe that anyone who knew what had happened there could doubt the existence of God's adversary.

Ironic that the concentration camp was so close to Weimar. On vacation from Glasgow University in the early 1920s he had made the pilgrimage to the gracious small town which had been home to so many writers and thinkers. A huge statue of the two giants of German literature, Goethe and Schiller, stood in front of the theatre there, birthplace of the ill-fated Weimar Republic.

It occurred to him that the two extremes of modern

Germany being a mere mile or two apart was a chilling metaphor for the two faces of man: Dr Jekyll and Mr Hyde writ monstrous large. He thought about writing something about that but in the end the horror was too awful to do anything but simply report it as it was, making his language as restrained as possible.

Last autumn, while he was reporting from the British zone of occupation, a letter from Jo had reached him. She had sent him the cuttings from the newspapers in which the article had appeared, thanked him gravely for what he had written and told him what an impact it was having on people. She had typed her letter, signed off simply with her first name and said absolutely nothing about what she felt for him. Then again, why should she have? There were no fairytales.

Unable to summon up the courage to reply, he had immersed himself in his work. Watching Allied soldiers handing out chocolate and chewing gum to timid German children, he had wondered if they too were to be damned and held responsible for the sins of their fathers. Roderick Cunningham had no answers, only lots and lots of questions. He put them to as many people as he could find who were willing to answer them, and at night he tried to block it all out by relaxing with two old companions: alcohol and women. The former was sometimes difficult to find. There was no shortage of the latter.

The German girls offered themselves in exchange for food, sometimes even a packet of cigarettes. In one town they visited, a big bear of a Russian laughed uproariously as he told them that the local going rate was just four single cigarettes. That evening the American disappeared into the back room of a half-destroyed inn with a young woman. Half an hour later Roddy spotted her sitting on a wall not too far away, puffing on a cigarette. Even from a distance he could see how much her hand was shaking.

As he walked over to her she looked up warily. He tried

offering reassurance in his rudimentary German that he wasn't approaching her for the reason she thought he was. Then he spotted the three cigarettes lying in her lap. That was the night he gave up smoking, handing the two full packets and one half-empty one he had on him to the bemused girl before turning and walking away.

He continued travelling with the American because he would have been stuck with no transport otherwise and because he was in no position to take a high moral stance. At the beginning he too had drunk of the cup which was being so freely and so cheaply offered. When they were flinging themselves at you, what were you supposed to do? Especially when you were as bitter and as lonely as they were.

Despite his reputation, he liked to think that he had never been a promiscuous man. He supposed he hadn't been very discerning during the London Blitz, but everyone had gone a bit mad then. There had never been as many affairs as he had allowed people to think. None of them had come within a million miles of giving him what that one night and day with Jo had.

What she had lacked in experience she had made up for in an eagerness to please him which had come as the most joyful of surprises. And she had surrendered herself to him with an abandon which had exceeded his wildest expectations and a trust which had brought tears to his eyes. He had never felt so loved or so accepted: and he had destroyed it all with his own savage tongue.

What was going on here was a travesty of lovemaking. He wasn't even sure it had anything very much to do with sex. That at least would have been an honest exchange. When he came to the conclusion that it was a witches' brew of power and revenge and survival and yielding to the conqueror, he stopped participating. He was in Dresden by then.

He had travelled there too, back in the '20s. He

remembered beautiful Baroque buildings and pavement cafés and museums full of the finest Meissen porcelain. Now the place which had been known as Florence-on-the-Elbe was little more than a pile of rubble, destroyed by British bombs and the resulting firestorm in a raid mere months before the war had ended.

There was a girl watching him as he picked his way through the ruins. He would have walked past her with nothing more than a nod of acknowledgement if she hadn't spoken to him, addressing him in English. 'You are American?'

He shook his head. 'British. A journalist,' he expanded, not sure why he wished her to know that. He didn't want to start all this again; he really didn't. But standing among the wreckage of what had once been a lovely city, he felt lost and alone and empty, and he was missing Jo and longing for her more than he could afford to admit. He looked at the girl. 'You want something to eat?'

She nodded. 'Come on then,' he said, reaching for the enormous leather grip which lay beside her. Even in these surroundings being a gentleman was a habit which died hard. She got there before him.

'I will carry it myself.'

Everything she owned in the world, he supposed. He took her back to the jeep being guarded by some urchins whom he had bribed with chocolate. Then he drove to the outskirts of the city, to an old guesthouse where the Russians had allowed him and the American to carve themselves out a piece of territory.

He had a mattress, a broken-down table, two upright chairs and a door he could close. On the floor below, the American was sleeping off last night's vodka-drinking bout with their hosts – an event in which Roddy had declined to participate. They were heading back west tomorrow morning at six o'clock.

'Sit down,' he instructed the girl. 'I'll make us

something to eat.' He'd acquired a small camping stove and pan on his travels, exchanging them with a German housewife for a couple of cans of food. Opening a tin of British Army field rations, he emptied it into the pan. It contained some indeterminate form of meat stew.

He would throw in some baked beans too and open the tin of Spam he'd been saving. The girl looked as if she could do with a good feed. When he turned round she was still standing but she had shrugged off her jacket, put the two upright chairs together and placed her large bag over both of them.

'Please,' she said, 'if you want to take me to bed you do it now. Then you give me some food. Then I go.'

Her eyes kept flickering from his face to the pan of food. She walked over to stand in front of him and began unbuttoning her blouse. Roddy put his own hand over hers, stilling the movements of her fingers. 'You don't want to do this.'

She attempted a smile. 'You're a handsome man.' She continued to undress, pushing his hand away. He raised it to her shoulder, meaning to give her a gentle shove backwards.

'Hit me then,' she said, in a voice which had all the weariness of the world in it. 'I know some of you like to. Call me names too if you want.'

Appalled, he stared down into her face. 'I've never hit a woman in my life. Or used foul language in front of one.'

She smiled bitterly. 'Not even a dirty German whore? A Nazi slut?'

'Sit down at that table,' Roddy said, his voice not quite steady. 'Sit down at that table and we'll eat together. Like civilised human beings.'

Her laugh was harsh. Then her eyes locked with his. What she saw in them he didn't know but she gave him a funny little nod and moved to comply with his request.

Still unable to stop being a gentleman, he strode over to remove the leather holdall from the two chairs and give her a seat. The girl uttered a cry of protest. At exactly the same moment as the baby inside the bag did.

Fifteen minutes later, the child cradled in his arms while he sat and watched its mother eat, he had the whole terrible story. Her tiny daughter was the product of rape.

'Russians,' she explained. 'Seven of them, or maybe eight. I think I lost consciousness at one stage. The mind does that, you know. Blanks out the unacceptable.'

Roddy glanced up from the baby, currently sucking some heavily diluted condensed milk off his little finger. 'You speak very good English.'

'I was a student of psychology,' she said. 'Now I'm nothing. A slut. A whore.'

He winced. 'Don't call yourself that.'

'It's what I do now,' she said. 'It's how I survive.'

'You feel you have to hide your child?'

She shrugged. 'Men like virgins. Especially Russian men. They're easily fooled. But not if you're holding a baby in your arms.'

Dear God in heaven, he thought, more ashamed of his own sex than he ever had been in his life. 'How can I help you?' he asked. 'Is there something I can do for you?'

'If I could get to my sister,' she said, the words coming out jerkily in her fear that he might be tormenting her. 'She is near Bremen. She would help me.'

'And the baby?'

'She is innocent,' she said fiercely. 'She cannot help her birth.'

'No,' he agreed. He stood up and went round the table. Her baby in one arm, he slid the other around the girl's thin shoulders. 'Come on,' he said. 'Come and lie down.'

She had that resigned look on her face again. 'As long as we can put the baby somewhere safe while you have me.' Her words were slurred with tiredness.

'No, no,' he said, 'you misunderstand. I will take the chairs. You and your child will sleep in the bed. You can feed her there.'

Her eyes were searching his face. 'You ask for nothing in return?'

Smiling down at her, he shook his head. He felt elated. Cleansed.

As he pulled the grubby blankets up over mother and child, the girl reached up and touched his unshaven chin with her thin fingers. The touch was light as thistledown. 'I think you are what they call an English gentleman.'

'A Scottish gentleman,' he corrected gently.

He watched over both of them throughout the night, occasionally slipping into a fitful doze as he sat uncomfortably on one of the upright chairs, his long legs stretched out on the other. By the time the dawn came up the next morning, his body was stiff and cold. His head was clearer than it had been for months.

He stood up and stretched to get rid of the stiffness. Looking down at the still sleeping mother and child, he was thinking about Jo. He'd been thinking about her all night. Separated from this girl by nationality, she was united to her by experience. Jo too had been left with her life in ruins. She had fought her way out of them, with no resources other than sheer guts and determination.

He hoped this young mother would find the same sort of strength and he was grateful that he'd been given the chance to help her on the first stage of her journey. Surely her love for her child would do the rest. Love, he thought, it's a hell of a powerful thing.

Powerful enough to apologise. Powerful enough to forgive.

It was time to go home.

Chapter 40

'I like your hair like that, Miss Shaw,' observed the receptionist on the front desk.

'Why thank you,' Josie said, patting her crowning glory, piled loosely on top of her head. 'I delude myself that I look taller when I put it up.'

She smiled at the girl and headed for the stairs. She was feeling rather smart today. With their elegantly wide legs, the soft black wool trousers she'd found at a recent sale of second-hand clothes must be pre-war, although they'd obviously never been worn.

She had teamed them with a crisp white shirt and the red bolero-style cardigan Carrie Campbell's neighbour had knitted for her. Florence Cooke was a real crafts-woman. The cardigan was as smart as anything you would find in an exclusive shop, the shoulder pads which the old lady had sewn in giving it the required look of businesslike efficiency, although there was a touch of frivolity in the way the knitted jacket was fastened, with a woollen cord laced through the neckband and tied in a bow at the front.

Still smiling as she walked into the Features Department, Josie thought about the evening at Carrie's house during which Mrs Cooke had instructed her and April Campbell in the esoteric arts of French knitting and the making of pom-poms. She glanced up at the picture of Sally. 'Smart but feminine,' she said softly. 'I hope you approve.'

The day was as busy as it always was. Only in the late

afternoon did Josie get the chance to sit down and read some articles which had been sent in on spec. Her pulse quickened when she found one she definitely wanted to publish and another which was extremely well written. Like several she'd received lately, it dealt with how individuals, families and the country were coping with the transition from war to peace.

The joy of victory last year had given way all too soon to a realisation of just how difficult that transition might be. For a start, everyone was going to have to live with shortages, privations and rationing for a good while yet. Then there was the small matter of moving industry from a war footing on to a peacetime one. So much investment was needed in so many areas of the economy, and where that was going to come from was anybody's guess.

Although all of that impinged greatly on the lives of ordinary people, the psychological adjustment required now that the war was over was equally as significant. The article in which Josie was currently engrossed gave advice on how to deal with a crucially important aspect of that, one which was rapidly becoming a talking point.

Now that so many men had finally been discharged from the forces after serving the regulation *duration plus six months*, it was becoming clear that homecomings weren't always unreservedly happy affairs. Husbands and wives who hadn't seen each other for years could find it difficult to settle down to living with each other again. Children who'd been used to having their mother's full attention didn't necessarily take too kindly to having to share it with a man they hardly knew. The article examined the problem from the point of view of the returning men.

They will have changed, the writer had written, *more than one can imagine. We women have also been through the fire, but we have not faced what they have faced. Their country has not only asked them to be prepared to die, it has also asked them to be prepared to kill.*

Some will want to talk about their experiences. Many will not. They will all need careful handling by those around them: patience and understanding; compassion and consideration for what has been required of them; a realisation of the horrors which they have been compelled to witness.

It was an excellent piece, thoughtful and thought-provoking but more suited to a woman's magazine than an evening newspaper. Josie turned to her typewriter and wrote the author a letter suggesting two or three outlets and adding a few words of encouragement about the standard of the writing and the sensitive way in which the subject-matter had been dealt with.

After she had tossed the envelope containing her letter and the returned article into the wire basket for outgoing mail, she made a start on the filing. Piled up in another basket, the one sitting on top of the bank of filing cabinets in the Features Department, it was beginning to reach impending avalanche proportions. Crouching down to put some papers away in the bottom of one of the cabinets, she stood up again and kicked the drawer shut with her foot.

'Love the trousers,' came a voice from the doorway. 'Very chic.'

She whirled round, pom-poms flying. He was lounging against the door frame in the way that only he could, the picture of rumpled elegance. Josie took in the soft-collared shirt which looked as if it had been slept in and the herringbone tweed coat with the broad lapels, worn casually open.

'I was just wondering,' he said. As though he were picking up the threads of a conversation they'd been having half an hour before.

'What were you wondering?' She sounded like a frog with a sore throat. Maybe it was a miracle that she could speak at all.

'If it's true that time and tide wait for no man. What do you think?'

431

'I don't know,' she said. 'Did you get my letter?'

'What letter?'

'The one I sent to your flat in London three months ago.'

'I haven't been there. I came straight here.' He straightened up and folded his arms across his chest. 'What did you write in your letter?'

'Words,' she said. 'Why were you wondering about time and tide?'

He transferred his gaze to the wire basket on top of the filing cabinets. 'I see that's in its usual state of neglect.'

'Why were you wondering about time and tide?' she repeated.

He turned his fair head and met her eyes. 'Because I'm wondering if it's too late to say sorry.'

She opened her mouth to reply but before she could say anything he had dropped his arms and the nonchalant air, words tumbling out of his mouth. 'I'm wondering that. And I'm wondering if it's too late to ask for the chance to prove that the leopard really can change his spots. And I'm wondering if there's even the remotest chance of your ever forgiving me.'

He ran a hand through his hair. 'Och, Jo,' he breathed. 'I know I'd have an awful lot of bridge-building to do.'

'Tell you what,' she said, 'why don't you start building that bridge from one side and I'll meet you in the middle?'

A spark of hope leaped into his eyes. 'Jo . . .' he began, and then stopped.

'What's the matter?' she asked lightly. 'Don't you understand English? Maybe we should try a very short sentence, then. One which contains only three words.'

The spark became a candle, its flame burning cautious but bright.

'A small but crucial combination of two personal pronouns and one verb?' he queried, trying once again for the nonchalant air. The hunger in his face gave the lie to that.

'You say it first,' she whispered

'We'll say it together,' he said.

By the time the *I love yous* were out they were in each other's arms. A few minutes later he put another few simple words together. 'Will you marry me, Jo?'

Her eyes were full of love for him. As she pointed towards the floor, they were also brimming with mischief.

'Down on one knee, Cunningham, down on one knee.'

Epilogue

1953

The editor of the *Glasgow Evening Dispatch* came round the corner of his house loosening his tie and smiling at the sight which greeted him. His wife was sitting on a blanket in the middle of the grass playing with their younger son. Accompanied by Darwin the dog, their elder boy was being chased around the garden by his twin sister in what looked to Roddy like a game of cowboys and Indians. The only problem was that *both* of his offspring seemed to be wearing paper headdresses.

'How can you play Indians and Indians?'

Issuing blood-curdling cries, the twins did a war dance around their father, accepted a kiss apiece and headed off again.

'Neither of them wants to be the cowboy,' Josie explained.

Roddy lowered himself down on to the blanket beside her, patted Darwin, did his duty by the baby and gave his wife a somewhat more leisurely kiss. 'Trust children brought up by you to be supporters of the underdog, Miss Shaw.'

'Speaking of which,' she said, 'in my capacity as Miss Shaw it's my duty to inform that you that freelance rates are going up again.'

He groaned. 'Whatever possessed me to marry a member of the National Union of Journalists? Nothing but troublemakers, the lot of you.'

'Filthy capitalist,' Josie said lovingly, kissing him again.

'Stop trying to distract me.' He looked pointedly at her typewriter, stood on a camping table set under the shade of a tree. 'When am I getting the last of those articles about the boarded-out children? Should you in fact be sitting here playing with your children when you have a deadline to meet?'

'I'll meet your deadline, Mr Editor. Have I ever missed one?'

Roddy smiled. Then he put his hand inside his jacket and extracted a letter.

'Is that the invitation to Alan's book launch?' Seeing that the baby was asleep, Josie placed him carefully into the wicker Moses basket which lay beside the blanket. 'Apparently Deirdre's been teasing him about being a fashion model ever since Ben took his photo for the cover.'

She turned. Her husband's face bore an unusually grave expression. 'It's not the invitation to Alan's do,' he said, handing her the letter. Roddy waited until she had opened the envelope and read it, watching as her face grew pale and serious. 'Is it what I think it is?'

She nodded, and handed it to him.

'Near Garelochhead,' he observed. 'We could go up there next weekend.'

'Yes,' she agreed.

Roddy slid an arm about her. 'D'you think we can get a babysitter?'

She laid her head against his shoulder, appreciating what he was trying to do. Offers of help with the children were never hard to come by. 'I won't ask Mick and Bridget this time, though. I don't want Ella Paterson to know about this until we're sure that it's going to be all right.'

'I think that's very wise.' He dropped a soft kiss on to the top of her head.

'He might only want to meet me the once. Find the last piece of the jigsaw.'

'He might,' Roddy said equably. 'He might not. We'll have to wait and see.'

Josie raised a hand to his face. 'I love you,' she said.

'More than anything?'

'More than anything in the whole wide world.'

Claiming to be glad of the break from the city centre hotel where they both lived and worked, Charlie and his new wife came to spend the afternoon with the children. Josie and Roddy left Glasgow, following the Clyde until Helensburgh. Then they drove past all the great grey battleships laid up in the Gare Loch. When they reached the village at the head of the narrow stretch of water they stopped to ask directions.

Ten minutes later they pulled up in front of a rambling cottage which was clearly in the process of being renovated. The young man perched on the dyke in front of it jumped down from the wall and came forward to greet them as the car stopped. The fair-haired girl sitting beside him stayed where she was.

As he approached her, Josie drew her breath in sharply. The resemblance was unmistakable. He stopped when he was a few feet away from her.

'I don't think I can call you Mother.'

'That's all right,' she said. 'I wasn't expecting you to. Call me Josephine,' she offered, thinking he might be more comfortable addressing her in a slightly formal way. She glanced over to where Roddy had gone to introduce himself to the young woman. Both of them were trying to look casual and unconcerned. Both of them were failing miserably.

She herself was finding it hard to stop smiling.

'Do you like horses?' she asked suddenly.

He looked at her in surprise. 'We've a couple of Highland ponies round the back. We're hoping to get a Clydesdale soon.' He unbent sufficiently to give her a grave smile. 'I've always had this big thing about Clydesdales.'

Josie examined her surroundings. Someone had been busy in this garden, giving it loving care after what looked like years of neglect. There were clumps of flowers and the earth under a flourishing rowan tree close to the front door was freshly turned over and free of weeds.

There was a voice in her head: a voice from the past. *A nice wee house by a loch somewhere. A bit of land and a couple of horses.*

'Will you come inside?' the young man asked. 'My wife's baked a cake. There are some things I'd like to ask you. Quite a lot of things. Would you mind?'

'No,' Josie said gently. 'I wouldn't mind at all.' She lifted her head and smiled across at Roddy.

As the young couple led the way into the house he came over and looked down into her face. 'It's all right, then?' he asked.

'Oh yes,' she said, 'it's all right!'

And as they smiled into each other's eyes a tiny robin perched in the rowan tree by the door began to sing its sweet song.

Author's Note

The tenement houses which lined the old Drygate are no more, swept away in the great demolition frenzy of the 1960s. However, this ancient Glasgow street lives on as part of a thriving modern housing development and community which also spreads out over the site of Duke Street Prison. Remnants of that grim place remain, including a substantial amount of the old prison wall.

The Wellpark Brewery too has expanded over the centuries but essentially occupies the same site it has done for the past half millennium or so. Brewing had been taking place there for almost two hundred years before Bonnie Prince Charlie and his men called past for a refreshment around Christmas 1745.

It's sixty years now since carters routinely drove their Clydesdales through the streets of Glasgow to deliver the brewery's products, and a long time since a horse has been anywhere near the place. Nevertheless, there are those who work there today who maintain that on a quiet and still night they've heard quite clearly soft whinnying and the clip-clop of heavy hooves on cobbles.

Now Or Never

Lynda Page

When Maddie Ashman is deceived into giving up her baby for adoption she is utterly devastated. Her mother has convinced Maddie that she has no choice – the child is illegitimate and the father has deserted her. But this act of cruelty is the final straw for Maddie and she knows she must leave home. It's now or never. But who can she turn to for help?

Catching the train to Leicester, she goes in search of the one person who might take her in – even though she has no idea where he lives. And when she gets a job in a funeral parlour she discovers that life is full of surprises – for love and laughter can be found in the most unlikely places!

Don't miss Lynda Page's other sagas, also available from Headline.

'You'll be hooked from page one' *Woman's Realm*

'Full of lively characters' *Best*

'Lynda Page creates strong charactes and is a clever and careful storyteller' *LE1*

'Lynda Page . . . writes with skill and style; her characters are strongly drawn and thoroughly believable . . . it keeps the reader enthralled from start to finish' *Hull Daily Mail*

0 7472 6122 9

headline

Now you can buy any of these other bestselling books from your bookshop or *direct from the publisher*.

FREE P&P AND UK DELIVERY
(Overseas and Ireland £3.50 per book)

My Sister's Child	Lyn Andrews	£5.99
Liverpool Lies	Anne Baker	£5.99
The Whispering Years	Harry Bowling	£5.99
Ragamuffin Angel	Rita Bradshaw	£5.99
The Stationmaster's Daughter	Maggie Craig	£5.99
Our Kid	Billy Hopkins	£6.99
Dream a Little Dream	Joan Jonker	£5.99
For Love and Glory	Janet MacLeod Trotter	£5.99
In for a Penny	Lynda Page	£5.99
Goodnight Amy	Victor Pemberton	£5.99
My Dark-Eyed Girl	Wendy Robertson	£5.99
For the Love of a Soldier	June Tate	£5.99
Sorrows and Smiles	Dee Williams	£5.99

TO ORDER SIMPLY CALL THIS NUMBER

01235 400 414

or e-mail <u>orders@bookpoint.co.uk</u>

Prices and availability subject to change without notice.